# A CHRISTMAS RAILWAY MYSTERY

December, 1860: The morning shift at the Swindon Locomotive Works is about to begin, and an army of men is pouring out of the nearby terraced houses built by the GWR. Frank Rodman should have been among them, but he is destined for the grave sooner than he might have expected — or he will be, once his missing head is found. However, Christmas is fast approaching, and the last thing Inspector Colbeck needs is a complex case, mired in contradictions. As he wrestles with one crime, he is alarmed to hear of another — the abduction of Superintendent Tallis. Colbeck and Leeming find themselves in a hectic race to solve a brutal murder before rushing off to Kent in a bid to save the superintendent's life.

# A CHRISTMAS RAILWAY MYSTERY

## EDWARD MARSTON

LARGE
PRINT

First published in Great Britain 2017
by
Allison & Busby Limited

First Isis Edition
published 2019
by arrangement with
Allison & Busby Limited

HEREFORDSHIRE
LIBRARIES

*A catalogue record for this book is available
from the British Library.*

ISBN 978–1–78541–801–3 (hb)
ISBN 978–1–78541–807–5 (pb)

Published by
F. A. Thorpe (Publishing)
Anstey, Leicestershire

Set by Words & Graphics Ltd.
Anstey, Leicestershire
Printed and bound in Great Britain by
T. J. International Ltd., Padstow, Cornwall

This book is printed on acid-free paper

# CHAPTER
# ONE

## December, 1860

Betty Rodman was in torment. Anxiety was gnawing at her like a rat eating its way into a sack of grain. Unable to sleep, she was suffering both physical and mental pain. Where on earth was her husband? She was used to his coming home late with the stink of beer on his breath but he'd never been out this long before. It was well past midnight. The early shift began at six in the morning. If he was not there on time, he'd get more than a stern reprimand from the foreman. His job might be in danger and that prospect troubled her more than anything else. Though their house was among the smallest, she liked living in the Railway Village. They'd been there long enough to feel that they were permanent members of the community. They belonged. Betty never stopped telling herself that — in spite of everything — they had a roof over their heads and a place to bring up their three children.

Suddenly, their whole future was in doubt. She felt it in her bones. After brooding for hours, her fears were drowned beneath waves of fatigue and she drifted off in the vain hope that she'd open her eyes to find her husband snoring beside her. It was the baby's cry that eventually brought her out of her slumber. The child was shivering in the biting cold. Betty clambered out of bed to take her daughter out of her cot and soothe her with quiet words and a warm embrace. When the baby fell asleep again, she put her gently down, covered her with a blanket then dressed in the darkness. Groping her way to the bed, she shook her elder son.

"Wake up, Davy," she said.

The boy stirred resentfully. "Leave me be . . . I'm tired."

"I need you to look after Martha and Leonard."

"You can do that."

"I have to go out."

"Then ask Daddy."

"Your father's not here," she told him in a voice that brought him fully awake. "I'm going out to find him."

And leaving a six-year-old boy in charge of the baby and his younger brother, she let herself out of the bedroom and padded downstairs. After putting on her coat and hat, she wrapped a shawl around her shoulders as an extra barrier against the winter weather but she still shuddered when she stepped out into the street. Betty scurried off past the serried ranks of houses built for its employees by the Great Western Railway Company. Though it was too dark to read the name of the street she was after, she found it by instinct. By the time she reached the house she wanted, she was panting heavily. She banged on the door with both fists and looked up hopefully at the bedroom above. When she saw a glimpse of candlelight, she heaved a sigh of relief. Seconds later, the door was

2

opened by a sturdy man in his thirties, wearing a nightshirt.

"Is that you, Betty?" he asked, peering through blurred eyes.

"Where's Frank?"

"I've no idea."

"But he went off to the pub with you."

"He was still there when I left."

"What time was that?"

"Look, you shouldn't be out there in the cold. Step inside."

"I just want to know where my husband is."

"He should have come home hours ago."

"Well, he didn't. So where can he be?"

"I wish I knew," said Fred Alford, scratching his head. "Frank can usually hold his beer but p'raps he had too much this time and passed out somewhere. I'll put my clothes on and help you to search."

"Did anything happen at the pub?"

"No, no. He just had a drink with us."

"You know what I'm asking," she said, meaningfully.

"There was nothing like that, Betty."

"Are you sure? He's come home with blood on his face so many times."

"Frank was on his best behaviour. There was no fight."

Wanting to reassure her, he suppressed the fact that his friend had got into a heated argument with another man from the Works. They'd reached the stage of growling threats at each other. Alford had dried to drag Rodman away but had been shrugged off. The row could easily have descended into violence but Alford didn't want to alarm Betty by telling her that. She needed hope.

"Wait until I put some clothes on," he said, easing her into the house, "and stop worrying about him. He'll be fine, I'm sure. Frank's got his faults, as we all know, but he can look after himself."

The naked body was flat on its back, the ankles bound and the palms tied firmly together as if he was praying for the return of his missing head.

# CHAPTER
# TWO

When the call came, they were in Colbeck's office, reviewing their latest case and wondering why the killer had chosen to commit suicide rather than face arrest.

"It was a dramatic confession of guilt," said Colbeck, "and it saved us an appearance in court. The man hanged himself in private to avoid the ordeal of being hanged in public."

They were interrupted by the messenger who stressed the urgency of the summons. It set off alarm bells for Leeming.

"I knew it," he said, mournfully. "With only ten days to go to Christmas, the superintendent is about to send us hundreds of miles away from London."

"You're being unduly pessimistic, Victor."

"It's happened before. Three years ago, we spent Christmas Day arresting a man in Cornwall. The same thing could happen again."

"That's highly unlikely," said Colbeck with a smile. "That particular individual paid the ultimate price for the murder of his wife. Of one thing you may be certain — there'll be no need for us to go to Truro again."

"You know what I mean, sir."

"I do, Victor, and I share your concern. There have been occasions when the festive season didn't exist for us. I'm hoping that we can at least salvage part of it this year. Our daughter will be enjoying her first Christmas, remember. I want to be there to celebrate it with her."

"I don't blame you. It's the one day of the year when a family *should* be together. The superintendent doesn't realise that because he lives on his own."

"He does so by choice."

"It's unnatural. Everyone needs company."

"He's the exception to the rule. In fact, he's the exception to *most* rules." Leaving the room, he led the way along the corridor. "Let's hope that he has an assignment for us here in the capital."

"No chance of that!" murmured Leeming.

After knocking on his door, they went into Edward Tallis's office and stood side by side in front of his desk. By way of a greeting, he growled at them.

"What kept you?"

"We were detained for a few moments, sir," said Colbeck.

"You were too busy gossiping to obey an order," said the superintendent. "A summons is a summons. I'll brook no delay."

"You have our apologies."

"I'd rather have you responding instantly to a command."

"We're here now, sir," Leeming pointed out.

"Thank you for telling me," said Tallis, sarcastically. "I hadn't noticed."

"Do you have another case for us, Superintendent?" asked Colbeck.

"Why else should I send for you?"

"Can we work in London this time?" pleaded Leeming.

"You'll go where you're needed."

"It's not Scotland again, is it?"

"If you'll shut up," said Tallis, quelling him with a stare, "I'll tell you." He picked up a telegraph. "This was sent by the manager of the GWR Works in Swindon. He asks specifically for the Railway Detective."

"That's very gratifying," said Colbeck. "What are the details?"

"Very few, I regret to say. The headless body of an employee has been found on the premises. We have no name of the deceased, no address, no description of him, no suspects."

"And no head," said Leeming, involuntarily.

Tallis grimaced. "That observation is in the worst possible taste, Sergeant."

"I'm sorry, sir," whispered the other. "It slipped out."

"We need to be on the next train to Swindon," said Colbeck. "That means travelling on the broad gauge of the GWR. It's less than eighty miles away in total and we have a favourable gradient all the way." He extended a hand. "May I see the telegraph, please?" Tallis gave it to him. "Thank you, sir."

"We've got only ten days to solve the crime," moaned Leeming.

"Then we mustn't waste a minute of them."

"If there's been no arrest by Christmas," warned Tallis, "you must stay on in Wiltshire until you track down the culprit."

"We'll do our best to avoid that situation," said Colbeck. "Come on, Sergeant."

Tallis raised a hand. "One moment . . ."

"Was there something else, Superintendent?"

"Yes, there was. This weekend, I'm vacating my command here in order to attend a reunion of my regiment. As a matter of fact," he went on, straightening his shoulders, "I am to receive a prestigious award."

"Congratulations, sir."

"I'll be here until Friday morning then I'm away until Monday. In my absence, you'll report to the man I've appointed as Acting Superintendent."

"The obvious man to replace you," said Leeming, "is Inspector Colbeck."

"The obvious choice is not always the *best* choice."

"Whoever he might be," said Colbeck, ignoring the slight, "we'll report to him in your stead. May we know his name?"

"Inspector Grosvenor."

Leeming was aghast. "It's not Mouldy Grosvenor, surely!"

"His name is Martin," said Tallis, acidly.

"*I'd* be a better choice than him."

"Do you dare to question my decision?"

"The sergeant respects it as much as I do, sir," said Colbeck, anxious to get Leeming out of there before he provoked the superintendent into unleashing one of his

8

blistering tirades. "Time to go," he continued, taking his colleague by the arm and more or less pulling him to the door. "We'll be in touch, sir."

And before Leeming could speak again, he was hauled out of the room.

The Erecting Shop was a large building where the multiple parts of a locomotive were fitted carefully together. As a rule, it was a clamorous place, obliging those who worked there to shout over the pandemonium of pounding hammers, clanking chains, hissing steam and the resounding thud of cranes. Today, however, it was eerily silent. Because the corpse had been discovered there that morning, work had been suspended for a while out of respect for the dead man. Even places like the Foundry and the Boiler Shop — both of them a source of continuous tumult — were muted. It was possible for once to hold something akin to a normal conversation.

At first glance, the two men appeared to be wearing the same uniform but, in fact, they belonged to different police forces and had very different powers. Edgar Fellowes was employed by the GWR and his authority was limited to railway property. He was a grizzled man in his fifties with a pockmarked face. Jared Piercey was ten years younger, a tall, cadaverous, sharp-featured inspector in the local constabulary. He was stationed in what was now known as the Old Town of Swindon to distinguish it from the New Town, the railway community, close to a mile away. When news of the discovery reached him, he'd been buoyed by the

**9**

thought that he'd be in charge of his first murder investigation, only to learn on arrival that the manager had been in touch with Scotland Yard.

"We could handle this case ourselves," he asserted.

"Mr Stinson wanted the best man for the job," said Fellowes.

"I *am* the best man."

"The Railway Detective has a good reputation."

"We don't need him blundering around here. I have local knowledge and a feel for what goes on in this community."

"I live here," said the other, inflating his chest. "You don't."

"Were you a friend of the victim?"

"Frank Rodman didn't have any friends."

"Who identified him?"

"I did," said Fellowes.

"Even though someone had cut off his head?"

"I recognised him immediately by the tattoos on his arms. He always worked with his sleeves rolled up because of the heat in the Brass Foundry. They call it Hell's Kitchen."

"Why did he have no friends?" asked Piercey.

"He was much better at making enemies."

"Oh?"

"Rodman was always spoiling for a fight."

"Then how did he manage to keep his job?"

"Oh, he never struck a blow while he was at work and, by all accounts, he was very good at what he did. Off duty, it was a different story. If you crossed him in a pub, you'd find him waiting outside for you."

**10**

"Was he ever violent with you?"

"I kept out of his way," said Fellowes, "just like most of his workmates."

"So there won't be many tears shed over his death."

"There'll be little sympathy for Rodman himself. It'll be reserved for his wife, Betty, a long-suffering woman if ever there was one. She'll be left with horrible memories of his murder and with three kiddies to support."

"You speak as if you know her."

Fellowes gave a wan smile. "Everyone knows Betty Rodman," he said. "She's a lovely woman and was saddled with that angry husband of hers. We'll be sorry to lose her from the village."

Hands behind his back, Piercey walked across to the spot where the body had been found and where there was an ominous pool of blood. It was in the shadow of a half-assembled locomotive. Having examined the corpse alongside the Works doctor, Piercey had had it covered by a sheet and removed. He stared meditatively at the blood for some time before turning to Fellowes.

"Have you any idea who might have killed him?"

"No, I haven't."

Piercey looked around. "How did they get in here?"

"There are ways and means, Inspector."

"Someone is on duty all night, surely?"

"We have regular patrols and, of course, there'll be a nightwatchman on duty to keep everything alight."

"Then why did nobody see anything?" demanded Piercey. "Someone carrying a dead body is bound to be conspicuous."

"There's your first clue."

"What do you mean?"

"Shame on you, Inspector," mocked the other. "A man in your position should have spotted it right away. I bet that the Railway Detective will see it immediately."

"I've no idea what you're talking about."

"Look at the circumstances," said Fellowes, enjoying the inspector's patent discomfort. "A corpse is lugged in here during the night and trussed up. The blood on the floor tells you that Rodman's head was severed on that exact spot. A stranger wouldn't know how to get into this place without being seen. In other words," he went on, pausing before delivering his conclusion, "the killer is one of us."

Before they left, the detectives each dashed off a letter to their respective wives, to be delivered by hand, explaining their departure and likely absence for some time. Both had learnt from experience to keep changes of clothing at Scotland Yard in case they had to leave the city without warning. A cab took them to Paddington and they boarded a train to Plymouth that would stop at Swindon. It was only when they'd settled into an empty compartment that they were able to reflect on what Tallis had told them. Leeming was still simmering.

"It's an insult to you, sir," he said.

"I didn't see it as such, Victor."

"Mouldy Grosvenor can't hold a candle you."

"Evidently, the superintendent believes that he can. Nothing we can say will alter that. It's kind of you to take up the cudgels on my behalf but perhaps you should see the advantage of having Inspector Grosvenor as the acting superintendent."

"There *is* no advantage."

"Think again."

"Even if it's only for a weekend, I hate the thought of Mouldy having power over us. Mark my words — he'll use it to punish us."

"What would happen if *I'd* been chosen to replace the superintendent?"

"Justice would have been done."

"That may be so but it would have chained me to a desk. I was in that position once before, if you recall, and I felt like a fish out of water. I don't want promotion, Victor. I already have what I desire and that's to be leading a murder investigation with an able sergeant beside me. The truth of it is that Inspector Grosvenor is a better choice because he'll relish the role."

"I still don't see any advantage for me."

"What would happen if *I* were the acting superintendent?"

"I'd have to work with another inspector."

"Precisely," said Colbeck, "and the most likely person is . . ."

Leeming's face fell. "Mouldy Grosvenor!"

"You've been saved from that grisly fate, so there's no need to generate any righteous indignation on my behalf. It's all for the best, Victor. We carry on together.

I know full well that the inspector is a nasty, egotistic, ambitious, small-minded man who bears grudges, but his elevation in rank will only last for three days at most." He removed his top hat and set it down beside him. "I think we're clever enough to keep out of his way for that long, don't you?"

# CHAPTER
# THREE

When she first heard the news, Betty Rodman felt as if she'd just been hit by a locomotive travelling at speed. She was in a complete daze. It was only when the shock slowly began to wear off that painful questions began to form in her mind. Who had murdered her husband? Why had they done it? What would happen to her children? How could she shield them from the ugly truth? When would she be turned out of the house? Where could they all go?

Fortunately, she was not left alone. The neighbours quickly rallied around her. Women who'd been afraid of Frank Rodman and kept their distance from his family now took pity on her. They fed the children then took them off Betty's hands, leaving her alone with her one true female friend in the village. Liza Alford was the wife of Frederick Alford, the only man who enjoyed spending time with Rodman and who'd saved him over the years from many situations when the latter's temper was roused. On the previous night, he'd left his friend alone at the pub so that he could get home early to his wife.

"Fred blames himself," said Liza. "He should have stayed with Frank."

"It's not his fault. Nobody could have been kinder to us. When I needed help, Fred was the only person I could turn to. He's been a rock. Who else would have got out of bed like that and helped me to search?"

"He loves you, Betty — both you and Frank."

"I can't thank him enough," said the other, dabbing at her tears with an already moist handkerchief. "What's going to become of us? We have no future here. They'll want this place for another family." She shuddered. "It's frightening. We could end up in a workhouse."

"Don't keep fearing the worst. If they force you out, you and the children can move in with us for a while."

"But there's already six of you in that house."

"We'll squeeze you in somehow."

Liza Alford was a motherly woman in her early thirties with plain features and a spreading girth. Betty, by contrast, had kept her youthful shapeliness. Distorted by misery now, her face still retained much of the beauty that had made her so popular with the other sex. In marrying Rodman, she'd frightened other suitors away. They had to be content with watching her wistfully from a distance.

"Who can it be, Liza?" she asked.

"Don't keep asking that."

"Who could have hated my husband so much that he did *that*?"

"I don't know."

"What does Fred think? Did he suggest any names?"

"There's no point in making wild guesses."

"I have to *know*," said Betty, grimly. "I won't rest until then."

16

"You just think about yourself and the children."

"That monster killed my husband."

She burst into tears again. All that Liza could do was to enfold her in her arms and rock her to and fro. It was minutes before the sobbing ceased. Pulling away from her friend, Betty began to dry her eyes once more.

"I'm sorry," she said.

"There's no need."

"I have to be strong for the children. They mustn't see me like this."

"You have to grieve, Betty. It's human nature."

"They'll grow up without a father."

"But they have a wonderful mother. One day, they'll appreciate that."

"I don't feel very wonderful at the moment. I feel so . . . hopeless."

"You'll pull through somehow and we'll be there to help."

"Thank you."

"Lean on us, Betty."

"He might still be here," said Betty, sitting upright. "The murderer might still be among us with a smile on his face. Who is he, Liza? Will they ever catch him?"

"Oh, he'll be caught. There's a rumour that someone famous is coming from London to solve the crime. I don't know anything about him except that he always finds the killer, however long it takes."

Oswald Stinson was the general manager of the Works, a stout, pale-faced man of middle years with a bushy moustache diverting attention from his bulbous nose and watery eyes. While introductions were made, Colbeck admired the cut of the man's frock coat and the way that his tailor had designed the waistcoat to diminish the size of the paunch. They were standing beside the spot where the lifeless body had been found. Close by was a patch of vomit. Edgar Fellowes stepped forward.

"I can explain that," he said, importantly. "Zeb Reynolds, the man who actually discovered the corpse, emptied his stomach there and then."

"How soon were you called?" asked Colbeck.

"I was here within minutes."

"Then you'll have valuable information to give us. Please go with Sergeant Leeming and he'll take a full statement from you."

Fellowes was disappointed. "Don't you need me here?"

"Not at the moment."

Colbeck nodded to Leeming who led the railway policeman away.

"It was good of you to come so quickly," said Stinson.

"An emergency like this deserves an immediate response, sir. I know how anxious you'll be to get this place operative again."

"We work to a tight schedule, Inspector. This locomotive, for instance, is due to be finished and dispatched by tomorrow morning. The sooner we let the men back in here, the better."

"When I've familiarised myself with the layout of this Shop, you'll be able to recall your staff. Where is the body now?"

"I had it removed," said Piercey. "When you're ready, I'll take you to see it."

"Thank you."

"Needless to say, you'll get full support from us."

"That's heartening. We're not always made welcome by local constabularies."

"You'll have no complaints against us, Inspector."

Though he was writhing with envy, Piercey maintained an expression of polite subservience because he was keen to remain an active part of the investigation.

"I've already established most of the relevant details," he said, airily. "That should save you some valuable time, Inspector."

"I look forward to hearing what you found out."

"What puzzles us is how the killer managed to get the dead body in here."

"Aren't you making a dangerous assumption?" asked Colbeck. "How do you know that the victim wasn't alive when he came here?"

"Is that likely?"

"It's a possibility you mustn't discount. Put yourself in the position of the killer. Would you prefer to carry a heavy body into the Works or would you take the more sensible option of making him walk in here with you?"

Piercey gaped. "Are you saying that the murder took place *here*?"

"That would be my guess."

"The victim would never come of his own accord, surely?"

"Granted, but if a man has a gun pressed against his head, he'll have a tendency to cooperate with the person holding it."

"That sounds a persuasive theory to me," said Stinson.

"But it is only a theory, sir," Colbeck reminded him. "Instead of worrying about how they got in here, I'd prefer to find out how the killer got out. When he hacked off the victim's head, he left this pool of blood. How did he carry off his trophy? He'd hardly tuck it under his arm like a football. The likelihood is that he had some kind of canvas bag or sack. Blood would still be dripping from the neck and, in all probability, it would soon seep through." He fixed Piercey with a steely gaze. "Have you searched in here for a trail of blood?"

"No, I . . . haven't had the time to do so."

"Then I'll be grateful if you'll both leave me alone to conduct my own search. When it's completed," said Colbeck, turning to Stinson, "I suggest that you get someone to throw sawdust over this mess then sweep it up and remove it. Once that's done, you can get this place back into production."

"Thank goodness for that," said the manager with a sigh of relief.

"What about me?" asked Piercey. "Shall I help in the search?"

"I'd rather do that by myself," replied Colbeck. "Please wait right here until I've finished. You can then take me to view the body." He glanced from one to the other. "Are there any more questions?"

The two men were too bemused to speak.

Though he was quickly aware of the man's shortcomings, Leeming grew to like Edgar Fellowes. He might be pompous, assertive and have an irritating habit of gesticulating frantically while he spoke but the older man was also intelligent, perceptive and conscientious. Called to the scene, he'd quickly taken charge, cleared everyone out of the Erecting Shop and set about taking statements. His pocketbook was a mine of useful information. Of particular use to Leeming was the list of names garnered. He singled one out immediately.

"Tell me about Fred Alford," he said.

"Insofar as Rodman actually had a friend, Alford was him."

"What sort of a person, is he?"

"He's a good, honest, hard-working foundryman."

"I'd like to meet him."

"Then I can give you his address."

Fellowes did so without having to refer to his pocketbook. Leeming jotted it down then looked up at the railway policeman with interest.

"Is he a neighbour of yours?"

"No, Sergeant, I live a hundred yards away but I have a knack of remembering details about people." He tapped his skull. "I've got dozens and dozens of addresses locked away in here. In Alford's case, I once saw him leave the Glue Pot — that's the pub on the corner of Emlyn Square — and walk to his house. I made a mental note."

"What's the beer like in the Glue Pot?"

"It's very good."

"That's the most useful thing you've told me so far."

Exposing a row of yellowing teeth, Fellowes cackled. They were in the hut that the railway policemen used. It was makeshift but snug, a refuge where they could rest, exchange gossip and have basic refreshments. Leeming warmed to the man.

"Let's go back to Alford," he said. "According to you, he was drinking in the pub with Rodman last night."

"That's right."

"So it must have been the Glue Pot."

"No, it was the Queen's Tap. Frank Rodman was barred from the Glue Pot months ago. He shifted to the Queen's Tap."

"Alford left him there arguing with someone."

"That's what he told me."

"Did he give you a name of the other person?"

"No, but I've a good idea who it might have been."

"Go on."

"It was somebody by the name of Jones, Evans, Thomas or Williams."

Leeming laughed derisively. "That's a great help, I must say!"

"Listen to what I'm telling you. It was one of those Welshmen. They've been a damned nuisance ever since they came."

"I don't follow."

"Earlier this year, the new rolling mills were opened and Mr Stinson needed people to work in them. He imported steelworkers from over the border — about twenty in number. They brought their children with them."

"That sounds reasonable. You'd expect whole families to come."

"There was no proper accommodation for them, Sergeant, so they were dumped in the barracks."

"I didn't know you had an army stationed here."

"We don't," said Fellowes. "There's a building that used to be occupied by single men and we called it the barracks. It was half-empty so bits of it were converted into units big enough for a family. Then the invasion began."

"I wouldn't call twenty families an invasion."

"You don't have to live beside them."

"Has there been friction?"

"There's been nothing else," said Fellowes, bitterly. "They share the communal facilities of washing, cooking, the bakehouse and so on with families already here. Rows break out every day. Those Welsh women are nothing but screeching harpies. They terrify their neighbours."

"I'm not sure that I believe that," said Leeming, tolerantly. "I've met lots of Welsh people and worked alongside some of them. They get a bit morose at times but they're usually friendly and they're not afraid of hard work."

"Go to the barracks and you'll soon change your mind."

"Supposing you're right . . ."

Fellowes was categorical. "I *am* right, Sergeant."

"Then Rodman got into an argument with someone from the rolling mills."

"I'm certain of it."

"Alford will be able to confirm that."

"He may have left before the trouble started."

"Are you saying that the murder was revenge for something?"

"That would be my guess."

"You're making a very serious accusation."

"I've been brooding on it," said Fellowes. "When I was asked by Inspector Piercey for any likely names, I couldn't give him any. But the more I think about it, the more certain I am that one of those leek-eating bastards was involved. Frank Rodman was a tough man. It would've needed someone big and powerful to kill him. Some of those Welshmen are as strong as an ox. Wait till you see them. That's where you and Inspector Colbeck should start looking," he insisted. "The villain is living somewhere in the barracks."

# CHAPTER
# FOUR

Edward Tallis was a solid man of sixty with a backbone so straight and vertical that it seemed to have been welded into position. Robust for his age, he had short, grey hair and a neat moustache thrown into relief by his ruddy complexion. He exuded authority. As he sat in his office and thought fondly about the weekend ahead among old army friends, he allowed himself the luxury of a cigar. Smoke was still curling around him when there was a tap on the door and it opened to reveal Inspector Martin Grosvenor.

"Is this a convenient moment?" asked the visitor.

"It's as good as any other."

"Then I'm at your command, sir."

Closing the door behind him, Grosvenor gave the sly smile for which he was well known among his colleagues. Dark-haired, stooping and of medium height, he had an apologetic air about him in the presence of a superior.

"Have you told Inspector Colbeck?" he asked.

"He and Sergeant Leeming have both been informed."

"How did they react?"

"That's neither here nor there, Inspector. It was my decision and they have to accept it. I've sent them off to Swindon to investigate a gruesome murder."

"Oh . . . I'm sorry to hear that."

Hoping to crow over his rival, Grosvenor was piqued that Colbeck was no longer at Scotland Yard and might be away for some time. One of the main attractions of being promoted above him — albeit for a weekend — was that it gave him a chance to bark orders at the man who'd become so prominent in the Detective Department.

"I was hoping to have a word with him about his appearance."

"Colbeck has always been a dandy. It's in his nature."

"He dresses in a way that's wholly inappropriate."

"I used to feel that but I've learnt to live with his idiosyncrasies. If he continues to solve heinous crimes the way that he does, I don't care if he wears a loincloth and has a bone through his nose."

Grosvenor gave a tinny laugh but he was squirming inside. He made a virtue of being nondescript. His apparel was smart yet intentionally dull, a shell into which he could withdraw from time to time like an apprehensive tortoise. Colbeck's poise and brimming confidence had always exasperated him. There was a long history of tussles between them and Grosvenor had always come off worst from the encounters. He'd been looking forward to getting his own back on Colbeck.

"Right," said Tallis, indicating the sheaf of paper in front of him, "everything you need to know is here. All the cases are listed with the names of the detectives deployed to handle them. In the short time before I leave, I can guarantee that a number of other crimes will come to our attention. Even as we speak, some sort of nefarious activity is taking place. I'll assign the new cases but, when I leave on Friday morning, you'll have to deal with all reported crimes that flood in."

"I'm fully prepared for that, Superintendent."

"That's why I selected you. I wanted a safe pair of hands."

"Thank you, sir."

"Also, if truth be told, I've always thought that you'd be more productive behind a desk than working out in the field. Your record of arrests hasn't exactly been impressive."

Grosvenor winced. "Nobody has been more industrious than me."

"I agree but you've yet to convert industry into consistent success. Try to follow Colbeck's example. He has an uncanny knack of catching villains."

"Fortune has always favoured the inspector, I agree."

"There's more to it than that. His methods are highly questionable and do infuriate me at times but they do yield results."

"I'm not sure that the end always justifies the means, sir."

"That's a judgement you'll have to make over the weekend. Meanwhile," said Tallis, handing him the sheaf of papers, "I advise you to study everything that

I've set down. When you sit in this chair, you must be fully prepared."

"I will be, Superintendent." The sly smile returned. "Where did you say that Colbeck was at the moment?"

"Swindon."

"Swindon!" said Caleb Andrews with disgust. "He's working for the GWR?"

"Robert has to go wherever he's sent, Father."

"I feel betrayed, Maddy."

"Don't be so silly."

"He knows how I feel about Brunel and his despicable railway company."

"Robert has a great respect for his achievements and you should remember that Mr Brunel passed away last year. Never speak ill of the dead."

Madeleine Colbeck knew that trying to defend the late Isambard Kingdom Brunel was a forlorn exercise. Because he'd spend his entire working life with rival railway companies, Andrews despised the GWR and poured scorn on its obsession with the broad gauge. The retired engine driver had spent most of his career on the footplate of locomotives from the LNWR, boasting for year after year that it had no peer. When his son-in-law was engaged to help another company, he was always critical but, when it happened to be the GWR, he was incensed.

"Robert is their best detective," he said, jabbing a finger at her.

"That's one thing we *can* agree on, Father."

"Then he should be in a position to pick and choose his cases."

"Well, he's not. If there's an appeal for his help, he'll respond to it. This time it happens to come from Wiltshire."

"But we're only ten days from Christmas."

"I'm well aware of that."

"Trust the GWR to spoil it for you. While you and I are having Christmas dinner with my gorgeous little granddaughter, Robert will be tied down in the Railway Village in Swindon."

"I have more faith in him," said Madeleine, loyally. "He'll solve the murder in time to be home for Christmas."

"What if he isn't?"

She left the question hanging in the air. Though she was always pleased to see her father, there were occasions when his prejudices offended her. Had the murder victim been an employee of the LNWR, Andrews would have been gushing with sympathy. Since he was in the pay of the GWR, however, the man aroused no compassion whatsoever in him. Andrews was a short, wiry individual in his sixties with a fringe beard threatening to turn from grey to white, but his fiery nature was undimmed by time. He'd been delighted when his daughter, a young woman of humble birth, had met and married the Railway Detective. Even after all this time, however, he was never at home in the fine house in Westminster with its many rooms, relative opulence and efficient servants. It was a far cry from the place where Madeleine had been born and brought up. While she had slowly come to accept it as the place where she deserved to be, Andrews still felt uneasy.

"I thought you came here to see Helen," she said, "not to lose your temper."

"I'm sorry, Maddy. I didn't mean it."

"If you're likely to start ranting about the GWR, I'm not taking you up to your granddaughter."

"Try stopping me."

"I'm serious, Father."

"So am I. Robert's parents are both dead and so is your dear mother — God bless her. In short, I'm the only grandparent that Helen has and that gives me special rights. None of us will live for ever, Maddy," he went on, "so make the most of me while I'm still above ground. Helen needs to have *someone* from my generation in her little life. Don't you agree?"

"Of course," she said, kissing her father on the cheek. "Let's go up to the nursery, shall we?"

Linking arms, they went happily up the stairs together.

During his years as doctor at the Works, Gordon Burnaby had seen some grotesque sights. By its very nature, it was a place beset by hazards. In the course of their work, men had been blinded, severely burnt, left with serious fractures, suffered hideous disfigurement or, in some cases, died from wounds they'd picked up during their shift. Inured to the horrors of the job, he'd nevertheless been shaken when he first saw the corpse of Frank Rodman. It now rested on a table in the room used as his surgery. After issuing a warning to Colbeck, he pulled back the sheet to reveal the body. The inspector had visited too many morgues to be unsettled. While the doctor had looked at the victim as a pitiable human being, Colbeck treated him primarily as a source of clues. He first noticed the man's muscularity, realising that Rodman would never have been easily overpowered in a fight. His eyes then roved over the vivid tattoos on both arms and on the bare chest. There were mermaids, an anchor, a whale and a variety of fish. A five-masted clipper had pride of place on his chest. On the back of one hand, two hearts overlapped.

"He was a seafaring man at one time, I see," said Colbeck.

"That was my deduction as well."

"There's no sign of a fatal wound on the body."

"You'd have found plenty on the head," said Burnaby. "My feeling is that he was killed by repeated blows with a blunt instrument before being decapitated. If we ever find it, the skull will be in a dreadful state."

"That's borne out by the blood spots I saw in the Erecting Shop. They're so profuse that they couldn't all have come from the severed neck. The whole head must have been smashed to a pulp and turned red."

"What does that say about the killer?" asked Piercey, standing nearby.

"It says that he needs to be caught as soon as possible. Rodman was the victim of a savage attack. Why his ankles and wrists were bound like this, I can only surmise but in time, I hope, all will become clear."

"He wasn't just killed, he was slaughtered like an animal. It's revolting."

"Inspector Piercey advised me to keep the body here until you'd seen it," explained Burnaby. "I'd rather not have it on the premises any longer than it need be. Once the word gets around, ghoulish workmates will ask for a chance to gape."

"We don't want that."

"I agree," said Colbeck, "and we don't want full details of his injuries released to the press." He gave a nod. "Thank you, Dr Burnaby. I've seen enough."

"Will there have to be a formal identification by someone in his family?"

"Ideally, yes. I'm told that he was married but I'm not going to put his wife through the nightmare of seeing him in this state. Someone else will have to do it," said Colbeck before turning to Piercey. "You can have Mr Rodman removed to the morgue now, Inspector."

"I'll arrange it at once," said the other going out.

Colbeck looked at Burnaby, appraising him for the first time. Wearing a white coat that had seen better days, the doctor was a slim, tired-looking man in his forties with a bald head and a brow that was permanently corrugated. Having responsibility for the health of all the employees at the Works had clearly taken its toll.

"Thank you for leaving the body in the state in which you discovered it, Dr Burnaby. You must have been tempted to cut away those cords."

"I felt that you should see exactly what we found."

"I'm glad that you did. The killer was sending a signal."

"When you find out what it was, please tell me."

"I will," said Colbeck. "Before he's taken away, I suggest that you cut the cords binding his ankles and wrists. Whoever identifies him can be spared those particular details of the murder." Burnaby used a pair of scissors to cut off the two pieces of twine. "I'll keep those. They're evidence."

The doctor passed them over. "What happened to his clothing?"

"The killer must have taken it with him."

"Why did he have to strip his victim naked?"

"I imagine that it was an act of humiliation."

"It was so unnecessary."

"He didn't think so."

"And why make off with the head?"

"It was a souvenir of his triumph."

"What's he going to do with it?"

Colbeck gritted his teeth. "I dread to think."

The next moment, he recoiled from a sudden explosion of noise. There had been a steady drone of sound in the background but it was now augmented by a veritable cacophony as the Works came back to life. The relentless buffeting of the steam hammer made the floor tremble. Burnaby didn't turn a hair.

"They've started up," he said, calmly. "The whole place is operating at full pelt again."

Thanks to Edgar Fellowes, the garrulous railway policeman, Victor Leeming had learnt a great deal about the history of the community. At the start of the century, Swindon had been little more than a sleepy country town with a population of less than 1,200 souls. When the census was taken in 1841, numbers had still not increased markedly but the GWR changed all that by settling on the area for its new manufactory. While the Old Town remained defiantly rural, the Railway Village brought the din, stink, grime and general commotion of industry. Swindon underwent a revolution.

"We got bigger and bigger," said Edgar Fellowes, "and the two separate halves grew closer and closer. Twenty years ago, two constables were enough to look after the town. They have Inspector Piercey in charge of a small team now."

"How much crime is there?" asked Leeming.

"Oh, we have our fair share of petty offences. Drunkenness and causing an affray are always worse at the weekend when the men can get a little boisterous. Pilfering and trespass is what I deal with most of the time. There's far too much of it on the site. Since there are single men, of course, we have a brothel here. There's a police raid every so often and it closes down, only to open up very quickly in another part of the village. Laws to control men's natural urges never really work. What we've never had before," he said, solemnly, "is a murder. Until it's solved, the whole town will be on edge."

"Then we'll do our best to catch the man responsible very quickly. To do that, of course, we'll need somewhere to stay."

"Mr Stinson will arrange that, surely. He's got a very big house."

"If we're offered accommodation there, Inspector Colbeck will certainly turn down the invitation because we'd have to eat our meals with the manager and issue regular reports. We work best when nobody is looking over our shoulder. We like to be able to come and go as we please."

"Then your choice is between the Glue Pot and the Queen's Tap."

"Which one sells the best beer?"

"The Glue Pot," said Fellowes, "but the beds are softer at the Queen's Tap."

"Then that's the one we'll choose. It's going to be tiring work so we'll need a good night's sleep."

"Try to get rooms at the back. It's quieter there."

They were on their way to the Brass Foundry where Frank Rodman had once worked. Instead of waiting until the end of his shift when the man left the Works, Leeming wanted to see Fred Alford now. After his long chat with Fellowes, the sergeant felt that he was better prepared to carry on the investigation. He just wished that his companion would stop giving him unsought advice.

"You'd be better off going to the rolling mill," said Fellowes. "That's where you'll find the Welshmen."

"I'd rather speak to Mr Alford first."

"He's not the killer, I can tell you."

"He's the nearest thing Rodman had to a friend so he'll know things about the victim that nobody else can tell us."

"That's true," conceded the other, "but I still think that —"

"Think what you will," said Leeming, cutting him short. "My decision is final. Mr Alford is the one I want to meet."

"Oh, very well . . ."

"And I don't need you trailing behind me."

Fellowes was hurt. "I'm sorry," he said. "I don't mean to be in the way."

"You've been very helpful but I can manage on my own now."

Reluctant to go, Fellowes had no choice. After urging Leeming to get in touch with him if he needed more help, he moved away. The sergeant went briskly on to the Foundry, introduced himself to the foreman and discovered that he had to shout to make himself heard. When Alford was released to talk to the detective, the two of them stepped outside. Leeming was curious.

"How can you work in a place like that?"

"You'll have to speak up. I'm a bit deaf. Most of us are."

"I'm not surprised," said Leeming, raising his voice. "I understand that you and Mr Rodman were friends."

"Yes, Frank was good company when you got to know him."

"I was told that he was too fond of a brawl."

"He wasn't that bad, Sergeant."

"When did you learn about his murder?"

"It was when I arrived for work. We were turned back. This place went dead silent for once. It was creepy."

"What did you do, Mr Alford?"

"I ran straight home and told my wife that she had to get to Frank's house as soon as possible. Betty was already in a terrible state because he'd gone missing. We were up half the night looking for him."

"Who told her that her husband had been murdered?"

"That would be my wife, Liza."

"Mrs Rodman must have suspected that something had happened."

"None of us foresaw anything as bad as this, Sergeant. Betty is a strong-minded woman but this will be too much for her. Apart from anything else, she'll be forced to leave that house of theirs. I hope you're not going to ask her to identify the body," he went on, a hand on Leeming's arm. "It would be cruel."

"We'll need a relative or close friend."

"Then it will have to be me, I suppose," said Alford. "But why is it necessary? Someone's already identified him, haven't they?"

"That was Constable Fellowes, the railway policeman."

"You can rely on anything Edgar tells you."

"He recognised Mr Rodman by his tattoos."

"Well, yes, I suppose he must have known about those."

"There's something you need to be told," said Leeming, sadly, "and it's something I'd rather you keep from Mrs Rodman at this stage. According to Fellowes, the victim's head had been hacked off and taken away."

"Jesus!" exclaimed Alford, stomach beginning to heave. "Why, in God's name, would anyone do that?"

"We don't know, sir, but you can understand why that particular detail would distress Mrs Rodman beyond bearing. In time, naturally, she'll have to be told but she needs to be protected from the truth for a while."

"I understand. That's very considerate of you, Sergeant."

"We've had rather too much experience of grieving widows, sir. In the early stages, we always try to . . . soften the blow, so to speak. However," he continued, "let's put that aside and concentrate on the man behind this unspeakable crime. Fellowes feels certain that he was someone who got into a row with Mr Rodman."

"Quite a few people have done that," admitted Alford.

"We'll need names, sir."

"Then the first one I can give belongs to a man Frank was arguing with last night at the Queen's Tap. The two of them were squaring up to each other. I tried to tear Frank away but he ignored me, so I left."

"Was the argument getting heated?"

"I'm afraid so."

"And who was the person Mr Rodman was arguing with?"

"It was Gareth Llewellyn," said Alford. "He works in the rolling mill."

# CHAPTER
# FIVE

Marriage to Robert Colbeck had transformed Madeleine's life. Under his guidance, there'd been two major developments. From time to time, he'd been able to involve her in an investigation, taking great care to hide the fact from Edward Tallis, a man who'd never countenance the use of female detectives. It had given Madeleine great pleasure to work alongside her husband, albeit covertly, but the second development brought her even more joy. Discovering that his wife had artistic talent, Colbeck had encouraged her to seek instruction from a professional artist. Her progress had been so remarkable that she'd reached the point where her paintings were good enough to be sold. Since she took her inspiration solely from railways, she earned the unstinting approval of both her husband and her father. Being immersed in her latest project had always been a way to stave off loneliness when Colbeck was working elsewhere.

The birth of their daughter had changed everything. It robbed her of the chance to be part of an investigative process but meant that she never felt deserted when her husband was assigned to a distant part of the country. Looking after the baby kept her fully occupied. In the early stages, the responsibilities of motherhood had also deprived her of the time and urge to immerse herself in her work. The studio had been left empty for months. At long last, the situation had changed. She was at her easel when a visitor came in.

"I'm not disturbing you, am I?" asked Lydia Quayle.

"Not at all," said Madeleine. "I was hoping you'd call. That's why I left word that you should be shown up to the studio."

"I thought you'd given up painting for a while."

"That was Helen's doing. I felt that I needed to be on duty for her."

"But babies spend most of the time asleep, don't they?"

"Helen doesn't and, even though we've got a nanny to help us, I thought I'd be letting her down if I sneaked in here and picked up a paintbrush."

"So why are you here now?"

Madeline shrugged. "I just wanted to start work again."

She was delighted to see her friend. Lydia Quayle provided the female companionship that she lacked. The women had met in grim circumstances. Colbeck had been in charge of the investigation into the murder of Lydia's estranged father and he'd sought his wife's assistance. When Madeleine met Lydia on his behalf, the two of them had been drawn slowly together and were now firm friends. Since the birth of the baby, Lydia had been a regular visitor to the house.

"Christmas is almost here," said Lydia, thrilled. "I was in Oxford Street yesterday and the shops were very busy. There's an excitement in the air."

Madeline was sad. "I wish I could share in it."

"What's the problem — has Robert been sent away again?"

"Yes, Lydia, he's trying to solve a murder in Swindon and he won't leave there until the job is done. Searching for evidence doesn't stop for Christmas."

"But he *must* be here — for Helen's sake as much as for yours."

"I'm praying that he will be, Lydia. It's another reason why I came back in here. Painting helps me to forget all my worries. If I was sitting downstairs, I'd be worrying about Robert. The studio is my escape."

"Then I ought to let you get on with your work."

"No, no," said Madeleine, wiping her hands on a cloth, "I was about to break off, anyway. Helen will be waking up soon."

"Is she always aware of it when her father is not at home?"

"Oh, yes. She misses him as much as I do."

"How do you know?"

"I sense it and her eyes are darting about, looking for her father."

"Is ten days long enough to solve a murder?"

"That depends. Some cases have dragged on for weeks. We'll just have to hope that this isn't one of them. It isn't only Robert who'll be fighting against time, of course. There's Victor Leeming as well."

"Yes, he's a family man, too. He'll be desperate to see the smiles on his children's faces on Christmas morning."

"What will you be doing?"

"Well," said Lydia, soulfully, "I certainly won't be spending Christmas with any of my family. It's a time of the year when I feel very much an outcast."

When he left the surgery, Colbeck went straight to the general manager's office, a large, cluttered, rectangular room with charts and designs hanging on the walls. Above the fireplace was a framed photograph of Isambard Kingdom Brunel, smoking a cigar and staring at something with intense pride.

"That photograph was taken in the Erecting Shop," said Oswald Stinson. "You can see the sense of achievement in his eyes. I don't think he'd look quite so pleased if he were in there now."

"It's finally back in action, sir. He'd have been pleased with that."

Colbeck told him about his visit to the surgery and how he'd sanctioned the removal of the body. He also confessed that he'd spent some time exploring the Works to get his bearings.

"I've always been fascinated by the way that locomotives, carriages and wagons are actually constructed. When I handled a case in Derby, they gave me a tour of the Works that was instrumental in helping me to solve the crime. It was a very interesting case."

"Excuse me for being selfish," said Stinson, levelly, "but I'm only interested in solving the murder that took place here. Can you give me any hope?"

"There's always hope."

"I'd like more reassurance, Inspector."

"Then I can guarantee that the killer will be caught. What I can't predict is how long it will take us to catch him."

"Until you do, there'll be a dark shadow over the entire Works."

"I understand that, sir. All I ask is that you give us the freedom to get on with our inquiry. Not to put too fine a point on it, we prefer to work without interference."

"You'll get none from me."

"That's good to hear."

"I'll help in any way that I can."

"Then perhaps you could loan me a ground plan of the Works," said Colbeck. "I enjoyed my tour but I wasn't entirely sure what all the buildings were."

Stinson opened a drawer. "Let me give you this," he said, taking out a plan and unfolding it. "This will tell you all you need to know." He spread it out on his desk. "The only thing you won't find on it is the new rolling mill."

"Oh, I think that I heard that, loud and clear." He pored over the plan and was struck by the clarity of the architect's drawing. "The body was found here," he said, tapping the paper with a finger, "and the killer made his escape this way. The blood spots go all the way to the exit then they skirt the Engine Shed and disappear here." His finger indicated the spot. "What are these buildings?"

"Those are offices and stores, Inspector."

"Did he have a key to get in, I wonder?"

"I doubt it. They're kept locked at night."

"Then you need to review your security arrangements, sir. The simple fact is that two men were able to stroll in here at night and gain access to the Erecting Shop. One of them was murdered there and the other walked boldly out of the Works without being seen. In your position, I'd be alarmed."

"I'm very disturbed, Inspector. Heads will roll over this." Realising what he'd said, he gestured an abject apology. "Do forgive me. In view of what happened to the victim, that was a dreadful thing to say."

"It was unintentional, Mr Stinson." He folded up the plan. "This will make our job much easier. Ever since I heard about the creation of this Railway Village, I wanted to see it. I just wish it could have been under happier circumstances."

"Solve this terrible crime and I'll show you around in person."

"I may hold you to that."

"Until then," said Stinson, stroking his moustache, "my wife and I would like to extend hospitality to you and your sergeant. We live well away from the Works so we can offer you peace as well as comfort."

"That's very kind of you, sir, but we'd rather stay there, if you don't mind. We need to mix with your employees and get to know what life in the village is like. Mr Rodman was killed by someone who knows this place intimately. This is where we'll find him. As it happens," said Colbeck, "I asked Sergeant Leeming to find some suitable accommodation for us. The chances are that's he's doing that right now."

Having been designed in his office in 1842, the Queen's Tap was an important part of Brunel's legacy. Occupying a corner site, it was a solid structure built of local stone and boasting an impressive portico on the front elevation. Ales, wines and spirits were advertised in bold letters. The pub was an integral part of the village, not least because of the personality of its landlord, Hiram Wells, a man with a beaming smile and a welcoming manner. He was a tall, strapping character in his sixties with flowing grey hair and a full beard. Wells was delighted that the detectives were interested in staying at his pub. When Leeming called there, the landlord took him straight upstairs and showed him two rooms furthest away from the street. They were small but cosy and spotlessly clean. On the walls of one room were pictures of locomotives built at the Works. For that reason, Leeming decided that Colbeck should stay there. The sergeant elected to sleep in the other room, its walls adorned by framed watercolours. Since he hated railways, he felt that the restful landscapes of Wiltshire were more suited to his needs.

Once terms had been agreed, they shook hands.

"We left our luggage at the station," explained Leeming. "We'll pick it up later and drop it off."

"That's fine with me," said Wells.

"Needless to say, we can't tell you how long we'll be here."

"I'll do my best to make your stay a happy one, sir. To that end, I won't pester you for details of what you find out. That'd be a real nuisance. You and the inspector need peace and quiet to think deep thoughts."

"Thank you."

"I'll make that clear to my customers."

"That will be a great help." Leeming studied him. "Are you a local man?"

"Yes, sir," replied the other with a soft West Country burr, "I was born and bred not five miles away."

"It's the first time I've heard a voice like yours. Everyone I've met at the Works seems to have a different accent."

"That's because this is a rural area with no history of heavy industry. The Works are sited in lovely green fields I used to walk across as a boy. They had to get labour from places where there was a tradition of manufacture. I reckon that Mr Brunel poached some of his men from other railway companies."

"That sounds like him."

"Go to the Works and you'll hear voices from far afield."

"The one I'd like to ask you about," said Leeming, taking his cue, "comes from the other side of the Welsh border. Does the name Gareth Llewellyn mean anything to you?"

"Yes, he was in here last night."

"I'm told that he was seen arguing with Mr Rodman."

Wells chuckled. "That was just friendly banter."

"Not according to my information. I heard that they squared up to each other."

"It was only in fun, Sergeant. Everyone knows my rules. Lively argument is allowed but, if you want a fight, you step outside."

"So they didn't start trading punches?"

"No, they just called each other a few rude names."

"What were they arguing about?"

"I can show you," said Wells, heading for the stairs. "Follow me."

Leeming went after him, descending to the ground floor then going into the bar. Wells pointed to a large poster pinned up on the wall.

"This is the latest musical entertainment at the Mechanics' Institution," he said, proudly. "They're regular events. People in the village love their music. As you can see, the band will play an overture from a Mozart opera then there's a whole list of performers. The one that might interest you," he went on, pointing to an item in the programme, "is this one right here. Someone was going to sing 'The Standard Bearer'."

"Why should that interest me?"

"The soloist's name is Frank Rodman."

Leeming was taken aback. "The murder victim?"

"He has a wonderful voice — or, at least, he did."

The sergeant took a closer look at the list of items in the entertainment and was amazed by its length and variety. Music, song and recitation made up the bulk of the evening. Rodman was due to have appeared near the end of the concert.

"They always put Frank there," said Wells, "because he could stay onstage and lead everyone in the singing of the national anthem. I gather that there was a spot of bother last time he tried to do that."

"Was there?"

"Some of the Welsh lads were in the audience and they claimed to have their own anthem. So they refused to sing 'God Save the Queen'."

"And was Gareth Llewellyn among them?"

"I expect so."

"What exactly happened?"

"I wasn't there myself but it seems that it all ended peacefully. The Welshmen agreed to sing our anthem if they were allowed to sing theirs first."

"I didn't know they had one."

"It was written three or four years ago, it seems."

"How did Mr Rodman react?"

"He was annoyed at first, being interrupted when he was about to sing. I know that because he was still going on about it last night."

"Is that what he and Llewellyn were arguing about?"

"Yes," replied Wells with another chuckle. "Gareth was teasing Frank about his voice and saying that he couldn't compare with a Welsh tenor. He was goading him but not in a spiteful way. They had a lively argument but there was never any danger of a brawl. In fact, they ended up drinking together and singing a duet. Like I told you, it was all in fun, really."

48

On arrival in Swindon, Colbeck's first instinct had been to contact the victim's family to offer sympathy and to promise retribution. As it was, he decided to visit the Works first to see the scene of the crime and gather what evidence he could. Hours had now passed since Rodman's wife had been told of the murder so he hoped that she'd had time to adjust to it slightly. Armed with the address given him by Stinson, he walked along streets of red-brick houses arranged to form a grid pattern. Though the terraces appeared identical, there were varying classes of dwelling, ranging from the small, two-room cottages to larger, three-storey houses occupied by more well-paid employees. The accommodation was let by means of differing rental agreements. When he reached it, Colbeck saw that the Rodman abode was among the cheapest in the village.

The appearance of someone of his elegance had already aroused interest. Women peered through windows at him and those he passed in the street assumed that he belonged to the management. Knocking on the front door, he got no response. He knocked even harder the second time and heard sounds from within. Eventually, the door inched open and a pair of eyes looked out at him.

"Are you Mrs Rodman?" he said, gently.

"No, no, sir — I'm Liza Alford. Betty is inside."

After introducing himself, he asked if he'd be able to speak to Rodman's wife.

Liza was flustered. "I don't know, Inspector . . . I'll ask her."

She vanished into the house and was gone for a couple of minutes. When she returned the second time, she opened the door wide. Betty had agreed to see him but, she warned, the woman was in a very delicate state. He promised not to keep her long. Removing his hat, Colbeck followed her in. Betty Rodman was seated on a chair with a shawl around her. She was in an attitude of complete misery. Arm protectively around her, Liza sat beside her friend.

"First of all," said Colbeck, softly, "allow me to express my profoundest sympathy. It's a terrible thing to happen to anyone. I've not long left Mr Stinson. He sends his sincerest condolences."

"Thank you," said Betty, voice barely rising to a whisper.

"He acted with commendable speed and got in touch with Scotland Yard. I've been dispatched to deal with this tragic situation. I have a lot of resources at my disposal, Mrs Rodman, and I'll deploy them to the full until we catch the man who killed your husband."

"Frank didn't deserve to die like that," said Liza.

"I agree, Mrs . . ."

"I'm Liza Alford."

"She's my best friend," added Betty. "I don't know what I'd have done without her." She squeezed Liza's hand in gratitude. "Who did this, Inspector?"

"That's what I'm here to find out," said Colbeck. "I'm wondering if you — or Mrs Alford, for that matter — might be able to help me. You both know this village very well. I don't. On the surface, it seems like a nice place to live."

"It was," affirmed Liza, "until this happened."

"It all started last night," said Betty, speaking slowly and staring at the floor. "Frank didn't come home. He was a good man, Inspector. If he gave his word, he kept to it. When he didn't turn up at the time he promised, I knew something was wrong. All I could do was to sit here and fret."

"In the end, Betty came and knocked on our door," said Liza, taking over. "Fred, my husband, scoured the whole village with her but there was no sign of him. Then Fred went off to work and they told him there'd been a murder. He wouldn't leave until he knew who the victim was."

"He must already have guessed."

"He kept praying that it wasn't Frank."

"After what happened last night," said Betty, "I expected bad news but nothing like this. I thought he'd had an accident or something."

"Most people would have thought the same, Mrs Rodman," said Colbeck. "Now then, I'm going to ask both of you a question and I'd like you to think carefully before either of you gives me an answer. Do you understand?" The women nodded in unison. "Can you think of anyone — anyone at all — who might have had a reason to kill Mr Rodman?"

There was a long pause. The taut silence was eventually broken by Betty.

"A lot of people didn't like Frank," she confessed. "That wasn't his fault. They didn't know how kind he could be and what a wonderful father he was."

"Did anyone ever threaten him?"

"I don't think so," said Liza, "because they'd be too afraid."

"Mr Rodman had been in the navy, hadn't he?"

"That was when he was much younger."

"Why did he turn his back on the sea?"

"I made him," said Betty, woefully. "He was happy as a sailor. It's all he ever wanted to be. But I didn't like the idea of a husband who went away for months on end. So I made him give it up. This is my reward," she went on, lower lip quivering. "Instead of an absent husband, I've got a dead one. It's my fault, Inspector. If I hadn't forced him to leave the navy, he'd still be alive. I'm as much to blame as the man who killed him."

Bursting into tears, she brought both hands up to her face.

# CHAPTER
# SIX

One of the most striking buildings in the village was St Mark's Church, a large, imposing, neo-Gothic structure that served the spiritual needs of the community. Constructed of limestone, it was roofed in tile and lead and surmounted by a crocketted spire that soared to a height of 140 feet and looked down on the industrial sprawl below it with a watchful eye. To the Rev. Howard Law, it was at once a home and workplace. He was a familiar figure in the area, admired for his dedication, scholarship and ability to relate easily to people of all ranks of society. Law was a slender man in his forties with a youthfulness that made him look ten years younger. His face was unlined, his back straight and his movements unusually lithe. In the years that he'd been in the Railway Village, he'd made himself popular even among those who worshipped elsewhere on a Sunday.

The church had a capacious interior, comprising a five-bay nave with a clerestory, a north aisle and a south aisle with a three-bay chapel and a three-bay chancel. When Jennifer Law came in, therefore, it was impossible to see her husband at first because there were so many hiding places in the gloom. The vicar's wife was a plump woman with dimpled cheeks and an emerging double chin. Time had been far kinder to her husband. Unlike him, her face was wrinkled, her shoulders rounded and her mobility restricted. In trying to hurry, she was almost out of breath. Eager to speak to her husband, she was tempted to call out for him but she knew that would have been quite improper on consecrated ground. She therefore began a desperate search, finally running him to ground in the vestry.

"There you are, Howard," she gasped. "Thank God!"

"What's the trouble, my dear?"

"I have some terrible news."

"Well, at least get your breath back before you tell me what it is," he said, taking her by the shoulders and easing her down on to a chair. "You look as if you've been running."

"I came as fast as I could."

"Why — what's happened?"

"When I went into the shop, everyone was talking about it."

"Talking about what?"

"There's been a murder. A dead body was found in the Works."

"Heavens!" he exclaimed.

"You'll be shocked when you hear who the victim is."

"Why?"

"It's Frank Rodman."

He was stunned. "Are you sure?" he asked at length.

"There's no question about it. I thought you ought to know at once."

54

"I'm very grateful that you told me, Jenny," he said, "though I wish you hadn't forced yourself to race back here. It wasn't good for you. Frank Rodman, was it?" he went on, still trying to absorb the news. "Who could possibly have had a reason to kill him?"

"We're going to miss him, Howard."

"Now, now, my dear, we mustn't put our needs first. Frank was the mainstay of the choir and will be a great loss. His death is . . . highly inconvenient, to say the least. But we should be thinking of his wife, poor woman. She's the one who's really suffering. Betty Rodman's been left with three children to care for."

"My heart goes out to her."

"I must get over there at once to offer what solace I can. Before that, however," he said, "we must pray for his wife and family."

Lowering himself to the floor in front of her, he knelt on the cold paving stone with her hands clasped in his. Eyes closed and voice low, he sent up a fervent prayer to the Almighty.

"Do you remember that hatbox in Crewe?" asked Leeming.

"I remember it very clearly, Victor."

"In that case, we had a head but no body. This time, we've got a body without a head. Do you think it will ever turn up?"

"I'm certain that it will reappear," said Colbeck, "when we least expect it."

"How do you know?"

"The killer loves to cause a shock."

It was the first time the two of them had been alone since they'd arrived in Swindon and they had a lot of information to exchange. They were in a small, cold, nondescript office at the Works made available to them by the manager. Privacy was in short supply in the bar of the Queen's Tap so they were grateful for a lair into which they could withdraw. Stinson had even arranged for light refreshments to be served to them. Colbeck talked about his discovery of the blood spots, his inspection of the corpse and his chat with the manager. When he recounted his visit to Betty Rodman, his face clouded.

"The woman is in utter despair."

"Alford told me that his wife was looking after her."

"Thankfully, Mrs Alford is offering her real comfort. She's a redoubtable woman. Without a close friend like that beside her, Rodman's wife would have collapsed completely."

"What about her children?"

"The neighbours are taking care of them. The two boys should be at school but they're being held back today and, wisely, they haven't yet been told what happened to their father."

"They'll be distraught when they finally find out," said Leeming. "My sons would be, in their position. How do you explain to young lads that they'll never see their father again?"

Having heard Colbeck's news, he gave his own, recalling his help from Edgar Fellowes, his interview with Fred Alford and his visit to the pub. When he'd secured two rooms at the Queen's Tap, he'd retrieved their luggage from the station and left it with the landlord, Hiram Wells.

"He's larger than life," said Leeming, approvingly.

"Like Superintendent Tallis, you mean?"

The sergeant groaned. "Not *that* large, sir."

"So which of them do you believe?"

"What do you mean?"

"Well, you've given me opposing views of Mr Rodman. According to the pub landlord, he was no trouble last night and hadn't been on the verge of a fight with anyone. That railway policeman, Fellowes, takes a different view. He thinks that, in effect, Rodman was his own worst enemy. If he was challenged by anyone, he wouldn't back down. He'd settle every argument with his fists."

"I'd rely on Fellowes. He knew Rodman better than the landlord."

"Mr Wells sounds like a shrewd man to me. You have to be, in that trade. A sixth sense with regard to trouble is vital and the landlord didn't think it was brewing between Rodman and that Welshman."

"His name was Gareth Llewellyn, sir."

"Then I fancy that we can eliminate him as a suspect."

"He was seen having a row with Rodman."

"Yes, but it was a good-humoured row, apparently."

"That was only the landlord's opinion. Fellowes said that there was nothing good-humoured about Rodman. Even his friend, Alford, more or less admitted that. Put together the testimony from Fellowes and Alford and it outweighs everything the landlord told me."

"So you believe that Rodman was killed by a Welshman?"

"I do, and we know his name — Gareth Llewellyn. To be honest, sir, I can't understand why you dismiss him as a suspect."

"It's because I don't think that Llewellyn would be quite so stupid. If he had designs on someone's life, the last thing he'd do is to be seen threatening him in public. Suspicion would fall on him immediately."

"He'd been drinking heavily, sir."

"That does release a man from his inhibitions, I grant you."

"They might have seemed jolly enough inside the pub but, when they got outside," Leeming contended, "the argument could've turned nasty. When men are drunk, they lose all reason. My guess is that Rodman and the Welshman went for each other tooth and nail. The murder happened on the spur of the moment."

"That's where you're quite wrong, Victor. Seconds ago, you said that drunken men lose all reason. I agree. But you'd need a great deal of reason to get into the Works without being seen and to kill someone there before beheading him and melting into the night. You'd need iron control. The killer was no inebriated Welshman. He was as sober as you or me."

"I still say that we should talk to Llewellyn."

"That's vital. He may have been the last person to see Rodman alive — apart from the killer, that is."

"Fellowes was adamant. One of the Welshmen is to blame."

58

"You may be right on that score, Victor, but the villain was definitely not Gareth Llewellyn. More to the point, Rodman wasn't killed on the spur of the moment." He took the twine from his pocket and held it out on his palm. "Do you know what these are?"

"They're pieces of string, sir."

"This is the twine that was cut from Rodman's wrists and ankles. In my view, it's compelling evidence that the crime was premeditated," said Colbeck. "The killer not only bided his time, he knew exactly how he intended to leave his victim. So he took the twine along with him. Nothing like this is used at the Works. I checked up on that. It was brought for a specific purpose. There was no drunken brawl," he concluded, slipping the twine back into his pocket. "It was a clinical execution."

Helen Rose Colbeck was in her element, giggling in her crib and kicking her little legs in the air as her mother and her honorary aunt gazed at her in adoration. The child loved attention and responded to it readily. Her facial expressions were so eloquent that they knew exactly what she was thinking. The two women stood there until their necks began to ache and until the baby started to yawn. Withdrawing to the sofa at the far end of the room, they picked up their earlier conversation.

"It was a kind invitation," said Lydia, "but I couldn't possibly accept it. When I told you that Christmas was a difficult time for me, I wasn't dropping a hint that I'd like to join you all here."

"We'd be delighted to have you."

"You need to be alone with your family, Madeleine."

"What family? Apart from Father, all I have are a couple of aunts and two cousins and they'll have their own Christmas dinners. If Robert is unable to get away from Swindon, there'll just be the two of us and the baby."

"It will be a magical time for Helen."

"Do you think she's old enough to appreciate it?" asked Madeleine.

"I'm certain that she is. Helen is so aware."

"We think she's the most beautiful little child in the world but I suppose that all parents feel that about their first-born. It's only natural. Father believes that Helen takes after him but Robert insists that she's just a younger version of me."

"Your husband is the better judge." Lydia looked around the room. "Oh, it's lovely to be able to come here," she said. "It's such a happy place."

Madeleine laughed. "You haven't been here when Helen is howling like a she-wolf because she wants to be fed."

"You can't expect a baby to be patient."

"That's what my father said."

"How *is* Mr Andrews?"

"He's still fuming because Robert is working for the GWR."

"From what you told me, he had no choice."

"It's the same for everyone, Lydia, from inspectors such as Robert down to constables like Alan Hinton."

Madeleine saw the slight colouring in Lydia's cheeks at the mention of Hinton and hoped that she hadn't embarrassed her friend. There'd been a mutual attraction between Lydia and the young detective. Madeleine had hoped that it might develop into a romance but, it seemed, it had not. Detective Constable Hinton had come into Lydia's life when she was distressed by the attentions of a stalker. In addition to following her from place to place, the man had actually stolen one of her dresses from her hotel room. Lydia had been so anxious that she'd moved into the Colbeck home for safety. When the persecution continued, Colbeck had confronted the superintendent and insisted that it was a case worthy of the attention of the Detective Department. Hinton had been given the task of finding the stalker and, in time, had arrested him. Lydia could relax at last. She was deeply grateful.

"I haven't seen him for a while," she said, almost dejectedly.

"He has to work very long hours, Lydia."

"I know that."

"He may not even be here in London."

"That's true."

"I'm sure he hasn't forgotten you."

"No," said Lydia, brightening slightly, "he did take the trouble of calling on me to explain what had happened to that awful man. Constable Hinton told me that he'd gone to prison for twelve months."

"Courtney's sentence won't end there," Madeleine told her. "He's brought shame on the family. His father will be livid and won't ever give him the same freedom again. Courtney won't be anywhere near London. His father will want him back in Nottingham where he can keep an eye on him. Well, you know what wealthy businessmen are like because you come from that world."

"Reputation is everything," said Lydia. "That's what my father used to say. Because of what he did, Courtney tarnished the company name."

"You have Constable Hinton to thank for arresting him."

"I'll never forget that, Madeleine. He set me free again."

"Oh, I think the case meant a great deal to him as well. That's why I'm certain that he'll be in touch again. Christmas is a time when we remember our friends. Alan Hinton is certain to remember you."

A smile flitted across Lydia's face.

Betty Rodman was so touched that the vicar had come to see her that she let out a cry of relief. Having the utmost faith in him, she looked upon him as the father she'd never known. Her manner was therefore at once familial and deferential.

"Thank you so much for coming," she said.

Liza Alford smiled. "I told you he would, Betty."

"I've come to offer what help I can," said Law, a hand on Betty's shoulder. "My wife and I are appalled at what happened. The first thing I did when I heard the news was to offer up a prayer on Frank's behalf and, before I leave, I'll pray with you as well. What I really want to do, however, is to offer practical help. Just tell me what you need and I'll provide it."

"What I want to do first," said Betty, pathetically, "is to find out who killed my husband and why he did it."

"That's the one thing I can't tell you, I'm afraid."

"Inspector Colbeck will catch him," said Liza, firmly. "He's come all the way from London to take charge of the chase."

"Then I'll make it my business to speak to him. He needs to understand the role that Frank played at church. It was such a joy to see him bringing you and the children every Sunday before singing so beautifully in the choir. It's a consolation to me that he lived to see Martha christened." He glanced around. "Where is the baby, incidentally?"

"She's next door with Mrs Hankin," replied Betty, "and so are the boys."

"Do they know what . . .?"

"No, Father, we haven't told them. Davy knows that Frank didn't come home last night but that's all. I was hoping . . ." She bit her lip. "I was hoping that, in time, you could speak to him."

"Of course I will."

"It might be better coming from you. Davy loves it when you teach them at school and so does Leonard. They respect you."

"We all do," added Liza.

"That's kind of you to say so, Mrs Alford. You've been a wonderful friend to the Rodman family," he went on. "In her hour of need, we knew that you'd be here to comfort Betty."

"I'd have been helpless without her," said Betty, turning to her friend with a grateful smile. "Liza's been here since the moment she heard the news. And the neighbours have been kind to me as well."

"That makes a change," muttered Liza under her breath.

"In times of adversity," he said, "people come together and show their best sides. When they see someone in pain, they want to alleviate it. But let's go back to what I said about practical help. There must be something I can do."

"I don't suppose you could speak to Mr Stinson, could you?" asked Betty, nervously. "I know we'll have to leave this house but I don't want to be turned out immediately."

"That's very unlikely to happen," he said, soothingly. "But, yes, I'll certainly have a word with Mr Stinson. These are unusual circumstances. I'm sure he'll be compassionate. However, if you are required to quit this place, Betty, you mustn't worry. You and the children will be more than welcome to stay with us at the parsonage."

She was overawed. "Would you really take us in, Father?"

"It's the least we can do and, I suspect, it's what Frank would have wanted. Don't hesitate to call on us, Betty. My wife and I will be delighted to have you and the children."

Since he'd interviewed Fred Alford before, it fell to Victor Leeming to intercept him at the end of his shift in order to take him off to the police morgue. Alford had agreed to identify the body of Frank Rodman but he was clearly not looking forward to the task. Having seen so many murder victims laid out on a cold slab, Leeming was hardened against the horrors that could be inflicted on the human body. Because Alford was not, he was likely to be deeply upset at the sight of his former friend. On the way, therefore, the sergeant did his best to prepare his companion, emphasising that a glance was all that was needed if he was certain of the victim's identity. Though he'd been forewarned, Alford was still badly shaken by what he saw when the shroud was pulled back. Repelled as he was, he nevertheless kept staring at the corpse as if unable to look away. It was only when Leeming gave the signal to the police doctor that Frank Rodman was covered up again.

Rooted to the spot, Alford continued to stare at the outline of his former friend. Leeming had to take him by the arm to get him out of there, leading him straight to the main door. Alford was grateful to be able to breathe fresh air again.

"Thank you, Sergeant," he said. "I'm sorry if I —"

"Don't apologise, sir. It was a natural reaction. I did tell you that a glance would be enough for you to confirm that it was Mr Rodman."

"Oh, there's no question about that."

"Did you recognise him by his tattoos?"

"I hardly noticed those. As soon as I saw him, I knew it was Frank. We used to swim together in the canal, especially in the summer. I'd know that body anywhere. When you spend all day in the Foundry, you long for a dip in cold water."

"I'm grateful to you, Mr Alford. I know that Edgar Fellowes was the first to identify him but he wasn't as close to the deceased as you were. You may not be a family member but you're the next best thing."

"I'd do *anything* to keep Betty from seeing what I just did," said Alford with sudden passion. "She's suffered enough already."

"Have you had time to think about the crime?"

"I've thought about nothing else."

"What I'm asking," said Leeming, "is if you can put a name to the killer now that you've had time to mull it over. Also, of course, I'd like your opinion of what could drive a man to butcher someone like that." Seeing that Alford was momentarily tongue-tied, he pressed on. "Since you can't provide a name, let me suggest one to you. It was put forward by Fellowes."

"Who is it?"

"Gareth Llewellyn."

Alford was pensive. "Well . . ."

"He was the man you saw arguing with Mr Rodman last night."

"It wasn't the first time. They don't like each other."

"The landlord at the Queen's Tap tells a different story. He claims that it wasn't the kind of argument that led to blows. In fact, after you'd left the pub, the two of them shook hands and had a drink together."

"That means nothing. Llewellyn is two-faced."

"Are you telling me that he's a likely suspect?"

"I'm not picking anyone out just yet, Sergeant," said Alford, choosing his words carefully. "But I've done a lot of thinking about it and . . . well, you may be looking in the wrong direction."

"If you know the *right* direction," said Leeming, "we'd be eternally grateful if you could point us that way."

"You're after someone who hates Frank."

"He did have a habit of upsetting people. You conceded that."

"Yes, but he might have upset someone in a way you haven't considered."

"And in what way was that, sir?"

Alford fell silent as if changing his mind at the last moment. He seemed to be wrestling with his thoughts. Leeming prompted him.

"What way was that?"

"He married Betty Marklew."

Leeming was baffled. "I'm none the wiser, sir."

"In her younger days," explained Alford, "Betty was a beautiful woman. She still is, in some ways. Frank wasn't the only man trying to court her. He had rivals and they weren't happy when she chose him instead of them."

"How long were they married?"

"It must be seven years or more."

"Could someone nurse a grudge *that* long?"

"Oh, yes, there's no doubt about that. I might be wrong," Alford continued, raising both palms. "I'm no detective. I'm just saying that the killer could be someone who hated Frank because he stole Betty from him."

# CHAPTER
# SEVEN

Howard Law was as good as his word. After spending an hour or more consoling Betty Rodman, he went across to the Works and was in time to catch the manager before he left. They knew each other well. Although he found the vicar a trifle locquacious at times, Stinson invited him into his office and listened patiently to his plea. His answer was evasive.

"It's too soon to set a date for the family's departure," he said.

"Let's call it what it is, shall we?" said Law, evenly. "We're talking about the summary eviction of a woman in dire straits. She's been left with three children and meagre resources."

"Her husband is no longer one of our employees."

"That's a rather cruel euphemism, I must say."

"I'm just being practical."

"The man was murdered on your premises. You make it sound as if he simply reached the end of his employment contract with you."

"In effect, he has," said Stinson, caught on the raw by the criticism. "Unlike you, I don't have the luxury of viewing the situation in emotional terms. When someone goes — for whatever reason — I have to make

**68**

a judgement about replacing him or leaving a vacancy. It's a simple business procedure."

"Is that how you describe the expulsion of a family in distress?"

"We can't leave them in the house indefinitely."

"That's not what I'm asking, Mr Stinson," said the other. "All I need from you is an idea of how long Mrs Rodman and her children can stay there without fearing a knock on the door."

"We do have a waiting list for accommodation," said the manager.

"You still haven't given me a date."

"The family will be informed in due course."

Law was becoming exasperated. He'd assured Betty Rodman that the manager would be compassionate, only to discover that Stinson was not as amenable as he'd assumed. It would be highly embarrassing for him to return to her with bad news. He therefore tried a different tack.

"I'm appealing to you as the good Christian I know that you are."

"Don't patronise me, Vicar. I've been a churchgoer for more years than you."

"Granted."

"And before you start accusing us of hard-hearted behaviour," Stinson went on, "let me remind you that it was the directors of the GWR who felt it important to have a church, school and parsonage built for this village. That's why you're able to deliver your sermons every Sunday in St Mark's."

"I'm very grateful for that."

"When this village was created, religious observance was felt to be one of its cornerstones. For that reason, a church capable of holding a congregation of 800 people was constructed. You and the other members of the clergy at St Mark's are the beneficiaries of the foresight of the GWR."

"I willingly acknowledge it."

"We don't interfere with your sphere of activity. Why interfere in ours?"

Law bridled slightly. "I've never heard the worship of God being described as a sphere of activity before," he said, disapprovingly, "but I'll let it pass. I didn't come here for a theological debate."

"No, you came — in good faith — on behalf of a family in grave difficulties."

"They need help, Mr Stinson."

"Nobody is denying that."

"Then why can't you tell me how long they can stay?"

The manager looked him in the eye. "At most, it will be a matter of weeks."

"And at least . . .?" Getting no reply, Law pressed on. "Do you have a policy with regard to this situation?"

"We've never had an employee murdered before."

"You've had deaths on-site and a number of accidents that left people crippled and unable to work. Apart from eyeing up their houses," said the vicar, pointedly, "do you have any means of offering some relief?"

"As you well know, the Sick Fund was set up to provide assistance during illness and for the payment of funeral expenses. It was a pioneering scheme, as was our Medical Fund, which exists specifically for the benefit of all employees and their families. Among other things, it's helped to rid the town of most of the insanitary conditions that made it vulnerable to epidemics of diseases like typhus and cholera. Please bear these initiatives in mind," stressed Stinson. "They prove that the GWR looks after its employees."

"What I was hoping for was an additional fund for the provision of financial aid in special cases. Mrs Rodman's case, I venture to suggest, is a very special one."

"I agree with you."

"So is there money available to her?"

"I fear not," said Stinson with genuine regret. "As you'll recall, way back in 1847, there was a dramatic fall in the demand for locomotives and repair work. We had to reduce our Swindon staff by two-thirds and that meant laying off twelve hundred men. It caused widespread suffering. Three years ago we had another recession and were forced to resort to short-time working and the closure of the entire operation over the weekend. Rodman was one of the lucky ones who kept his job."

"In essence, then, there's no fund for emergencies."

"Let me put it more bluntly — we have to watch every penny."

"I understand."

Law abandoned his attack and wished that he hadn't been quite so outspoken. When all was said and done, Stinson and his wife were regular members of his congregation even though they didn't live in the village. He shook hands with them every Sunday as they left the church. Accustomed to winning arguments by means of his charm and eloquence, Law had to accept that he'd lost this particular one. He switched to another topic.

"I'm told that you've summoned detectives from Scotland Yard."

"We asked for Inspector Colbeck himself," said Stinson. "Nobody else could compare with him."

"He won't have tackled anything quite like this before."

"I can see that you don't follow his career. His name often appears in the national newspapers. Some years ago, a severed head was found on Crewe Station. Inspector Colbeck tracked down the missing body and, as a result, investigated a crime that related to the running of the Derby. Trust him, Vicar. There's very little he hasn't done before."

"Betty Rodman was impressed by him."

"So was I. Expenses will be incurred, of course. We'll have to pay for his accommodation and any meals he and his sergeant require. Careful as we are with any expenditure, we're happy to take care of any bills. Do you object to that?"

"Not in the slightest," said Law.

"So, in that sense," argued the manager, "we are treating Rodman's death as a special case. Because we're investing money in the investigation, his widow will, in due course, have the satisfaction of seeing her husband's killer caught, convicted and sent to the gallows."

When he came to the end of a punishing shift in the rolling mill, all that Gareth Llewellyn wanted to do was to go home to his family and enjoy a meal with them. He was irritated, therefore, when his foreman told him that he had to speak to someone before being allowed out of the Works. The Welshman was even more annoyed by the fact that he was given no details. All the way to the temporary office occupied by the detectives, he complained bitterly to the foreman. When he actually met Colbeck and realised that he was being treated as a murder suspect, he was enraged.

"It's a rotten lie!" he yelled.

"Calm down, sir."

"Some bastard is trying to get me into trouble. Who was it?"

"Your name was mentioned, that's all," said Colbeck. "It doesn't matter by whom. We felt it was our duty to speak to you."

"Right, you've done that. Now let me have my turn. I'll swear on the Holy Book that I had nothing at all to do with Frank's murder. Diu! I was drinking with the man last night."

"Yes, you were drinking and engaging in a heated debate."

Llewellyn laughed. "You call *that* heated?"

"I hear that you also caused a scene at the Mechanics' Institution."

"A man is allowed to stand up for his country, isn't he?"

"There's a time and place for patriotism, sir."

"You weren't even there," snarled Llewellyn. "Who are you to tell me what I should and shouldn't do? I'm Welsh and proud of it."

Colbeck could see that it was going to be an arduous conversation. The other man was big and brawny with a huge, bristly chin, a broken nose and two fiery eyes. Tufts of dark, curly hair stuck out from beneath his hat. His stance was challenging, his manner truculent. Llewellyn had little respect for authority.

"I've got my rights," he said in a deep, lilting voice. "If someone is accusing me of murder, I'm entitled to know his name."

"Nobody is accusing you, sir," said Colbeck, gently. "But it seems that you were one of the last people seen with Mr Rodman."

"There were others in that bar. Are they suspects as well?"

"I can't say."

"So why have you picked me out?"

"You do seem to have got yourself noticed, Mr Llewellyn. Having met you face-to-face, I can see why. You have a strong personality."

"I like to stand up for myself, that's all."

"There's nothing wrong with that as long as self-assertion is kept within reasonable limits. I'm not sure if that was the case at the Mechanics's Institution."

74

"I made a polite enquiry, that's all," insisted the other. "If we have to listen to *their* national anthem, they should have the grace to listen to ours. Apart from anything else, it's much better than that dreadful dirge about saving the Queen. Ours at least has some life in it and a proper melody."

"I didn't know that there was a Welsh national anthem."

"It's only quite recent but none the worse for that."

"Technically, Wales is part of Great Britain so it's perfectly normal for you to sing 'God Save the Queen'."

"We prefer our own anthem."

"Does that justify interrupting a concert?"

"Yes, it does."

Colbeck weighed him up. He'd met people like Llewellyn before, combative individuals who could not be cowed by intense questioning. Any accusations would be shrugged off. The Welshman seemed to embody aggression. He'd admit nothing and justify everything. To prise information out of him, another approach was needed.

"Do you like working here?" he asked, pleasantly.

"I'd rather be in Wales."

"Why aren't you?"

"There were no jobs in the steelworks there so we were sent here."

"I sense a lot of resentment in your voice."

"We were happy where we were."

"But this is a very fine Locomotive Works," said Colbeck. "And I speak as someone who's been to

Derby, Crewe, Wolverton, Doncaster and Ashford, Kent — all of them, railway towns. Swindon can compete with any of them."

"It happens to be the wrong side of the Welsh border."

"It's given you a job. Aren't you grateful?"

"We take what we can get."

"Your foreman told me that you're all hard workers."

"It's a matter of pride with us."

"You sound as if you're the spokesman for your countrymen."

"Someone has to be."

"There are tales of friction between the Welsh and the local community."

"Don't believe a bleeding word of them."

"It seems to be an established fact."

"You've only listened to one side of the story." He yawned extravagantly. "Can I go now? My wife is expecting me home."

"One last question, sir — what did you feel when you first heard the news about Mr Rodman's death? Were you upset?"

"A bit of me was. I came close to liking Frank. Another bit of me was glad."

Colbeck was shocked. "You were *glad* that someone was murdered?"

"Yes," said Llewellyn, grinning. "I might have the chance of replacing him at the next concert. My solo will be in Welsh, of course, then people will realise what a wonderful language it is."

76

While most of his colleagues found Inspector Martin Grosvenor an unprepossessing character, they all admired his efficiency and commitment. Nobody liked working under him because he routinely took all of the credit for a successful investigation, submitting reports that rarely mentioned other officers involved. Yet even the most aggrieved detectives accepted that he'd earned the rank of inspector. When they learnt that he was about to be the acting superintendent, however, they were on their guard. Grosvenor was known to have a malicious streak. He'd use his new power to strike back at those who'd mocked him in the past.

When he called on Tallis at the end of the day, he'd absorbed the information he'd been given about the current cases and was able to discuss each one of them without referring to the documents. The superintendent was full of praise.

"You have a remarkable memory, Inspector."

"It's an asset in our profession."

"Oh, I agree. The only detective we have with a greater power of recall is Colbeck. In addition to remembering details about the activities of various criminals, he has an extraordinary capacity to recognise their faces. No matter how clever the disguises they might employ, Colbeck picks them out at once."

"I've done that myself many times," said Grosvenor, peevishly.

"He's developed it into an art. However," said Tallis, "let's deal with your role as my replacement. There's one change to the information I gave you. That burglar

77

in Whitechapel has now been arrested. We have Detective Constable Hinton to thank for that. He's young and eager and might one day aspire to a higher rank."

"Yes, I've worked with him, sir. He's sometimes too eager. When he has more experience, Hinton will understand the virtue of patience."

"He's still a young man to watch."

Tallis shuffled the papers in front of him. In the course of the day, reports of various crimes had come in and officers had been sent to look into them. He gave Grosvenor a brief description of each one before passing the sheaf to him. After glancing through them, the inspector looked up.

"No word from Colbeck, I suppose?"

"He'll be in touch when he's ready."

"Does that mean he'll be coming back here this evening? If he does, I'd like to be here when he delivers his report."

"That won't be necessary."

"Why not?"

"Colbeck and Leeming will be staying in Swindon."

"But a train would get them back here in little over two hours."

"They prefer to remain where they are," said Tallis, "and I agree with the decision. If they are to solve this grotesque murder, they need to mingle with the people who live in the Railway Village in order to win their confidence."

Grosvenor winced. He'd been thwarted.

★   ★   ★

There was no need for an appeal to the public. Information about the murder came in from a number of anonymous sources. Everyone seemed to know by now that the detectives had taken rooms at the Queen's Tap. Leeming called in there and found a selection of messages waiting for them. Most simply contained the putative name of the killer but a few tried to offer what they felt was crucial evidence. After sifting through them, Leeming thanked Hiram Wells for looking after the unsolicited mail.

"Do you have any idea who sent these?" he asked.

"No," replied the landlord. "They were slipped under the door."

"We'll need to study them carefully."

"Don't be misled. Some people here are known for their hoaxes."

"Yes, I spotted one of those straight away. According to him, we should be arresting Prince Albert. That wouldn't go down well in the Queen's Tap, would it?"

Wells guffawed. "I don't think Her Majesty would be too pleased, either."

"It's always the same. We get ridiculous suggestions, especially when there's a big reward on offer. They'll tell any lie to get their hands on the money."

"Is there going to be a reward this time?"

"I'm sure that the GWR will advertise one. The false claims will really start to pour in then. By the way," said Leeming, "I want to thank you for keeping everyone at bay for us. Since I've been here, nobody has come up and asked how we're getting on even though they're dying to know."

"That goes for one man in particular."

"Who's that?"

"The killer — while you're looking for *him*, he'll be sure to watch out for you and the inspector. The chances are that he'll have drunk in this pub at some point."

"That's a good reminder," said Leeming. "If he's bold enough to commit murder in the way that he did, he won't hold back from coming in here to weigh us up." He held up the letters. "He may even have written one of these. There's no better way to throw suspicion off yourself than by shifting it to someone else. That's why we have to tread carefully."

"I don't envy you your job, Sergeant."

"Well, I envy *you*. I'd love to work in a place where I had the smell of beer in my nostrils all day long."

"There's more to it than that," warned the other.

"I daresay there is, Mr Wells."

Leeming glanced around. There were only a few customers in the bar and they were taking no notice of him. The landlord's wife was polishing glasses behind the counter and their son was bringing in a crate of beer. There was a friendly atmosphere to the Queen's Tap. It was difficult to imagine a murder being hatched there on the previous night.

"How many Welshmen come in here?"

"Very few, as a rule," said the landlord. "They seem to prefer the Glue Pot for some reason. That doesn't worry me. We've got more than enough regulars."

"What about Mr Llewellyn — was he one of them?"

"No, he only popped in now and again. They earn a decent wage in the rolling mill but they all have families to support, Llewellyn included. If they manage two nights a week in a pub, that's their limit."

"What about single men?"

"We see more of them. They only have themselves to think about."

"Have you seen more of Llewellyn in recent weeks?"

"We have, as a matter of fact."

"Why come here when most of his friends are in the Glue Pot?"

"You'll have to ask him, Sergeant."

"I'm asking myself at the moment," said Leeming, "and the answer is obvious. The Welshman came here because Rodman was barred from the other pub so was forced to drink here. Before that, I'll wager, you hardly saw Llewellyn."

"That's true," admitted Wells, realisation dawning. "It's almost as if . . . as if he was stalking a victim."

In the event, Howard Law didn't have to go in search of Colbeck because the inspector came to him. He arrived at the parsonage to be given a cordial welcome by the vicar and his wife. He was then shown into the study, a large room that was exceptionally tidy and which still had a strange newness about it.

"I know what you're thinking," said Law. "It feels as if we just moved in."

"When was the church consecrated?"

"Just over fifteen years ago. I could have wished for something less decorative and not quite so redolent of medieval tradition but, then, I'm not the architect. It's a fine church that makes a clear statement about its position in the village."

"I was very taken with the park opposite, Mr Law. It gives you a lovely aspect and is an ideal place for families to walk and play games."

"In summer months, it's largely the preserve of cricket teams. However," he went on, "you didn't come to discuss our leisure activities. A darker incident brought you." He indicated a chair and they sat opposite each other. "First, let me say how grateful I am that you took the trouble to call on Mrs Rodman. When I was there, she said how kind and considerate you'd been."

"I did what I could, Vicar. It's very important for the victim's family to believe that someone is working hard to bring a killer to justice. While it may not alter the misery of her situation, an arrest will bring her a measure of relief. What I'd really like to ask you about," said Colbeck, "is Frank Rodman. Until I spoke to his wife, I had no idea that he was a member of your choir."

"He was the lynchpin of it, Inspector."

"I also hear that he used to sing at occasional concerts."

"The programme was never complete without a solo from Frank. He was a good man at heart. Yes, he had a temper but he was learning how to curb it. People misunderstood him. In defiance of his bellicose manner, he was a very devout man."

"That surprises me."

"I've seen him kneel in prayer for an hour or more."

"Was that out of piety or in expiation of a sin? The reason I ask that," he went on quickly, "is that it might explain something. When the body was found — and these details will not be released to the press — it was completely naked and the head had been cut off. The ankles were bound together and the hands tied as if in prayer."

"Good Lord!"

"You said that your church makes a statement. Was the killer doing the same?"

"I really don't know, Inspector."

"You must have an opinion."

"If you pressed me," said Law, slowly, "I'd have to say that he was mocking Frank's devotion to the church. I'm trying to picture it in my mind and I find it a revolting image."

"I saw it in reality."

"And what was *your* judgement?"

"I didn't have one at first," confessed Colbeck, "because I couldn't understand it. On reflection, however, I've come to see that it was a deliberate act of ridicule. It's as if the killer is treating Christianity with contempt. 'Prayer is useless,' he seems to be saying. 'It can't stop me killing you.' It's a derisive message and it tells us something very significant about the man who sent it."

"And what's that, Inspector?"

"He's an atheist."

# CHAPTER
# EIGHT

Caleb Andrews called at the house while the baby was being fed so he had to wait some time before his daughter came down from the nursery. He passed the time by picking up a newspaper and reading an article that was unduly critical of Scotland Yard, questioning its effectiveness in fighting crime. Thrown on the defensive, he tossed the newspaper on the table and simmered. Madeleine entered to see him pacing up and down.

"Hello, Father," she said, kissing him on the cheek. "How nice it is to see you again."

"I wish I hadn't come now."

"Why not?"

"Because I wouldn't have seen that article about Scotland Yard if I'd stayed at home. Someone has the gall to claim that the Detective Department is a failure. They even wrote some nasty things about Robert."

"Oh, take no notice of that," she told him, blithely. "They always expect too much of the police. Robert ignores articles like that."

"Well, I don't, Maddy."

"You mustn't take it so personally."

"It's unfair," said Andrews. "I know how hard he works. When is he coming home, by the way?"

"I've no idea."

"But Swindon isn't all that far away. He managed to slip home when he was working in Dorset and that was four hours on the train. I know that because I made the journey there to warn him that you'd gone into hospital."

"Please don't remind me of that, Father. It was . . . very frightening at the time. However, all's well that ends well," she said, brightening. "Think of Helen. You've got the most delightful granddaughter."

"And I've got a son-in-law who's laughed at in a newspaper."

"Robert will vindicate himself, have no fear."

"Do you think that —?"

"No," she said, cutting him off. "You are not to write to the newspaper on his behalf. Robert would never allow that. Forget the article and come over here. I have something good to tell you." They moved to the sofa and sat down. "It's about Lydia."

"Has she been here?"

"Yes, she was bemoaning the fact that she's desperately lonely at Christmas."

"It's her fault, Maddy. She walked out on her family."

"Lydia was driven out by her father," corrected Madeleine, "and her elder brother didn't want her in the house again. That's all history now, anyway. The fact is that I've invited her to come to us."

"Won't she be in the way?"

"No, of course she won't. She's wonderful at fitting in."

"Your aunts will call in on Christmas Day and so will your cousins."

"Lydia will be very pleased to meet them. I'm certainly not going to hide her away. She's on her own, Father," said Madeleine, "and she's been such a staunch friend to me. I didn't hesitate to invite her here. Ideally," she continued, smiling, "I'd like someone else to put in an appearance at some point."

"Who are you talking about?"

"Detective Constable Hilton."

"Ah, yes, she owes a lot to that young man."

"Lydia appreciates that. She'd hoped to see more of him."

Andrews grinned. "Did she really like him that much?"

"Oh, yes, and he was certainly drawn to her but . . . nothing happened."

"Are you surprised?"

"Frankly, I am," she admitted. "A romance seemed to be on the horizon. I think Lydia believed that as well, but her hopes were dashed."

"You can't blame him for that."

"Why not?"

"Look at the situation. Lydia is a very pretty young woman. Any man would be attracted to her and I'm sure that Constable Hinton was. But there's a yawning gap between them," he pointed out. "He's just a humble detective while she's a wealthy woman in her own right."

"So?"

"They're worlds apart, Maddy."

"Robert and I were worlds apart once," she said, smiling, "but not any more."

Howard Law had never met anyone quite like Colbeck before. In his meticulous attire and with his educated vowels, he seemed an unlikely policeman. When he heard that Colbeck had once abandoned a promising career as a barrister in order to join the Metropolitan Police Force, the vicar was amazed. His only dealings with the police had been with Inspector Piercey, an industrious but limited man with no experience of a murder inquiry. Unlike Colbeck, he didn't inspire confidence and he certainly didn't have the former's knowledge of the Gospels.

"Matthew, Mark and Luke all record the way that Jesus was mocked on the cross," said Colbeck. "He was ridiculed by the soldiers, the chief priests and the elders alike. They taunted him, saying that he could save others but not himself. If he was the Messiah, why didn't God come to his aid? John makes no mention of the derision but the other Gospels are of one voice. Is that what we have here?" he asked. "Was the killer sneering at him for his beliefs?"

"Frank Rodman was no Christ-like figure, Inspector."

"Yet you told me he was devout."

"That was only when he was sober," said Law. "I know that some of his workmates thought him a nuisance because he used to sing hymns at them, but that would hardly constitute a motive for murder."

"It could in some circumstances." Colbeck's thoughts drifted to Llewellyn. "I suppose that none of the Welsh families worship here?"

"No, Inspector. This is an Anglican church and they're Nonconformist by nature. We have a Baptist church here and a Primitive Methodist church was built halfway between Old and New Swindon to draw in people from both. I assume that the Welsh can be found at one of those on a Sunday, though I daresay they'll want to build a chapel of their own one day."

"Is it true that they've stirred up trouble since they came?"

"I'm afraid so, though there are faults on both sides. The newcomers were not welcomed, especially when they were heard speaking in their own language. For their part, the Welsh were very envious."

"Why was that?"

"Most of the workers here have proper houses, built especially for them by the GWR. The Welsh have been crammed into the barracks."

"Yes, Sergeant Leeming mentioned those."

"They must have fifty or sixty children in there. It's not ideal accommodation."

"Have you ever come across a man named Gareth Llewellyn?"

The vicar pulled a face. "Oh, yes, we've all met him."

"I hear a note of censure."

"When they first arrived here, Llewellyn attended a service at St Mark's with his family. He accosted me afterwards and told me that there was no fire in my sermon and that the choir couldn't sing in tune."

"I don't think Mr Rodman would have liked that."

"If we hadn't been in a church," recalled Law, "Frank would have hit him. To avoid any trouble, I hustled Llewellyn and his family outside."

Colbeck was interested to hear of another clash between Rodman and the Welshman. It made him wonder how many more there'd been. Most newcomers to an area tried to blend in. Llewellyn, it seemed, enjoyed sticking out.

"I've just been thinking about your comment that the man you're after may be an atheist," said the vicar. "Over the past year or so, we've had some vandalism here. Thankfully, it's only been small-scale so far but it could be the work of someone who doesn't believe in God and who's therefore offended by those of us who do."

"What sort of damage?"

"Some of the headstones in the churchyard were defaced, causing great upset to the relatives of the deceased. White paint was splattered over a statue of an angel and there were more minor incidents."

"Did you contact the police?"

"Inspector Piercey had one of his men on guard here at night for over a week in the summer. Nobody turned up but the message is clear. Someone doesn't like us."

"I'll bear that in mind."

Since the vicar knew the village inside out, Colbeck took the time to find out as much about its people and their way of life as possible. For his part, Law was glad to have a serious conversation with a man of such manifest intelligence. Inevitably, they came back to the tragedy confronting Betty Rodman.

"Her situation is hopeless," said Law. "Just imagine what it will be like for the children to spend Christmas without their father."

Colbeck was hoping that his daughter wouldn't be in the same situation. He got up and thanked the vicar for his help. About to leave, he was struck by a thought.

"It may be that atheism is nothing to do with the murder," he said. "There's another explanation why the victim was beheaded."

"Is there?"

"Think of John the Baptist. Against his will, Herod ordered his decapitation at the request of Salome."

"There's an account of it in Mark, chapter six. 'I want you to give me at once the head of John the Baptist on a platter.' What a terrible demand that was!"

"Have we stumbled on the answer?" asked Colbeck.

"I don't understand."

"Is a woman responsible?"

The passage of time had not soothed Betty Rodman. She was more disturbed than ever. While she'd managed to control her weeping, she could do nothing to ease the pain of a broken heart. As soon as he was able, Fred Alford had come straight to the house, allowing his wife to go home to feed their children. Mabel Hankin, the neighbour who'd looked after Betty's sons and daughter, brought the baby back to

**91**

her mother, hoping Betty would draw succour from the feel of the child in her arms. At the same time, she feared for the future, wondering how she'd be able to house, feed and clothe Martha and the two boys. Her prospects were bleak.

"Everything will work out," he said, putting an arm around her shoulders. "I don't quite know how but it will."

"I've been left almost destitute, Fred."

"Didn't Frank have any savings?"

"They went on drink. He was always sorry afterwards but that was no use. I begged and begged him to stay at home but he wouldn't. When he'd come back late, it was either because he'd drunk too much or because he'd been to church."

"It would have been closed at that time of night, Betty."

"He'd kneel in the porch and pray for forgiveness."

"I kept telling him that he had to put you and the family first. It's what I would have done. I like a pint of beer as much as the next man but I'm always home early and I put savings aside every week."

"Yours is one life, Fred, ours was another."

"Yet he always seemed happy." He became tentative. "Were you?"

"I loved Frank but . . . oh, he could be so difficult at times."

"We realised that."

"Now I'll have to learn how to live without him."

There was a long, brooding silence. He was savouring their closeness but all she was thinking about was the hardship that lay ahead. The baby started to cry. Betty rocked her slowly asleep, forcing Alford to remove his arm.

"Would you like a cup of tea?" he asked.

"No, thank you. Liza made one for me earlier on."

He peered at the baby. "How is Martha?"

"She's lucky. She doesn't know what's happened to us."

Pretending to look at the baby, Alford was really studying her. He'd always admired Betty and was bound to compare her with his own wife. Liza had become rather flabby and the attractive figure that had first caught his eye had now more or less disappeared. Betty, however, was still essentially the same shape she'd been when she was eighteen. Her body was hunched now and the colour had drained out of her face but he was still looking at a beautiful woman.

"Did the vicar call?" he asked.

"Yes, I had two visitors," she replied. "The first one was Inspector Colbeck. He was kindness himself. He'll do everything in his power to catch the man who . . ." The words trailed off. "Then the vicar turned up. I know it's a silly thing to say but I felt honoured that he took the trouble."

"He's the one who should have felt honoured."

"Mr Law is a true Christian. He invited us to stay in the parsonage."

"Well, I hope you didn't agree," he said, quickly. "You can move in with us. Liza told you that, surely? Count on us for everything."

"It would be an imposition, Fred. Besides, you could never fit us all in. There's plenty of room at the parsonage. Mrs Law showed us around once."

Alford was hurt. "I was banking on you to stay with us," he said. "Davy and Leonard get on so well with our children. It's the obvious answer. Yes, I know it will be a squeeze to have ten of us under the same roof but Walter Hughes has an identical house to ours and there's twelve of them living there."

"Mrs Hughes says it's like Bedlam sometimes. You don't want that."

"We're your friends, Betty. We simply want to show our love."

She reached out to squeeze his hand. "There's one way you can do that."

"Tell me what it is and I'll do it."

"I want to know *everything*, Fred."

"You already do."

"No, I have this awful feeling that people are hiding things from me. Inspector Colbeck wouldn't give me any details because he was afraid to upset me. But Frank was my husband," she said, firmly, "so I have a right to know."

"That . . . may not be wise."

"Is it that bad?"

"I had to identify the body, I was so glad you didn't have to do it."

"Why?"

"Because you've got to be protected, Betty, that's why."

"Won't I ever be told the truth?" she asked, anguish clouding her eyes.

"Be patient, Betty," he suggested. "It won't be long."

Conversation in the bar at the Queen's Tap that evening was fuelled entirely by the murder. Everybody had an opinion on the subject and a number of potential suspects were mentioned. Seated in the next room, Colbeck and Leeming could hear names drifting through to them. Having chosen a table in the far corner, they sampled what turned out to be rather basic fare. However, the place was clean, the landlord's wife was an attentive waitress, the food was edible and — thanks to the stern supervision of Hiram Wells — they were left in peace. They delayed any discussion until the meal was finished and the plates had been cleared away. Leeming then sipped his beer while Colbeck opted for a glass of whisky.

After comparing notes, they concentrated on the anonymous mail that had been delivered to them at the pub. Leeming had had time to read through it and separate the wheat from the chaff.

"Six of them named someone called Albert Crann," he said, "and I thought we had a real suspect at last."

"Is that what he is?"

"No, sir, he's just a blind alley."

"So why did six people pick him out?"

"It's because he's the most unpopular foreman in the whole Works. According to the landlord, Crann is barely five feet in height. He couldn't even reach

Rodman's head, let alone slice it off. His enemies simply wanted to set us on to him to give him a fright."

"Spare me the hoaxes, Victor. Who should we take seriously?"

"I think there are three contenders," said Leeming. "I'd have added Llewellyn's name but you ruled that out."

"Start with the prime suspect."

"That must be Hector Samway. Two of these letters point to him and they both tell you why." He handed them over. "He had a fight with Rodman some weeks ago and he came off worst. Samway was heard vowing to get his own back."

"Does he have a history of violence?"

"Yes, he's been banned from here and from the Glue Pot."

"Who else?"

"There's a man named Danny Gill who deserves looking at. He lost his job as a smith when they laid people off and reckons that Rodman was responsible. One of them had to go so Gill was sacked while Rodman stayed. He's been seen hanging about the village and, of course, having worked there, he knows the geography of the Locomotive Works very well."

"Does he have a job?"

"Yes, he's employed by a butcher in the Old Town. Do you see why I singled him out, sir? Butchers know how to chop things in two with a cleaver."

"Gill sounds more promising than Samway."

"I don't think so."

"We must agree to differ. If you favour Samway, question him tomorrow."

"What about Gill?"

"I'll tackle him," decided Colbeck. "It will give me a chance to see the Old Town. What's the third name?"

"Simeon Cudlip," replied Leeming, "but he wasn't suggested by any of the people in this pile of letters. It was Mr Alford who mentioned him. He was one of the men who was very fond of Rodman's wife before she was married. Cudlip had hopes of calling her Mrs Cudlip one day but she turned him down."

"What manner of man is he?"

"Alford said that he was quiet and determined. He works as a clerk."

"Is he physically capable of tackling someone like Rodman?"

"So it appears."

"Does he have a family?"

"No, it's possible that he's still pining for Betty Rodman."

"Well, we've got a start, anyway," said Colbeck. "I'll speak to Mr Stinson to see what he has to say about these three individuals, then we can split up and talk to them in person."

"What about Superintendent Tallis?"

Colbeck smiled. "Oh, I don't think that he qualifies as a suspect, Victor."

"He'll expect a report of our first day."

"Then he'll get it tomorrow."

"On Friday he's going off to the reunion. I was very pleased to hear about it at first. I breathe much easier when the superintendent is away," said Leeming. "Then he told us who'd take his place."

"Inspector Grosvenor will cope very well."

"I don't want him having any power over us."

"It's only for the weekend."

The sergeant scowled. "A lot can happen during a weekend, sir."

Summoned to the superintendent's office, Grosvenor responded at once. He found Tallis seated at his desk and studying a copy of *Bradshaw*. He had to wait a couple of minutes before the older man eventually looked up.

"You sent for me, sir," said Grosvenor.

"Yes, yes, I did."

"Is there a problem?"

"No," said Tallis, "but there's a change of plan. I've had an invitation from an army friend. He lives in Kent and is within easy reach of the barracks where the reunion will take place. The invitation came at short notice because Captain Wardlow was unsure if he'd be well enough to attend. Fortunately, his arthritis has relented somewhat so he's offered me hospitality. I'm going to stay with him tomorrow night. That means I'll catch an afternoon train."

Grosvenor was delighted. "So I'll be in charge sooner than I thought?"

"I've spoken to the commissioner. I'll leave here at midday." Tallis became nostalgic. "It will be wonderful to see Captain Wardlow again. We fought in the First Sikh War together. I still bear a few scars from that.

People complain that the streets of London are not safe. If they want to know what real danger is, they should join the British army and fight against the Sikhs. It was a brutal campaign in every way but we held sway in the end. War is a terrible thing but it does mould a man's character. After coming through the battles that I did, I feel able to take on anything. I like to think that I've had my triumphs in the Detective Department but they pale beside the thrill of conquest on a battlefield." He sat back in his chair and wallowed in his reminiscences. "Did I ever tell you what impelled me to join the army?"

"No, sir," said Grosvenor. "I'd be interested to hear why."

But he was not listening to the superintendent. As Tallis regaled him with a series of military escapades, all that the inspector was thinking about was the fact that he'd replace him at noon on the following day. He'd at last have the power to give orders, issue reprimands and wreak his revenge on his enemies.

The face of Robert Colbeck came into his mind.

# CHAPTER
# NINE

Oswald Stinson was an early riser. As the manager, he felt that he should set an example and arrive at the Works as the men were streaming in at the start of another day. What he hadn't expected that morning was that someone would get to his office before he did. Seated outside it, looking relaxed and debonair, was Colbeck. He raised a hand in welcome.

"What the devil are *you* doing here, Inspector?" asked Stinson.

"I'm hunting for the man who killed Frank Rodman."

"Well, you won't find him in my office, I can assure you of that." Unlocking the door, he led Colbeck into the room then turned to face him. "Before we go any further, I must tell you something. I had a visitor late last night. He'd been in Bristol all day and had only caught up with developments here when he got back. His name is William Morris."

"William Morris, the poet and artist?"

"This is a different man with the same name but he also makes a living with his pen. He's the editor of the *Swindon Advertiser* and wanted details of the murder. Since we agreed to keep certain aspects of it back, I told him enough to give him something to print and took the opportunity to place a reward notice in the newspaper. I also insisted that he wasn't to bother you at such an hour."

"Thank you, sir."

"That means you'll find him on the doorstep of the Queen's Tap when you get back there. Morris is very persistent."

"He's only doing his job, sir."

"Be prepared," said Stinson. "Now, do you have any news for me?"

"Yes, I'm full of admiration for the way that you manage to get to the Works at this unearthly hour. It must take a great effort."

"I was asking if there were any signs of progress."

"Progress is always difficult to quantify."

"Please explain what you mean."

"Well," said Colbeck, frankly, "in any investigation, you have to start by gathering evidence and meeting relevant witnesses. Without realising it, you may actually make headway from the very start. By the same token, you can expend an enormous amount of energy pursuing lines of inquiry, get the impression that you are very close to solving a crime then find that you're back where you started."

"Which is it in this case?"

"We're advancing slowly, sir, to put it no higher than that. What we've done so far is this . . ."

Colbeck went on to tell him about the information he and Leeming had amassed between them and how they were still trying to collate it. He mentioned the anonymous letters that had come in. He also told the manager how enlightening his visit to Howard Law had been.

"You're lucky to have such a man as your vicar, sir."

"That's what I've always felt, Inspector. Howard Law is everything you want in a good shepherd. His sermons are uplifting and he's renowned for his pastoral care. Yesterday, alas, I came up against a less pleasing side of his character."

Colbeck raised a disbelieving eyebrow. "Really?"

"He tried to harass me into extending Mrs Rodman's stay at the house."

"I would have thought you'd do that without being asked."

"Being asked is one thing, Inspector," said the other, "but I was subjected to undue pressure and made to feel as if I was being cruel to the Rodman family in planning for their departure. The GWR is not a charitable institution. Other families are waiting to move into a house. Mrs Rodman and her children must go."

"Agreed, sir, but I do feel that a show of sympathy is in order."

"The vicar wanted more than that. It was almost as if he expected me to let them stay in perpetuity — and that's out of the question." He shot Colbeck a warning glance. "I hope *you* haven't also come to tell me how to do my job."

"I wouldn't presume to do so, Mr Stinson. I just wanted to see if you recognised the names of any of the three people we've picked out as credible suspects.

**102**

They may, of course, have nothing whatsoever to do with the murder," Colbeck added, "but in the interests of thoroughness, we need to speak to them."

"Hundreds of men work here, Inspector. I don't know them all."

"What about a coppersmith called Hector Samway?"

Stinson frowned. "Oh, I've heard of him."

"What can you tell me?"

"He used to be quite disruptive until I hauled him in here and threatened to dismiss him unless he behaved himself. He's a rather surly character and he's not a man to cross. There are rumours about him taking on Rodman in a fight outside the Glue Pot. Samway came to work with a black eye next day."

"What age would he be?"

"Much the same age as Rodman, I fancy. He does, however, have a gentler side to him. Samway came to me last summer to beg for some time off to organise his wife's funeral. A very sad business — she died of tuberculosis." His eyes flared momentarily. "I should have reminded the vicar of that. He'd have been forced to admit that we can be compassionate on occasion. I gave Samway a whole week off with pay."

"Let's move on to Daniel Gill."

"That name is vaguely familiar to me, Inspector."

"He was laid off a few years ago and now works for a butcher."

"Lots of people had to leave, I'm afraid. Gill must have been one of them."

"That takes us on to our third suspect," said Colbeck. "Simeon Cudlip."

"I do recall him because of the unusual name. He's a clerk here and a good one, by all accounts. Unlike Samway, he's had no history of causing trouble. He's quiet, industrious and gets on with his job. I wish more of them were like that."

"Thank you, sir," said Colbeck. "Your comments have been helpful. I'm sorry that you had nothing to say about Gill. I can't explain why but he strikes me as the most interesting of the three."

Daniel Gill walked jauntily along Victoria Road until he came to Newspaper House, where he paused to glance at the front page of the *Swindon Advertiser* on display in the window. Beneath the stark headline — MURDER AT THE LOCOMOTIVE WORKS — was the name of the victim. Gill laughed all the way to the butcher's shop.

Hector Samway was unhappy at being dragged from out of the burning heat of the Foundry into the cold air outside. He grumbled under his breath. Victor Leeming weighed him up. Samway was a chunky man in his forties with a neck so short that his head appeared to grow out of his shoulders. His face was a portrait of resentment. When he saw the sergeant waiting for him in frock coat and top hat, he assumed that he was part of the management and manufactured an expression of mute obedience. It was only when they got to the office assigned to the detectives that he understood who the stranger was.

"You're that inspector from London," he said, warily.

"I'm only a sergeant, sir, as it happens, and I'm glad to be so. I'm Detective Sergeant Leeming from Scotland Yard."

"What do you want?"

"I just wanted a little talk with you, sir."

"I've got work to do."

"So have I," said Leeming, "and talking to you happens to be it. Would you mind telling me where you were the night before last?"

Samway stiffened. "Why d'you want to know that?"

"Just answer the question, please."

"I was at home."

"Would that be all night?"

"What's going on? Am I in trouble or something?"

"You could be, sir."

"Hey," said the other, voice hardening, "you don't think I had anything to do with . . . what happened here?"

"We're just making enquiries."

"Why pick on me?"

"I'm still waiting to hear if you were at home all night."

"Yes, I was — are you satisfied now?"

"No, Mr Samway, and I won't be until someone confirms what you just told me. I'll need to speak to your wife."

"You can't do that."

"Does that mean you're not married?"

"No."

"Then why can't I speak to your wife?"

Samway's face crumpled. "Jean died last August."

"Oh," murmured Leeming, "I'm sorry to hear that."

Seeing the other man's patent grief, Leeming felt sorry for him at first and wished that he hadn't mentioned the wife. But he had to put duty before sympathy. Samway needed to be questioned. He might still be in mourning but that wouldn't rule him out as the killer. Indeed, he believed, it might be a reason to strengthen his suspicion of the man. Leeming had known others in the past who tried to compensate for a tragic loss by striking out violently at an enemy. Had Samway coped with one death by being responsible for another?

"You knew Mr Rodman, didn't you?"

"Yes," grunted Samway.

"And you didn't like each other."

"He was a bastard."

"Is that why you had a fight with him?"

"No, Sergeant."

"Then what was the reason?"

"It doesn't matter."

"It matters a great deal, sir. I need to know."

"Then go and ask him," said Samway, curling his lip.

"That's a very cruel suggestion, sir."

"I hated the man. Rodman was a bully. He picked on people."

"Why did he single you out?"

"Who cares? I've forgotten all about it."

"I don't believe that, Mr Samway. I sense that you're the kind of man who never forgets a thing. He goaded you, didn't he?"

"It's none of your business."

**106**

"He goaded you to the point where you lost your temper."

"Don't keep on about it," said Samway, bunching his fists.

"Mr Rodman knew what would hurt you most, didn't he? I think that he exploited your weak point," said Leeming, "and we both know what that is. He taunted you about the loss of your wife, didn't he?"

"Be quiet!" yelled Samway, throwing a punch.

Leeming stepped back quickly to avoid it, then he grabbed the man by the shoulders and pinned him against the wall. When Samway tried to escape, he found himself too securely held. At length, his rage began to cool. When Leeming felt it was safe to do so, he let go of him.

"I could arrest you for that, Mr Samway."

"It was your fault."

"If I reported it, you could lose your job."

"I didn't mean it," pleaded Samway. "You just kept on and on at me."

"Perhaps I did," said Leeming. "But I still want to hear the truth. Please don't attack me again or you'll leave this office in handcuffs. Is that clear?"

Samway nodded sulkily. "Yes . . ."

"All I want is a simple answer. He taunted you about your wife, didn't he?"

"No, he didn't."

"Then what was the fight about?"

The words dripped slowly out. "It was about Betty Rodman."

Betty Rodman sat beside the crib and looked sadly down at her sleeping daughter, wondering what sort of future the child would have now. Held back from school once more, her two bemused sons were being looked after by their neighbour, Mabel Hankin. All they'd been told was that their father had gone away. Betty's only adult companion was Liza Alford, as kind and supportive as ever. She'd carried the crib downstairs so that Betty could have the baby beside her. Tired and listless, Betty sipped the tea that her friend had made for her.

"I could never thank you enough, Liza."

"You'd do the same for me."

"You and Fred have been saintly."

"It was his idea that I should spend the night here with you. We didn't want you to be alone."

"I had the children," said Betty.

"You needed help and so I came. I slept quite well in that chair."

"I didn't get a wink of sleep."

"That's a pity. You need it."

"I keep thinking about Frank."

As they drank their tea, there was a long, companionable silence. No words were spoken or required. The restful interlude was soon interrupted by a knock on the door. It startled both of them.

"I don't want to see anybody," said Betty, shrinking back.

"Let me see who it is first." Liza peered out of the window. "It's the vicar."

"Oh . . . well, that's different."

"Shall I let him in?"

In response to a nod from Betty, she opened the front door and invited Howard Law to step in. There was a brief exchange of greetings then he handed Betty a gift. In the small basket was a clutch of eggs.

"Thank you," she said, "but I couldn't eat a thing."

"You must keep your strength up," he argued. "The children depend on you."

"Is there any news?" asked Liza.

"None that I know of, Mrs Alford, but I had the pleasure of a long talk with Inspector Colbeck yesterday. He's an extraordinary man and I have full confidence in him to find out who was responsible for this hideous crime."

"Did you speak to Mr Stinson?"

"Yes, I did," said Law, guardedly.

"Did he say how long Betty could stay here?"

"He couldn't give me an exact date but I'm hoping it may be weeks."

"And then what?" asked Betty. "What's to become of us?"

"You'll move into the parsonage."

"We can't stay there for ever."

"We'll find somewhere for you all."

"I want to stay in the village."

"I'd have thought you'd prefer to go well away from here. It will have unfortunate associations for you."

"My friends are here," she said. "I don't want to lose touch with people like Liza and Fred. They're part of the family."

"And we always will be," affirmed Liza.

"Let's cross those bridges when we come to them," advised Law. "There are some practical problems to solve first. The inspector told me that there'd be a post-mortem and that the body wouldn't be released until after the inquest. However sensitive a subject it may be, we do have to discuss the funeral."

Betty took a deep breath. "I'm ready."

"If you find it too upsetting, you can always break off."

The vicar had been in charge of a large number of funerals at St Mark's and he'd learnt that it was impossible to predict the behaviour of surviving spouses. He'd seen strong men reduced to tears by the loss of their wives and apparently frail women showing unexpected courage in coping with the death of a husband. In one sense, Betty Rodman was under greater pressure than the others. The beloved spouses of others had all died of natural causes. Her husband had been murdered.

"We have to decide on the order of service," he explained.

"I'll leave that to you, Vicar."

"Don't you want to choose the hymns?"

"I'd like to have Frank's favourites."

"Are they entirely suitable for a funeral?"

"Does that matter?" asked Liza. "You just asked Betty to choose the hymns. She can have what she wants, can't she?"

"Yes, of course," replied Law, making an attempt to sound obliging while keen to exert some control.

**110**

"Frank's favourite was that lovely hymn written by Cecil Francis Alexander — 'There is a Green Hill Far Away'. It's an essentially Easter hymn and might seem rather incongruous so close to Christmas."

"We're having no Christmas this year," said Betty, faintly.

"Yes, you are," said Liza. "You're all coming to us."

"It won't be the same without Frank."

"Think of the children. They must have *something* good to remember."

"That's an excellent piece of advice," said Law, seizing on his cue. "They're too young to understand the implications of what's happened to their father but they're old enough to experience at least a little of the joy of Christmas. Thank you, Mrs Alford," he added, turning to her. "I fully endorse what you said."

The manager's warning had been accurate. Leaving the Works, Colbeck got back to the Queen's Tap to find William Morris waiting for him. Though the pub was closed that early in the morning, the landlord had invited the editor in out of the swirling wind. Morris was a well-dressed man in his thirties with a full beard, an open face and wide, enquiring eyes. After introductions had taken place, he shook hands with the zeal of a true believer, squeezing hard and saying how — on the strength of what he'd been told about him by Oswald Stinson — he admired Colbeck for his astonishing run of success as a detective. It was a full minute before the inspector was able to detach his hand.

They moved to a table and sat down. Morris produced a notebook at once.

"I didn't hear about the murder until late last night," he said.

"Mr Stinson told me that he was about to go to bed when you called. I don't really have much to add to what he must have said."

"There must be something."

"How often is your newspaper printed?"

"The *Swindon Advertiser* is a weekly publication," said Morris, proudly. "It was first printed six years ago as a broadsheet and sold for one penny. I was the writer, editor, printer and — believe it or not — delivery boy. The second edition was twice the size because I included advertisements of local businesses."

"That was very enterprising of you, sir."

"I used a hand press in my father's shop in Wood Street. After a year or so, I'd made enough money to move to bigger premises in Victoria Road and, in time, was able to add a printing shop at the rear."

"You've worked hard, obviously."

"My mission is to keep Swindon well informed, especially when something as important as this falls into my lap."

"You won't have been misled by Mr Stinson."

"He took the liberty of quoting you, Inspector."

Opening his valise, he took out the latest edition of the newspaper and handed it over. Colbeck studied it with interest, pleased that the manager had given only the outline details of the crime and offered no speculation about possible suspects. He was praised by

Morris for having the wisdom to summon the Railway Detective. The article was well written, though there were a few typographical errors.

"I stayed up half the night reprinting the paper," said Morris. "Such are the perils of being an editor. I was just about to release a new edition to the public when a major story suddenly popped up."

"By the next edition, you'll have a lot more to report."

"Does that mean you anticipate an early arrest?"

"I can't be that specific about that."

"But you remain hopeful."

"I'm cautiously hopeful."

Morris lowered his voice. "Is it true that the body was naked?"

"Who told you that?"

"I bumped into Inspector Piercey earlier today."

"He's not deeply involved in the case."

"He gave me the impression that he was."

"I'll need to speak to him," said Colbeck, face impassive. "As it happens, I was thinking of going to the Old Town today. When I visit a different part of the country, I like to get my bearings as soon as possible."

"I can offer you a lift in my trap," volunteered Morris, "and we can have a longer conversation on the way."

"That's very kind of you, Mr Morris. I accept your offer."

"We can go as soon as you wish."

"As for what Inspector Piercey told you, I'd treat it with some scepticism. I'll make a point of speaking to him when I'm in the Old Town."

Colbeck was careful to conceal his reason for visiting the older part of Swindon because he didn't want to disclose that the butcher's assistant was a suspect in the case. Unable to make use of it himself, Morris might be tempted to pass on the information to a national newspaper. In that event, reporters would start to converge on the Locomotive Works and would inevitably hamper the investigation. Much as he liked Morris, he vowed to keep him at arm's length. After a second glance at the latest edition, he handed it back.

"You have a gift for journalism, Mr Morris."

The newspaperman laughed. "My gifts pale beside yours, Inspector," he said. "Only a genius could do what you do. What made you join the police?"

"The work appealed to me."

"Do you really find ruthless, cold-hearted killers *appealing*?"

"Oh, yes," said Colbeck, "they always fascinate me. The urge to kill is something that many people feel at some stage in life but, fortunately, only a tiny proportion of them actually commit murder. Each case is different, each killer is highly individual. Their appeal to me is quite irresistible."

"What interests you about this particular man?"

"He's unpredictable. I'd like to see what he does next."

Making sure that nobody was about, he slipped furtively into the woods carrying a bloodstained sack. When he came to a tree stump, he took a head out of the sack and set it down. The face was comprehensively smashed in and the distorted cranium was covered in dried blood. Lowering his trousers, the man goaded him.

"Come on, Frank," he said, smirking. "Let's hear you sing."

Then he urinated all over the head.

# CHAPTER
# TEN

William Morris was a pleasant companion. As he drove Colbeck away from the village, he provided him with a brief history of the Old Town and recalled how radically the community had been changed by the arrival of the GWR Locomotive Works. Early hostility from the inhabitants of Swindon had slowly given way to resigned acceptance. In the early years, the market had benefited from the presence of a large number of new customers a mile away but shops had slowly started to open in the New Town, saving people a long trudge across the fields to buy food.

"Are you related to the other William Morris?" asked Colbeck.

"I didn't know there was another one."

"He's written on architecture and is also a poet. I remember enjoying one of his poems printed in a magazine — 'The Haystack in the Floods'."

"I'm no poet, Inspector. I'm unashamedly prosaic."

"You do a valuable job, Mr Morris, and you should be proud of that. From what you've told me, you do it more or less on your own."

"I do have one or two people to help me, as it happens, but I make sure I'm involved in every stage of the process. The *Advertiser* is my baby and I love to cradle it in my arms. Do you think that's evidence of megalomania?"

"Far from it," said Colbeck, smiling. "It shows that you still care very much about your newspaper and rightly so. I'm grateful that you spoke to Mr Stinson and to me. There are some editors in London who'd send reporters to interview a grieving family in a murder case. That's an unacceptable intrusion, in my view."

"I'd never dream of doing anything like that."

"National newspapers are not quite so considerate."

"You sound as if you've had difficulties with some of them."

"They bark at my heels like a pack of hounds sometimes. That can be very distracting when I'm trying to focus on a crime."

They'd left the village behind now and were into open country. Colbeck could see what a beautiful part of Wiltshire it was but he could also understand why the GWR had chosen the site. It was ideally placed to link London to the West Country and the presence of the Wilts and Berks Canal meant that coal, iron and timber could be easily brought in during the early stages of construction.

"Would you like me to show you around the Old Town?" asked Morris.

"No, no," said Colbeck, "I'd prefer to be on my own."

"But I could introduce you to people."

"I'd rather wander around incognito, Mr Morris."

"I understand," said the other. "The murder will dominate conversation. If people knew that you'd been sent to solve it, they'd pester you unmercifully. By the way," he said, "what was the name of that poem you mentioned? I'd like to read it."

"It's 'The Haystack in the Floods' and you'll find an odd coincidence in it."

"What's that?"

"It features a cruel murder."

Inspector Grosvenor was too impatient to wait until noon. So keen was he to take on the superintendent's mantle that he arrived at Tallis's office almost an hour in advance. He was wearing his new frock coat for the occasion.

"Good morning, sir," said Grosvenor. "How are you?"

"The honest answer is that I can't wait to get away."

"Don't let me hold you up."

"Everything has to go in this record book," said Tallis, placing a palm on the ledger in front of him, "as I showed you. I expect accuracy of information and neat calligraphy."

"You'll get both, sir."

"This time tomorrow I'll be back with my old regiment."

"When is the reunion dinner?"

"That will be on Saturday evening. Wine and spirits are always served in the most generous quantities. That's why I'm allowing myself Sunday to recover. As for your work here," added Tallis, "don't forget to crack the whip. You have to remind those under you that you are in charge."

Grosvenor's sly smile came into view. "I'll enjoy doing that," he said. "How do I get in touch with Colbeck?"

"There's a telegraph station at Swindon Junction. Send a message there and it will be passed on to him. Why do you wish to contact Colbeck?"

"I think he needs a rap on the knuckles, sir. He's been there for the best part of twenty-four hours and we haven't heard a peep from him."

"Yes, we have."

"Oh?"

"A report came by courier first thing this morning," explained Tallis, opening a drawer to take out two sheets of paper. "It's a perfect example of how a report should be written — clear, concise yet covering every aspect of the case. Read it, Inspector."

"I'll be a superintendent soon, sir."

"Even at the higher rank, you should still be ready to learn from a master of the art. As you'll see, it's a highly complex case but Colbeck has it well in hand."

"I'll need more evidence of that," said the other, grumpily.

"Then here it is." Tallis gave him the report with an ambiguous smile. "I regret to say that I was quite unable to find a single fault in it."

Simeon Cudlip was one of the many clerks working in the building where the detectives had their office. When he was summoned by Leeming, therefore, the man only had to walk up a flight of stairs and along a corridor. He was mystified as to why he'd been called to speak to the sergeant.

"Are you sure you've got the right person?" he asked, guardedly.

"Yes, Mr Cudlip."

"I'm just one of the clerks here."

"This is nothing to do with your status."

"Why have you asked for me?"

"I wanted to have a good look at you, sir."

Cudlip was very much like the other clerks he'd seen flitting about the building — smart, subdued and uniformly nondescript. What set Cudlip apart from his colleagues was that he didn't have the same rounded shoulders and deferential manner. He was a handsome man in his thirties with broad shoulders and a barrel chest. He clearly had the physique to take on someone like Rodman. Unlike most of the employees, he looked Leeming in the eye.

"How long have you lived here, Mr Cudlip?"

"It must be eight years now."

"Do you like it here?"

"Yes, I do."

"The wonder is that you've never married."

Cudlip blenched. "That's my business, Sergeant."

"Wouldn't you like to have a family? It means that you always have someone to go home to."

"I've seen too many unhappy marriages."

"What about Frank Rodman? Was he unhappily married?"

"It's not for me to say," muttered the other.

"But you *knew* him, didn't you?"

"I knew of him but I wasn't a friend of his. In fact, it must be years since I even spoke to him. I'm not a drinking man, Sergeant. He was. That's never a good thing for a man with responsibilities."

"I believe that you know Mrs Rodman."

"That was a very long time ago."

"When did you last speak to *her*?"

"I've no reason to do so." His eyelids narrowed. "Someone's been talking to you, haven't they? I'm a suspect."

"You obviously object to that."

"I object very strongly."

"Tell me why Mr Cudlip."

"I lead a quiet, law-abiding life, Sergeant, and I happen to prefer my own company when I'm off duty. When I'm here," he stressed, "I'm in the same office as five other clerks so I'm not starved of company. I hear them complaining about their wives and moaning about their children and I'm thankful that I never made the mistake of getting married. They've all put a ball and chain around their ankle. I'm free to do exactly what I want."

There was an almost exultant note in his voice. Leeming wondered how he could sound so happy when he boasted that he had no social life. If his time was divided between work as a clerk and sitting at home alone, there was no cause for celebration. What it did mean, Leeming realised, was that he would have been able to move freely about the village — and the Works

— on the night of the murder. With nobody else to answer to, he would be invisible.

"Are you a churchgoer, sir?" asked Leeming, remembering what Colbeck had surmised with regard to the killer. "I'm told you have a lovely church here."

"Churches are never lovely to me."

"But St Mark's was built especially for this village."

"I never go near the place."

"Is there a reason for that?"

"It's because I don't believe in God."

"So that's why you never got married."

"What do you mean?"

"Well, if you take a wife, you have to make promises in church. You and your beloved are joined in the sight of God. If you don't believe that He exists, of course, you could never even think of taking part in a wedding." He saw Cudlip wince slightly. "Was there ever a time when you *were* a Christian?"

"I was brought up to believe certain things as a boy. When I was older, I felt that I'd been cheated. It was all nonsense."

"Did you think it was nonsense when you met Betty Marklew?"

The fact that Leeming asked the question so casually gave it added impact. It silenced Cudlip completely. Painful memories had clearly been reignited. When he eventually spoke, his voice was deliberately slow and emphatic.

"I did not kill Frank Rodman," he said. "I did not help anyone who did kill him. I had no connection whatsoever with the murder."

"What did you do when you heard the news?"

"I felt sorry for Betty . . . for Mrs Rodman, that is. This will destroy her."

"Do you intend to get in touch with her?"

"It's not my place to do that, Sergeant."

"What about the funeral?"

"It's in a church. I won't be there."

"Do you ever go to concerts at the Mechanics' Institution?"

Cudlip nodded. "Now and then . . ."

"So you'll have heard Mr Rodman singing."

"That's not why I went."

"Then why did you go? Was it to see *Mrs* Rodman?"

"I don't know who's been telling you tales," said Cudlip, hotly, "but you've been given the wrong information. There was a time when I . . . was fond of Betty Marklew but I lost interest when she chose someone else. I wasn't the only one who liked her, Sergeant. Why don't you talk to some of them instead? When she got married, Betty disappointed quite a few of us."

"Would you care to name them, sir?"

"I'll name the man who was far more upset than me."

"Who was it?"

"Fred Alford."

During his morning break, Alford left the Foundry and walked quickly across to the Erecting Shop, acknowledging greetings as he went in. He stopped near the spot where the murder victim had been found. The blood had been washed away now but the area had some chairs around it to keep people at bay. It exerted a macabre fascination on some men as they passed it. Alford's interest was more intense. He stared fixedly at the spot until it was time to return to the Foundry.

Colbeck didn't mince his words. Calling at the police station, he spoke to Jared Piercey in the privacy of the inspector's office and berated him for telling the editor of the *Swindon Advertiser* that the dead man had been naked. Though Piercey had been warned to be discreet, he'd given away a crucial piece of information.

"Fortunately," said Colbeck, "Mr Morris has not printed that detail in the latest edition of his newspaper but that's no thanks to you."

Piercey was abashed. "I'm sorry," he said. "It was a slip of the tongue."

"It was a stupid mistake, Inspector, and I ought by rights to report you to your chief constable. Full details will obviously come out at the inquest but that will not be for a while so they won't have the same searing impact. Just imagine how Mrs Rodman, the widow, would feel if she knew everything at this stage. She's already struggling to cope with the enormity of the shock. Your indiscretion would only increase her anguish."

"It won't happen again," said Piercey.

"It should never have happened at all."

The stinging rebuke left the inspector thoroughly chastened. Hoping to play a telling part in the investigation, Piercey would now be confined to the outer perimeter. In talking to William Morris, he'd engineered his own fate. It left him feeling bitter and rueful. Colbeck, meanwhile, strode out of the building and walked along Wood Street. When he'd arrived in the Old Town, he'd noticed the butcher's shop on the corner. He was in luck. As he looked through the window, he saw that there were no customers there. The only person in the shop was a tall, wiry man in his early forties wearing a blood-spattered apron. Colbeck went in.

"I'm looking for Daniel Gill," he said.

"That's me."

"Then I'd like a word with you, if I may, sir. I'm Inspector Colbeck from Scotland Yard and I'm in charge of the investigation into the recent murder at the Locomotive Works."

Gill went pale. "It was nothing to do with me."

"That may well be the case, sir, but I'd still value a word with you."

"Wait here," said the other, thinking quickly. "I'll need to speak to the boss. He's out the back, getting another carcass. I don't suppose . . ."

"Don't worry," said Colbeck, understanding his predicament "I'll wait outside. I don't want to embarrass you in front of your employer."

"He's my uncle."

"I won't take much of your time."

"Thank you."

Colbeck left the shop and walked a dozen yards or so along the street. He didn't have long to wait. Gill came out to join him. He seemed to have recovered from the initial jolt and was more composed. The butcher's nephew had small, dark, mobile eyes either side of a beaky nose. He had a local accent with a pronounced burr.

"I can't see why you're bothering with me, Inspector," he said.

"Your name came to our attention, Mr Gill."

"Who gave it to you?"

"We don't know," replied Colbeck. "In the wake of the murder, we received a number of anonymous suggestions as to who the killer might be. Two people gave us your name."

Gill was furious. "Then they had no right to do so."

"They both said you loathed Frank Rodman."

"That bit is true."

"And that you think that you lost your job unfairly."

"I did. The foreman was too scared of Rodman to sack him so he got rid of me instead. When he saw me leaving, Rodman laughed. I'll never forget that sneer on his ugly face."

"What did you do about it?"

"Nothing," said Gill. "What could I do?"

"You might have tried to get your own back," suggested Colbeck. "According to the people who gave us your name, you vowed that you'd do just that."

"Oh, I was just blowing off steam, Inspector."

"How often do you go to the New Town?"

"Never — this is my home now."

"You must have earned more at the Works than you could ever get from being a butcher's assistant."

"I'm more than that," insisted Gill, thrusting out his chin.

"Uncle Eric is getting on. He's got no sons, only daughters. I'll take over the business one day."

"In that sense, then, you've fallen on your feet."

"Yes, I had a good job to go to."

"So why did you feel so vengeful towards Mr Rodman?"

"We never liked each other. He'd been looking for a chance to get rid of me and leant on the foreman. Being sacked is upsetting. It hurts your pride."

"Would you describe yourself as a proud man, Mr Gill?"

"Yes, I would," said the other, eyes glistening.

Colbeck stepped back to allow two people to walk past on the pavement. A few flakes of snow began to fall. He looked up at the sky.

"It could be a white Christmas," said Gill.

"I daren't look that far ahead, sir. I have to keep my mind on the present." He raised his hat as an elderly lady went past. "Have you read today's *Advertiser?*"

"The only time I read newspapers is when I'm using them to wrap up a shoulder of lamb or some pork sausages."

"You might find the latest edition rather interesting."

"Why's that, sir?"

"It contains a reward notice for information leading to the arrest of the man who killed Frank Rodman. The GWR is offering a substantial amount."

"That's their business. If I had that kind of money," said Gill, vehemently, "I'd rather give it to the man who actually did the deed. When he killed Rodman, he did us all a big favour."

"You're being very unkind, Mr Gill."

"I'm being honest."

"Where were you on the night of the murder?"

"I was in bed with my wife — ask her."

"I'm prepared to take your word for it — for the moment, that is."

Gill glanced towards the shop. "Can I go now?"

"Now that you've been warned, you can."

"I didn't hear any warning."

"It was in the mention of the reward," explained Colbeck. "We always get a good response, you see. Names of possible suspects are sure to roll in. If yours is among them again, Mr Gill, we may have to speak to you again."

Madeleine Colbeck tried an experiment. Wanting to work in her studio, she took the crib in with her so that she could have the child beside her and enjoy the sound of her burbling quietly away. It worked well at first. Helen seemed quite content and her mother was able to address herself to her easel. The baby then began to cry, forcing Madeleine to put down her brush, wipe her hands clean then move to the crib. She was still trying to calm the child down when there was a knock on the door and Lydia Quayle was shown in by the maid. Almost immediately, Helen stopped crying.

"There you are," said Madeleine. "The moment you arrive, she's happy."

**128**

"Oh, I don't think I can take the credit for that." The women embraced and exchanged a kiss. "But it's nice to pretend that I can." She looked into the crib. "Good morning. How are you today?"

There was a long, satisfied burble by way of reply. The friends laughed.

"I've got some good news for you, Madeleine," said Lydia.

"Oh, wonderful — does it concern Constable Hinton?"

"I'm afraid not. If you've been engrossed in a painting, I know you wouldn't have glanced out of the window. It's trying to snow."

"Is it?" Madeleine peered out at the garden. "I can't see anything."

"It's very faint at the moment. Look at those clouds. There's snow up there."

"I believe you're right, Lydia."

"Just think — Helen's first Christmas will be a white one. She'll love that."

"I'm not sure she'll appreciate it. She's too young. And I can't say that I'll appreciate it either."

"Why ever do you say that?"

"I'm thinking of Robert. Snow is wonderful to look at but, if there's too much of it, there'll be a lot of disruption. The last time we had a heavy snowfall, trains were cancelled and roads in some parts of the country were impassable. I don't want my husband marooned in Swindon by four feet of snow."

"Have you heard from Robert?"

"Yes, I had a letter earlier this morning."

"What did he have to say?"

"Well, it's an intriguing case, it seems, but it won't be easy to solve. That's his way of saying that he can't make any promises."

"They'll let him home for Christmas, surely?"

"Not unless he's arrested the culprit," said Madeleine. "Superintendent Tallis was very clear on that point. Robert must stay there over the new year, if need be."

"What a dreadful thought!"

"He did promise to come home before then, if only for an hour or so."

"Didn't you tell me that the superintendent was going to be away this weekend at a regimental reunion?" Madeleine nodded. "That's the ideal time to slip back here, isn't it? When the cat's away, the mice will play. He and Sergeant Leeming will have a lot more freedom when Superintendent Tallis is not on duty."

Colbeck got back to their temporary office to find a telegraph waiting for him on the desk. It had been sent by Acting Superintendent Grosvenor. The message was curt and faintly threatening.

YOU ANSWER TO ME NOW

# CHAPTER
# ELEVEN

Jennifer Law was not merely the vicar's wife, she played an important part in his ministry. Apart from running the parsonage, acting as hostess to an unending stream of parishioners and helping her husband with secretarial duties, she had a regular round of visits to make to those who were sick, bereaved or too old to get to church any more. A new name had been added to her list. It was that of Betty Rodman. The door of the Rodman house was opened by Liza Alford who invited her in at once. There was an exchange of greetings then Jennifer looked down at the crib.

"What a beautiful baby!" she said. "And Martha is such a lovely name."

"But what kind of a life can I offer her?" asked Betty, hopelessly.

"It will be much better than you fear. Always remember that the Lord will provide. That promise may sound rather hollow at the moment but you have to keep faith in it. As for the immediate future, you can move into the parsonage with Martha, Davy and Leonard."

"That's so generous of you, Mrs Law."

Liza marvelled at the way that their visitor had remembered the names of the children. The vicar's wife had made it her business to know all of the families in the congregation even though it meant committing hundreds of names to memory. It was one way of showing that she cared about people. Liza had been willing to take the Rodman family into her own little house but she accepted that the parsonage would offer greater space and more comfort.

"I know that my husband has asked you this," said Jennifer, "but I'll repeat the question nevertheless. Is there anything practical we can do for you now?"

"No, Mrs Law," replied Betty. "I've got Liza. She's been a godsend."

"You can call on us night and day," said Liza.

"She and her husband are wonderful friends."

"That's what you need in a crisis like this," said Jennifer. "The unconditional love of friends will help you through these dark days." She noticed a number of books on a shelf in the corner. "What have you been reading?"

"Oh, they're not mine, Mrs Law," said Betty. "The only book I ever read is the Bible."

"Do they belong to your husband?"

"No, he borrowed them from the library in the Mechanics' Institution. Frank was always trying to better himself. He didn't want to do the same job for the rest of his life so he studied a lot."

"For a person in his circumstances, that was admirable."

"My husband is the same," said Liza. "Fred is always borrowing books."

"That library is a great asset to the community," remarked Jennifer. "People who've had limited schooling in their youth can educate themselves. And it's all because of the enterprise of those who run the Institution. Then there are the concerts they offer, of course. I'm told that they are excellent."

"Frank used to sing a solo in them," recalled Betty, her face almost managing a smile. "Though he loved being in the choir, he always enjoyed singing at a concert. He said that he felt more at home at the Institution."

"He never looked out of place in church."

"That's because it meant so much to him, Mrs Law."

"When are we going to know the truth?" asked Liza.

"I don't understand what you mean, Mrs Alford."

"Well, we've listened to Inspector Colbeck — and to the vicar, of course — but there are things we still don't know. Betty is entitled to hear everything. She doesn't like the feeling that . . . things are being kept from her."

"I don't," said Betty. "Why are they holding things back?"

"I'm not sure that that's what anybody is doing," said Jennifer. "You were rightly informed of what had happened almost at once, then the inspector called on you to pass on certain details. This is a new situation for the village. None of us has been through it before. There's bound to be confusion."

"The vicar said that there'd be an inquest."

"There'll be a post-mortem before that, Mrs Rodman. That's an examination of the body to ascertain exactly how your husband died."

Betty gasped. "Are they going to cut him open?"

"They're looking for clues that will help them to catch the man who killed him. It's quite normal in cases of unnatural death. Once that's done, they can move on to the inquest."

"I'd like to be there."

"Do you think that's wise? It could be rather harrowing."

Betty was defiant. "I'm going," she asserted. "If Liza is with me, I can face anything. I want to know the full truth."

The train rolled into Canterbury Station and came to an abrupt halt. Having just risen from his seat, Edward Tallis had to put a hand against the wall to steady himself. He gathered up his bag, put on his top hat then ducked low as he followed the other passengers out of the compartment. The platform was awash with people waiting to get on to the train or meeting those who alighted. Drawing himself to his full height, Tallis waited for a few seconds before someone emerged from the crowd to hobble towards him. It was a tall, angular man in his sixties with luxuriant side whiskers acting as bookends to a face with more than a hint of nobility about it. Tallis was sad to see that his old friend now needed a walking stick.

The former Captain Terence Wardlow shook his hand warmly.

"You're looking well, Edward," he said.

"I survive."

"I may hang on for a few years myself but then I had the sense to retire. You still help to rid London of its vile criminals. How will they manage without you?"

"They won't," said Tallis with disdain. "I'm sure I'll find a mess on my return. But let's forget about the future, Terence. We meet to talk about the past and to share precious memories. I can't tell you how delighted I am to see you again."

After exchanging pleasantries, they made their way toward the exit. Before they reached it, however, they heard the cathedral bells ringing. Wardlow laughed and patted his companion in the back.

"Did you hear that welcome? It's a perfect tribute to the gallant Major Tallis."

After a long day of moving around the area and questioning various people, the detectives finally met up at their office. While Colbeck felt that their hard work would eventually yield dividends, Leeming was less positive.

"We have too many suspects," he moaned, "and that worries me."

"All we have to do is to eliminate them one by one. Before we take a closer look at each of them, let me tell you about William Morris."

Leeming's face puckered. "Not *another* suspect, surely?"

"No, Victor, he's the editor of the *Swindon Advertiser* and he could be very useful to us."

"I don't trust anyone who works for a newspaper. They twist your words."

"Mr Morris is not like that."

"Then what *is* he like?"

Colbeck told him about his meeting with Morris and how, when he discovered that a murder had occurred at the Works, the latter had worked all night to reprint his newspaper so that it was up to date. Leeming was befuddled by mention of a poem.

"He writes poetry as well, sir?"

"No, Victor, that's the *other* William Morris."

"Which other one are you talking about? There are lots to choose from. I grew up with a Willie Morris and there's a Bill Morris who sells vegetables in our market."

"I'm referring to the author of 'The Haystack in the Floods'."

"Oh, he's a farmer, is he?"

"It's a poem about thwarted love set in the Hundred Years' War. The young woman is desperate to be reunited with the soldier she adores but, before he can even give her a kiss, he has his head lopped off by an enemy. She ends up standing beside the wet haystack."

"Are you making this up, Inspector?"

Colbeck smiled. "No, it's all true. It's just a weird coincidence that we're involved in a crime featuring decapitation when that also happens in Morris's poem."

"Does the killer get arrested?"

"There was a war going on, Victor — our country against France. The soldier is simply one more victim of it."

"I think you've confused me enough, sir."

"All that I'm telling you is that William Morris — the one in the Old Town — is trustworthy. That doesn't mean we have to confide everything in him but we mustn't shut him out of the investigation."

"I'll remember that."

"Right — tell me about Hector Samway."

Referring to his notebook, Leeming reeled off details of his meeting with the coppersmith. He described him as aggressive and overbearing but regretted the fact that he'd asked Samway if Rodman had taunted him about his dead wife. When the man threw a punch at him, Leeming came to understand why and spared him arrest on a charge of assault. Colbeck was interested to hear what had caused the tussle between the two men.

"So it wasn't about Samway's wife — it was about Rodman's."

"That's what he told me."

"He must have made an insulting reference to her."

"That's not the impression I got, sir," said Leeming. "He was hinting that he knew Mrs Rodman better than he should have done. He gave one of those sly smiles you always see on Mouldy Grosvenor's face."

"Ah," said Colbeck, "I meant to warn you about that. You're likely to see that smile sooner than you'd like to. Acting Superintendent Grosvenor sent a telegraph to tell us that we now are under his undeserving thumb."

"But Superintendent Tallis is not leaving until tomorrow."

"He's already gone, by the look of it. Beware, Victor."

Leeming rolled his eyes. "And there was me, thinking that things couldn't possibly get any worse . . ."

"Go back to Hector Samway. His remark about Mrs Rodman is revealing."

"Something went on between them, I'm sure."

"Then we need to discover what it was."

"Samway has to remain a suspect in my view," said Leeming.

"The same goes for Daniel Gill," said Colbeck. "I questioned him earlier."

"How would you describe him?"

"He was slippery."

Colbeck gave him a brief account of the meeting with the butcher's assistant and said that they'd need to contact his wife in order to verify Gill's claim that he was at home all night at the time the murder took place. He also recalled that he'd strolled around the Old Town to get a feel of it. There'd been snow in the air at the start but it had slowly petered out.

"I was glad to see it go," said Leeming. "I hate snow."

"Don't be such a spoilsport, Victor. Your sons would love it — so will Helen when she's old enough to play in it. I'll wager that you revelled in snow as a boy."

"I did, sir, but I know how badly it can hamper travel. If we get a blizzard, we could be stuck here for ages."

"There are worse places to be marooned in than the Queen's Tap."

"What about Christmas?"

"We'll be home by then," promised Colbeck. "So far, we have only two confirmed suspects yet you said we had too many. Are you going to increase the number?"

"Yes, I'm going to add three more names."

"*Three*? Where did they all come from?"

"You know one of them already. It's that Welshman, Llewellyn. Something about him troubles me. I know you think he's innocent but I keep remembering what Edgar Fellowes said about him. Llewellyn. He's a law unto himself."

"Have you actually spoken to him?"

"No, but I have this nagging suspicion."

"Then I'll respect your instincts. Samway, Gill and Llewellyn need more investigation. How did you get on with Simeon Cudlip?"

"I disliked him, sir."

"Why was that?"

Leeming told him that Cudlip was an irritating man with a belief that he could outwit anyone who tried to question him too closely. The clerk had been proud of his atheism and scornful of those — like Rodman — who were regular churchgoers. While he admitted his hatred of the man, he denied any involvement in the murder. Of all the things that came out in their conversation, the most significant was the name of another suspect.

Colbeck was astonished. "Fred Alford?"

"That's him, sir."

"But he's Rodman's closest friend."

"Cain was Abel's brother yet he still killed him."

"Let's not get carried away by biblical allusions, Victor. They can be very misleading. Rely on what we know for a fact. Mrs Rodman was so disturbed by her husband's absence on the night in question that she went out and called on Fred Alford. He joined in the search at once."

"He could have been only *pretending* to search."

"What possible motive could he have for murdering his friend?"

"I don't know, sir. Killers choose their victims for a lot of different reasons. We've known some that didn't need any motive at all. They just do it."

"When you met Alford, did you get any sense that he was guileful?"

"No, I didn't. He seemed honest and open. When I took him to identify the body, he was really upset by the horrible state his friend was in."

"Then why should we be taking this allegation against him seriously?"

"We have to, sir. Cudlip has known Alford for years. He also knew and was fond of Mrs Rodman. In fact, I think that she's the reason he never married. Cudlip is still carrying a torch for her. Could that be what Alford was doing as well? He might be another one of her rejected suitors."

"I'm not happy about this," said Colbeck, pursing his lips. "Something doesn't ring true."

"Alford is an unlikely suspect, I agree, but we can't overlook him."

"When is he supposed to have committed the murder?"

140

"It was some time in the night."

"But we know that he left the pub early and went back home."

"That's what he told us."

"I've met his wife, Victor. She's a very strong and capable woman. If her husband didn't come back until the early hours, she'd want to know why. And there's another factor," said Colbeck. "It was Fred Alford who first raised the possibility that the killer was one of Betty Rodman's disappointed admirers. Why should he draw attention to them if he was attracted to her as well?"

"I think he needs looking at more closely."

"Is there any point? From what you tell me, Cudlip sounds like a highly unreliable source. There's clearly a streak of arrogance in him as well. He's probably just trying to get his own back on Alford for some imagined slight."

"On the other hand," said Leeming, seriously, "he may actually have been giving us a valuable piece of information. I believe that Alford must join the other four suspects." He rapped the desk with his knuckles. "I say that we should talk to Fred Alford as a matter of urgency."

Struck by the sergeant's determination, Colbeck got to his feet.

"He may be home by now. I'll call on him at once."

Fred Alford was part of the human torrent that poured out of the Works then went off in different directions. Heading for the Rodman house, he suddenly felt a powerful hand on his shoulder. He turned to confront a grinning Gareth Llewellyn.

"Your friend has done me a favour," said the Welshman.

Alford tensed. "Don't you sneer at Frank Rodman."

"I'm not sneering. I'm grateful to him. You'll find out why on Saturday night."

"I haven't a clue what you're talking about."

"It's the concert. They've lost one soloist so they need someone in his place. I persuaded them to use me. I'll show this village what a real singing voice sounds like. Make sure that you and your wife are there."

"I'm not interested in listening to you."

"You'd better get used to the idea, Fred."

"Why?"

"I'll be the regular soloist at the Mechanics' Institution from now on. Once they hear me, they'll beg me to sing at every concert. I'm sorry to see Frank die that way — a pity, really."

"Don't pretend you actually care about him. You hated Frank."

"I love him like a brother now," said Llewellyn, grinning broadly, "because his death has been a bonus for me. The Welsh are a musical nation, you see. We were born to sing. I've been given the chance to prove myself in front of an audience and it's all because of your old friend." Looking up, he blew a kiss up to heaven. "Thank you, Frank. I appreciate your kindness in stepping aside for me."

He laughed harshly and lumbered off down the road.

142

\* \* \*

Colbeck got to the house to find that Liza Alford had just been reunited with her family. Since she'd spent most of the day with Betty Rodman, she'd had to ask her neighbours to look after the children for her. They were now demanding to know where she'd been. When her visitor arrived, she'd sent them upstairs so that she could talk in private with Colbeck. He was interested to hear that she'd spent the night with Betty Rodman and that her husband would call there before coming home. Colbeck was glad of the opportunity to question her alone.

"How is Mrs Rodman?" he asked.

"She's still dazed by what's happened but, then, any woman would be."

"You've been a tower of strength to her."

"We've always been friends, Inspector. I can't let her down. Mrs Law called on her this morning and the vicar was there again this afternoon. Other people have offered their help as well."

"But you're her mainstay, Mrs Alford. Tell me," he went on, "do you remember a man named Simeon Cudlip?"

"Yes, he's a clerk at the Works."

"What do you know about him?"

"I know that he was a terrible nuisance to Betty before she was married. She had lots of admirers but Mr Cudlip was the one who bothered her most."

"Did he continue to bother her *after* she was married?"

"I don't think he'd dare. Frank was very protective."

"But he wasn't always there, was he? It seems to be common knowledge that he spent a lot of time in the pub, then there'd be choir rehearsals and other reasons to keep him out of the house. Didn't that make his wife feel lonely?"

"You're never lonely if you have children, Inspector."

"The vicar told me that Mr Rodman was a troubled soul," said Colbeck. "It sounds as if he was guilt-stricken. Why do you think that was?"

Liza became guarded. "I really don't know."

"Was he worried about something — or about someone?"

"You'd have to ask my husband."

"I'd have thought that Mrs Rodman would have confided in you."

"Betty did say that . . . he spent too much money on drink," said the other, carefully, "but a lot of men do that. Luckily, Fred is not one of them. He knows that we have mouths to feed. He can't afford to drink his pay away."

"Is that what Mr Rodman did?"

There was a lengthy pause. "You'll have to ask Betty."

"I think that you know the answer, Mrs Alford," he said, "but I won't press you on the subject." He saw her stifle a yawn. "Ever since you heard the grim news about Mr Rodman, you've been on duty with his wife. You must be exhausted."

"I do feel weary. My back hurts from sleeping in a chair."

144

"That's understandable," said Colbeck. "You'd have been much better off on the floor."

"I tried that but there was a terrible draught coming in."

"So you spent the entire night perched on a chair?"

"I can sleep *anywhere*, Inspector," she boasted. "If my husband didn't wake me up when it was time for him to go to work, I'd sleep throughout the whole day. When Fred, or one of the children, gets up in the night, I never hear a thing. Once I nod off, I could sleep through a thunderstorm."

After his encounter with the Welshman, Alford went straight to the Rodman house. Betty was alone. When she let him in, she was so pleased to see him that she flung herself impulsively into his arms.

"Hold me, Fred," she told him. "Hold me tight."

# CHAPTER
# TWELVE

Those who worked under him at Scotland Yard joked that Edward Tallis was never off duty and routinely arrested criminals in his sleep. Had they seen him that evening, however, they might have revised their judgement. Relaxed, contented and actually smiling for once, he was enjoying the hospitality of his friend, Terence Wardlow. The two men were ensconced in leather armchairs in the study of a rambling country house just outside Canterbury, trading memoirs of their army careers and sampling an aperitif before dinner. A fire crackled in the grate of the book-lined room. Above the mantelpiece was a portrait of Wardlow in uniform, staring at the horizon with the defiant gaze of a British soldier confronting the enemy on the battlefield. Tallis had been impressed by the glass-topped cabinet in one corner of the room with its display of medals and its memorabilia from the various campaigns in which they'd both fought. He, too, had a similar collection.

There was no thought of the Detective Department now. The superintendent was comprehensively off duty, luxuriating in the company of a close friend with shared memories that had bonded them for life. When they'd left the army, however, their paths had diverged.

**146**

Wardlow had returned to his wife and family and was now revelling in his retirement. Tallis, on the other hand, had accepted a new challenge.

"It was the late Colonel Rowan who persuaded me," he explained. "He was appointed alongside Richard Mayne as one of the first commissioners of the newly established Detective Department and he brought all the virtues of a military background into Scotland Yard. He was an Ulsterman of Scottish descent and a man of proven abilities. What he saw in me were the strengths that he himself possessed. The colonel was decisive, authoritative and industrious."

"That sums you up perfectly, Edward."

"Those qualities are yours as much as mine."

Wardlow chuckled. "We were hewn from the same rock," he said, slapping his thigh. "Oh, it's such a treat to see you again and find you in such robust health. My gain is Scotland Yard's loss."

"Don't even mention the place. I'm back in the army now."

"And you're obviously very glad to be there — just like me."

They raised their glasses in celebration then emptied them in one gulp.

Victor Leeming was also interested in alcohol that evening. Alone in the back room at the Queen's Tap, he was just about to take a first sip of his beer when a bearded man swooped down on him with a smile of recognition.

"You must be Sergeant Leeming," he said.

"That's right. How did you guess?"

"They don't get many customers here dressed like you and Inspector Colbeck. This pub was built to serve GWR employees and they don't tend to wear top hats and frock coats as a rule." He offered his hand. "My name is William Morris, by the way."

"Ah, yes," said Leeming, taking the outstretched palm. "I'm pleased to meet you, Mr Morris. I hear that you're a poet."

"That's the *other* William Morris."

"Then you must be the editor of the *Advertiser*."

"It's a title I bear with pride."

Though his visitor seemed pleasant and well spoken, Leeming nevertheless remained wary. His lingering fear of the press remained. During previous cases, he'd been deliberately misquoted in national newspapers and didn't want the embarrassing experience repeated.

"If you've come in search of an interview," he said, quietly, "I'll have to disappoint you. I don't talk to journalists on principle."

"That's fine with me, Sergeant. I didn't come to bother you. I just wanted to deliver these." He handed over a small sheaf of letters. "I printed details of the reward in today's edition and this is the result. All that some people saw in the reward notice was the amount on offer and they promptly wrote down their claims and put them through our letter box. Had they been more attentive, they'd have seen that you and the inspector could be contacted at an office in the Locomotive Works."

"Thank you very much, Mr Morris. It was good of you to take the trouble."

"I can't promise that any of those letters will be genuine."

"Have no fear," said Leeming, glancing at them. "We're used to sifting through bogus claims and ridiculous guesses. Among the earlier suggestions we had was the information that the killer was the late Mr Brunel."

Morris laughed. "Did he pop back from the grave to carry out the murder?"

"Nobody has ever managed to do that, sir."

"On the other hand," said the other, thoughtfully, "I suppose that you could argue that Brunel was a sort of accessory before the event. If he hadn't created the Works in the first place, the crime could never have taken place. However," he went on, looking down at the tankard, "I'm keeping you from that excellent pint of beer. It's from Arkell's Brewery and worthy of its popularity. If I get any more mail relating to the reward notice, I'll pass it on to you."

"Thank you, Mr Morris."

"And I leave you with a sad confession. I *did* try to write a poem once. It was unbelievably terrible. The other William Morris is much better at it."

Leeming waved him off and thought how much less predatory the provincial journalist was than his London counterparts. It had been a pleasure to meet and talk to Morris. The sergeant hoped he'd see the man again.

To stave off the feeling of loneliness, Madeleine Colbeck had invited her father and Lydia Quayle to join her for dinner. The meal was over, the baby had been put down for the night and the three of them were now in the drawing room. Wherever they looked, the impact of the festive season was evident. Christmas cards stood on the mantelpiece and on every other available surface, a tree decorated with baubles occupied a place in the window and around its base were piles of boxes wrapped in brightly coloured paper. It would be Madeleine's second night without her husband and she was acutely aware that Christmas Day was getting closer than ever.

Aware of her friend's anxieties, Lydia had taken care to keep off the subject but Caleb Andrews had no such concern for his daughter's feelings.

"He's not going to be here on the day itself," he prophesied, gloomily.

"Don't say that, Father."

"We have to face the truth."

"Robert's letter was quite optimistic."

"He was only trying to cheer you up, Maddy."

"From what I know of him," said Lydia, "I believe that he'll move heaven and earth to be here in time to celebrate Helen's first Christmas. Have faith in your son-in-law, Mr Andrews."

The old man stroked his beard. "Maybe I should go there to help him."

"No," said Madeleine, firmly. "Don't even think of it."

"This is a crime committed in a Locomotive Works. Nobody knows as much about such places as me. They were my world. I can still hear that deafening clatter. I

**150**

can still smell that awful reek. I'd see things that Robert didn't."

"You'd be in the way, Father."

"I like to feel useful."

"The most useful thing you can do is to stay in London and to stop moaning. It's better if you don't even mention Robert."

"Am I supposed to pretend he doesn't exist?" asked Andrews in disbelief.

"You have to exercise discretion, as Lydia has been doing."

"Your husband is going to ruin Christmas for you. Admit it."

"No, it's not true."

"Look around you, Maddy. He's not here."

"Perhaps we should talk about something else," suggested Lydia.

"Everyone thinks about their family at Christmas."

"*I* don't, Mr Andrews."

The conversation came to an abrupt halt. Lydia had spoken without bitterness or regret. She simply stated a fact. Madeleine felt profoundly sorry for her friend's alienation from her siblings. Lydia's parents might both be dead but her two brothers and her sister were still alive as were several cousins, nephews and nieces. Members of the wider family had also lost touch with her. To be cut off from them all at such a time seemed unnatural. Lydia's plight also saddened Andrews. Though he couldn't fully understand how it had come about, he could see how isolated she must feel at such a time. He reached out to touch her arm.

"You belong to *us* now," he said, softly, "so you *do* have a family."

After an acceptable but uninspiring meal at the Queen's Tap, the detectives leafed through the correspondence provided by William Morris. None of it was either useful or convincing. Most of the correspondents simply suggested a name, supplied no evidence to support the allegation then asked when they could collect the reward money. The only name offered that was already on their list was that of Hector Samway. There was no mention of Daniel Gill, Simeon Cudlip or Gareth Llewellyn. One man, writing in a shaky hand, assured the detectives that he knew who the killer was but that he'd only yield up the name when they handed over the money.

"That's barefaced fraud!" protested Leeming. "He'd take the money and run."

"Track him down and give him a scare."

"I'll give him more than that, sir."

"With so many men employed at the Works," said Colbeck, sighing, "you'd have thought that at least one of them might have come up with evidence we can actually use."

"Not everyone has read the *Advertiser*."

"Mr Stinson has had reward notices put up in the Old Town as well as here. Everybody in Swindon will know that there's money at stake."

"That means we'll have more rubbish like this flooding in."

"We shall see, Victor."

They went back to their original list and discussed each suspect in turn. When they came to Alford's name, Colbeck admitted that he'd been sceptical about the inclusion of the murder victim's best friend. His conversation with Alford's wife had forced him to reappraise the suggestion. Since Liza Alford had admitted she slept very soundly, it would have been possible for Alford to leave the house at night without her being aware of it. Colbeck learnt that he'd courted Betty Marklew, as she then was, assiduously and even proposed marriage. When she turned him down, he was deeply upset. While she didn't put it into words, it became clear that his wife felt that she was second best. Until the relationship with Betty had ended, Alford had never looked at the woman he went on to marry.

"What did Alford stand to gain by the murder?" asked Leeming.

"It would bring him closer to Mrs Rodman. He knew she'd turn to him."

"But he already has a wife."

"Yes," said Colbeck, "and do you know what she told me? Her husband was very angry when he heard that the vicar had stepped in to offer the family a refuge at the parsonage. Alford was keen for them to move into his house."

"It would've been far too small, surely?"

"Betty Rodman would have been under his roof. That's what he wanted. Let me add one more significant piece of information," Colbeck went on. "Mrs Alford had returned to her own house earlier on because she knew that her husband would call on Mrs

Rodman on his way back from work. They'd agreed between them that one of them should be with her at all times."

"So Alford would have been alone with Mrs Rodman."

"I fancy that he'd savour the situation."

"Maybe he does deserve closer attention, then."

"All four main suspects do, Victor. I'm excluding the Welshman."

"Well, I'm not," said Leeming. "I don't suppose you happened to see that poster for the concert when you came in here this evening?" Colbeck shook his head. "I think that you ought to look at it, sir."

"Why?"

"There's been a change in the programme. Frank Rodman's name has been crossed out and Llewellyn's has been written in its place."

"That's probably just a bit of fun on the Welshman's behalf."

"No, it isn't. I spoke to the landlord about it. They couldn't find anyone else to take part in the concert at such short notice so they agreed to give the Welshman his opportunity."

"Thank you for telling me. It's an additional reason for us to go to the Mechanics' Institution on Saturday night."

Leeming was surprised. "We're attending the concert?"

"Of course," said Colbeck, seriously. "Has it never occurred to you that we're likely to be in the same room as the killer?"

154

"Are we?"

"He might even be singing a solo."

Edward Tallis awoke on Friday morning with a sense of release. He was free from responsibility for once, he was staying with a close friend and he'd be going to join his old regiment at their barracks in Hythe. After a hearty breakfast with Wardlow and his wife, he was offered the chance to visit Canterbury and he promptly accepted. A religious man, Tallis was keen to see the cathedral, to admire its soaring architecture and to draw strength from being at the very heart of the Anglican Church. He was also interested to see the city itself, retaining much of its medieval geography and replete with relics of the past. When his friend joked that he might wish to call in on the local constabulary, the suggestion was met with a firm refusal. Tallis was on holiday. He intended to relish every moment of it.

When they were ready to depart, they found the dog cart waiting for them outside the front door. Wardlow took up the reins and they set off down the drive. Tallis was glad to be alone with his friend once more. Mrs Wardlow had been a charming and attentive hostess but the superintendent was ill at ease in the company of women and lacked the ability to converse with them. Marriage had never appealed to him and he'd resolved that his bachelor status would remain intact until his death.

They were soon discussing which of the sights of Canterbury they should see and in what order. As they joined the winding road to the city, they were so

155

immersed in their debate that neither of them noticed that they were being watched from the cover of a nearby copse.

When the detectives got to their office that morning, the first person who came to see them was Inspector Piercey. Still mouthing apologies for revealing information about the murder victim to William Morris, he asked for an opportunity to redeem himself. Colbeck saw a chance to unload on to him a task he'd asked Leeming to undertake. Handing the inspector the relevant letter, he told him to find out who'd written it and to arrest him for wasting police time and trying to obtain money by fraudulent means. Piercey was delighted to be a functioning part of the investigation and set off to prove that he, too, had skills of detection.

The tempting prospect of a reward had produced a flurry of letters but all of them were based on guesswork rather than on evidence. Hector Samway's name cropped up twice and so did that of Simeon Cudlip. Other suspects on the detectives' list were not accused by anybody. One letter was three pages long.

"Someone has written a whole life story," he observed.

"Yes, Victor, and every line is riddled with malice. I don't believe that he's seriously suggesting that this man, Arthur Caldicott, really is the killer. He just wants us to give him a nasty shock by hauling him out of the Wagon Shop to question him."

"Should we set Inspector Piercey on to him?"

"That's exactly what we'll do," said Colbeck, smiling. "A man in uniform gives most people a jolt and that's what's needed in the case of the spiteful individual who wrote this letter."

When they'd finished trawling through the correspondence, they decided that nobody would actually turn up in person because they were all at work. Colbeck suggested that it was time for him to meet Samway and Cudlip while Leeming went off to the Old Town to form his opinion of Daniel Gill. Before they could leave the office, however, they had an unexpected visitor. She was a short, dark-haired, shapely woman in her late twenties with anxious eyes set in a pretty face. In her sing-song accent, she told them that her name was Rachel Griffiths and that her husband worked in the rolling mills.

Since she was clearly unnerved by the sight of the two detectives, Colbeck offered her a seat then spent a few minutes trying to make her feel more comfortable.

"Thank you very much for coming to see us, Mrs Griffiths," he said, gently. "Whatever you say will be treated in confidence so you may speak freely. Let me remind you that we're dealing with a truly horrific crime that has poisoned the atmosphere of the whole village. We've seen its effect wherever we've been. If it remains unsolved, the murder is going to blight Christmas for everyone here."

"That includes us," Leeming put in.

"Anything you can tell us — anything at all you think might be of practical use to us — will be welcomed. Don't be afraid of repercussions. Nobody needs to know that you came here but, if you do still feel afraid, you'll get police protection."

There was a protracted silence. She studied both of them in turn.

"Take your time, Mrs Griffiths," said Colbeck. "We can wait."

"I'm not afraid," she whispered. "I'm ashamed."

"Why is that?"

"You did say that nobody would know I'd come here, didn't you?"

"The sergeant and I give you our word."

"That's true," said Leeming. "You can trust us."

"What if you despise me?" she asked, worriedly.

"We're not here to sit in judgement," Colbeck assured her. "Our only interest is in acquiring information that will lead to the arrest of the man who murdered Frank Rodman. Something brought you along here this morning and I'm fairly certain that it was not the promise of a reward." She shook her head vigorously. "Then please tell us what it was."

After another pause, she forced herself to speak, words coming out haltingly.

"My husband is a good man, Inspector. I want you to know that."

"Go on."

"But he's a lot older than me. That's not an excuse," she added, "so please don't think it is. The truth is that I *have* no excuse."

"Are you telling us that someone else . . . took an interest in you?" said Colbeck.

"There's been more than one. I was plagued with them. It's one of the reasons I got married in the first place. I hoped it would stop all that."

"Patently, it didn't."

"You get used to things," she said, resignedly.

"Do you live in what they call the barracks?"

"We all do. They herded us in there like sheep."

"You don't like it, do you?"

"There are some good things about it," she conceded, "and I thought that he was one of them." She bit her lip. "I met someone and we . . . became friends. Since we all live on top of each other, it was very difficult for us to meet but there's this empty room and he managed to get hold of the key."

"Keep going, Mrs Griffiths," said Colbeck. "You met this person from time to time, I suspect. Is that right?"

"Yes, Inspector."

"And did you arrange to meet him two nights ago?" She lowered her head. "Please tell us what happened."

"He didn't turn up. He'd never let me down before. I couldn't just wait there. I had to keep going back to our own rooms. When I heard my husband snoring again," she said, "I went out for the last time and . . . Gareth was there."

"Would that be Gareth Llewellyn?" asked Leeming.

"Yes, it would."

"And did he say where he'd been all night?"

"No, Sergeant," she replied, looking up, "but his hands were covered in blood."

The effort of making her confession was too much for her. Having betrayed her husband by having

**159**

assignations with another man, she had now betrayed her lover and was in despair. She burst into tears and began to shake uncontrollably. Colbeck put a consoling arm around her and told her that she'd been very brave to do what she'd just done. It was several minutes before she stopped weeping.

"You must think I'm wicked," she wailed.

"We think you did the right thing," said Colbeck.

"But I'm a married woman with a child. What I did was terrible."

"Nothing is quite as terrible as a murder, Mrs Griffiths."

"I just can't believe that Gareth would have . . ."

"He may yet be innocent and that will put your mind at rest. I can see how much you must have agonised over this. When you first heard about the murder, it must have been like a blow from a sledgehammer. It's to your credit that you felt you had to tell us what you knew."

"I feel like a traitor. How can I ever face Gareth again?"

"You may not have to," said Leeming, bluntly.

Colbeck stepped in quickly. "What the sergeant means," he said, "is that you might be advised to keep out of Mr Llewellyn's way for a while."

"I'll do that," she agreed.

It was another ten minutes before she'd recovered from what was plainly an ordeal for her, confessing that she'd committed adultery then naming her lover as the likely killer. When she felt able to get up, Colbeck accompanied her to the door and left her with a few last comforting words. She thanked him for his kindness then left.

"That wasn't what I meant at all," complained Leeming. "I said she wouldn't have to face Llewellyn again because we'd put him behind bars."

"We're not going to do that, Victor."

"But we've just had solid evidence."

"All we know is that he arrived for a tryst with blood on his hands."

"Yes, he was late turning up because he'd been killing Rodman."

"It's a possibility," agreed Colbeck, "but it's very far from being a probability. I can think of all kinds of reasons why a man would have blood on his hands. Daniel Gill's hands were bloodstained when I met him."

"He's a butcher."

"I'm not convinced that Llewellyn is."

Leeming was astounded. "Are you saying that we should . . . do nothing?"

"We have to watch and wait, Victor. Before we do anything as rash as making an arrest, we should get more proof. To do that, we need to find out a great deal more about Llewellyn and his movements that night. In any case," he continued, "we don't want to commit an unforgivable crime ourselves."

"What do you mean, sir?"

"If we take him into custody now, he'll be unable to perform at the concert. We can't deprive a Welshman of the chance to sing," he said with a twinkle in his eye. "That would be tantamount to wilful cruelty."

# CHAPTER
# THIRTEEN

There were two of them. Concealed among the trees, they'd been keeping the house under surveillance since early that morning. When Wardlow and Tallis finally emerged from the drive in the dog cart, the men gave them time to get well past the copse before coming out of it. They followed their quarry at a discreet distance. There was never any danger of being seen. The old soldiers were deep into their memoirs once more and were oblivious to all else. When the dog cart pulled up in the cathedral precinct, the men who'd trailed behind it were given an unexpected bonus. They saw Wardlow alight from the vehicle with some difficulty then reach for his walking stick. Tallis seemed unimpaired but he slowed his pace to match that of his friend. The two men exchanged a look.

"Nobody told us he couldn't walk properly," said one.

His companion grinned. "Are you complaining?"

"No."

"Nor me."

"What do we do?"

"We bide our time. And then . . ."

They sniggered. Their task had now become easier.

It was the second time that Hector Samway had been hauled out of the Foundry and it annoyed him. When he confronted Colbeck in the detective's office, he was forthright.

"You're costing me money," he protested.

"I may not have to keep you long. Mr Samway."

"You shouldn't have needed to see me at all. I told that sergeant of yours everything. Why are you bothering me again? If I'm away from my job for any length of time, the foreman will dock my wages."

"I'll make sure that doesn't happen."

"Rules are rules."

"If I speak to him, Mr Stinson will be able to bend them in your favour."

Samway muttered grudging thanks. Physically, he was exactly as Leeming had described and there was the constant sense of a temper just being kept in check. Not wishing to provoke it, Colbeck's manner was more emollient.

"I'm sorry to take you away from your work again," he began.

"Why couldn't you wait until my shift was finished?"

"We'd like to clear up certain things as quickly as possible, Mr Samway."

"I can't help you."

"Don't be too certain of that."

"I had nothing to do with the murder. I can't understand why my name came up in the first place."

"We're acting on an anonymous allegation about you."

"Then the man who made it is a liar!" snarled the other.

"In actual fact, more than one person named you in connection with the crime. We don't know who they are but all of them felt strongly enough about it to put pen to paper. Unfortunately, they held back their identities."

"Cowards!"

"Their claims are consistent, Mr Samway. Each of them asserts that there was bad blood between you and Mr Rodman. According to Sergeant Leeming, you don't deny it. Is that true?"

"What if it is?"

"Can you account for your movements on the night of the murder?"

"I was in bed asleep."

"Will anyone confirm that?"

"My neighbours saw me go into the house at the usual time and they know I'm always exhausted at the end of a shift. When I'd had some food, I went straight to bed. We have an early start in the Foundry."

"Why do you think people are naming you as a suspect?"

"We all have enemies — even you."

Colbeck smiled. "Oh, I have a lot more of them than you," he said, wryly. "If you wish to make yourself very unpopular, you simply have to become a policeman. At a stroke, you create an army of enemies."

"Did any of these people who wrote to you have proof that I was the killer?"

"No, they didn't."

"Then you might as well let me go back to work."

"There's a question I must put to you first. If you are not the culprit, somebody else is. Can you suggest who that somebody else might be?"

Lost in thought, Samway screwed his face up until it became a mask of cold anger. His expression would intimidate most people. The fact that Rodman had got the better of him in a fight said a lot about the strength and determination of the murder victim. At length, Samway spat out a name.

"Danny Gill."

"But he doesn't work here any more."

"That's why he'd hate Rodman almost as much as I did. Danny was sacked but Rodman stayed on. They got rid of the wrong man."

"Who made the decision?"

"It would have been the foreman but Mr Stinson would have had the final say. He goes to church regular so he'll have seen Rodman singing his bleeding head off every Sunday. That counted in Rodman's favour. Danny couldn't sing a note. Also," said Samway, "he's really mean when he wants to be. You should talk to him."

"I already have," said Colbeck. "He remains a suspect."

"What about me?"

"We'll have to keep you in mind."

"But I've told you that I'm innocent. Bring a Bible and I'll swear on it."

"How often do you go to church?"

Samway looked sheepish. "It's not as often as I ought to."

"Is there a reason for that?"

"Every time I go to church, I'm reminded of my wife's funeral. So I keep away most of the time. The vicar told me that I'd feel better if I went every Sunday but it's not true. My stomach churns whenever I go in there and hear Mr Law spouting a sermon." He straightened up and wagged a finger. "I'm not saying it *is* Danny Gill, mind, but it could be."

"Can you offer another name?"

"No, Inspector."

"What about Simeon Cudlip?"

"I don't know him."

"He's a clerk and he didn't get on with Mr Rodman."

"Neither did lots of us — he could be very nasty."

"Yet he sang in the church choir and educated himself from books in the library at the Mechanics' Institution. He can't just be dismissed as an ogre. Mr Rodman was a complex man."

"You never met him."

"I've built up a fairly detailed picture of him — and, of course, I've met his wife." Colbeck studied him. "You knew her before she was married, I gather."

"If you lived in the village, you couldn't miss Betty Marklew. She was lovely."

"Did you make efforts to court her?"

"Yes, I did, and I'm not ashamed of it."

"Yet you went on to marry someone else."

"Betty was . . . no longer within reach."

"But you continued to admire her, I daresay," said Colbeck, "and that kind of admiration can sometimes exert a powerful influence on a man. Is that why you and Mr Rodman fell out? Did you try to pester Mrs Rodman?"

Samway was roused. "I'd never do that to her, Inspector," he insisted. "Even after my wife died, I never went near Betty. I was just sickened at the way that Rodman treated her. While he was getting drunk in the pub, she was always left alone with the children without enough money to feed and clothe them properly. It wasn't fair on her. When I had that row with him, I told him the truth to his face. I said that Betty deserved someone far better than him. Rodman thought I was talking about myself."

Colbeck regarded him coolly. "Weren't you?"

Though she had the three children and though Liza Alford had spent a second night with her, Betty Rodman felt that the house was strangely empty. When the vicar called on her again, she told him about it.

"The emptiness is in your heart, Betty," he said, "and not in your house."

"Will it ever go away?"

"The feeling will shrink with the passage of time. I'm speaking from personal experience. When my father died, I was devastated. Something of vital importance had just been stolen from my life. At the time, I never thought that I'd get over it but, with God's help, I have."

"That's different," Liza interjected. "Your father wasn't murdered."

"No, he died peacefully from old age."

"Betty's case is not the same."

"I agree," he said. "Perhaps it was foolish to make such a comparison."

He'd brought some scones his wife had made especially for the children. Since he intended to stay an hour at least, he offered Liza the opportunity to slip away if she wished to do any shopping. After discussing it with Betty, she accepted the offer but promised to return before the vicar left.

"Somebody ought to be with her all the time," she said.

"Nights are the worst," admitted Betty. "I couldn't manage without Liza."

"I'll sleep here as long as I'm needed."

"You've got your own family to look after. It's what Fred was saying when he called in yesterday. He didn't like the idea of you sitting in that chair all night. Fred told me he'd rather sleep there himself so that you could be with the children."

Unable to hide her disapproval at the suggestion, Liza bade them farewell. Howard Law waited until she was out of the house.

"You can come to us as soon as you wish," he said.

"As long as they'll let me," she replied, "I'd rather stay here. This house has . . . memories I cling on to." Betty became fearful. "When you spoke to Mr Stinson, did he give you a date when we had to leave?"

"No, he couldn't be that specific but I'll put gentle pressure on him to make sure that it's as long as possible. The GWR is a caring company. They'll pay for the funeral, of course, and, as I told you, that's something we must discuss."

"I'm not ready yet."

"No, no, I understand that."

"And I'm not sure that I ever will be."

Law backed off immediately. "Then let's forget about it for now. I'll have to make certain practical decisions regarding the service but I needn't bother you with those." He sat beside Betty and squeezed her hand. "My wife said that you were being very courageous in the face of a malign act of fate."

"Who killed my husband?" she asked faintly.

"Inspector Colbeck will find that out."

"But it must be someone we *know*. That's what frightens me. He's still here, living among us, carrying on as if nothing has happened. I'm afraid to go out at the end of the working day in case I pass him in the street."

"It's freezing out there, anyway, so you're better off in here. When I call in tomorrow, I'll bring some more coal for the fire. It's important for you to be in the warm."

"You and Mrs Law have been so good to me."

"We'll help you through the difficult days that lie ahead, Betty. Until you get back on your feet, so to speak, the parsonage is yours. And it will mean you won't have to impose on Fred and Liza Alford."

"They both begged me to go to them," said Betty. "Fred was here yesterday evening and said that they'd find room for us somehow. We're very close, you see. Moving in with you will be . . . well, we'll find it very strange."

"You'll be in the best possible place."

Though she forced a grateful smile and nodded, she still had reservations about moving into the parsonage because she'd feel constrained and out of place. Betty would be embarrassed by the luxury of having servants. She simply wouldn't know how to deal with them. Law saw her confusion.

"Put your trust in the Lord," he said, "and all will be well."

"I'd rather put my trust in Inspector Colbeck for the time being. I have to know who destroyed our lives and I trust the inspector to catch him in the end. Then," she went on, face contorted by an upsurge of hatred, "I can go to court to watch my husband's killer being sentenced to death. I'll enjoy that."

There was a short queue in the butcher's shop when he got there. Leeming had to stand behind two women and an old man. He looked incongruous in the setting and collected stares of amazement from the other customers. When he'd served the women and the old man, Daniel Gill produced a smile for the sergeant.

"What can I get you, sir?"

"You can get me someone to look after the shop while we have a chat," said Leeming. "Inspector

Colbeck asked me to speak to you. I'm Sergeant Leeming and I don't much care for the stink in here or the sawdust under my feet."

"That's a good, healthy smell," argued Gill.

"I'd rather be out in the fresh air. If I stay here, we'll have to talk in front of your uncle. Does he know that we're interested in you?"

"No, he doesn't and there's no reason why he should."

After gesturing for Leeming to get out, he went off into the back room and invented an excuse to leave the premises for a short while. Then he went outside and wiped his hands on his apron. The sergeant was twenty yards away. Gill was grateful.

"The inspector advised me to keep out of sight of your uncle," he explained. "We don't want to put you in an awkward situation, Mr Gill — unless, that is, you happen to be the man we're after."

"I had nothing to do with Frank Rodman's death," affirmed the other.

"Would you *like* to have been involved?"

"I'd have loved it."

"Thanks for your honesty — it's a good start."

"This is a waste of your time. The inspector has already questioned me."

"There was one small point that needed to be clarified."

"Oh, what was that?"

"Where were you on the night of the murder?"

"I was fast asleep with my wife."

"I wish that I'd been in bed with *my* wife," said Leeming, mordantly. "I hate being away from home, especially at this time of year."

"Why pester me? I have an alibi. If you don't believe me, speak to my wife."

"I've already done that, sir."

Gill was shaken. "You spoke to Anne?"

"Yes, I did."

"But you don't know where we live."

"I solved that problem by calling on Mr Morris, the editor of the *Advertiser*. He seems to know where everyone lives. That's how I got to meet Mrs Gill."

"You had no right to go there behind my back," protested Gill.

"We had every right, sir. Indeed, you invited Inspector Colbeck to speak to her because she would verify what you'd told him."

"And did she?"

"Oh, yes," said Leeming, "she repeated what you told her, word for word."

"There you are then." Gill tapped his own chest. "I'm in the clear."

"Not quite, I'm afraid. When someone talks to me parrot-fashion, I never believe what they tell me. Mrs Gill behaved like a dutiful wife and I don't blame her for that. She was only obeying orders from you."

"Anne told you the truth."

"Yes, she did — eventually. When I pointed out to her that misleading the police with false information was an offence, she changed her tune completely. It seems that, on the night of the murder, you didn't spend the whole time in bed with her because you got back hours after midnight."

"My wife is mistaken. I was there not long after eleven o'clock."

"On balance," said Leeming, levelly, "I'd trust her word before yours."

Gill quailed. His defence had just crumbled to pieces. The sergeant was looking at him with an accusatory stare. He realised that he'd underestimated the detectives. His mind was racing as he sought to save himself from arrest. As a last resort, he fell back on a small portion of the truth.

"I was very late," he confessed, "but it wasn't because I went anywhere near the Locomotive Works. I've got good reason to hate the place. As for Frank Rodman, I haven't seen him for years."

Leeming stepped in closer. "Where were you on the night in question?"

"I was too drunk to know what I was doing, Sergeant. I'd been to the pub on the corner and . . . had too much. The landlord will back me up. He had to turn me out. I managed to stagger home somehow," said Gill, "then I collapsed in the doorway. All I remember is that I eventually woke up shivering, unlocked the door and crawled upstairs. My wife will have told you the state I was in."

"Mrs Gill said that you stank of beer."

"And I didn't ask her to tell you that. How am I supposed to have murdered Frank Rodman when I couldn't even stand up properly?"

"Killers often need a strong drink before they go after their victim."

"It wasn't me," howled Gill. "I swear before God. And I do that as a true Christian. My wife and I go to St Mark's every Sunday."

"Yet you told me a little earlier that you hadn't seen Mr Rodman for years. If you go to church, you're bound to have seen him singing in the choir. Every time you did that, you'd be reminded why you hate him so much. Stop telling me lies, Mr Gill," warned Leeming, "or I'll bring your uncle into the conversation. It may be time that he realised his nephew could be a vicious criminal."

It was not difficult to watch the two men. All that they had to do was to mingle with the crowds that had flocked into the cathedral. Wardlow and Tallis were moving so slowly that they were easy targets. There was so much to see and they'd clearly resolved to see most of it. They even explored the crypt, then climbed the circular stone steps of the tower. The effort eventually took its toll on Wardlow and he excused himself, settling down in a pew and indicating that he'd stay there and enjoy a respite until Tallis returned. The superintendent was content with the arrangement but the two men behind him were even happier. Detached from his friend, Tallis was much more vulnerable. They simply had to wait for the right moment.

It came when Tallis wandered out into the cloisters, the place where the sandalled feet of generations of monks had walked in the past. There was a divine serenity about the whole area that would have encouraged contemplation. A scattering of other visitors were there so the two men had to stay their hand. They watched Tallis go into every nook and cranny before strolling on to the tunnel that led to King's College, the famous school attended by many luminaries from past centuries. To get there, Tallis had to duck his head and go into dark shadow for a few moments. They caught up with him in a flash. One of them pushed him face first against the wall while the other thrust a pistol against his back.

"This is loaded," he warned. "Cry out and I'll pull the trigger."

"Who are you?" demanded Tallis.

"Be quiet! We'll do the talking."

"There's a way out through the school gate," said the other man. "We're going to walk towards it. If you so much as blink, you'll be shot in the back and I'll slit your throat to make sure you're dead."

He reinforced his warning by running the blade of a dagger across Tallis's neck. The superintendent winced but no blood was drawn.

"I have to speak to a friend," he said, trying to turn.

"Stay where you are," ordered the man with the pistol, thrusting it deeper into his ribs. "Captain Wardlow will have to do without you."

"How do you know his name?"

"It doesn't matter."

"Are you going to rob me?"

"Oh," said the second man, "we're going to do a lot more than that. Now do as you're told. Hold your tongue and walk just ahead of us as if nothing is amiss. Don't give me an excuse to use my dagger."

"Now, let's go," said his companion.

He turned Tallis towards the school and nudged him forward. They were either side of their prisoner and slightly behind him so that he was unable to see them. As they walked towards the gate, they didn't even earn a glance from the boys they passed or from the gardener clearing away leaves. All that onlookers would have seen was a trio of men, ambling along together as if they were friends. Tallis was helpless.

He was their prisoner.

# CHAPTER
# FOURTEEN

As they walked along the street abreast, they presented a curious sight to the observer. Caleb Andrews was in the middle, marginally shorter than either of the two women and far less smartly dressed. Madeleine Colbeck and Lydia Quayle combined beauty and elegance. While they glided along, Andrews seemed on the point of breaking into a trot in order to keep up with them. He looked and felt like a large weed between two exquisite roses. Notwithstanding that, he was enjoying the afternoon outing.

"I never thought that I'd one day be shopping at Hamleys," said Madeleine.

"When you were born," recalled her father, "we couldn't afford to shop anywhere. We made the toys you had for Christmas. Your mother knitted all kinds of things for you to play with and I made you some wooden dolls."

"I've still got them somewhere."

"What about you, Lydia? Have you still got keepsakes from your childhood?"

"One of two," she replied, "but it's not a time I look back on very often. With two elder brothers competing with me, I was always kept in the shade. It got much better when they were sent off to school and I was alone with my sister."

Andrews was apologetic. "That's another thing we couldn't do, Maddy — send you off to school."

"And I'm very glad," said Madeleine. "I wouldn't have liked being brought up among strangers. Besides, I've been lucky enough to repair some of the gaps in my education. Robert has a wonderful library and his recommendations are always very wise." She turned to Lydia. "But you used to borrow books from a much bigger library, didn't you?"

"Yes, I did."

As soon as she asked the question, Madeleine regretted it because she knew that it would awaken memories best left dormant. When she'd first met Lydia, the latter was living with an older woman because she was in flight from her family. As the friendship with Madeleine burgeoned, tensions arose between Lydia and her companion. In moving in with the older woman, Lydia had not only signalled a break with her parents, she'd given up all thought of having children herself. Now released from what she'd come to see as a kind of comfortable incarceration, Lydia felt able to have the same aspirations as any other young woman. Hitherto, she'd never have even thought about visiting a toy shop yet here she was, turning into High Holborn, and striding eagerly towards one of the most famous toy shops in the world.

"I would have thought you'd already bought enough for Helen," she said.

"Oh, yes," agreed Madeleine, "but I just love the thrill of being in Hamleys. It's such a magical place. I've come to look rather than buy."

"Well, I intend to buy something for my grand-daughter," said Andrews.

"What did you have in mind, Father?"

"What else but a toy engine?"

Madeleine laughed. "She's far too young for that."

"Besides," said Lydia, "it's not really suitable for a girl."

"I made one for Maddy when she was a girl," said Andrews, "and she loved playing with it."

"It's true," said Madeleine.

"That's what happens when you come from a railway family."

"But that's not Helen's position," argued Lydia. "Her father's a celebrated detective and her mother — when she can get the time — is an artist."

"That makes the choice more difficult," he said.

"What would you suggest, Lydia?" asked Madeleine.

"You could always get her a magnifying glass and a box of paints," said Lydia.

"What I'd really like to get her is something that even Hamleys can't supply."

"What's that, Madeleine?"

"I want her father back home in time for Christmas."

Warned about the man's hostility towards the church, Colbeck expected to see some real fire in the clerk. Instead he found Simeon Cudlip in a subdued mood. It was as if the man had calculated that he stood to gain more by cooperating with the detectives than by raising his voice. When he was summoned to the office, he made no complaints about being taken away from his desk. He was quiet and composed, noting how much more well spoken, well groomed and sophisticated the inspector was than his sergeant.

"Do you know why you're here?" began Colbeck.

"You're not happy with what Sergeant Leeming told you about me."

"That's only part of the reason, sir. I wanted to see you in person to ask you why you tried to shift the blame for the murder on to Fred Alford?"

"I didn't accuse him directly," said Cudlip, defensively. "The sergeant kept prodding me with questions about Betty Rodman as if he believed the killer simply had to be someone with strong feelings for her."

"That's one possibility. There are others."

"I felt cornered. Simply because I liked the woman, the sergeant thought I had a reason for killing her husband. If that was the real motive, I suggested, the person to look at was Fred Alford. He worshipped Betty."

"He also befriended Mr Rodman."

"It was a way of staying in touch with her."

"Mr Alford has a wife of his own."

"Stand her beside Betty Rodman and she'd disappear."

"I don't agree," said Colbeck. "Mrs Alford has many virtues, not least of which is her compassion.

She's the person who's helping Mrs Rodman through this crisis."

"I'm glad that someone is. I don't want her at the mercy of the vicar."

"What do you have against Mr Law?"

"It's not him I despise, it's his breed. They're all the same. However," he went on, lowering his voice, "my views on religion don't matter."

"They could do."

"My faith — or lack of it — is a private matter."

"How long have you been an atheist?"

"I'd rather not go into that."

"You spoke freely to Sergeant Leeming about your opinions."

"That was a mistake."

"Are you afraid that you gave yourself away?"

"No, of course not," said Cudlip, sharply. "There was nothing to give away. My position is simple. I've nothing at all on my conscience. I didn't kill Rodman and I've no idea who did."

"What about Hector Samway?"

"I've never met him."

"Have you ever met Daniel Gill?"

"Yes," admitted the other. "When I first came here and was still drinking, I used to play cards with him sometimes. Then I stopped."

"Why?"

"Danny was a cheat. I also stopped drinking."

"What was the reason for that?"

"It's . . . personal."

"Where do you live, Mr Cudlip?"

"I've got my own house at last," said the clerk with a touch of pride. "I saved up long enough. Before that I was in the barracks."

"Really?" said Colbeck with interest. "What was it like?"

"It was used by single men like me and the conditions were poor. It was bad enough before the Welsh families moved in. After that, it was even worse. They were so aggressive, especially the women. I was glad to move into a place of my own."

"While you were in the barracks, did you get to know any of the newcomers?"

"I had no choice. They were always complaining about something or other and they formed a choir that used to practise twice a week. I couldn't stand that."

"Did you ever come across a man named Gareth Llewellyn?"

"Oh, yes," said the other, curling a lip. "He was the biggest and loudest of them. I had a row with him about the noise they all made. Llewellyn always had to be the centre of attention. I felt sorry for his wife and children."

"Why was that?"

"He neglected her and he bullied his two sons."

"Did you ever meet Mrs Llewellyn?"

"Yes, I did. She wasn't like the others. She was quiet, pleasant and she always managed to smile even though she was in pain."

"What was wrong with her?"

182

"I don't know, Inspector, but one thing is certain. Mrs Llewellyn is not going to live for three score years and ten. I'd be surprised if she reaches the age of forty."

Martin Grosvenor had always been ambitious but he accepted that he might have to wait a long time before promotion. To be singled out as the temporary replacement for Edward Tallis had filled him with a warm glow. It was his chance to impress. If he showed the exceptional talent he believed he possessed, he'd be putting down a marker against the day when the superintendent would retire for good, leaving the chair in which Grosvenor was now sitting enticingly vacant. There would be other contenders for the post — Colbeck among them — but it would be Grosvenor's stint as acting superintendent that would be in the commissioner's mind. If he could handicap the Railway Detective in some way or expose his shortcomings, he'd make his future even more secure. The rank, the office, the chair and even the box of cigars might then be his for the rest of his working days.

He picked up the report that had arrived from Swindon that morning, hoping to find a reason to reprimand Colbeck and to criticise his handling of the case. Though he'd read it a dozen times, however, there was no discernible mistake on which he could pounce. As on the previous day, Colbeck's account was lucid, detailed and comprehensive. The one thing it lacked was a promise of an early arrest. Grosvenor slapped it back down on his desk and considered the possibility of making an unexpected visit to the town to catch his rival unawares and to take charge briefly of the investigation. If nothing else, it would annoy Colbeck intensely.

Someone knocked on the door and, in answer to his summons, entered. It was a tall, slim, well-proportioned fresh-faced young man.

"You sent for me, sir," said Detective Constable Alan Hinton.

"Ah, yes, come on in, Hinton. I hear good things of you."

"Thank you, sir."

"Part of my job is to deploy my detectives wisely. To that end, I'm assigning you to work with Inspector Vallence."

Hinton's face fell. "Oh, I see."

"The inspector is a fine detective."

"He's outstanding and it would be a privilege to work with him. But Inspector Vallence is only dealing with cases of fraud at the moment and I was hoping that I might be involved in a murder investigation."

"You're not ready for that, Constable."

"I believe that I am, sir. Inspector Colbeck thinks the same."

"His opinion is irrelevant. I make operational decisions, not him. You'll report to Inspector Vallence at once. He's expecting you."

"Yes, sir."

Grosvenor snapped his fingers. "Off you go, man."

Hinton got as far as the door then turned around.

"When will Superintendent Tallis be back, sir?"

"Not until Monday morning," said Grosvenor, complacently, "so I'm in charge for the whole weekend. You can forget about the superintendent. He's attending a reunion with his old regiment and is probably having a high old time."

Stripped of his hat and frock coat, Edward Tallis was face down in a mixture of straw and horse dung. There was a large lump on the back of his head and a stream of blood trickling down from his temple.

Having made the journey to the Old Town, Leeming decided to take a proper look at it. He therefore strolled around the streets, enjoying the country air and freedom from the stifling crowds in London. In retrospect, he felt satisfied with the way he'd scared Daniel Gill and intended to keep him under suspicion. At the same time, he was sorry for the man's wife who would have to face some vehement reproaches when her husband returned from work. In telling the truth, Anne Gill had destroyed his alibi. Leeming wondered what new version of events she'd now be forced to rehearse and what threats would be used against her.

As he was approaching Victoria Road, he saw Inspector Piercey coming towards him. The latter had the radiant smile of a man about to make a significant arrest. When he saw Leeming, he quickened his step.

"I have good news for you to carry back to Inspector Colbeck," he said.

"Have you found out who sent that letter?"

"I believe so."

"What's his name?"

"It's one of four people. I simply have to visit each of them in turn."

"How did you narrow it down to four suspects?"

"I had the sense to involve Mr Morris, who edits the *Advertiser*. Since the letter I was given was posted through his letter box, I reasoned that its author lived in the Old Town. He had to be a regular reader of the newspaper or he'd never have seen the reward notice."

"He might have seen one of the posters."

"They were put up after the *Advertiser* came out. The anonymous letter in question was the first to arrive, immediately after the newspapers had been delivered. My guess is that the man dashed it off as soon as he saw how much money was on offer."

"That's logical," said Leeming, approvingly. "And I daresay Mr Morris was able to tell you the names of everyone who has a copy of the paper delivered to him."

"Exactly — all that I had to do was to go through his list of subscribers and let him explain who each of them was. According to Morris, only four people could be deemed to be responsible. It's my job to find out which one it was."

"Inspector Colbeck will be very grateful to you."

"Please pass on my regards to him."

"I daresay that he'd like to thank you in person, Inspector. In fact, he may well have another task for you."

"Then I'll accept it gladly. We must catch the killer."

"We must also punish those who are trying to mislead us," said Leeming. "We can't concentrate on the search if we keep getting letters designed to hamper us."

Piercey lowered his voice. "Have we . . . made any headway yet?"

"We continue to amass evidence."

"But you must have picked out suspects by now."

"Certain people have aroused our interest."

"Might I know who they are?"

"I'm not at liberty to tell you."

"But I'm involved in the investigation, Sergeant."

"We've learnt never to release names too soon," Leeming told him. "It's a strict policy. Evidence must be overwhelming before we strike."

"Can't you even give me a hint?"

"I'm afraid not, sir. You'll have to ask Inspector Colbeck."

After speaking to two of the suspects, Colbeck spent an improving hour with Stinson, assuring him that they were confident of success and checking on the employment records of the five people he and Leeming had identified as potential culprits. He then returned to their temporary office and wrote their names on a sheet of paper, listing everything that they'd found out about the men and searching, in each case, for motive, means and opportunity. It had occurred to him at the very start that more than one person might have been involved in the murder but, as he studied the accumulated details of the five men, he couldn't see how any two of them could possibly have colluded with each other. Rodman had therefore, in all likelihood, been killed by a single individual with a plan to remove the man's head and to leave him tied up in a strange position that might, or might not, have religious implications. Of the suspects, only Simeon Cudlip was a self-declared atheist. Had the clerk created the grotesque scene of horror and humiliation that was found in the Erecting Shop? What had he achieved by doing so?

Hector Samway and Daniel Gill both had enough hatred of the victim to drive them on to murder and the butcher's assistant would have ready access to a cleaver for decapitation. It was, however, difficult to see how he'd compelled Rodman to enter the Works in the dead of night. Earlier on, Leeming had been inclined to install Gareth Llewellyn as their prime suspect and Colbeck had opposed the idea. Given what he'd learnt from Rachel Griffiths, however, the inspector had begun to change his mind, recalling that the Welshman had deserted his countrymen in the Glue Pot in order to go to the Queen's Tap, the pub where Rodman was still allowed to drink. There seemed to be no other explanation as to why Llewellyn had left a place that reputedly sold the best beer in the village. He wanted to be close to Rodman, ready to pounce.

Fred Alford was the most puzzling suspect and there were moments when Colbeck felt that he shouldn't even be considered alongside the other four men. On the face of it, Alford was a happily married man with a family and had no apparent reason for wanting to slaughter a close friend. If he still cared for Betty Rodman as much as had been claimed, why would he subject her to the unspeakable agony of losing her husband in such a cruel way? It might make her turn to him for help but her dependence on him was all that he stood to gain. As long as his own wife was alive, Betty was hopelessly beyond his reach. Even if Liza Alford died — by natural or other means — would her husband really want to take on responsibility for a woman with three children when he already had four children of his own to feed? Fred Alford seemed like the ideal friend to have in a crisis. And yet there was something about the man that made Colbeck doubt his innocence. He wished that he knew what it was.

His deliberations were soon interrupted by the arrival of Victor Leeming. The sergeant passed on the message he'd been given by Inspector Piercey, then described his confrontation with Daniel Gill.

"He was lying through his teeth, sir."

"That's his normal mode of speech," said Colbeck. "Gill is unacquainted with the concept of truth."

"I felt sorry for his wife. She was so meek and mild."

"You were right to apply pressure on her, Victor. It may have seemed unkind at the time but you got the desired result."

"When I told Gill I'd spoken to her, his eyes nearly popped out of his head."

"We've both established that he's a congenital liar. Is he also a killer?"

"He could be, sir."

"We'd never secure a conviction with 'could be'. There are four other men who *could* be guilty. We need incontestable proof."

"I'm beginning think that it was Hector Samway."

"What makes you believe that?"

"He's strong and aggressive. Losing his wife made him very bitter. It must have rankled with him that Rodman went home to a lovely woman every night while he was sleeping in an empty bed."

"We don't know that it was always empty," suggested Colbeck. "I remembered something that the railway policeman told you."

"Edgar Fellowes? He knows this village inside out."

"You said he mentioned that there was a brothel here. There's no shortage of single men here and a lonely widower like Samway could also be tempted to look for female company even if it meant paying for it."

Leeming gave a mirthless laugh. "The last time I took part in a raid on a brothel, most of the men in there were married. It was disgusting."

"We're not moral guardians, Victor. We're after a killer. If you think his name could be Hector Samway, you might find it useful to visit the brothel and speak to the local prostitutes. Find out if he was a regular client of theirs and if — this is important — he was there on the night of the murder. And while you're at it," added Colbeck, "see if Simeon Cudlip is known to them. I don't believe that he lives like a monk when he's off duty."

**190**

"Neither do I, sir. It will be interesting to see if *he* was paying for pleasure on the night when Rodman was killed. If he was, he'd have an alibi."

"Cudlip would never use it. He has to keep up the pretence of being above that kind of thing. It's the reason he guards his private life so carefully."

"Until we know more, Samway is my man. What about you, sir?"

"Well, I've had second thoughts about Llewellyn."

Leeming was surprised. "You dismissed him completely."

"I was too hasty."

"I've never heard you admit that before. You're always so careful."

"Now that we know a lot more about the Welshman, I see him in a different light. He's violent, devious and vengeful. He mocked the way that Rodman sang in church and was desperately keen to replace him as a soloist in the concert."

"Is that a strong enough motive for murder?" asked Leeming, dubiously.

"Ordinarily, I'd say that it wasn't."

"And now?"

"I'll reserve my judgement," said Colbeck.

He looked down at the names in front of him, convinced that one of them was the man they wanted. All that they had to do was to keep digging into the immediate past of the quintet until they found the evidence they needed.

"What will you say in your report to Mouldy Grosvenor?" asked Leeming.

"I'll tell him that we're making slow but steady progress."

"If we don't make an arrest soon, he'll claim we're being incompetent."

"He's envious of our reputation, Victor. Ignore his jibes."

"That was easy when he was only an inspector like you. He's the acting superintendent now. That gives him power over us."

"Yes, but he'll have no idea how to exercise it. He wants us to fail so that he can berate us. We must ensure that we don't give him that opportunity."

"I know it's a strange thing to say," admitted Leeming, "but I'm starting to miss Superintendent Tallis. At least he never crowed over us and that's all that Mouldy Grosvenor ever does."

Without warning, the door was flung open and their superior strode in purposefully before taking up a combative stance.

"Did I hear my name being mentioned?" he asked.

Grosvenor's sly smile had been replaced by a triumphant smirk.

# CHAPTER
# FIFTEEN

Edward Tallis was in pain. His head was pounding and the handcuffs that held his arms together behind his back were chafing his wrists. He had no idea where he was or how he came to be there. All that he remembered was a stream of foul language followed by a crushing blow to his skull. Having lain unconscious in an awkward position for some while, he found that every muscle ached. The feel of the straw and the stench of manure told him that he was in some kind of stable. Only a few fingers of light poked through the gaps in the timber to soften the gloom. He rolled over on his back and looked upwards. Ropes and harness dangled above him. Tallis could just make out a trapdoor in the ceiling but he had no means of reaching it. His mind searched frantically for answers. Where was he? Who brought him there? And why had he been kidnapped in the first place?

It was infuriating. The promise of a whole weekend in the company of his old comrades had made his mouth water. He'd been looking forward to the reunion for months. Instead of being able to step back in time to his army days, he was held fast in a fetid prison.

Robbed of the pleasures he'd anticipated, he was utterly humiliated.

After clearing his throat, he put back his head and yelled.

"Is anybody there?"

His voice sounded dull and hoarse. He tried again.

"Who *are* you?"

Once again, there was no response. He fell back on a threat.

"Let me go or you'll suffer for it. Do you know who I am and *what* I am?"

He might have been howling in the wilderness. Nobody heard or came. Tallis made an effort to sound more reasonable. Struggling up into a sitting position, he rested his back against a stall.

"Let's talk this over, shall we? I think you'll find you have the wrong man."

This time he did provoke a reply but it was only the lowing of a disgruntled cow. There was no other sound, no babble of human voices, no noise of traffic rattling over the cobblestones of Canterbury. He surmised that he was in a remote spot in the country, well out of earshot of anyone. They'd stolen his hat, frock coat, watch, wallet and — worst of all — his gold cufflinks with the regimental coat of arms engraved on them. In their place was a set of handcuffs that were causing him sheer agony.

"Where am I?" he shouted.

But he didn't even expect an answer this time.

Martin Grosvenor enjoyed his moment. For the first time ever, he'd managed to secure an advantage over Colbeck, startling him with his sudden appearance and cowing him into at least a semblance of submission. If the inspector was shocked, Leeming was absolutely flabbergasted, staring at the newcomer as if he'd just returned from the dead and taking a few defensive steps backwards. The acting superintendent explained why he'd come to Swindon.

"I had the idea from my predecessor," he said.

"Superintendent Tallis is your superior, sir," Colbeck pointed out, "and not your predecessor."

"There's no need to be so pedantic."

"You have but a fleeting ownership of his mantle."

"And I mean to put it to good use. That's why I descended unexpectedly on you and the sergeant. It's something the superintendent used to do with great effect. He told me about the time he took control of a case in Derby."

"That's not quite what happened, sir."

"It wasn't," agreed Leeming. "Superintendent Tallis simply got in the way. Luckily, he injured himself and had to go back to London. As soon as he did that, we were able to solve the case."

Grosvenor sniffed. "He tells a different story."

"He would."

"I'll allow no disrespect of the superintendent."

"Which one, sir — you or him?"

"Both of us," snapped Grosvenor.

"We're very pleased to see you, sir," said Colbeck, adapting quickly to the situation. "It will save me the trouble of sending a report. We're honoured that you should favour us when there are so many other cases clamouring for your attention."

"This is the one that interests me, Inspector."

"May I ask why?"

"It's the one in which I feel I can make the most useful contribution," said the other, loftily. "At first glance, your last report appeared to be sound enough but I was soon able to see a series of lacunae in it."

Leeming frowned. "What are they?"

"Gaps, spaces, missing parts," said Colbeck.

"Carefully hidden as they were," continued Grosvenor, "I spotted them."

"Then perhaps you'll be good enough to point them out, sir." He indicated the chairs. "Why don't we all sit down and carry on the discussion in comfort?"

When the three of them were seated, Grosvenor delivered his critique of Colbeck's second report, claiming that it was too unstructured and that it gave him no confidence in the prospect of an early arrest.

"We've only been here two days or so," argued Leeming.

Grosvenor was acerbic. "I expected you to have made *some* advances."

"What advances did *you* make in two days when you were in charge of the Seymour case? It took you seven weeks before you worked out who the culprit was."

"That's history. This is the only investigation that matters now and I want a sign of industry from you. Where do things stand at this moment?"

**196**

Colbeck was tempted to tell him that his presence had brought their work to a complete standstill but he didn't want to anger Grosvenor any more than was necessary. He therefore gave him a cogent and comprehensive account of their movements that day and revealed the evidence they'd garnered. To his credit, Grosvenor showed that he'd read very carefully both of the reports sent to Scotland Yard. Indeed, on the strength of the known facts, he was ready to plump for the name of the killer.

"Daniel Gill ought to be in custody," he insisted.

"I agree," said Leeming. "That shop where he works is in a terrible state. His uncle ought to be locked up for keeping it so dirty and smelly."

"Everything points to Gill as the killer."

"Does it?"

"Who but a butcher would hack off someone's head?"

"You've obviously forgotten our adventures in Crewe," said Colbeck. "We found a severed head in a hatbox and it certainly wasn't put there by a butcher."

"That was a different case, man. Don't confuse the issue."

"What was Gill's motive?"

"He had a long-standing grudge against Rodman because the latter had kept his job when Gill was ousted."

"Several people here have been holding a grudge against Rodman, sir. We've whittled the list down to five."

"I've just whittled it down to one."

"Then you can have the pleasure of arresting Mr Gill," said Colbeck, easily. "If you stay here long enough, you may also be forced to release him."

"We don't think it's him," said Leeming, bluntly.

"When he's under lock and key," argued Grosvenor, "he can be interrogated properly. I'd soon get a confession out of him."

"It won't be a confession of murder, sir."

"Why not?"

"Gill has too much to lose. He has a pretty wife and two young children."

"So does this fellow called Llewellyn yet the inspector has just told me that the Welshman is the most likely killer."

"He simply became a prime suspect, sir," said Colbeck. "In essence, I still believe that any of the five people we've named could be guilty. Gill, Llewellyn, Samway, Cudlip and Alford deserve the same degree of scrutiny."

Grosvenor was defiant. "I'd like to meet Gill."

"Take a peg for your nose," advised Leeming. "That shop has a real pong."

"You can accompany me, Colbeck. I'll show you how to question a suspect until he cracks. You're far too polite with them."

"Perhaps that's why the inspector has made many more arrests than you, sir," said Leeming. "And all his arrests led to convictions."

Reminded of an uncomfortable truth, Grosvenor quivered with fury.

★　★　★

It had not been long before Terence Wardlow realised that something was amiss. His friend should have returned already. Hauling himself to his feet, Wardlow went out to the cloisters and hobbled around them, looking into every room. When there was no sign of Tallis, his first thought was that his friend had been taken ill or had some kind of accident. Had that been the case, he then decided, Tallis would definitely have sent word to him to put his mind at rest. Another possible explanation was that his old friend had simply wandered off somewhere and lost his way. It was something that had happened to more than one of Wardlow's older acquaintances. Their grasp on reality was slipping badly. Yet that wasn't a charge that could be levelled against Tallis. He was fit, healthy and remarkably alert. If there'd been any loss of mental power, he'd have been unable to keep such a taxing job.

That left only one explanation and it filled Wardlow with anxiety. Tallis must have been the victim of foul play. As his host, Wardlow blamed himself for getting parted from his friend. He should have braved the discomfort and stayed with him. He'd never forgive himself if anything serious had happened to the former Major Tallis. To make amends, he had to institute a proper search immediately. In spite of the pain it caused him, he almost ran to the police station to raise the alarm, gasping for breath when he finally got there. When they heard that the missing person was a detective superintendent from Scotland Yard, the local constabulary called in the meagre supply of police

199

officers at their disposal. A description of Edward Tallis was circulated among them along with details of where and when he was last seen. The uniformed policemen hurried off. They were soon asking questions of everyone in the vicinity of the cathedral. Wardlow's only regret was that he didn't have the strength to join in what would be a thorough search of the city.

"Why do you call him Mouldy Grosvenor?" asked Fellowes.

"Stand next to him," replied Leeming, "and you'll soon find out. His breath smells like mouldy cheese."

"And he just turned up out of the blue?"

"He thinks he knows how to solve this crime. However, that's not why I came looking for you. I need help. You told me that there was a brothel here."

Fellowes was shocked. "You're not saying that you'd like to —?"

"No," said Leeming, angrily. "I'm not asking for that reason. I have a lovely wife and would never dream of betraying her or my marriage vows. I need the address because I might learn something there that has a bearing on this case. So — where is it?"

"I'm not quite sure," said the other, evasively.

"Don't lie to me. You know everything that goes on here."

"Well, I have heard a rumour."

"Just give me the address and I'll be off."

The railway policeman shuffled his feet then told him where he believed the brothel might be located. Once Leeming had established where the street was, he went off quickly. He was still jangled by the arrival of Grosvenor. It had caught him and Colbeck completely off guard. He resented the way that the man had taken control of the investigation, relegating the detectives who'd being doing all the hard work to the role of assistants. If Colbeck and Leeming solved the case, they could now be sure that Grosvenor would claim that his intervention had made all the difference. It would allow him to gloat over them.

During his time in uniform, Leeming had policed some of the worst areas of London. The brothels where he'd made arrests were usually squalid places in ramshackle houses, devoid of even basic comfort, let alone allure. He'd always felt sorry for the women employed there because they were subject to the fantasies of random clients and at the mercy of the cruel men who'd controlled them. When he reached the house mentioned by Edgar Fellowes, he saw that it was very different from the malodorous slums he'd once visited. Leeming was standing outside a dwelling in one of the neat terraces built by the GWR. It made him wonder if he'd come to the wrong place.

That impression was reinforced by the sight of the person who opened the front door to him. She was a well-dressed, presentable woman in her fifties with a disarming smile and an aura of wholesomeness. He found himself tipping his hat respectfully. Thrusting her head out of the door, she looked up and down the street then plucked at his sleeve to bring him into the house.

"My daughter's asleep at the moment," she explained, "because she had a very busy night, but I can see to your needs, sir. Just tell me what they are."

Leeming was revolted. "I haven't come in search of your services," he said, testily. "I'm a detective sergeant and I'm investigating the murder that took place recently."

"Goodness!" she cried. "We had nothing to do with that, sir."

"You could be wrong on that score."

"Please don't arrest us again and turn us out. It took weeks to find this place."

"I've come here for information, Mrs . . ."

"Mrs Knight," she told him. "I'm Claire Knight and my daughter is Euphemia. Actually," she confessed, "her real name is Meg but gentlemen seem to prefer something a little less common." She eyed him shrewdly. "Are you sure that you're not here for pleasure, sir? I'm very experienced and there'd be no charge."

Leeming spluttered.

Colbeck had expected some sort of interference from Grosvenor but he hadn't foreseen a visit from him. It was a worrying development and would handicap rather than help the investigation. On the cab ride to the Old Town, he had to listen to his companion's boasts about how easily he'd taken to his new status as superintendent. Colbeck's fear was that Grosvenor would charge into the butcher's shop to arrest Daniel Gill without even bothering to question him first.

Having each given the man a decided scare, he and Leeming had chosen to leave him at liberty so that they could watch his reactions. Neither of them had marked him down as their chief suspect.

In the event, fortune favoured the inspector. When they got to the shop, they were told that Gill was not there. The butcher — a peppery old man with a red face and a rasping voice — explained that he'd sent his nephew to collect some meat from a farm that was miles away. He wanted to know why two detectives were interested in Gill but Colbeck assured him that they were only making routine enquiries. He then hustled Grosvenor out of there before the superintendent tried to question the butcher. On their way out of the Old Town, Colbeck drew the attention of his companion to the reward notice displayed in the window of the *Swindon Advertiser*.

"That's a large amount of money to offer," said Grosvenor.

"Unfortunately, it hasn't brought in the information we need, sir."

"Gill is your man. Get him before he makes a run for it."

"Where could he go?"

Having no answer, the other man lapsed into silence for several minutes. When he finally spoke again, he had a question about Leeming.

"I saw you whispering to the sergeant before we went out," he said. "What did you tell him to do?"

"I asked him to interview someone who may be able to help us."

"And what's the name of this individual?"

"To be honest, sir, I don't rightly know."

Notwithstanding his rooted objection to prostitution, Leeming was actually warming to Claire Knight. As they sat together in a cosy room, the heat of the fire was almost seductive. For the first time since they'd been in Swindon, he was really comfortable. He almost forgot what his hospitable hostess did for a living.

"I could offer you a glass of wine, Sergeant," she said, nudging him.

"All I want are answers, Mrs Knight."

"There's nothing Euphemia and I can tell you."

"There may be," he said. "Without realising it, you might have entertained someone who was planning a murder."

She laughed throatily. "There's only one thing they're planning when they come here." Sitting up, she shot him a look of apology. "I do beg your pardon."

"Cast your mind back to the night of the murder."

"Why?"

"Just do as I say. Did anyone come here that night?"

She regarded him warily. "You're not a *real* detective, are you?" she said, sharply. "You've been hired by some nasty, suspicious killjoy of a wife to see if her husband comes here because he doesn't get what he wants at home." She stood up. "I'll thank you to leave my premises." Leeming took something from his pocket and held it up in front of her. "What's that?"

"It's my warrant card, Mrs Knight. It proves that I'm a detective sergeant in the Metropolitan Police Force.

As such, I have the right to arrest you and your daughter for running a disorderly house."

"Oh, please don't do that!" she begged, sinking back down in her chair. "We're doing no harm, Sergeant. We fulfil a need. What's wrong with that?"

"I'll ask you once more."

"No, no, I heard you the first time. Someone *did* come here that night. In fact, there were three of them. They came at separate times."

"Was one of them Hector Samway?"

"No, we haven't seen him for weeks."

"He's a regular visitor, then?"

"I can't tell you that. I swore to protect all our clients."

"Do you want to protect a killer from arrest?"

She was astounded. "Is that what Hector is?"

"It's a possibility, Mrs Knight. That's why it's so important that you're honest with me. Who were the three who did come here that night?" He narrowed his eyelids. "If you won't tell me, I'll go upstairs and ask your daughter instead."

"You can't do that," she protested. "Meg needs her sleep, poor dear."

He took out his notebook. "Give me those names."

After a long delay and a battery of excuses, she at last told the truth.

"One was Josiah Daley, the cobbler." He wrote down the name. "The second one was . . . oh," she said, hands clasped together, "he'll be so angry if I tell you that he came here. We have . . . an arrangement, you see."

"What sort of arrangement?"

"Edgar trusts me."

His ears perked up. "Are you talking about Edgar Fellowes, by any chance?" Her face was a confession in itself. "Right," he went on, jotting down the name before looking up. "You told me that you had three clients. Who was the other one?"

"My daughter is the best person to talk about him. His behaviour was very upsetting. She said she never wanted him here again."

"Why was that?"

"He was like a mad thing, Sergeant. When he came here before, he was always quiet and considerate. Two nights ago, he was in a violent mood. He made Meg scream out loud in agony at one point and I couldn't allow that."

"What was his name, Mrs Knight?" She shook her head guiltily, afraid that she'd already given too much away. "Who *was* it?"

"Simeon Cudlip."

Having barged his way into the investigation, Grosvenor insisted on meeting the general manager and assuring him that everything was in hand. Oswald Stinson was pleased to hear that an arrest would soon take place, forcing Colbeck to step in and explain that, as yet, they had insufficient evidence to charge the man. Annoyed at the interruption, Grosvenor was adamant that, when he met the suspect face-to-face, he would be able to draw all the evidence that was necessary out of him. Colbeck could see how impressed Stinson was by the superintendent and accepted that Grosvenor was always able to make a favourable impact on first acquaintance. Unlike the general manager, he'd known and disliked the man for many years and knew all his defects, not least his tendency towards fatal overconfidence.

"I'm delighted that you came, Superintendent," said Stinson. "You seem to have injected some real spirit into the investigation."

Grosvenor basked in the praise. "I'm renowned for it."

"How long are you staying?"

"I'd planned to return to London this evening."

"If you change your mind, my wife and I would be delighted to offer you our hospitality." He glanced at Colbeck. "The inspector turned down our invitation."

"That was rather ungracious," said Grosvenor.

"We felt that we needed to be at the heart of the village, sir," said Colbeck.

"I'd question that decision."

He was prevented from going on to justify his criticism by the arrival of a clerk. After knocking on the door, the man entered carrying a telegraph.

"I'm sorry to disturb you," he said, "but this is urgent."

Stinson stretched out a hand. "Let me see it."

"Actually, sir, it's for the superintendent."

"Then I'd better have it," said Grosvenor, taking it from him. When he'd read the contents, he leapt up from his chair. "This is dreadful!"

"What's the trouble, sir?" asked Colbeck.

"I have to catch the next train back to London."

"Why — is there a problem?"

"There's a very big problem, I'm afraid. Superintendent Tallis has disappeared in Canterbury. They fear that he's been abducted."

# CHAPTER
# SIXTEEN

When her friend turned up unexpectedly on the doorstep, Madeleine Colbeck knew that there was good news for her to enjoy. On a cold, wintry day, Lydia Quayle was glowing. They sat side by side on a sofa in the drawing room.

"You've seen Constable Hinton, haven't you?" said Madeleine.

"How did you guess?"

"It's written all over your face. Am I right?"

"Yes, you are."

"Then tell me what happened."

After taking a moment to compose herself, Lydia said how surprised and delighted she'd been when Hinton had called at her house. Ostensibly, he'd come to see if she'd recovered from her ordeal, urging her to contact him at his home address if she was ever in difficulty again. It was clear to Madeleine, however, that he'd used the excuse as a means of seeing her again.

"Alan told me that he was working with Inspector Vallence now," said Lydia. "What he really wants to do, of course, is to be involved in a murder investigation and to work with Robert. He believes that he could learn so much from your husband."

"It's true. As well as being a good detective, Robert is an inspiring teacher. But tell me what else your adoring constable said to you."

Lydia tittered. "Oh, I wouldn't call him that."

"Why else would he go out of his way to speak to you?"

"He's concerned for my safety."

"Alan Hinton wants to be your protector. Do you object to that?"

"No, I don't."

"Then you can expect him to call again from time to time."

"Do you really think so?" asked Lydia, hopefully.

"Of course," said Madeleine. "Both of you obviously relish each other's company."

"We do."

"And you'd like to meet regularly."

"There's only one way that could happen, Madeleine."

"Is there?"

"Alan would have to be assigned to one of Robert's cases. He'd come here to the house then. If he proved his worth, he'd become part of the family in a way that Victor Leeming has. You'd see me here a lot more often if that were the case."

"That would be wonderful."

Pleased that her friend was so happy, Madeleine gave her a warm hug.

Terence Wardlow was in despair. A close friend had vanished into thin air. The police in Canterbury were

**210**

carrying out an exhaustive search but, after a couple of hours, they had nothing encouraging to report. It seemed that Tallis was no longer in the city. Where could he possibly be and who took him there? He'd only have gone under duress. That troubled Wardlow. Tallis would be no obedient prisoner. It was not in his character to submit to anyone. He'd be more likely to resist and therefore provoke his captors. In that sense, he'd be his own worse enemy. Though there were no sightings of him, Wardlow had at least hoped for a ransom demand that would prove Tallis was still alive. To secure his release, he'd be happy to pay the amount from his own pocket. But no demand came and there was no hint of the whereabouts of his guest.

It was time to try something else. While they were doing their best, the police had restricted resources. Wardlow therefore sent a telegraph to the commissioner at Scotland Yard, knowing that it would get an instant response. Desperate to do something of his own to help the hunt for his missing friend, he acted on impulse and headed for the railway station. If the police were unable to find Tallis, they needed to be reinforced and the best place to get those reinforcements was in Hythe. The crisis had only arisen because Tallis was attending a reunion as an honoured guest at his old regiment. Soldiers had to come to his rescue.

The shock of Grosvenor's arrival had been matched by the suddenness of his departure. No sooner had he taken control of the investigation than he was called back to handle an emergency. Colbeck and Leeming were simultaneously relieved and disturbed, glad to be rid of him while concerned for the fate of Edward Tallis.

"Who could want to abduct him?" asked Leeming.

"We don't know that that's what happened, Victor. The telegraph was brief. It seemed to be working on an assumption rather than on solid evidence. As to your question," Colbeck went on, "the answer is simple. He is a figurehead at Scotland Yard. Criminals identify him as a loathsome enemy because he's responsible for dispatching the detectives who hunt them down. Hundreds of villains have gone to prison, cursing his name."

"I curse his name sometimes but it doesn't make me want to kidnap him."

"Let's hope that it *is* a kidnap. It would mean that he's still alive and that a ransom will be demanded for his release."

"How much is he worth?"

"A hundred times as much as Grosvenor, in my opinion," said Colbeck with feeling. "Tallis is indispensable. He is not."

"Why doesn't someone abduct Mouldy and do all of us a favour?"

After his visit to the brothel, Leeming had returned to their office to learn of the latest development. Like Colbeck, he felt that they were in charge of the case again. He described his visit to Claire Knight's abode and how unlike it was to the establishments where he'd made arrests in London.

"The daughter is known as Euphemia."

212

Colbeck was amused. "That's singularly inappropriate," he said. "I seem to remember that Euphemia was a virgin saint martyred in the fourth century. It's hardly the right name for a prostitute."

"Mrs Knight didn't use that word," said Leeming. "She told me that she and her daughter were courtesans."

"I doubt whether it's a term that any of their clients ever use. Strictly speaking, I suppose, we should report the existence and location of the house to Inspector Piercey but I suspect that he's already aware of it and turns a blind eye."

"That's what Mrs Knight hinted to me."

"Then we don't need to interfere. Well, I can see that you had an unsettling time with her, Victor, but you learnt something valuable. Cudlip went there on the night of the murder in a state of wild excitement."

"I wonder if it was the act of killing someone that made him like that. We've seen it happen before. Some people are overcome with guilt after a murder but we've met others who are quite the opposite. They're wild and inflamed. It sounds to me as if Cudlip was in that state," said Leeming, confidently. "We should arrest him."

"No," decided Colbeck. "I'm not committing myself to an arrest on the word of a courtesan or whatever she claims to be. We have a suspect who was overexcited on the night when Rodman was killed but we also have one who came back to the barracks with blood on his hands. Cudlip or Llewellyn — which one of them did the deed? It's up to us to be sure we have the right man before we move in. In any case, you favour Samway and Superintendent Grosvenor still believes that it was Daniel Gill. He didn't even consider Alford and the others."

"We should forget Alford."

"I'm loath to rule him out, Victor."

"Yet there's no real evidence against him."

"It may yet emerge."

They discussed their five suspects for some time but the disappearance of Edward Tallis remained at the back of their minds. Conversation eventually moved once again to the missing superintendent.

"This will teach Mouldy a lesson," said Leeming. "When he replaced Tallis, he thought that he could be just as good at the job. Then he gets a telegraph from the commissioner and has to take control of a search. He won't know where to begin. I'll wager that he's sitting on the train at this moment, wishing that he'd never been promoted in the first place."

"I disagree, Victor."

"Mouldy will be shaking in his shoes."

"That may be his initial reaction," said Colbeck, "but he'll soon adjust to the emergency and he'll begin to see it in a rather different way."

Martin Grosvenor caught the first train to London and settled into a compartment. When one of his travelling companions tried to engage him in conversation, he studiously ignored the man. He was eager to be alone with his thoughts. An element of panic had set in when he stood on the platform earlier. He had no experience

**214**

of organising a manhunt or of dealing with a ransom demand. Tallis, by contrast, had done both and would therefore know exactly what to do. Grosvenor had to try to emulate him somehow. For the first time, he began to question his own abilities. If his deficiencies were exposed by such an important investigation, his occupation of Tallis's office would come to an abrupt end. Instead of earning kudos, he'd lose the commissioner's faith in him.

As time passed, however, he slowly recovered his confidence and came to look at the crisis in an alternative way. If he was dealing with a kidnap, it might work to his advantage. Those involved might not even want money in return for Tallis's freedom. The superintendent might already have been killed. Like most of those in law enforcement, Tallis had received anonymous letters in the past, threatening him with revenge and he'd cheerfully disregarded them. Had some of his enemies managed to carry out their threats at last? Had he been abducted in order to be murdered? It was a grim prospect yet Grosvenor stood to profit from the calamity. If one superintendent was killed, the most likely person to replace him was the man who'd been Tallis's temporary substitute. A promotion due to last a few days might be extended until his retirement from the Detective Department. He would have security of tenure and permanent authority over Colbeck.

It was a delicious possibility. If he led a successful hunt for Tallis and rescued him, Grosvenor would win plaudits from everyone. If, however, the superintendent had already been executed by vengeful criminals, his caretaker would stay in office. Either way, Grosvenor stood to gain. His anxiety melted away instantly. Instead of fearing his return to Scotland Yard, he couldn't get there quick enough.

When his shift was over, Fred Alford followed the same procedure as on previous days. He went straight to Betty Rodman's house, relieved his wife of the task of keeping her company and took on the duty himself. The moment that Liza had left, he enfolded Betty in his arms.

"How have you been today?"

"I'm bearing up, Fred."

"I'm always here for you — and you know why."

"Yes," she said, sadly. "My life would have been very different if I'd married you instead of Frank. He made lots of promises but stood by very few of them. You'd have been much more steadfast."

"I'd have done *anything* for you, Betty. I still would."

She smiled bravely. "I made my decision and it gave me three wonderful children. It also gave me a lot of bad memories but there are plenty of good ones as well. Frank *wanted* to be a better husband but he was . . . easily led astray."

"You don't need to tell me that. I watched it happen."

"It was like having two husbands, Fred. One of them was the man I loved who sang in the church choir and doted on the children. The other was a drunken fool who got into fights and neglected us."

**216**

"There were times when I simply wanted to knock some sense into him," said Alford, "but I knew you wouldn't like me interfering so I kept my distance."

She kissed him on the cheek. "Thank you, Fred."

He stood back from her so that he could look at her properly.

"Have you heard anything from Inspector Colbeck?"

"No, but I'm sure he's working hard to solve the murder. It's somebody we know, somebody who's carrying on as if nothing has happened. Who can it be?"

"Let the detectives sort that out. All you need to think about is the future for you and the children."

"We *have* no future, Fred," she said, gloomily. "It died with Frank."

"No, it didn't," he said, squeezing her hands. "As long as I'm alive, Betty, you do have a future. I know it's difficult at the moment but you must believe that there is a life elsewhere — better than the one you've been living. Keep that thought at the forefront of your mind. You'll always have *me*, remember."

She nodded. "Knowing that is the only thing that's kept me going, Fred."

He took her in his arms again and held her tight.

The novelty of Swindon had soon worn off for Leeming. Since he didn't share Colbeck's passion for watching steam locomotives, carriages and wagons being constructed, he simply found the Railway Village dirty, noisy and depressing. He was, therefore, delighted when he was told they'd be going back to London that evening.

"What changed your mind, sir?" he asked.

"Tallis's disappearance worries me, Victor," said Colbeck. "I'd like to know the details and see if I can offer advice."

"Oh, you can offer it but it would never be accepted by Mouldy Grosvenor."

"I'd go above his head to the commissioner."

"Does that mean we have a night at home?"

"It does, indeed, but we'll be on the early train back here tomorrow."

"It will be a lovely surprise for Estelle and the boys."

"I'm rather hoping that I'll get a cordial welcome from Madeleine. She'll have read the letter I posted yesterday but today's news can be delivered in person."

"Have you told Mr Stinson that we're leaving?"

"There's no need for him to know. We'll ask Mr Wells to keep our rooms at the Queen's Tap and be back there before Stinson realises that we went home." Gathering up some papers from the desk, he led the way to the door. "London can be noisy but it's positively deafening being in the middle of a Locomotive Works." As they left the office, he couldn't resist teasing the sergeant. "Are you going to tell Estelle about your visit to Mrs Knight, the courtesan?"

"No, I'm not!" retorted Leeming.

"It's not often you meet a mother and daughter like them."

"They shouldn't *need* to do . . . what they do."

They returned to the pub, collected their valises, then headed for the station. Though it was early evening, it was dark and bleak. They walked briskly to generate warmth. Colbeck was practical.

"Sometimes we need to get away from a place in order to view it in a new perspective. Since we've been here," said Colbeck, "we've immersed ourselves in the world of railways. Taking a short break from it will both freshen us and allow us time for reflection."

"Do we need it, sir? We know who the killer is."

"Are you still convinced that it was Samway?"

"No," said Leeming. "My money is on Simeon Cudlip now."

"I think it would be wise to restrict yourself to a very small wager."

"Why is that, sir?"

"Nothing can be considered to be positive," said Colbeck. "Yes, we have five credible suspects, each one of them capable of the vile act that brought us to Swindon. But we must always bear in mind the possibility — remote, I grant you — that all of them are entirely innocent."

Leeming was disheartened. "Do you mean that it could be someone we've never even thought of?"

"I mean exactly that, Victor."

Grosvenor's interview with the commissioner was relatively short. There were scant details of the abduction to pass on. The news that the local constabulary had been unable to find any clues as to Tallis's whereabouts was worrying. Grosvenor was told to send detectives to join the hunt immediately. He did his best to impress the commissioner by claiming that his visit to Swindon had more or less resulted in the identification of the killer but that news made no impact. The disappearance of the highly respected superintendent took precedence. Grosvenor was urged to forget about the murder investigation in Wiltshire and concentrate all his energies on finding Edward Tallis.

Grosvenor returned to his office to discover that someone was waiting to see him. Having reported the kidnap to their old regiment, Terence Wardlow had caught a train to London and had just arrived. He was able to pass on more details of what he believed must have happened.

"Are you absolutely *sure* that he was kidnapped?" asked Grosvenor.

"What else could have happened?"

"He might have been taken seriously ill."

"Edward was in rude health. Besides, if he had been taken ill or been involved in some kind of accident, it would have been reported hours ago."

"Have the police made no progress at all?"

"They're convinced that Edward is no longer in the city because they've scoured it from end to end. Since they're relatively few in number, I called on members of our old regiment to lend us their assistance. Soldiers are now searching Canterbury and the vicinity. They know about his distinguished military service."

Grosvenor was not sure whether to be reassured or worried. If the manhunt had reinforcements, the

220

chances of finding Tallis were increased. Detectives were all working at full stretch in London. Very few were available. Grosvenor decided that a couple would suffice to coordinate the search. What Wardlow had told him should have been construed as good news. Yet he didn't recognise it as such. While he didn't want any harm to come to the superintendent, he was hoping that, at the very least, he'd be able to hold on to his role at Scotland Yard for a few more days. A full week at the helm would give him enough time to establish his credentials for promotion. Though he told Wardlow that he'd do all in his power to rescue Tallis, he was secretly hoping that there'd be a delay.

"You must have some idea who is behind this," said Wardlow.

"I'm afraid that I don't."

"Because of his work here, Edward was bound to create enemies. He talked to me about the constant threats he received. Knowing him, I'm sure that he kept any abusive letters in a drawer somewhere. Couldn't you sift through them to find some that relate to recent cases? They might hold a clue as to who his captors might be."

"I'll look into it, Captain Wardlow."

"Inspector Colbeck would already have done so. Edward always spoke about him in such favourable terms. It's a pity that he's not sitting in your chair."

"I was chosen *above* Inspector Colbeck," said Grosvenor, wincing.

Praise for his rival was not simply irritating, it came as a surprise. Whenever Tallis spoke about Colbeck in

Grosvenor's hearing, he was more likely to criticise than commend him. The notion that he spoke so well of Colbeck in private was like a dagger inserted between the ribs.

"Colbeck is involved in a murder inquiry," he explained. "I will send detectives to Canterbury at once."

Wardlow was upset. "You'll go with them, surely?"

"I have responsibility for many other important cases. The manhunt is the most pressing, of course, but I can't abandon all the others and desert my desk."

"Yet one of your officers told me you'd done just that. You went off earlier today to Swindon and left all these other cases you talk about dangling in the air."

Grosvenor writhed in his seat. "A crisis arose there," he said, airily, "and I had to deal with it. News of the abduction brought me back at once."

"I'd feel happier if you went to Canterbury."

"You're not in the army now, Captain Wardlow. Inside this building, I'm the one who makes decisions and gives orders. I know that you're a close friend of the superintendent but that doesn't entitle you to question my authority."

Wardlow gritted his teeth. "So be it," he said.

"It was good of you to report to me in person but I now have all the available facts at my fingertips. That allows me to act accordingly." Standing up, he crossed to the door and opened it meaningfully. "Thank you for coming, Captain Wardlow. You can leave everything to us now. If the superintendent is still in Canterbury, we'll find him very quickly."

Edward Tallis had called out so much that he no longer had a voice left. His throat was burning, his whole body was aching and he was starting to lose hope. Having struggled to his feet, he now had freedom of movement but all he could do was to blunder about in the dark. The door was securely locked and all he'd achieved by hurling himself repeatedly against it was a series of painful bruises on his shoulder. It seemed as if he was being deliberately left alone there by his captors. There was no light and no means of sustenance. When he found a trough, the water in it was so brackish that he was forced to spit it out. Tallis could hear rats crawling in the straw but they were only a minor worry. What troubled him most was the way that the temperature had fallen. The biting cold was making him shiver. Somehow he had to find a way to keep warm. If he dared to fall asleep, he might freeze to death.

# CHAPTER
# SEVENTEEN

Having put her daughter to bed, Madeleine was tiptoeing away from the nursery when she heard the sound of a key being inserted in the front door. She came swiftly downstairs and saw her husband standing in the hall with his arms widespread. Suffused with delight, she ran into his embrace and kissed him full on the lips.

"Why didn't you tell me that you were coming home?" she asked.

"It was a decision made on the spur of the moment, my love."

"Does that mean you'll be going back to Swindon?"

"It does, I fear," he said. "Meanwhile, I'll be able to hold my beautiful daughter again before spending a night in your arms."

"Helen has just gone to bed."

"Then I'll just kiss her gently on the forehead."

"Before you do that, tell me what's been happening. You've given me some of the details in your letter but there must be a lot more to hear."

Taking off his hat, coat and gloves, he followed her into the privacy of the drawing room. Hands entwined, they sat side by side on the sofa. He gave her a brief summary of the latest events in Swindon before telling her that the investigation had, to some extent, been eclipsed by the disappearance of Tallis.

She was horrified. "Have they any idea where he is?"

"Apparently not," he replied.

"Do they think that . . .?"

"Foul play is always a possibility in this profession, alas. I've lost count of the number of officers who've been attacked over the years. I've always believed that Edward Tallis was able to look after himself. Patently, that's no longer true."

"What steps are being taken to find him?"

"I don't know, Madeleine. It's the other reason I decided to come home for the night. I need to confront Martin Grosvenor on the issue. I don't want him doing things that might inadvertently imperil the superintendent's life."

"This is dreadful news."

"We may yet be worrying unnecessarily."

"He can't just vanish like that."

"I agree." He stroked her hand. "But tell me your news. How is Helen and how is your father? Did he suggest that he came to Swindon as my assistant or was he put off by its association with Brunel?"

"Helen is well but missing you a lot. As for my father, he continues to sneer at the GWR but was ready to offer you advice all the same. I steered him away from doing that. Otherwise, life has carried on as normal. Oh," she recalled, "I've seen a lot of Lydia while you were away."

"That's good. How is she?"

"Oh, she's very happy at the moment because Alan Hinton called on her earlier today."

"Was it a social call?"

"He claimed that he was just checking up on her but she had the feeling that he was simply keen to see her again."

"That's not surprising. Lydia is a handsome young woman."

"She's going to be spending Christmas with us, Robert."

"Then she'll be very welcome — so would Hinton, of course," he added with a grin, "but I daresay that he has other commitments. Besides, we shouldn't try to play Cupid. I learnt a long time ago not to interfere in other people's private lives."

She kissed him again. "I'm glad that you interfered in mine."

"That's very gratifying, Mrs Colbeck." Her face puckered with concern. "What's the trouble?"

"I'm just terribly afraid that you won't be home for Christmas. But when I catch myself thinking that, I'm ashamed at being so selfish. I have a lovely home and family," she said. "I should be thinking of that poor woman in Swindon whose husband was murdered. Her situation must be unbearable. What sort of Christmas will she and her children have? It will be such an ordeal for her."

Though he'd had many calls to make that day, the Rev. Howard Law made sure that he spent a lot of time with Betty Rodman. He called at the house just as Fred

226

Alford was leaving, suggesting to him that he delayed sending his wife to be with her friend. Alone with Betty, he listened patiently to her concerns even though she was simply saying the same things in different ways. He waited for his moment then broached a topic that had been on his mind since the murder.

"Do you feel able to join us in church on Sunday?"

She was flustered. "I never even thought of it."

"The reason I ask is that I intend to mention Frank in my sermon. Everyone will expect me to say something because of his associations with St Mark's. If you did feel able to come, you'd feel the warmth and compassion of the whole community. People *care* about you, Betty."

She was uncertain. "I'll think about it."

"I'll be happy to arrange transport for you to and from the service."

"If I did come, I'd go with Fred and Liza but I wouldn't take the children."

"That's very wise. It would be overwhelming for them. Whenever you feel ready, I'll speak to the boys about what's happened. They must be asking."

"I've told them that their father had a bad accident, that's all."

"They deserve to know the truth."

"Then I'd be grateful if you told them."

"I will."

He went on to describe the plans he and his wife had made for the family when they had to leave the house. She was amazed at how much trouble they were taking on her behalf, removing all immediate financial worries and guaranteeing them bed and board at the parsonage for as long as they wished. Betty felt able to ask a question that had always haunted her.

"Did Frank ever come to see you?"

"He came to choir practices regularly."

"That's not what I meant. Did he ever . . . ask for your help?"

He gave a straight answer. "Yes, he did."

"What did he say?"

He pursed his lips. "Your husband had his demons," he began, "and they caused him a lot of heartache. Frank knew only too well that he had a loving wife and family yet he kept letting you all down. He couldn't understand why he was driven to do things like getting drunk and fighting that he afterwards regretted." He looked at her quizzically. "What was the best day of the week in your marriage?"

"Oh, it was Sunday," she replied. "There's no question of that."

"It was his day of repentance. He always stayed sober."

"He'd play all afternoon with the boys."

"It's what fathers do, Betty."

"He didn't pay much attention to them during the week. They couldn't understand it. Other boys used to tease them at school about Frank's reputation as a drunk. They came home crying sometimes."

"It must have been very hard on you."

"I had to get used to it."

"Those days are over, Betty," he said, gently. "You'll be leading a different kind of life from now on; you'll get support from all of us. It isn't only Fred and his wife who love you. We all do."

"Thank you." She looked him in the eye, "Who killed my husband?"

"We don't yet know."

"Was it because he hated Frank?" she asked, forcing the words out. "Or did *I* have something to do with it?"

"What a strange thought to have! You're completely innocent."

"I wonder."

"You're above reproach, Betty," he said, not understanding what she was trying to say. "As for naming the killer, all I can tell you is Inspector Colbeck will soon solve the mystery. He's working very hard to do so."

Colbeck didn't stand on ceremony. When he got to Scotland Yard late that evening, he knocked on the superintendent's door and went straight into the office. Grosvenor was behind the desk, smoking a cigar. He had the guilty look of a naughty child caught eating a cream cake on the sly.

"What the devil are *you* doing here?" he demanded.

"Superintendent Tallis asked me to keep an eye on his cigars," said Colbeck, sarcastically. "You're taking too great an advantage of his absence."

"I bought this box of cigars with my own money."

"You may ape his fondness for smoking but you still can't compare with him. I came back to London because I didn't have faith in your ability to take charge of a manhunt. The fact that you're still here is proof of that. You should be down in Canterbury, directing the operation."

"Don't tell me how to do my job."

"Somebody needs to, sir."

"Damn your impertinence!"

"What steps have you taken?" asked Colbeck. "If you don't tell me, I'll march straight to the commissioner's office. He needs to be involved in this discussion."

"Don't do that," said the other, worriedly, getting to his feet and stubbing out his cigar in the ashtray. "I have everything in hand. Captain Wardlow was here earlier. He was the superintendent's host and raised the alarm when he realised there was a problem. On his own initiative, he drafted in members of their old regiment into the hunt. I fancy that the superintendent will be touched by that. Soldiers are combing the city for him."

"Captain Wardlow is to be congratulated but we remain in charge of the search. It's your responsibility to take further action."

"I've already dispatched two detectives to Canterbury."

"Who are they?"

"Does it matter?"

"Yes, it does. I insist on knowing."

Grosvenor was on the defensive. "I sent Legge and Hinton."

"They're both detective constables," said Colbeck in disbelief.

"They'll be able to marshal the men at their disposal."

"Somebody more senior is needed."

230

"Nobody was available. I have every confidence in the two men I chose. Legge is an experienced detective and Hinton has definite promise. I'd ordered him to work with Inspector Vallence but have now redeployed him."

"Inspector Vallence is the person you should have redeployed. He'd have some standing in the eyes of the local police and of the soldiers."

"I think you'll find that my decision was the right one," said Grosvenor, haughtily. "Instead of harassing me, you should be back in Swindon, doing your job properly by arresting Daniel Gill."

"It would be a waste of time."

"Get back there and do what you were sent to do."

"I'm too concerned by this disappearance," said Colbeck with controlled anger. "I have great respect for Legge and Hinton but you've given them a task that's far too demanding for them. Higher ranked detectives should have been sent and you know it, sir." His voice hardened. "It's almost as if you don't *want* the superintendent to be found."

Grosvenor glared at him malevolently.

Terence Wardlow was exhausted. Still smarting from the brusque treatment he was given at Scotland Yard, he caught the train back to Canterbury and reflected on the cruel speed with which fortunes could change. After a thoroughly pleasurable visit to the cathedral with Tallis, he'd suddenly found himself reporting his friend as missing, thus setting a manhunt in motion. The longer it went on, the less faith he had that Tallis would be found. Wardlow was suffering. Having gone to London for reassurance, he'd come away feeling rebuffed. To make things worse, his arthritis flared up, making the train journey an exercise in pain and discomfort. When he finally got home that evening, all that he wanted to do was to slump in a chair and call for a large brandy.

An hour later, his wife came in to say that he had a visitor. Hopes rising, he asked for the man to be admitted, only to learn that it was a constable dispatched from Scotland Yard and given his address.

"I'm sorry to trouble you, Captain Wardlow," said Alan Hinton, politely, "but Superintendent Grosvenor told me to make contact with you to see if you'd remembered any details that you didn't pass on when you came to Scotland Yard. My colleague, detective Constable Legge, has gone to introduce himself to the local constabulary and to the soldiers involved in the hunt."

"Grosvenor should be here himself," protested Wardlow.

"He sent us in his stead."

"No disrespect to you, young man, but this kind of response would never happen in the army. In the face of a crisis, I would never send a callow recruit to what was clearly an incident requiring an officer."

"I can only do my best, sir."

"At least you've been kind enough to consult me. Once I'd informed the superintendent about the urgency of the situation, he more or less hustled me out of his office. Is he always so high-handed?"

Hinton was diplomatic. "It's not for me to say, sir."

"I will complain in the strongest terms to Major Tallis."

"We have to find him first and I believe that you may hold the clue to our doing that. If he really was abducted, it's unlikely to have been an opportunist crime. He'd have been watched and followed. It was only when he was on his own that his captors stepped in — that's what I assume, anyway."

"It's what I'm certain must have happened," said Wardlow.

"Then how did they know he'd be in the city in the first place?"

"I've no idea."

"He came here to attend a reunion at his old regiment," said Hinton, "and you were kind enough to invite him to stay here with you."

"That's right. This damned hip of mine decided to be benevolent for once, allowing me to hobble around without too much discomfort. I therefore contacted the barracks to say that I *would* be attending the reunion dinner, after all. I then promptly issued an invitation to Major Tallis to stay here ahead of the event."

"You wrote a letter to the regiment — is that correct?"

"Yes."

"So the person who opened it would have been aware that Superintendent Tallis would be staying here last night."

"Naturally."

"And who would that person be?"

"It's Captain Ardingley, who is organising the dinner."

"Do you know him?"

"Of course, I do. He's a first-rate soldier and an excellent fellow. As soon as I reported Major Tallis's disappearance to him, he arranged for his men to join in the search. Even in the dark, they're still at it."

"That may be the answer," said Hinton, pondering. "I'd like to meet Captain Ardingley in person."

"Then you'll have to go to the barracks in Hythe."

"I'll do that at once."

"Why this urgent need to see him?"

"The captain was clearly not the only person aware of your change of plan. Someone else learnt that the superintendent would be under your roof. In fact, he may well have kept your house under surveillance."

Wardlow started. "Good God!" he exclaimed. "That's monstrous."

"Who *else* would have been able to read your letter?" asked Hinton. "That's what I need to find out in Hythe."

"I feel so guilty. In inviting my dear friend here, I unwittingly made him a target. And the worst of it is — the possibility must be faced — that someone in our old regiment might be party to the abduction. It's terrifying."

Having groped his way around for hours in the dark, Tallis paused for a rest, gripping the side of a stall. He was about to doze off when he heard the sound of

234

approaching hooves. It made him rally and feel his way to the door. A horse came to a halt nearby.

"Let me out!" he yelled.

"You're still alive, then?" shouted a man's voice.

"Who, in God's name, are you?"

"You'll find out. Goodnight. Sleep well."

The horse was ridden away to the accompaniment of derisive laughter.

Robert Colbeck had brought the plan of the Works home so that he could study it once again. When it was spread out on the table, he pointed out the place where the mutilated body was discovered. Madeleine was interested in every detail. Having looked at the arrangement of the different shops and sheds in the complex, she asked about the realistic chances of an early arrest.

"I simply can't give you a date, my love."

"What does your instinct tell you?"

"For once, I'm not relying entirely on instinct."

"But that's Inspector Colbeck's secret weapon."

"*You're* my secret weapon, Madeleine," he said, slipping an arm around her. "As for Inspector Colbeck, he may not hold that rank for long."

"Why not?"

"I told Grosvenor exactly what I thought about his response to the emergency and I left him fuming. He's a vindictive man and will want revenge. If we've lost one superintendent, he may well be the replacement. In short, you may soon find that you're married to *Sergeant* Colbeck."

"The commissioner would never allow that."

"I'd hope not but Grosvenor can be very persuasive."

"Mr Tallis will be found alive, surely?"

"That's by no means certain."

"But he seems to be the victim of a kidnap."

"Then where's the ransom demand? It should have arrived hours ago."

Madeleine's voice was hushed. "Do you think he's been murdered?"

"I don't know what to think, my love," he admitted. "It's sensible to consider all options and one of them, alas, is that Grosvenor may be promoted. In that event, our work at Scotland Yard is going to be far less effective." He clicked his tongue. "Oh, I wish that I could supervise the manhunt. Legge and Hinton have no experience of dealing with such a situation. But I'm stuck down in Swindon when I should be in Canterbury."

"Could Victor handle the case on his own?"

"He'd never be allowed to do so, Madeleine. Grosvenor will see to that. He wants to keep me in Wiltshire until I listen to his advice and arrest the suspect that he — in his wisdom — has picked out as the killer."

"But he doesn't know anything about the case."

"He's read my reports. In his mind, that qualifies him as an expert. However, let's not talk about him. It's too depressing." He looked down at the plan and tapped it with a finger. "One of our suspects, a Welshman, works here in the rolling mill. It's unlikely that he's ever been inside the Erecting Shop yet that's where the body was found. The same is true of another suspect. He works as a clerk. As it happens, his office is close to the Erecting Shop, but would he ever venture into it?"

"It seems unlikely, Robert."

"I agree. Mr Cudlip is fastidious about his appearance. He'd certainly keep out of there during the day for fear of soiling his suit. If it wasn't the scene of the crime," he added, "I'd recommend that you visit it."

"Why?"

"It would inspire you, Madeleine. You'd love to paint it in operation."

"I'm rather preoccupied at the moment," she said, looking upward. "I may have to wait until Helen is a little older." She scrutinised the plan again. "To be honest, I'm not so much interested in the Works as in the houses built for the employees."

"They're quite impressive and better than some we've seen in other railway towns. Victor is quite taken with them. They're solid, well built and functional."

"That's why I'd hate to live in any of them. They look like a series of identical boxes enclosed within a much larger box. Everything is so relentlessly symmetrical."

"That's the artist in you speaking out," he said, laughing. "You hate straight lines. What you love to paint is the dirty, irregular, higgledy-piggledy world of locomotives with its endless variations. The New Town is a study in uniformity. There are few different shapes and sizes." As a thought struck him, Colbeck turned to her. "Perhaps you've picked out something that we missed."

"I doubt that."

"Well, I've been working on the assumption that there's a religious aspect to the murder but you've just touched on an alternative explanation. Living in a place like that must be reassuring for most of the workers because they've never known anything better. For someone, however, that regimented existence could be quite oppressive. Yes," said Colbeck, warming to his theme, "the Railway Village runs like clockwork. Every aspect of people's lives is controlled by the GWR. That's a comfort to the vast majority but there must be those who find it stifling."

"I'm not sure I follow your reasoning, Robert."

"What if this crime has nothing to do with religion but is a calculated assault on the Works and the way it forces everyone into a single mode of living and behaviour? Frank Rodman could have been murdered anywhere, yet the killer went out of his way to choose a crucial part of the Works."

"I'm beginning to see what you mean," she said.

"The man we're after wanted to administer a violent shock to the whole community and bring the Works to a dead halt. He succeeded. That's what we might have here, Madeleine. The murder could have been an act of rebellion."

The candle flickering beside it threw a lurid glow over the head of Frank Rodman. After watching the dancing flame for several minutes, the man made up his mind.

"I think it's time for you to make an appearance, Frank."

238

# CHAPTER
# EIGHTEEN

Hythe was a small but pretty coastal town that overlooked the Straits of Dover. Keen to get there as soon as possible, Alan Hinton gave thanks for the existence of the railway system. Like Colbeck, he'd come to appreciate its extraordinary value during an investigation. He was denied any pleasure from looking at the quaint cottages or the long beach of Hythe because he arrived in darkness. A cab took him from the station to the barracks. He was eventually admitted to the office belonging to Captain Philip Ardingley. After introducing himself, Hinton explained why he was there. The other man glowered at him.

"Frankly, Constable, I feel insulted."

"I didn't intend any insult, sir."

"You are suggesting that *I* am at fault in this instance."

"I simply asked if anyone else had access to your correspondence."

"It was an unnecessary question," said Ardingley. "Private correspondence is kept strictly private. From the moment it arrived and had been read by me, Captain Wardlow's letter has been under lock and key."

"Does anyone else have a key?"

"No, they don't."

Ardingley looked like a younger brother of Edward Tallis, with the same square jaw, stolid frame and arresting presence. He was angry to hear that a mere constable had been dispatched from Scotland Yard to solve what was to him a heinous crime.

"Were you the only officer at the superintendent's disposal?"

"No, sir, I travelled with Constable Legge. He's still in Canterbury."

"I expected half a dozen senior detectives."

"Unfortunately, none were free."

"Then they should have been liberated from their present duties to lend their assistance and expertise here. Kidnap, I hardly need remind you, is something that is intended to bring a quick profit. There's no time for a leisurely approach. If they feel they are being kept waiting, the abductors will simply kill their prisoner."

"Heaven forbid!"

"That's why we need the very best minds at work on the case."

"Someone found out that Superintendent Tallis was going to stay with his friend," explained Hinton, patiently. "The only way he could have done that was to read Captain Wardlow's letter."

"I accept that."

"Then why did you react so strongly when I asked if another pair of eyes had seen the letter here?"

"What I accept," said Ardingley, crisply, "is that someone *did* read the captain's letter but that he must have done so before it was actually sent. Look for no villainy here, Constable. You should be questioning the captain's domestic staff."

"Why should one of them betray his employer?"

"It may not have been a question of betrayal. He may not even have read the letter. Captain Wardlow could simply have told him that a guest would be arriving at the house and gone on to say who he was and why he was there. The manservant might inadvertently have released the information in a public place and it was seized on." Ardingley shot him a look of disapproval. "This is only supposition, of course. Heavens, man, do I have to do your detective work for you?"

"No, sir. I'm grateful for your help. The problem is evidently not here."

"This barracks is run with a firm hand."

"Then Superintendent Tallis would feel at home here," said Hinton with a smile. Seeing Ardingley's scowl, he became serious. "I do apologise for taking up your time, Captain. It was good of you to provide us with soldiers to help in the search. On behalf of the Metropolitan Police, I thank you for that."

"We were too late, unfortunately."

"What do you mean?"

"Major Tallis is no longer in Canterbury. I can guarantee that. If he had been, we'd have found him long before Scotland Yard had deigned to send two detective constables here. Don't you realise that, by the slowness of your response, you may have imperilled the major's life?"

"We can't really act until a ransom demand is made, sir."

"And what if one never actually comes?"

Hinton felt unable to reply. After thanking him again, he left the barracks and made his way back to the railway station, scolding himself for believing that the kidnappers could possibly have had a confederate inside a closely guarded barracks. He would have to look elsewhere.

As they left Swindon Railway Station on the following morning, daylight had still not dispersed some of the gloom. It took them a moment to recognise William Morris as he walked towards them. For his part, he picked them out by their distinctive profiles. They exchanged warm greetings with him.

"Thank you for your recommendation, Inspector," said Morris.

"I wasn't aware that I'd made one," replied Colbeck.

"You praised that poem by my namesake."

"Ah, yes — 'The Haystack in the Floods'."

"I managed to track down a copy. It's a fine piece of work."

"Who chops off whose head?" asked Leeming.

"A French soldier decapitates Robert, a British soldier, with a display of Gallic barbarity. It's not a poem to read to your children."

"They like nursery rhymes."

"Some of those have an underlying violence, of course," said Morris. "By the way, Sergeant, you got me into trouble."

"I didn't mean to, sir."

"When I gave you Daniel Gill's address, I didn't realise that he'd come to the office to yell abuse at me. I had to threaten to call the police to get rid of him. I was grateful that he hadn't brought his cleaver with him." Morris chuckled. "Inspector Piercey was in a much more amenable mood. One of the addresses I gave him led to the arrest of someone who sent a letter to you designed to obtain money under false pretences."

"Yes," said Colbeck, "he called in at our office and reported to me. I gave him a similar assignment and sent him off happy. You see the advantages of working as a partnership. The combination of detectives, local police and the editor of the *Swindon Advertiser* achieved a positive result."

"Is that a way of telling me that you're about to arrest the butcher's assistant?" asked Morris, scenting his next headline.

"We haven't got that far yet, sir."

"Let me know when you do. Meanwhile, I must be off to Bristol."

"Don't let us hold you up, Mr Morris."

"I'll see you both this evening."

"Will you?" said Leeming in surprise.

"You'll be at the concert, won't you? I never miss them. There's always a report of the Saturday concert in the next edition of the *Advertiser*. It will be a unique experience for both of you."

When the rolling mill was working at full throttle, the noise was a continuous onslaught on the eardrums. It made conversation almost impossible so the men often communicated with gestures. At one point, however, they heard another sound above the hullabaloo. It was very faint but they recognised it immediately. Rehearsing for the concert, Gareth Llewellyn was opening his lungs to give a full-throated rendition of a Welsh folk song.

Liza Alford was pleased with the slight improvement in her friend. Though Betty Rodman was still subdued, she no longer kept bursting into tears and wailing about her future. The vicar's visit on the previous evening had been a turning point. He'd not only soothed her, he'd stayed long enough to talk to her two sons and tell them what had happened to their father. They'd been stunned by the news at first but seemed to know instinctively that it was their mother who needed comfort and not them. Because they snuggled up against her in bed, she'd enjoyed the first real sleep since the murder.

All three children were now downstairs with her. The baby was in her arms and the boys were within reach. Liza was making a cup of tea in the kitchen. When something was slipped through the letter box, therefore, Davy was the first one to reach it. Picking up the letter from the floor, he took it to his mother. Betty saw that her name was written neatly on the missive. Wondering who had sent it, she put the baby down, tore open the letter and read the message inside.

When Liza heard her friend's cry of anguish, she came rushing into the room and saw that Betty had fainted. As if knowing there was a crisis, the baby began to howl piteously.

Caleb Andrews was approaching the house when he saw Lydia Quayle coming towards it from the other direction. They exchanged greetings and agreed that the weather was colder than ever and that the threat of snow still hovered. Admitted to the house, they were welcomed by Madeleine who whisked them into the drawing room and told them the good news about her husband's visit the previous evening.

"Robert was here?" asked Andrews. "Why didn't you send for me at once? I could have given him my opinion on what Brunel did wrong to the railway system."

"I think he can live without it, Father."

"But we could have discussed his latest case."

"Robert wanted a brief respite from it and a chance to see his daughter."

"Is he sanguine about the investigation?" asked Lydia.

"On balance, I believe that he is."

"Christmas is getting very close."

"It's what drives him on, Lydia. But he brought news of another awful crime," she told them. "Superintendent Tallis has been kidnapped in Canterbury."

"Who by, Maddy?" asked her father.

"Nobody knows."

"Didn't he have someone protecting him?"

"He was with an army friend, apparently, but they split up in the cathedral. Somehow and somewhere, he must have been overpowered."

"That's frightening," said Lydia. "You'd never expect someone in his position to be set on. Robert must have wished he'd been able to lead the manhunt."

"He did but it was left to Superintendent Grosvenor to send detectives to Kent. One of them, you'll be interested to know, was Alan Hinton."

"He's far too young," complained Andrews.

"Robert felt it should be someone more senior."

"Constable Hinton will do his best, I'm sure," said Lydia. "The very fact that he was sent to Canterbury shows you the esteem in which he's held."

"That's one way of looking at it," said Madeleine. "It's given Robert another reason to arrest a killer in Swindon as quickly as possible. He's determined to join in the search. My husband never does things by half measures," she went on with a smile. "He wants to solve *two* major crimes before Christmas."

Colbeck read the message that had caused Betty Rodman to swoon. Written in capitals, it told her that she'd get her husband's head back very soon. The crude simplicity of the letter had been too much for her. As she was still trying to cope with the gruesome fact of the murder, she was rocked by the news that his head had been hacked off.

"It took me an hour or more to calm her down," said Liza Alford.

"You've no idea who sent this, I suppose?"

"No, Inspector. I should have rushed to the door and flung it open in the hope of seeing the man running away. But I was too busy picking Betty up off the floor

246

and trying to soothe the children. When they saw what their mother did, they all started crying. Oh," she went on, angrily, "it was such a cruel thing to do to her."

Liza had come to the detectives' office to tell them about the anonymous letter and its effect. Colbeck was alone. He could imagine the searing pain inflicted on Betty Rodman. She was not only stunned by the information, she was hurt that it had been kept from her in the first place. Though he didn't confide his thoughts, Colbeck was relieved that the return of the head was imminent. When it was reunited with the body, a proper post-mortem could take place.

"How is Mrs Rodman now?" he asked.

"She's still shaking. The only reason I was able to slip away is that the vicar's wife called. Mrs Law is looking after her. She could see from Betty's face that something horrible had happened."

"Did Mrs Rodman have any idea who might have sent that letter?"

"She just kept saying that it was *her* fault."

"That's patently untrue."

"Betty believes that someone is trying to pay her back for . . . rejecting them."

"So she still thinks it may be an old admirer?"

"There were lots of them, Inspector," she said ruefully. "My own husband was one of them and Betty could probably name seven or eight others. It was never a problem that I had to put up with. I used to envy her, being so pretty when I was so plain. I don't envy her any more, I pity her."

"So do I, Mrs Alford."

"I felt that you had to see the letter."

"You did the right thing," said Colbeck. "Unfortunately, she's seen it. The fact that it's written in capitals means the handwriting is far more difficult to place. The sender wanted to make sure that Mrs Rodman didn't recognise it."

"Betty doesn't want it back in the house."

He put it down on his desk. "This is evidence. I'll take good care of it."

"Please catch him soon," she urged. "The murder's had a terrible effect on everyone, not just Betty. It's made people behave in strange ways. In fact —"

She stopped herself at the last moment but Colbeck had already guessed what she was going to say. Liza Alford knew from personal experience that the crime had had a profound impact on people. Her husband was one of them. She'd been about to confess that Alford had been behaving in strange and unsettling ways.

During the morning refreshment break, Alford ignored the banter of the other smiths and went across to the Erecting Shop. Making sure to get in nobody's way, he took up a vantage point from which he could stare at the exact point where his friend's headless corpse had been found. It aroused such deep emotions that he had to drag himself away again. When he got outside, he was running with sweat.

Victor Leeming was enjoying memories of his night at home with the family. His wife and children had been thrilled to see him and he was able to have a night for once that was not dominated by ceaseless speculation about the murder. Long after they'd arrived in Swindon, he still felt buoyant. Edgar Fellowes was struck by the sergeant's cheerful manner. When they met near the entrance to the Works, the railway policeman studied him shrewdly.

"Am I right in thinking congratulations are in order?" asked Fellowes.

"Yes," replied Leeming. "You can congratulate me on having the sense to spend a night at home."

"Oh, I thought you'd made an arrest."

"It won't be long before we do so."

"Who is it going to be — Llewellyn?"

"I'm not naming names. What I will tell you is that the inspector and I are not yet in total agreement. By the end of the day, we will be."

"Does that mean you favour different suspects?"

"It might do."

Fellowes grinned. "You don't give much away, do you? Well, it doesn't matter. I won't badger you. I'm the same. When I have my suspicions about someone who's been stealing coal from the wagons, I keep his name to myself until I'm ready to pounce."

"You told me that all you dealt with was trespass and pilfering."

"There have been more serious crimes. Someone broke into the Turning Shop one night and made off with some expensive equipment. We've had other substantial losses as well. Tools cost a pretty penny," he continued. "If someone is offered them at a lower price, they're likely to buy them without asking questions."

"Do you ever catch the thieves?"

"Two of them are already in prison but there are always others willing to chance their arm. They keep us busy."

Leeming was puzzled. Looking at Fellowes, he couldn't believe that he made use of the services provided by Claire Knight and her daughter. The railway policeman looked so staid and respectable yet he was, allegedly, familiar with the two women. It explained his hesitation in telling Leeming where they might be found. The sergeant decided to say nothing about his visit to the house but Fellowes asked him a direct question about it.

"You went to that brothel, didn't you?"

"Why do you say that?"

"You're like me, Sergeant. When an idea pops up, you'll follow it through. If you went there, you'll have met Mrs Knight."

"Her daughter was asleep upstairs."

"Euphemia is very popular, by all accounts. I call in there from time to time," said Fellowes, grandly, "to keep a fatherly eye on her. I disapprove strongly of what they do for a living but I don't think they deserve to be assaulted."

"Is that what happens?"

"Claire can handle most awkward clients. They never even get past the front door. But one or two have sneaked through and . . . thrown their weight about. So they turned to me for help."

"Shouldn't you have told Inspector Piercey where the house is?"

250

Fellowes nudged him. "I believe in live and let live," he said. "I'd never stoop to that kind of thing myself, you understand. I'm married so I don't need to. In any case, it's against my principles."

"So why do you bother to go there?"

"To be frank, it's for old times' sake. I knew Claire when I was much younger. She and her husband lived a quiet, honest, law-abiding life. It was only when he died that she found herself needing a source of money. She tried all sorts of legal ways to get it but somehow she just couldn't manage. As it happens," he confided, "I loaned her some money but that soon disappeared. The next minute, Claire and her daughter disappeared off to Bristol and learnt a different trade altogether. It was obviously profitable. When they came back here after a few years, Claire paid off my loan and set up in the village."

"Word about them must have got around, surely?"

"They were drummed out of one house by angry women so they found somewhere else and kept their heads down. They're very careful about the men they deal with. Because they only work at night, their clients arrive after dark. Yes," he concluded, "deep down, I can't condone what they do but, out of friendship, I lend them a hand now and then. Didn't Claire mention that?"

Leeming shook his head. Edgar Fellowes had been so smooth, confiding and plausible that he knew the man was mixing fact with a liberal amount of fiction.

When they were not in use, the altars in St Mark's Church were each covered by a green cloth to protect them from the droppings of the bats that had somehow managed to get into the building. Invisible during the day, they were clearly active at night. The vicar and his curates had learnt to accept them in the same way as they were resigned to the occasional presence of the church mice. The main altar had a large wooden cross set in the middle of it. Before a service, the sacristan removed it along with the green cloth. Underneath it was a gleaming white cloth thrown into relief by the decorative purple altar frontal, which hung in place for the Sundays during Advent. The wooden cross was replaced by the large one made of brass and brass candlesticks were placed either side of it. When the candles were lit, the main altar was a blaze of colour.

As he walked down the nave that morning, all that it collected from the vicar was a cursory glance. Howard Law went off into the vestry and was about to unlock a cupboard when he stopped to think. Without realising it, he'd noticed something very irregular about the main altar but simply couldn't remember what it was. He therefore retraced his steps and took a proper look. What he saw was alarming. The wooden cross had disappeared and been replaced by an object that was covered by some filthy sacking. The vicar was outraged. Striding forward, he grabbed the sacking and tore it away to reveal a human head plastered with dried blood.

Frank Rodman stared at him with a lopsided grin on his face.

# CHAPTER
# NINETEEN

Hiram Wells was bringing up a crate of beer from the cellar when he heard someone banging on the door. He opened it to find Daniel Gill standing on his doorstep.

"We're closed," he told him. "You should know that, Dan."

"I just wanted a word with you."

"What about?"

"If you let me in, I'll tell you."

The landlord stood back so that Gill could get in. He looked anxious.

"We haven't seen you for ages," said Wells. "Where do you drink now?"

"That doesn't matter. I need a favour from you, Hiram. In the past, I put a lot of money in that till of yours. I think you owe me something in return."

"That depends what you're after."

"Those detectives are staying here, aren't they?"

"Yes, but if you want to speak to them, you can go to their office. I can tell you how to get there."

"No, no," said Gill, nervously, "that's the last thing I want to do. Since they came here, they've made my life a misery. They got me into real trouble with my uncle and one of the buggers has been talking to my wife."

"So why have you come to me?"

"You've got closer to them than anyone."

Wells was guarded. "I wouldn't say that."

"You must have heard them chatting over their meals. What did they say? Have they any idea who the killer was?" He clutched the landlord's arm. "Have they ever mentioned *me*?"

"You sound like a man with a guilty conscience."

"I'm not, honestly. I'm just interested. I don't want them wasting time on me when it was someone else who murdered Frank Rodman."

"Have you told them that?"

"Yes — but they won't believe me."

"If they thought it was you, Dan, they'd have arrested you by now."

"Is that what they said? Am I really worrying about nothing?"

"You are. If you're truly innocent, you shouldn't have a care in the world. On the other hand . . ."

"I didn't do it, Hiram. I swear it. I'm not saying I wouldn't have liked to kill him. It crossed my mind more than once. But I never laid a finger on him. Come on," he said, grinning obsequiously. "We're old friends. You can tell me."

The landlord put a hand on his chest and eased him firmly away.

"I've run the Queen's Tap on the basis of one strict rule," he said. "As long as customers behave themselves, they can drink as much as they like and say whatever they wish without having me telling tales.

254

Inspector Colbeck and the sergeant have paid for privacy and that's what I've given them."

"Did you or did you not hear them talking about me?"

"I haven't heard them talking about *anyone*, Dan."

"Have you gone deaf?" demanded the other.

"It's what happens to me when I have guests staying here. They trust me."

Gill was embittered. "I thought that *I* could trust you."

"If you really want a favour," said Wells, "you can have one. I'm not going to say anything at all about this conversation. If I did, they'd come looking for you with an arrest warrant. That's the best I can do."

"Thank you."

"I don't know if you're the killer or not. All I can say is this. If you were involved in Frank Rodman's murder in *any* way, you might as well go and confess to Inspector Colbeck right now. Otherwise, you'll suffer agonies while you're waiting for him to come looking for you. He and the sergeant know what they're doing, Dan. There'd be no escape."

Without a word, Gill let himself out and closed the door behind him.

When he'd finally recovered his voice and his composure, Howard Law sent for the detectives. They came as quickly as they could. While Colbeck listened to the vicar's story, Leeming was transfixed by the head on the altar. The eyes seemed to be looking straight at him. Finding such a thing in a church was an abomination. He wasn't at all pleased when Colbeck told him to put the head back in the sack and take it to the police morgue so that it could be examined. Colbeck stressed that nobody else needed to be told what had happened. Leeming handled the head gingerly as if it was about to explode. It was only when he'd put it back in the blood-soaked sack that he felt safe. Holding it at arm's length away from him, he went out, leaving Colbeck to question the vicar.

"The church was locked all night, I presume?" he said.

"Yes, Inspector."

"Apart from you, who has a key?"

"The verger has one, of course, and the wardens. One of them usually unlocks the door in the morning. Because I needed something from the vestry, I unlocked the church today."

"Was everything as you expected — apart from the head, that is?"

"I think so."

"Have you checked?"

"Well, no, to be honest."

"Then I suggest that you get the verger to do so. A person with such a twisted mind might not be satisfied with leaving one item here. A thorough search of the church is needed to make sure there are no other horrors lurking in wait. You don't want the people in tomorrow's congregation stumbling on something designed to upset them in the way that you were."

"Oh, I wasn't upset," said Law. "I was incensed. It was an act of desecration."

"St Mark's was chosen for a reason. The killer wanted both to startle and to express his contempt for the Church."

"How could he possibly have broken in here?"

"We don't know that he did. He might have slipped in here during the day when the church was unlocked and hidden away until it was empty. When nobody was about, he arranged that macabre display on the altar. I'm assuming," said Colbeck, "that it's possible to open one of the doors from the inside to get out."

"It is, Inspector."

"I can't be certain but it's one explanation. The other is that he somehow got hold of a key and made a copy of it. An experienced smith would be able to do that without too much difficulty. He'd just need an impression of the key. One of our suspects is a smith. Three of the others have all been trained to work with metal."

"Then it has to be one of those four," decided Law. "And he has to have perverted ideas about religion." He shuddered. "The whole atmosphere in here has been poisoned. It doesn't smell like a holy place any more. It's almost as if this villain is trying to pollute the House of God."

"That's one thing he could never do."

"How should we react?"

"Remain calm and dignified," advised Colbeck. "For the rest of Advent, you must behave as you would normally do at this special time in the Christian calendar. Don't give him the pleasure of seeing you all in disarray because that's what he wants. Deny him any satisfaction."

"He'll expect to see a full report of this in the *Swindon Advertiser*."

"Then I'll make sure that Mr Morris doesn't print a word about what happened in here. Only a handful of us know about it. Let it remain that way."

"But that will only annoy him. He might strike again."

"How?" asked Colbeck. "His main weapon was the victim's head and he's just given it away. There's nothing left with which to scare this community. The killer has shot his bolt. Now, I have another theory to offer. I believe that the killer may be rebelling against the unrelenting sameness of the Railway Village because it's a place where variety of any kind is outlawed and where lives are, for the most part, forced to follow a common pattern."

"There's more than a little truth in that, Inspector."

"It was not simply religion that the killer despises. It's conceivable that rebelling against the way that industry has robbed people of any individuality and turned them into so many faceless worker ants coming out each day from their interchangeable houses."

"That's an interesting thesis," said Law.

"It means that we're not just looking for an atheist. If we were, Simeon Cudlip would be our killer. But I can't see him keeping a human head in his house for any length of time. The smell would offend him, for a start. There's a reason why he chose a job that allows him to go to work in a suit and give himself a false air of refinement."

"Let me ask you something," said the vicar. "When you and Sergeant Leeming came in here, you didn't seem at all surprised by the sight of a severed head. The sergeant turned away in disgust but you didn't."

"I was forewarned."

"How?"

Hand in his pocket, Colbeck took out the letter popped through the letter box of Betty Rodman's house. He showed it to Law, who winced as he read it.

"What a cruel thing to do!" he exclaimed.

"He was twisting the knife in the wound."

"Who is this excrescence, Inspector? He doesn't belong in a civilised world."

"I still can't put a name to him," admitted Colbeck, "but I'm getting ever nearer to being able to do so. Driven on to cause the maximum shock and offence, he's actually given us a few more clues as to his identity."

"Why punish Betty Rodman like this?"

"It gives him pleasure to do so."

"But this behaviour is inhuman."

"I agree. Having wrecked her life by killing her husband, he adds further torment by telling her that his missing head would soon make an appearance. Since the fact of the decapitation had been kept from her, you can imagine the pain it must have caused her when she learnt the truth."

"This is despicable," said Law, rancorously. "Betty Rodman is already in a fragile state. Someone is trying to shatter her completely."

"The one consolation," Colbeck pointed out, "is that she didn't come in here today. If she'd seen her husband's head set upon the altar like that, you might have been arranging *two* funerals in the Rodman family."

Betty Rodman sat in the chair and ignored the crying of the baby in her lap. Her mind was still on the letter sent to sharpen her grief. She couldn't believe that there was anyone capable of doing such a thing. To stop the child wailing, Liza took her from her mother and rocked her gently to and fro. Martha Rodman soon stopped crying. Unaware of the fierce blows dealt to her family, she dropped off to sleep and burbled contentedly.

Betty came out of her reverie and turned on her friend.

"Why didn't you tell me what he did to Frank?" she demanded.

"I didn't know," said Liza.

"You must have known. Fred was inside the Works when the body was discovered. They must have told him about the state Frank was found in. He'd have told you, Liza. You kept it from me."

"All right," confessed the other, "it's true. We tried to protect you from knowing."

"I was bound to find out one day."

"We wanted as long a delay as possible to give you chance to get over the news that someone had . . . murdered Frank. We hoped you'd rally."

"How can I do that when someone out there is determined to punish me? What's he going to do next?"

260

she shouted. "Will someone please tell me? Who is he and why is he trying to kill *me* as well?"

Her raised voice woke the baby up and she promptly started howling.

"My life is just not worth living any more," cried Betty.

Though he'd been told not to broadcast the information about the discovery at St Mark's Church, Leeming felt obliged to confide in Piercey. Now that he'd made a useful contribution to the inquiry, the police inspector deserved to be taken into their confidence. When he heard about the incident, Piercey grimaced.

"That was an appalling thing to do," he said.

"It's a measure of the man we're after."

"Are you any closer to catching him?"

"We believe so," said Leeming with more confidence than he felt. "To put the head on that altar in the way that he did, he had to take chances. People who do that always slip up in the end."

"I'd love to be the person to arrest him."

"So would I. He's sure to put up a fight and I'd be ready for him."

"There's a rumour that Daniel Gill is a suspect."

"He's one of the people who's come to our attention," said Leeming, carefully. "There are a number of others. Thanks to you, we haven't been diverted by false claims from anonymous sources."

"I've arrested two of those anonymous sources," said Piercey, proudly. "They're still languishing in one of our cells. People who try to make money out of someone else's tragedy are nothing but vultures."

"They always gather when someone is murdered. Inspector Colbeck and I are tackling this case with increased vigour. It isn't simply a question of clearing everything up in time for Christmas. We're eager to join another investigation."

"Has there been a second murder?"

"There may have been."

"Who is the victim this time?"

"We don't know for certain that he has been killed," said Leeming. "A hunt has been launched for our superintendent. He vanished without trace in Canterbury."

"Was he abducted?"

"Everything points that way, Inspector."

"Has a ransom note been sent?"

Leeming swallowed hard. "I sincerely hope so."

While he was flattered to be given so much authority, Alan Hinton was struggling to prove that he was worthy of it. His main problem was being younger than everyone around him. The policemen in Canterbury regarded him as callow and unassertive while the soldiers refused to take orders from anyone but their senior officer. Hinton had widened the search to the hamlets and villages outside the city but all to no avail. Terence Wardlow was becoming increasingly alarmed.

"Have there been no reported sightings at all?" he asked.

"None, sir."

262

"Major Tallis is a big man. Someone must have seen him being hustled away."

"If they did," said Hinton, "they didn't realise the significance of what they saw. He might have had a gun or a knife held against his back. Otherwise, he'd have fought back bravely."

They were at the police station in Canterbury. Although his arthritis was more painful than ever, Wardlow had forced himself to go into the city in order to find out what was happening. One piece of information was ominous.

"There's still been no ransom demand?"

"I fear not, sir."

"Has there been any contact at all from the kidnappers?"

"We've not heard a single word."

Wardlow sagged. "That's disturbing."

"It's unusual in such cases," said Hinton, "but we mustn't give up hope. It's something that Superintendent Tallis impresses upon us time and again. Never give up hope. Press on regardless. That's what we're doing."

"Did you meet Captain Ardingley?"

"Yes, I did."

"What did he say?"

"He gave me a flea in my ear and sent me on my way. When I suggested that someone at the barracks had learnt what was in the letter you sent, he was infuriated. It's been kept under lock and key since it arrived."

"It would be. Ardingley is a stickler for security."

Hinton was tentative. "He thought that the problem might have been . . . at your house, sir."

"I deny that most strongly," said Wardlow, bridling.

"One of your servants might incautiously have mentioned that you were having a visitor who was going to attend the reunion with you and . . ." Hinton could see the indignation rising in the other man. "But that's obviously not the case," he went on, trying to calm down his companion. "How the kidnappers caught wind of the fact that Superintendent Tallis would be coming to Kent, I just don't know. And yet they did somehow."

"Don't you dare accuse my domestic staff of being informers!"

"It was Captain Ardingley's suggestion."

"Then he should have known better than to make it. Instead of trying to blame me for what happened, you should be combing every blade of grass in the county in order to find Major Tallis. Now get off and do it!"

"I'll join the search myself."

Accepting the rebuke, Hinton went off with his cheeks burning.

His strong instinct for survival had kept Tallis awake for most of the night but he was increasingly weary. It reached the point where he slid downwards until he was in a sitting position. Fighting to remain alert, he eventually succumbed to fatigue. How long he slept he didn't know, but he might have slumbered on had he not felt a rat run across his thighs. The sensation brought him instantly awake and he put his back against the stall so that he could push himself upwards against it. When he looked around, he saw that nothing had changed. It was still freezing, he was still imprisoned in a stable and the handcuffs had chafed his wrists until they bled. There was no source of relief.

As his eyes became accustomed to the gloom, he took a closer look at his surroundings. Escape by means of the door was impossible. He'd discovered that when he'd struck it repeatedly with his shoulder. Tallis had the feeling that boards had been nailed across the door in order to strengthen it. Since there was no window, he'd need to find another way to get out. He therefore prowled the stable, searching for a weakness. He found it in a corner where more light was pouring in because there was a gap between the boards. Because it was low down, he was able to use his foot to kick at it. It troubled him that he was using the toecaps of his best shoes but, in the emergency, a damaged shoe was an acceptable casualty. Tallis kept pounding away until he heard the rewarding sound of a nail being driven out of the timber support. Turning around, he used his heel to kick away as hard as he could at the loose board and it eventually gave way completely.

The effort had made him pant heavily so he stopped for a rest, reasoning that if he took the wooden boards one by one, he might somehow kick his way out. It was a forlorn hope. He was suddenly aware that nails were being levered out of the timber as the boarding across the door was being removed. Someone was coming.

Tallis didn't know if he was being rescued or if his captors were outside. Fearing the worst, he took up a position near the door so that he could throw himself against anyone who came in and make a dash for freedom. That plan was immediately quashed.

"Stand back!" ordered a voice. "We're both armed."

Reluctantly, Tallis obeyed. He retreated to the far side of the stable. The last board was levered away, then he heard the sound of a key in the lock. The next moment, the door was flung open, allowing light to flood in. Unable to shield his eyes from the sudden glare, he lowered his head. When he lifted it, he was looking at the barrel of a rifle. The newcomers wore rough clothing and had their hats pulled down over their faces. They noticed the missing board in the wall.

"See what he's done?" asked one of them.

"We can't have that," said the other. He prodded the prisoner. "Turn around."

"What do you want with me?" challenged Tallis, still facing him.

"Do as I tell you!"

"At least, tell me who you are."

Tallis's brave defiance brought instant punishment. Jabbing him in the stomach with his rifle, the man used the butt of the weapon to club him to the ground. He turned to his accomplice.

"Tie his ankles together then nail that missing board back in place. He's not going to kick his way out of here again."

266

★  ★  ★

After his visit to the church, Colbeck made his way back to the Works and asked Stinson if he could study the employment records of the five people they'd singled out as suspects. The general manager had handed him the files and left him alone to peruse them. Since there were masses of employees, it took some time to pick out the relevant files. What Colbeck was looking for was a record of each man's hours at work that week. Someone on the night shift would not have had the time or the opportunity to break into the church after dark. Conversely, those on the day shift wouldn't have been able to sneak in there before it was locked early in the evening.

Suspicion quickly alighted on Hector Samway and Simeon Cudlip. Both left the premises a couple of hours earlier than the others and, since they had no wives waiting at home for them, they could easily have hidden in the church or, having waited until night-time, found a way in. Gareth Llewellyn had worked overtime on two occasions that week, suggesting a need for extra money. Alford's shift pattern matched that of the murder victim. Colbeck could find no motive that would impel Alford to cause the outrage in the church where he and his family were regular worshippers. Where would he have kept the missing head hidden for so long? Of the others, he was less certain. Cudlip might have relished the act and it might have appealed to Samway's warped sense of humour. The Welshman, too, was capable of such a bizarre act. But was he the culprit?

267

Daniel Gill was no longer at the Works but Colbeck took the trouble to look at his records. He saw that Gill had been warned about timekeeping and that his wages had been docked on one occasion because he'd been involved in a scuffle. What interested Colbeck most was the occupation Gill had been following before he joined the company.

He'd been a locksmith.

Victor Leeming, meanwhile, was doing some research on his own account. When he'd travelled to the Old Town in a cab, he'd kept the severed head as far away from him as he could in the confined space. While he had no wish ever to see the head again, he took an interest in the sack. It was not the kind of thing that would have been used for potatoes or some other vegetable. It was made of much thicker and heavier material. Wondering where it had come from, he made a tour of the Works. The detectives had been told by Stinson that they could go anywhere on the site as long as they took the obvious precautions and didn't hold up the manufacturing process in any way. Leeming took the general manager at his word, going from shop to shop and from shed to shed.

Sacks abounded — especially in the stores — but he could find none that were identical to the one used by the killer. Undaunted, he pressed on, enduring the heat of the Foundry, the ear-splitting din of the steam hammer and the death traps of the Erecting Shop where something seemed to have been deliberately strewn in his way at every point to trip him up. The sight of him blundering his way around caused a lot of amusement. After a comprehensive search, he walked past the hut used by the railway policemen. Three of them were enjoying a cup of tea inside. One of them was Edgar Fellowes.

"Hello, Sergeant," he said, getting up. "Would you like to join us?"

"No, thank you."

"What are you doing here?"

"I'm looking for a sack."

"Then you should go to the stores. There are masses of them there."

"I know," said Leeming. "I've been there. But they didn't have what I was after. The sack I have in mind is made of a much stronger material that could cope with almost anything."

"Then what you're talking about is a coal sack. They're reinforced to take a substantial weight."

"Where would I find one?"

"If you go down to the siding, you'll see dozens of them in piles. They're used for bringing coal out of the wagons and into the Works. It's loaded into sacks and brought here on a cart by one of the horses. We spend a lot of time guarding the coal wagons," said Fellowes. "When the weather is as cold as this, coal has a nasty habit of disappearing if you don't keep an eye on it."

"I'd like to see one of those sacks."

"Then I'll take you there." He fell in beside Leeming and they walked off together. "You should have been here a month ago. They had a competition to see who the strongest man here was. Sacks of coal were lined up. Whoever lifted the greatest weight was to be the winner. One man stood out a mile."

"What was his name?"

"Gareth Llewellyn."

# CHAPTER
# TWENTY

It had never happened before. While involved in solving one crime, Colbeck was now preoccupied with another. In the past, he'd always given the current investigation all his energy and concentration. This time he found it impossible. The fate of Edward Tallis kept looming up in front of him. The two men had had their differences in the past but there was an underlying respect for each other that had never wavered. In addition — as Colbeck now discovered — a hitherto dormant affection for Tallis had suddenly sprung to life. It was the main reason why the latter's plight played on his mind. Notwithstanding the man's glaring defects, he liked him. Colbeck was realistic. Until a killer had been arrested in Swindon, he was unable to lend his skills to the manhunt elsewhere. Reminding himself of his priority, he set off to question Hector Samway.

When he got to the house, he saw that it was among the smallest in the block. Samway was a rarity in that he lived alone. Colbeck knocked on the door but got no response. He knocked even harder then stood back to look up at the bedroom window. The curtains twitched, showing that Samway was at home. After waiting for a minute or so, Colbeck knocked again to make it clear that he was not going to leave until the door was opened. His persistence paid off. Samway eventually unlocked the door and opened it a matter of inches.

"What do you want?" he asked, gruffly.

"I'd like to speak to you, sir."

"Why do you both keep pestering me? I've nothing to add to what I've already said. You and the sergeant have caused me enough trouble already."

"I wasn't aware of that, Mr Samway."

"You questioned me at work. It means that everyone in the Foundry now knows I'm a suspect. That's changed the way they look and talk to me. Friends I've had for years now back away from me as if I've got a disease."

"I'm sorry to hear that."

"It's your fault, Inspector."

"Wouldn't it be easier if we had this conversation inside the house? If I'm seen standing here, your neighbours might realise who I am then they'll know that you're under suspicion. Is that what you want?"

"I want you to ask your questions then go," said Samway, inhospitably. "I'm certainly not inviting you into my house."

"Let's do it your way, then," said Colbeck. "The reason I knew you were likely to be at home on a Saturday afternoon is that I was studying your shift patterns earlier on. You seem to like having Saturday off then working overtime on Sundays."

"It saves me from having to go to church."

"The Sabbath is supposed to be the day of rest."

"Do *you* ever work on a Sunday?"

"Unhappily, I do. Crime happens seven days a week, alas." Sensing that Samway was anxious to get rid of him, Colbeck reeled off his questions. "Have you been out of the house today?"

"No, I haven't."

"Do you know where Mrs Rodman lives?"

"Why do you ask that?"

"Just answer my question, please."

"No, I don't," said the other, forcefully.

"That's very strange. The house is in the next street. Every time you go to work, you walk right past it. I can't believe that you've never seen Mr Rodman or his wife coming out of there."

"I knew Rodman lived somewhere in that street but I made sure I never bumped into him. If I'd seen him, I'd have ignored him."

"What about Mrs Rodman — did you ignore her?"

"I haven't seen Betty for years."

"Is that the truth?"

"Yes, it is."

"Do you still feel hurt at what happened between you?"

"*Nothing* happened between us, Inspector."

"That's my point, sir."

"Look, what are you trying to say?" asked Samway, irritably. "If you have any evidence against me, tell me. It's my right to know what it is, surely? There's something strange going on. Why are you here?"

"Earlier today, someone put a letter through Mrs Rodman's letter box that caused her great distress.

Since you weren't at work, you'd have been in a position to write and deliver that letter."

"I told you. I haven't been out of the house today."

"What about last night?"

Samway was wary. "I was here alone."

"Are you quite sure about that?"

"Yes, I am."

"So there's nobody who can vouch for you, then."

"You'll just have to take my word for it, Inspector."

Samway spoke as if issuing a challenge. Their eyes locked for a long time. Colbeck could see the anger, insolence and sheer defiance in the man. He didn't for one moment believe Samway's claim to be ignorant of Betty Rodman's address and he felt that the man was very capable of sending her a devastating message by way of retaliation for the way she'd once rejected his advances. Whether or not the man was also the killer, Colbeck was not certain. Would he hack off his victim's head then set it up on the main altar in the church? Gazing into the dark, unforgiving, malicious eyes, Colbeck thought he glimpsed the answer.

The next moment, Samway abruptly closed the door in his face. Colbeck turned away but, before walking off, he glanced up at the bedroom. He saw the curtains twitch again and knew that Samway couldn't possibly have got there yet. Somebody else was in the bedroom.

Edward Tallis was more confused than ever. Since light had largely faded, he couldn't even be certain what day it was. Waking up very slowly, he was immediately conscious of the excruciating pain in his skull. When he tried to raise a hand to the injury, however, he was reminded of the handcuffs cutting into his wrists. His ankles were also bound now, making it extremely difficult for him to sit up. He tried to piece together what had happened. Having tried to escape, he'd upset his captors. They not only restricted his movement even more, one of them had clubbed him to the ground and opened up another wound on his head. He felt as if someone was repeatedly hitting him on the same spot on his skull.

Who were they and why were they treating him so brutally? He'd been no random prisoner, Tallis was certain of that. He'd been picked on deliberately. That meant that one or both of the men had crossed his path in the past. Even though he couldn't really see them in the gloom, they'd taken care to pull their hats down to evade recognition. He concluded that he'd been involved in the arrest and conviction of the men and decided to work his way back through the cases in which he'd been instrumental over the years. There were several of them and many had involved threats of violence from criminals in the dock. Somewhere in the long catalogue of cases, he believed, were the two men who had captured, taunted and tormented him.

Before he could even begin to sift through his past, however, Tallis had to wait until the pain began to ease. With his head throbbing so remorselessly, his brain would simply not work properly. He also needed to change his position. Being face down in the dank straw was both unhealthy and hideously uncomfortable. Tallis therefore made a supreme effort to turn over by rotating his body. The first few attempts were miserable failures, compounding his agony, but he didn't give up. He kept going until he gave a determined heave then spun onto his back. With his full weight pressing down on his wrists, he had to endure more pain, but he felt that he'd secured a minor triumph.

By means of wriggling, he slowly made his way towards the stall. When he eventually banged his head against it, the pain burnt even more fiercely and he had to wait for several minutes before it began to subside slightly. At least he'd reached his destination. He could now work his body around so that it lay parallel with the stall. Once he'd done that, he tried to sit up by throwing himself upwards with all his power. But his strength had already been sapped by his earlier efforts. Instead of getting the upper part of his body upright, he simply flopped back down to the stable floor and bruised his shoulder.

As he lay there suffering, he tried to focus his mind on the possibility of rescue. His old friend, Captain Wardlow, would have raised the alarm and instigated a manhunt. The problem was that the detective who could lead it most effectively was engaged in a separate investigation in Swindon. It was maddening.

"Colbeck," he said to himself. "Where *are* you, man?"

Having established where the sack containing the severed head must have come from, Leeming's instinct was to confront Llewellyn at once, but he remembered Colbeck's earlier warning that it would be cruel to spoil a Welshman's opportunity to sing. In any event, he had no clear evidence that Llewellyn was the killer, merely that the man knew where to acquire a reinforced sack. He therefore decided to follow Colbeck's suggestion and call on Simeon Cudlip. On the night of the murder, the clerk had visited the brothel in such a state of excitement that he'd frightened Euphemia and annoyed her mother intensely. According to Claire Knight, she'd ordered him to leave and told him that he was barred from coming to the house again. Apparently, Cudlip had slunk away.

Cudlip, Samway and Fellowes were all clients of the brothel and there were doubtless others in Swindon who sought the place out. It was that particular trio, however, which interested Leeming, As a widower, Samway was not entirely a surprise visitor to Claire Knight's abode but it was a different matter with Fellowes. He was a married man and a representative of law and order, who ought to be reporting the existence of the brothel to Inspector Piercey instead of taking advantage of its services. Leeming wondered if he'd been seduced into sampling what was on offer in return for his silence. The crucial name to emerge from Leeming's own visit to the house was that of Simeon Cudlip, a man who seemed to enjoy keeping the detectives at bay as if murder was some sort of parlour game at which he believed he excelled. At their last meeting, Leeming felt that the clerk had all the answers prepared in advance. Caught off guard on a Saturday afternoon, he might be more vulnerable.

Predictably, he got a frosty welcome. When Cudlip opened his front door, he looked at Leeming with a mingled peevishness and contempt. He made an effort to control himself before he spoke.

"Good afternoon, Sergeant," he said, coldly.

"How are you, Mr Cudlip?"

"I was having a pleasant day until you interrupted me."

"I'm sorry to spoil it but there are a few questions I'd like to ask."

"In that case, you'd better step inside."

Standing back reluctantly, he let his visitor in then followed him into the living room. It was small, well furnished and impeccably clean. Beside the single armchair was a table on which a book was lying.

"What are you reading?" asked Leeming.

"It's *A Christmas Carol* by Charles Dickens. I always read it at this time of year. It reminds me that even bad people can have some good inside them."

"That's not been my experience, sir. The people I deal with are usually bad people with an abiding love of evil inside them."

"Is that how you see me?"

"Of course not," said Leeming. "I see you for what you are — a man who does his job efficiently and organises his life very carefully. That's what's on the surface, anyhow. What's underneath is what arouses my curiosity."

"And what do you *think* is underneath, Sergeant?"

"I think that you're a very lonely man."

"If you like reading, as I do, you're never alone."

"Do you spurn human company?"

"Most of the time, I do."

"Then let's talk about a time when you didn't," said Leeming. "Where were you on the night of the murder?"

Cudlip sighed. "We've been through this rigmarole before."

"It's different this time."

"Then the answer is that I was here, on my own, minding my own business."

"I have two witnesses who'd challenge that claim, sir."

"They're barefaced liars!"

"I choose to believe them," said Leeming, calmly. "That's unusual, I agree. People in that occupation rarely tell the truth to a policeman but, on this occasion, one of them did." Cudlip's face whitened instantly. "I'll name no names." The other man turned away and tried to collect himself. "I have to say that I was very surprised," continued Leeming. "After years of experience, I can often pick out the men who go to places like that. I didn't single you out, Mr Cudlip."

"It was a mistake," said the other, swinging round. "I'd never been there before and I don't intend to cross that threshold ever again."

"You won't be allowed to cross it. We both know why."

"It was . . . an aberration I prefer to forget."

"Mrs Knight and her daughter can't forget it that easily. You terrified them."

"I was drunk."

"I thought you told Inspector Colbeck that you'd stopped drinking."

"I have . . . occasional lapses."

"Don't you think it's an odd coincidence that you had one of your lapses on the very night that Frank Rodman was murdered?" Getting no reply, Leeming pressed on. "When I first became a policeman, there was an old sergeant who gave me some good advice. If I was ever called to a burglary or some other crime, he said, the first places I should go to were the local brothels. You'd be amazed how many criminals like to celebrate their success by jumping straight into bed with a woman. The married ones have wives, of course, but the others need to pay for their pleasure — just like you. As a matter of fact," he recalled, fondly, "some of my first arrests were made in brothels. Villains are less likely to make a run for it with their trousers off,"

Cudlip sounded contrite. "I'm ashamed of what happened, Sergeant."

"Ashamed of going to that particular house — or ashamed of what you did before you went?"

"I was drunk, I tell you."

"Yes, but why did you feel the need for alcohol? Did you have an urge to celebrate? Is that what happened? You were so elated by the thrill of committing a murder that you needed a drink or two to celebrate before going off to a brothel."

"No!" howled Cudlip.

"Then why did you behave like an animal?"

"I couldn't help myself."

"And why was that, sir?"

"I don't know."

"Is that the way you *always* treat a woman?"

"Euphemia has no complaints as a rule."

"I thought you'd only ever been there once."

"Well, yes ... I mean ... you're just trying to confuse me."

"No," said Leeming, confronting him, "I'm trying to do the opposite. I'm trying to make everything crystal clear but I need your help to do that. So please don't insult me by inventing any more lame excuses. I'm beginning to think that I may be standing face-to-face with the man who killed Mr Rodman." He took him firmly by the shoulders. "Am I right, Mr Cudlip?"

Betty Rodman was still upset by the anonymous letter that had popped through her letter box that morning. It had left her wondering if there were other shocks still to come. When Fred Alford replaced his wife at the house in the afternoon, Betty taxed him with keeping her in ignorance.

"You must have known, Fred."

"Yes, I did," he admitted.

"Then why didn't you tell me about them?"

"You were in enough pain as it was, Betty."

"I thought I could rely on you to be honest with me."

"I *was* honest," said Alford, worried by her accusatory tone. "All sorts of rumours were flying about. Most of them were probably complete nonsense. Would you have wanted me to tell you about them and cause you even more grief?"

"You let me down."

She lowered her head. They were seated opposite each other. The baby was in the crib and the two boys were playing together upstairs. Alford was delighted to have the chance to spend time with her and he'd expected her to lean on him for advice. Instead, she was treating him as if he'd betrayed her and that was wounding. He'd always considered himself part of the family. Rodman had spent leisure time with him and his two sons treated Alford as a kind of uncle. The real bonus was the fact that Betty turned to him in times of trouble. Unknown to Rodman — or to Liza, for that matter — Alford had occasionally given her money in an emergency. It had earned him Betty's thanks and deepened their friendship. All of a sudden, that friendship was in danger.

"I'm sorry," he said, touching her arm, "You know how I feel about you."

"I thought I did."

"Betty, I was trying to *protect* you."

"I was bound to find out sooner or later."

"Yes, I agree, but I don't know that you'd have been able to cope with the full truth at the start. One of the railway policemen told me that it had been a frenzied attack. It made my blood curdle when I heard that. I didn't dare tell Liza, let alone you. I suppose that I hoped someone else would do it — someone like the vicar or that Inspector Colbeck. It would come better from them. They've talked to people in your situation before. I haven't. I'd struggle to find the right words."

"I'd simply have liked to hear the truth."

"No matter how unpleasant it was?"

"Yes, even then. I feel as if there's been a conspiracy against me. I'm the one person who ought to know *everything* but people have ganged up against me and told me as little as possible. That includes you, Fred."

"I'd never deliberately hurt you, Betty."

"Well, you did."

There was a bruised silence. Neither of them spoke for several minutes. Betty was lost in her own thoughts while Alford was struggling to find a way to appease her. When she looked up, she changed the subject completely.

"Are you going to the concert tonight?"

"I'd rather be here with you."

"If you don't mind, I'd prefer Liza's company."

"Oh," he said, stung by the rebuff. "I'm sorry you feel like that."

"Go to the concert instead. You love music."

"You used to love it as well, Betty. You never missed it when Frank was singing as solo. He was happiest when he could open his lungs and let out that glorious voice of his. I'm going to miss that."

"I'll miss far more than his voice." Head to one side, she studied him for a moment. "What would you have done, Fred?"

"I don't follow."

"If you'd been there when Frank was attacked, what would you have done?"

"I've have gone to help him, of course."

"And what would you have done to the other man?"

"I'd have killed him," he said with a surge of passion. "If Frank was in trouble, I'd have murdered the bastard attacking him."

Reunited at their temporary office, the detectives took it in turns to describe their respective visits. Colbeck talked about his conversation with Samway, noting that the man seemed to have company at the house, possibly that of a woman. After telling him about his discovery relating to the coal sack, Leeming recounted the revealing interview with Simeon Cudlip.

"I came very close to arresting him," he confessed.

"What stopped you, Victor?"

"It was a warning you once gave me, sir. Suspicion needs to be supported by the kind of evidence that will hold water in court and we don't have that yet. I'd hate to arrest Cudlip, only to see him released in due course."

"Do you believe that he really *was* the killer?"

"I'm seventy per cent certain."

"Wait until we reach one hundred per cent."

"That's why I stopped myself reaching for the handcuffs," said Leeming. "What about you, sir? Did you get the feeling that Samway was involved in the murder somehow?"

"Yes, I did. At least, I felt that he *could* have been. He's patently a man with a lot to hide. Samway wouldn't even let me inside the house. He kept me shivering on the doorstep."

"Perhaps he didn't want you to find out about the woman upstairs."

284

"I'm not certain that it was a woman. You must find out for me, Victor."

Leeming was taken aback. "I can't tell you who she was."

"If you pay another visit to that house, you may be able to. Samway is not the most prepossessing character. If he wants a woman, he has to resort to Mrs Knight and her daughter. See which one of them called on him today."

"I will," said Leeming. "What about this evening?"

"That's already fixed. We're going to the concert."

"Earlier on, you said that all five suspects will be there as well."

"They probably will."

"I doubt that."

"Llewellyn *has* to be there because his solo is in the programme."

"What about Cudlip and Samway? Why should either of them go along?"

"They'd do so from force of habit, I daresay. What else can you do here except go to the pub? The concert is a major event. Everyone looks forward to it. I fully expect Alford to be there with his wife, though he's going to be put out when he hears the Welshman taking the place of his old friend."

"What about Daniel Gill?"

"He'll turn up so that he can find out how the investigation is going. Only a guilty man would come for that reason. I found out something very interesting about Gill. He served his apprenticeship as a locksmith."

Leeming slapped the table. "So it could have been him who managed to get into the church. Mouldy Grosvenor was right, after all. Gill is our man."

Colbeck laughed. "Have you deserted Cudlip so easily? A moment ago, you were seventy per cent sure that he was the killer."

"I'm not so sure now."

"Then let's press on hard until we know for certain. I'm dying for a resolution here so that we can get to Canterbury and find out what's going on."

"Has there been no telegraph?"

"No," said Colbeck, "and that's disturbing. Grosvenor would only contact me if he had success to report and could take credit for it."

"But you told me he hasn't even gone to Canterbury."

"He sent two constables instead — Hinton and Legge. I fear that they've been promoted beyond their competence."

"Mouldy has definitely been promoted beyond *his* competence."

"The commissioner hasn't found him out yet."

"He soon will. Sir Richard doesn't suffer fools gladly."

"It's ironic, isn't it? Tallis appointed Grosvenor without realising that he might well be anointing his successor."

"Is the situation really as dire as that, sir?"

"All I know is that the superintendent is still missing," said Colbeck, sadly. "I have a horrible feeling that they may be looking in the wrong direction."

"What do you mean, sir?"

"They'll go for the obvious explanation, assuming that Tallis is the victim of criminals with a grudge against him. It may well be the case, of course, but I've been thinking about another threat from his past. This could relate to his days in the army."

"But he retired as a soldier over a dozen years ago, sir."

"Some people have long memories."

"They'd have struck well before now, wouldn't they?"

"Not necessarily," explained Colbeck. "To begin with, they might have had no idea where Major Tallis, as he once was, could be found. If the men who kidnapped him — and there's no certainty that that *did* happen — are based in Canterbury, they'd have seen mention of him in the local press. He told us that he was due to receive a prestigious award from his regiment. That might well merit an article about him. His enemies, whoever they may be, would have seized gratefully on that information. Somehow they learnt that he'd be staying with Captain Wardlow beforehand and planned to ambush him."

"You've worked it all out," said Leeming, approvingly.

"No, Victor, I'm just groping in the dark. That's why we must get back to lend our assistance as soon as we can. I want to get at the truth. Edward Tallis is imperilled in some way. I feel that very strongly. The longer it goes on, the less likely it is that he will remain alive."

# CHAPTER
# TWENTY-ONE

When he'd been given this unexpectedly important task, Alan Hinton had tackled it with all the energy he could muster. Unfortunately, nobody had warned him about the pitfalls. He and his colleague, Constable Legge, had been dogged by setbacks from the start. Their knowledge of Kent was limited and neither had any flair for exerting authority. They were therefore at the mercy of the local police and the army, acting on the advice of both of them yet making no progress whatsoever. Hinton had the additional problem of having to cope with Captain Wardlow whose steely determination to rescue his friend brought out the soldier in him. Even when asking a question, he sounded as if he was barking an order on the parade ground.

"Is there nothing at all to report?" he demanded.

"I'm afraid not, Captain."

"Are you sure you've deployed the men properly?"

"I did what the inspector here suggested," replied Hinton, "and that was to organise a more thorough search in the vicinity of the cathedral. Policemen or soldiers have knocked on every door within a hundred yards of the precinct in search of someone who may have witnessed the kidnap."

"Did that produce any results?"

"We found a man who remembered seeing someone who might well have been Major Tallis in the crypt with a friend who had a walking stick."

"That was *me*," said Wardlow.

"As long as you were together, the superintendent was safe."

"What else did this man tell you?"

"Nothing," admitted Hinton. "There was just that single sighting of you."

"Is everyone *blind* in this city?"

"It's not their fault, Captain. Nobody visits the cathedral to look at other people. They've usually got their heads in a guidebook or are looking up at that magnificent ceiling."

"Well, they should be more perceptive — and so should you."

"We're doing our best, sir."

"But that's palpably untrue, Constable. You're young and willing but that's all I can say in your favour. When you're older, you may eventually acquire an aptitude for command. At the moment, however, it's woefully absent."

"I'm sorry to disappoint you, sir," said Hinton, uncomfortably. "I'm only obeying orders and doing so to the best of my ability."

"Well, it's not good enough. I made that point clear in a telegraph to Scotland Yard. When one needs action, one goes to the very top. On that basis, I approached the commissioner himself."

Hinton's heart sank. He feared repercussions. If he was described by the captain as being inadequate, it would affect his chances of a career in the Detective Department. He might even be put back in uniform, his hopes of working with Colbeck disappearing like so many wisps of smoke. They were back in a room at the police station, seated at a table on which a map of Kent was spread out. The ever-widening search continued but was now hampered by darkness. Hinton's one initiative had been the visit to the barracks but he'd been met with a dispiriting response from the man charged with organising the reunion. He longed to be back in the crime-ridden streets of London. He was at home there. In an army barracks, he felt, he was on enemy territory.

Wardlow was about to issue another stream of insults when the door suddenly opened and Grosvenor strode in purposefully. He took up a stance in the middle of the room.

"I'm taking charge now," he declared.

"Thank heavens somebody is," said Wardlow.

"Hinton."

"Yes, sir?" Hinton stood to attention.

"I want a full report of what steps you've taken so far."

"Yes, sir."

"And I want to know who's in charge of those soldiers I've seen in the streets."

"I can tell you that," said Wardlow.

"I'm very glad that you're here, Captain. I can assure you that the hunt will continue with a greater intensity now that I'm controlling it. On the train journey here, I've been working out my plan of campaign."

Grosvenor spoke as if it had been his decision to take over from Hinton. In fact, it was Wardlow's telegraph that had brought about the change. Instead of developing a master plan on his way there, Grosvenor had been smarting at the caustic criticism he'd received from the commissioner. Sir Richard Mayne had insisted that he caught the next train to Canterbury in a bid to vindicate himself. His future was in jeopardy.

"Well, come on, Hinton," he snapped, taking out his anger on the constable. "Bring me up to date with the situation. I want to put some real zest into this search. Speak up, man!"

Though he had no real appetite for going, Daniel Gill forced himself to attend the concert. He and his wife, Anne, set out with the horse and cart borrowed from his uncle. It was not the most comfortable way to travel but it had to suffice. Anne Gill was a small, delicate, submissive woman with the long-suffering look of someone dominated by her husband. Having been roundly chastised for telling Leeming the truth about Gill's whereabouts on the night of the murder, she was too afraid to open her mouth without her husband's permission. She therefore sat beside him with a shawl around her shoulders and a hat pulled down over her ears. Anne listened to the jingle of the harness as they went along and wished that the cart didn't smell quite so pungently of meat and offal.

When they reached the New Town, they saw the silhouette of St Mark's Church to their left. It prompted memories of their wedding there and she couldn't help thinking of all the solemn promises Gill had given her on their wedding night. Without exception, none of them had been kept. Hers had been a marriage of continuous disappointment. He, meanwhile, was enjoying memories of a different kind. At the sight of the church, he smiled quietly to himself.

Calling at the Knights' house for the second time, Leeming hoped that he wouldn't be mistaken for a client again. In his opinion, prostitution was a sin as well as a crime. He'd been brought up with Christian values and a respect for women. It was impossible to have any respect for Claire Knight and her daughter. Unlike so many prostitutes, however, they were not victims of a tyrannical master who forced them into the trade. It had been their choice and they'd somehow found a way to develop a profitable business without scandalising the neighbours. As long as there were men like Samway, Cudlip and Edgar Fellowes, they'd never lack for clients.

Claire Knight answered the door in a red velvet gown and an array of cheap jewellery. She reeked of perfume. Inviting him in, she batted her eyelids at him and asked if he'd changed his mind. Leeming was offended.

"I'm investigating a murder," he told her. "That's the only reason I'd ever come near this place."

"Oh, we don't only operate here, Sergeant. Euphemia and I pay calls on certain people. If the neighbours saw a stream of men coming here night after night, there'd be ructions. As it is, because we're very discreet, we're looked upon as a mother and daughter who live quiet, orderly lives and go to church every Sunday." She cackled. "I could tell you stories about some of the husbands we see there with their wives on their arms."

"I'm only interested in one person at the moment, Mrs Knight."

"Who is it?"

"Hector Samway."

"What about him?"

"Earlier today, Inspector Colbeck called on Mr Samway. He became aware that someone was in the bedroom. Was it your daughter?"

She was categorical. "No, it wasn't."

"It's important that you tell me the truth."

"Euphemia hasn't been out of this house all day."

"Well, someone was in that bedroom with Samway."

"Yes," she said, smiling sweetly. "It was me. Since he lives alone, he usually prefers one of us to go to him. We're quite happy with the arrangement because it allows us to charge a little more."

"What state was he in?"

She cackled again. "There's only one state men are in when I'm alone with them. They have a need. I satisfy it."

"That wasn't the case with Simeon Cudlip. The last time he came here, he was in a violent mood, according to you."

"It's true. Hector can be wild as well but in a way that I don't really mind, whereas Simeon came here with his eyes blazing."

"Do you or your daughter ever visit his house?"

"Yes, we do. It's always so clean and tidy. I can't say the same of Hector. He doesn't know how to look after the place properly. His sink was disgusting today. When I tried to wash in it, there were bloodstains everywhere. I have standards, Sergeant," she said, chin uplifted. "I made that clear to Hector Samway."

Since she needed good light in her studio, Madeleine had abandoned her latest painting as soon as shadows began to close in. She was now sitting alone in the drawing room in front of the fire, knowing that neither her father nor Lydia would be calling again. More to the point, her husband wouldn't be making another surprise return. Colbeck had vowed to solve the murder before he left Swindon and even then he wouldn't be coming directly home. He'd go straight on to Canterbury to take part in the search for the missing superintendent. Madeleine shared his anxiety. Tallis had been a hard taskmaster but an extremely efficient leader of the team of detectives under his control. He couldn't easily be replaced. Because he preferred investigating crimes on the railway system, Colbeck had no interest in a job that would keep him, for the most part, in London. If a vacancy occurred, therefore, it would be filled by someone like Inspector Grosvenor. That prospect made her shudder. From what she'd heard about him, he would exploit his position to bully and belittle her husband. It would be a very unpleasant Christmas present for Colbeck and, by extension, for Victor Leeming.

She hoped that Tallis would be found alive but knew that his chances were slim. If he was in the hands of villains bent on revenge, he might already be dead or kept alive for their sport. While she was pleased that Alan Hinton had been one of the detectives sent to Canterbury, his inexperience was unsettling. Ideally, she thought, he would acquit himself well and return to Scotland Yard to receive praise from the commissioner. There might even be a way to reunite him with Lydia Quayle. If he came back to London as a proven failure, however, there'd be a very different result. He might be castigated, or even demoted, and would feel too embarrassed to take up any invitation from her. Everything depended on rescuing Edward Tallis alive in a way that showed Hinton in a good light. It seemed impossible. Madeleine braced herself to cope with a more tragic outcome.

Though it had only been opened six years earlier, the Mechanics' Institution played a central part in the community and seemed always to have been there. It was a massive neo-Gothic structure with local stone for walling and Bath stone for dressings. It looked at first glance like a church or temple but some of the activities that occurred there would not have been entirely suitable to a place of worship. The ground floor comprised the reading room, the library, a coffee room, the men's mess room and the council and housekeeper's rooms. Hot and cold baths had also been built for the members. The concert was due to be performed on the upper floor, which housed the capacious assembly hall whose main feature was a large stage, capable of holding the Mechanics' Institution Band.

Crowds flocked to the building. Some of the plays that were performed there from time to time had been poorly received but the musical entertainments were always a success. When they looked at their programme, the detectives saw that the band would be kept busy. The first half of the concert consisted of the overture from *The Magic Flute* by Mozart, followed by a song from the choir, a polonaise, a ballad, a polka, a duet, a comic song, a waltz and another Mozart overture. Since they were sitting next to William Morris, the detectives were able to get informed answers to any questions they posed.

"How would you describe the band?" asked Colbeck.

"Oh, it's more than serviceable," said Morris. "They can't match the orchestras you're likely to hear in London, perhaps, but they have talent and take their music very seriously. If anyone is late for a rehearsal, they're fined a penny. If they're absent, the fine is doubled."

"What happens if they're persistently absent?" said Leeming.

"They're replaced. There's a waiting list to join the band. They're part of a substantial organisation, you see. When the Institution was founded way back in 1843, they had only fifteen members at the Annual General Meeting. I know that because I've studied their records."

"How many members do they have now, Mr Morris?"

"It must be over seven hundred."

"Then it's clearly a thriving society," observed Colbeck.

The room was filling rapidly. The babble of many voices was drowned out by the grating of chairs, the clacking of hundreds of feet on the bare boards and the noise of the musicians, practising a few bars. Most of the men had brass or woodwind instruments and there was a large bass drum being carried onstage by the smallest musician in the band. They wore dark uniforms but waistcoats of varying styles and colours. Their peaked caps were set at differing angles on their heads.

As he looked around, Colbeck saw that he'd guessed correctly. All five suspects were there. Gareth Llewellyn was seated with his wife and a group of his compatriots, boasting that he would bring the concert to a rousing conclusion when it was his turn to sing. Yet there was no sign of Rachel Griffiths, the woman who'd been his secret lover and who'd reported something disturbing she noticed about Llewellyn on the night of the murder. Daniel Gill had also brought his wife and they were sitting at the rear. When he caught Colbeck's eye, Gill looked away quickly. Hector Samway had obviously come on his own, as had Simeon Cudlip, noticeably smarter than most of his work colleagues. Fred Alford was there without his wife and Colbeck assumed that she was keeping Betty Rodman company once more. It would be a poignant evening for the murder victim's widow because she'd be reminded that her husband should have been singing at the concert.

The detectives recognised a number of other people. Howard and Jennifer Law were there seated close to Oswald Stinson and his wife, though the general manager looked as if he was there under sufferance rather than because he expected to enjoy the event. In the row behind them were Dr and Mrs Burnaby. Leeming was interested to spot Edgar Fellowes, divested of his uniform and wearing his best suit. When he entered the room, he had his wife beside him, a big, bosomy, middle-aged woman. Mrs Fellowes had an air of potency about her and Leeming was bound to wonder how she would react to the news that her husband was both an adulterer and a man who frequented a brothel. At that moment in time, he appeared to be an exemplar of respectability and he went out of his way to say a few words to the vicar and his wife.

Thunderous applause greeted the arrival of the conductor, a tall, spindly man in his fifties who bowed to acknowledge the ovation. He made sure that he had the attention of every musician before deciding that they were ready to begin. Baton held high, he gave them their cue and let Wolfgang Amadeus Mozart weave his magic spell.

**298**

★ ★ ★

In a sitting position against the stall, Tallis was in a marginally less painful position but his head was still aching and his limbs were under attack from cramp. To stave off his torture, he'd been thinking about the person who might have been behind his capture and finally settled on a name. It was Sam Byard, who'd travelled in a first-class carriage in order to pull a gun on his fellow passengers and rob them of a large amount of money. When one of them had refused to hand over his wallet, Byard had knocked him senseless. Since the crime had occurred on the railway, Colbeck had taken charge of the investigation but Tallis had been with him when Byard and an accomplice were arrested in Rochester. Along with Colbeck, he'd given evidence at the trial and been rewarded with a mouthful of abuse from the men in the dock. Byard had issued a chilling threat that the detectives had duly ignored, knowing that both men would be locked away for many years.

Tallis couldn't remember if they'd served their sentence or if they'd escaped from prison. What he did recall was the voice of the man who'd earlier come to see him then returned with someone else and knocked him out with the butt of his rifle. It sounded very much like the voice that had roared at him during the trial, though that was so long ago that he couldn't be entirely sure. Tallis was perplexed. Believing that he might be being held by Byard, he tried to work out how the man could possibly know that he'd be in Canterbury. A spasm of pain made him cry out as he realised how it must have happened. Captain Wardlow had kindly sent him a cutting from the local newspaper in which details of the regimental reunion were given. Various luminaries from the military world were attending but Tallis was singled out because, retrospectively, he was being awarded a special medal for his gallantry in the field while in India. The fact that he was a close friend of Wardlow was mentioned.

Was that how it had happened? Had Byard, who'd lived in Kent, seen the item in the press? Could he have found out where Wardlow lived? Or had he simply put the railway station under surveillance for days before the event on the supposition that Tallis was bound to arrive by train? That was it, he believed. Byard had actually witnessed the reunion between the two old friends. On their journey back to Wardlow's house, they must have been followed.

Tallis's fevered thoughts were suddenly swept aside by a crisis. As well as the pain, the cold, the hunger pangs and the nagging fear that he'd never get out of there alive, there was a more immediate problem. Needing to relieve himself, he was in great discomfort. The wants of nature couldn't be stemmed indefinitely.

The detectives had taken care to sit in a position that allowed them to keep an eye on most of the audience. When the interval came, they watched their suspect carefully. Morris was too busy making notes for the review he intended to write so they were not distracted by him. Colbeck looked first at Hector Samway, self-confessed enemy of Frank Rodman and a man

**300**

who, in physical terms, looked capable of a savage murder. Why was he there? Colbeck decided that Samway wanted to use the crowd as a form of camouflage, mixing with them on a Saturday night as if he was going through a normal routine. Nothing about him suggested that a prostitute had earlier paid him a visit. Samway was chatting easily to the people next to him and seemed very much at home in the gathering. Leeming had brought back the information that Claire Knight had found bloodstains in the man's house. How had they got there? Could it be that the sack containing the head had been kept there before being transferred to the church? As well as finding a way to avoid St Mark's since the death of his wife, had Samway developed a hatred of a place that had failed to help him through his bereavement? It was certainly a possibility.

Switching to Gareth Llewellyn, the inspector watched him preening in front of his friends and studiously ignoring his wife. Like Samway, the Welshman also had a double life, presenting one image to the public while conducting an illicit affair with another woman. Her evidence that he'd come back to the barracks on the night of the murder with blood on his hands couldn't be disregarded. Leeming had established that a new coal sack must have been used and Llewellyn knew very well where he could find one. Had he used his superior strength to take Rodman into the Works and to commit murder there? Colbeck was prepared to believe that he could but he had the gravest doubts about the Welshman being responsible for the outrage in the church. A religious man at heart, Llewellyn was highly unlikely to do anything so starkly blasphemous. Yet the question remained. Two suspects had blood on their hands: which one of them had acquired it from Rodman?

"Look at Gill," whispered Leeming in his companion's ear.

"Why?"

"I've never seen anyone so obviously guilty."

"Why did he come?" asked Colbeck. "He must have known we'd be here."

"I've been watching him for minutes, sir. Every so often, he glances in my direction then turns his head away quickly. We know he got home late on the night of the murder but he still hasn't given us a convincing alibi."

"Ask him again, Victor."

"What — now?"

"Wait until the concert is over. We don't want his wife to miss the entertainment. Speak to him when she is not present. I'm sure that Mrs Gill will have been told to keep silent but she's an honest woman and, as you discovered, can't control her facial expressions as easily as he does. Press him hard. Oh, and find out if he's been using his skills as a locksmith of late."

"I will, sir. What about you?"

"I fancy that another word with Samway is needed."

Colbeck turned to watch the man again. Leeming, meanwhile, switched his attention to Simeon Cudlip, the person most likely to have left a severed head on the main altar in St Mark's. An avowed atheist, he'd scorned religion of any kind. But how did the fastidious clerk get Rodman into the Erecting Shop in the first place and then have the strength to kill him?

Colbeck's eye finally alighted on Fred Alford, the putative friend of the dead man. In her younger days, Betty Rodman had had many admirers and Alford had been the most devoted. Even his wife had admitted that. Others might have yearned for her in the past but it was Alford who was still in love with her and who had access to her that none of the others did. On the night of the murder, Alford had left the Queen's Tap while his friend was having an argument with Llewellyn. Knowing that Rodman would be drunk when he left the pub, had Alford lain in wait for him, determined to kill him in order to release Betty from her suffocating marriage to a wayward Christian?

The other suspects would have killed Rodman out of hatred, revenge or a mixture of both. Alford's motive was that he cared deeply for the man's wife. Was he acting out of pity for her? Had he persuaded himself that the only way to make her life more bearable was to rid her of Rodman? If so, why had he found it necessary to behead the man and leave a mutilated corpse? It was easy to see why the other four suspects might have been driven to commit murder. There was a cold simplicity about their motives. Alford's case was far more problematical. He was, ironically, the most pleasant of the five men. Four had lied to the detectives while he had appeared to be telling the truth. Was his apparent desire to help the investigation really a clever

smokescreen? Neither of the detectives knew th
answer.

Members of the band had slipped off for a revivin
glass of beer in the interval and were now drifting bac
to the stage and picking up their instruments.

"What comes next, sir?" asked Leeming.

Colbeck looked at his programme. "It's an overtur
by Rossini."

"I've never heard of him."

"It's from his opera, *The Italian Girl in Algiers.*"

"That's a funny title."

"It will be instructive to find out how the band cope
with the piece. None of them will ever have been t
Italy and I doubt if they even know where Algiers is."

"What sort of place is it?"

"Rossini is about to tell you, Victor."

Leeming looked around. "Is the composer here?"

"No, but his music is. When the band plays, you'
hear Algiers being conjured up in front of you. All yo
have to do is to sit back and listen."

There were four of them in the room at Canterbur
police station. Wardlow, Hinton and Legge sat at th
table while Grosvenor remained on his feet so that h
could strut about and gesticulate. While he was still i
charge, Grosvenor was keen to demonstrate his abilit
as a leader.

"The moment I heard about the abduction," he saic
"I began to wonder how we could identify the perso
or persons responsible. On the train journey fror
Swindon to London, I thought of nothing else."

"So I should hope," said Wardlow.

"The answer lies in the superintendent's past."

"That seems obvious."

"Let me finish, Captain. It's a strange thing to say of a grown man like Edward Tallis but, when he stayed at your home, you were in loco parentis, so to speak. The responsibility for his safety therefore lay with you."

Wardlow scowled. "Balderdash!"

"You should have kept an eye on him at all times."

"It was Major Tallis who was looking after me, I'm the weak link here. I simply had to sit down to rest in the cathedral and had no qualms about doing so. Who would expect someone as big, powerful and experienced as the major to be at risk when alone?"

"Nobody," said Hinton. "You're not to blame, Captain Wardlow."

"I wish that I could feel that."

"The pair of you were being followed by someone who was waiting for the moment when you were split up."

"That's enough from you, Constable," said Grosvenor. "You've been here in Kent and achieved nothing. I, on the other hand, do have an achievement to report. Sitting in my office, I'm fairly certain that I may have found out the name of the man behind the kidnap."

Wardlow sat up. "Who is it? Tell us, man."

"Let me first explain how I came by it. Before I replaced the superintendent, he talked in fulsome terms about the demands of the position and how he'd occupied it with such distinction. He talked about various cases in which he played an active role. The one that stood out was a robbery on a train. He was directly involved in the arrest."

"When was this?"

"Oh, it was several years ago."

"Who was the villain?"

"His name was Sam Byard."

"I've heard of him," said Hinton, quickly. "It was one of Inspector Colbeck's first cases."

"Colbeck was promoted to that rank far too early, in my opinion. As it happened, he did solve the crime but needed the help of the superintendent to make the arrest. I looked at the transcript of the trial. Byard was vociferous in the dock. Some of the expletives were omitted, according to the superintendent. He'd never heard such a volley of abuse as that directed at him and Colbeck."

"Was there a specific threat of revenge?" asked Wardlow.

"It was aimed at the superintendent."

"Then Byard might well be our man."

"There's a clinching detail," said Grosvenor.

"What is it?"

"Sam Byard was released from prison earlier this year. As a local man, he'll certainly be living somewhere in Kent."

# CHAPTER
# TWENTY-TWO

The second half of the concert got off to a disappointing start. Having excelled himself with Mozart, the conductor — emboldened by a pint of beer during the interval — started Rossini off at too fast a tempo, losing all the finer nuances of the music and making his band struggle to maintain the pace. Those unfamiliar with the overture thought it was played superbly but Colbeck was among a minority of listeners who knew the truth. After a solo, a duet and a choral piece, the band redeemed themselves with the overture to *The Thieving Magpie*, sticking to the tempo prescribed by Rossini and rousing the audience to cheers. Nobody clapped as loud as Leeming.

When they reached the penultimate item in the programme, the conductor turned and waved the audience into silence. He explained that Gareth Llewellyn would be taking the place of Frank Rodman but felt that they should all spare a thought beforehand for the murder victim who'd entertained them so well over the years. Howard Law was invited up onstage to say a short prayer in memory of the dead man. While the majority of people lowered their heads and closed their eyes, Colbeck and Leeming were curious to see how the five suspects reacted to the situation. They noticed that Simeon Cudlip didn't even bother to listen to the words. Sitting up with his arms folded, he affected disdain. Daniel Gill was also less than committed to the prayer, looking up and smirking. Samway had lowered his head respectfully but it was Alford who responded most eagerly. Hands together and head on his chest, he knelt on the bare boards in an attitude of exaggerated grief. When the prayer was over, he was the last to get to his feet.

Colbeck had taken particular note of Llewellyn, pretending to join in with everyone else but really bursting with eagerness to get onstage. When he was finally introduced, he bounded out of his seat to a fusillade of clapping from the Welsh contingent there. It was countered by sounds of discontent and a couple of people walked out in protest but the majority stayed to hear him. It was Llewellyn's own decision to sing unaccompanied. After taking a deep breath, he threw himself wholeheartedly into a rendition of "Clychau Aberdyfi", a famous Welsh folk song. When he counted the bells of Aberdovey one by one, his friends in the audience joined in. Though the singer was unpopular with most people, they were ready to acknowledge that he had a wonderful voice, deeper and richer than Frank Rodman's. His performance was supremely confident and his breath control astonishing. When he'd counted the bells for the last time, there was a concerted shout of joy from his compatriots supported by polite applause from everyone else.

Llewellyn was not finished yet. Once the band had played the national anthem, he jumped back up onstage and led his makeshift choir in what he believed was the Welsh equivalent, introducing a contentious note to what had hitherto been a very harmonious evening. Colbeck had watched with fascination and listened with awe to an extraordinary voice. Early in the investigation, he and Leeming had wondered if any human being could commit murder for the sole purpose of securing a chance to sing in public. In the Mechanics' Institution that evening, they had their answer.

Daniel Gill and his wife were among the first to leave. Most of those in the audience lived in the New Town and could walk back to their houses. The Gills were almost a mile away and were keen to ride home in the cart. As they came out of the exit, however, they found Victor Leeming waiting for them.

"Did you enjoy the concert?" he asked.

"Most of it," replied Gill. "We could have done without that Welshman."

"That was the best part of the evening for me." Leeming turned to the wife. "What about you, Mrs Gill? Didn't you think he sang well?"

Too embarrassed to answer, she nodded earnestly in agreement.

"It's late," said Gill, pointedly. "You'll have to excuse us."

"I'm afraid I can't do that, sir. I need to speak to you again."

"Can't it wait until the morning?"

"No, it can't," replied Leeming.

Gill asked if he could first conduct his wife to their cart. Leeming was happy to agree though was appalled at the uncaring way he lifted her up on to the vehicle as if loading a side of beef on to it. Gill took him several yards away so that they were out of earshot of his wife.

"What is it this time, Sergeant?" he asked, warily.

"You still haven't told us where you were on the night of the murder."

"Yes, I did. I got drunk and fell asleep."

"But there are no witnesses to support that story."

"It's not a story, it's the truth."

"It's also the excuse we hear time and time again in investigations like this. People who are stone-cold sober every other day of the year claim to have been in a drunken stupor on the night a crime was committed."

"That's exactly what happened."

"Were you celebrating something, Mr Gill?"

"I enjoy a tankard of beer now and again, that's all."

"But you're claiming that you had several tankards. A confirmed drinker like you would know exactly what his limit was and take care not to go beyond it. Also, there's the problem of cost. You're only a butcher's assistant," Leeming reminded him. "That can't bring you the same wage you earned at the Works. Put simply, you can't afford to spend too much money in a pub, can you?"

"I have to be careful," mumbled Gill.

"So why did you scatter your money so recklessly *that* night."

310

"I was upset about something. I drowned my anger in beer."

"I have a strong feeling that you were upset about *somebody* and his name was Rodman. When everybody was showing respect to him by joining in that prayer, you were smirking to yourself. I watched you."

Gill was jolted. "I've never been much of a one for prayers."

"You haven't been much of a one for truth either," said Leeming. "You're so used to telling lies that you can't do anything else." He saw Gill run a tongue over dry lips. "I'm told that you were once apprenticed to a locksmith."

"So?"

"Why did you give it up?"

"I was offered more money at the Works."

"But you still possess your old skills, I expect. Could you pick a lock?"

"Why should I need to do that?"

"Could you?"

"That depends on the lock. I have helped friends in the past when they've locked themselves out of their houses and left the key inside."

"What about a large lock like the one they have on church doors?" Gill made no answer. "You must have seen the one at St Mark's many times. Could you get inside that church when it was locked?"

"I'd have no reason to do so, Sergeant."

"You might have wanted to get in there during the night."

"For what purpose?"

"It's because you wanted to leave something there."

"I don't know what you're talking about, Sergeant."

"It's the murder of Rodman," said Leeming, "and I'll keep on talking about it until we catch the man responsible." He lowered his voice. "Where were you on the night of the murder?" Gill glanced towards the cart. "And it's no use claiming that you were home in bed. Unlike you, Mrs Gill is an honest person. She told me how late you were that night."

"I was drunk." Leeming grabbed him by the throat. "Hey! You're hurting me!"

"One last chance — where were you?"

When the sergeant released him, Gill rubbed his throat. He took a moment to recover and to assemble his thoughts. Until he was completely honest, he realised, he'd never shake off the detectives.

"I was . . . with a couple of friends," he admitted.

"They were both women, weren't they?" said Leeming, thinking of Claire Knight and her daughter. "Is that how you treat your marriage vows?"

"They were both men. You can have their names, if you insist."

"Why haven't you told me about them before?"

"It's not something I care to remember because it was a terrible night for me. We were playing cards into the small hours. I usually do well when I gamble but not this time. I lost more money than I earn in a month and I drank far too much while I was doing it. When I staggered home," said Gill, "I felt ashamed at being so stupid. Why should I play cards and get drunk when

312

had a lovely wife waiting for me at home? I let her down, Sergeant, and I let myself down."

Leeming took out his notebook. "I'd like those two names, sir."

Gareth Llewellyn had stayed to enjoy the congratulations of his friends. As they drifted away, Colbeck stepped in to speak to the Welshman. Llewellyn immediately sent his wife off with the others so that he was alone with the inspector.

"You sang superbly," said Colbeck.

"I always do."

"You won many new friends with 'The Bells of Aberdovey' then promptly lost them with the Welsh national anthem."

"I'm proud of my country, Inspector."

"And so you should be but you misjudged the feelings of the audience. It was a time when patriotism was out of place. However," he went on, "that isn't what I wanted to talk about."

"Are we back to Frank Rodman again?" asked the other, feigning a yawn.

"It's a subject that may bore you, Mr Llewellyn, but it excites me because it gives me the chance to send a killer to the gallows."

"Then you'll have to look elsewhere for him, Inspector."

"I thought I caught a glimpse of him tonight."

Llewellyn's eyebrows shot up. "He was *here*?"

"We knew that he would be. That's why we came."

"So why didn't you arrest him?"

"We want to be absolutely sure that we have the righ man."

"Well, you're wasting your time if you're looking a me."

"On the contrary," said Colbeck, "you're a rewardin subject of study. I watched you during the prayer fo the murder victim. You not only spurned it, you sa there with an expression of joy on your face."

"I was eager to sing my solo."

"It wouldn't have hurt you to spare a thought for M Rodman."

"Why should I want to remember him?" askec Llewellyn, tapping his chest. "I came here to prove hov much better I was at singing than him. He's dead anc gone. They've got me now."

"That's only if you happen to be available."

"Why shouldn't I be?"

Colbeck met his stare. Their silent conversation wen on for minutes. Behind the defiance, the inspector sav something else. It was the quiet conviction that th Welshman was innocent but that he wanted to b arrested in order to embarrass the detectives. For hi part, Llewellyn saw something in Colbeck's eyes tha explained why he'd cornered him. It surprised him a first but he adjusted to the shock and gave a slow grin

"So that's it," he said. "Someone has been talkin about me."

"A lot of people have been doing that, sir."

"Only one person could have told you that I got bacl late to the barracks that night. She'd also have told you that I had blood on my hands. What a certain woma didn't know — because she ran away before I could tell her — was that the blood wasn't mine. Most of it came from the big nose of a man called Samway who tried to ambush me that night. He got in some good punches," said Llewellyn, "but he was no match for me. I left him with bruises all over his body and a bloody nose."

"We've spoken to Hector Samway. Why has he never mentioned a fight?"

"Nobody wants to talk about losing a brawl, Inspector."

"I'll need to confirm your alibi with him."

"Please do so. Would you like me to come with you?"

Llewellyn's grin broadened and Colbeck knew he was telling the truth. At a stroke, the Welshman had removed two names from their list of suspects. Neither Llewellyn nor Samway had killed Rodman. It had to be one of the others.

Grosvenor was so convinced that he'd identified the man behind the kidnap that he stood over the inspector at the Canterbury police station until he'd opened the ledger used for recording criminal convictions. Byard's name was there beside that of his accomplice. Both of them hailed from Rochester but there was only an address for Byard. The accomplice was listed as being of no fixed abode. Armed with the address, Grosvenor and the two constables went straight to the station to catch a train to Rochester. They were going from one beautiful cathedral city to another but darkness prevented them seeing the glories of either place. On the train journey, Grosvenor couldn't resist praising himself and denigrating his companions. Hinton and Legge, he told them, should have adopted his approach and looked for enemies in Edward Tallis's past.

"We couldn't do that, sir," Hinton pointed out. "You packed us straight off to Canterbury. All the records of cases in which he was directly involved were kept at Scotland Yard."

"You should have used your initiative and returned to London."

"Captain Wardlow was putting too much pressure on us, sir. He wouldn't let us leave Canterbury until we found Major Tallis."

"Luckily, I did that job for you."

"We're very grateful. Do you think . . . he's still alive?"

Grosvenor was impassive. "We can but pray that he is."

When they got to Rochester, they asked for the stationmaster's help to locate the address they'd been given. They were warned that the house was in one of the rougher areas of the city and that they needed to keep their wits about them. The three detectives set off through a maze of streets. Though they passed a number of men loitering on corners, they felt in no danger of attack. Even in silhouette, their brisk movement and sense of urgency marked them out as policemen. When they finally reached the house in a street that corkscrewed its way along, they saw that it was little more than a hovel. Candlelight showed that there was someone at home. Anxious to make the arrest himself, Grosvenor made sure that he was at the front

He banged on the door with his fist, setting off an outburst of curses from within the house.

After a few moments, the door was opened by a stooping old man.

"Who are you?" he demanded, peering from one to the other.

"We're detectives from Scotland Yard," said Grosvenor, grandly, "and we've come in search of Sam Byard."

"Well, you won't find him 'ere."

"Why not?"

"I won't 'ave 'im inside this 'ouse ever again," said the old man, savagely. "Sam brought shame on me and my wife. She died cos of it. I've 'ad to live with it. Our son ruined our lives."

"So where is he now?"

"Who cares?"

"This is important, Mr Byard. It could be a matter of life and death."

"Then I 'ope the little bastard dies."

"Please listen to me," said Grosvenor. "I won't waste time going into details. Let me just say that we are very anxious indeed to find your son before he does something terrible. If you have any idea where he might be, please tell us."

The old man shrugged. "I don't know where 'e is."

"Didn't he come back here when he came out of prison?"

"No, 'e wouldn't dare."

"You're his father. You must know something."

"All I can tell you is the rumour I 'eard."

"Go on?"

"Someone said 'e was living with a woman i[n] Faversham."

"Did they say *where*?"

"I didn't ask cos I didn't want to know."

Stepping back into the house, he closed the doo[r] firmly behind him.

On their walk back to the Queen's Tap, all tha[t] Leeming wanted to talk about was the concert. He'[d] been struck by the quality of the band and thought th[e] facilities in the Institution were exceptional. Colbec[k] had to guide him back to the investigation.

"We're working as usual by a process of elimination,[" he said.

"I've certainly eliminated Gill. That will upse[t] Mouldy," he added with a chuckle. "He insisted tha[t] the killer was Daniel Gill."

"I ruled out Llewellyn and Samway in one fe[ll] swoop," said Colbeck. "I wish that that sort of thin[g] happened in every case. Anyway, we're left with Cudli[p] and Alford."

"Cudlip would be my choice because he lives alone.[""]

"So did Hector Samway but he wasn't the killer."

"Alford seems unlikely. He's such a kind man."

"Murder has been committed out of kindness befor[e] now, Victor. Think of the many people we've know[n] who killed family members to end their suffering fro[m] intolerable pain or incurable diseases."

"Rodman wasn't in pain."

"His wife was," said Colbeck, "and Fred Alford kne[w] it. Did you notice what happened during the prayer?[""]

**318**

"Yes, Gill was smirking."

"I was referring to Alford. He got down on his knees and prayed fervently as if he was making a confession. When he got up again, he had a hunted look. He left the concert before we heard 'The Bells of Aberdovey'."

"That wouldn't go down well with Llewellyn."

"What's the evidence against Cudlip?" asked Colbeck. "It's hardly damning. All we know is that he didn't like Rodman and that he was in a violent mood when he went to the brothel."

"He frightened Mrs Knight and her daughter. It would take a lot for anyone to do that, sir. I just don't trust Cudlip."

"Then answer an awkward question. How did he persuade Rodman to go into the Works with him at night?"

"He could have had a gun," replied Leeming.

"Yes, it's the only way he would have got him there."

"The same thing goes for Alford, sir."

"No, it doesn't," said Colbeck. "I've been thinking about that. Alford wouldn't need a gun. Rodman was a friend. He would have gone there with Alford of his own volition. He was then caught unawares."

"But they'd have no reason to go into the Works at night."

"I can think of one, Victor."

"What is it?"

"They were going there to steal something. Didn't that railway policeman tell you that there was pilfering on the site? Perhaps Alford is not as honest as he looks. Both of them could do with extra money," reasoned

Colbeck. "Alford used that fact as a ruse to get his friend to the place where he'd determined to kill him."

"So what are we going to do, sir — challenge Alford?"

"No, I'll take your advice first. Let's call on Simeon Cudlip."

Grosvenor was livid. When they'd left Canterbury, the train had stopped at Faversham before taking them on to Rochester. They now had to retrace their steps to Faversham and that involved a long wait on a windswept railway platform. Sensing his irritation, the two constables remained silent and kept out of his way. The train finally arrived, then set off again in a cloud of steam.

"I've been wondering," said Hinton.

Grosvenor turned on him. "Speak when you're spoken to."

"It's just a thought, sir. If they kidnapped the superintendent in Canterbury, how did they get him to Faversham? They'd hardly risk going on a train."

"They had transport of their own. That's obvious."

"How could Byard afford it?" asked Hinton. "We've seen where he used to live. He'd have no money when he came out of prison and his father doesn't have two pennies to rub together."

"Stop asking inane questions," said Grosvenor, angrily. "Byard would do what any criminal does when he wants something he doesn't have. He'd steal it. All those years behind bars makes a man desperate. He'll stop at nothing."

320

Wishing that he hadn't spoken, Hinton kept his head down and his mouth shut for the rest of the journey. Faversham was as cold and blustery as the other places they'd visited. Since they had no address for Byard, they couldn't rely on a friendly stationmaster for directions this time. They simply asked his Faversham counterpart the way to the police station. When they got there, they were in luck. The duty sergeant, a stout man with a walrus moustache, had a sharp ear and a good memory. He'd overheard someone in a pub saying that Byard had served his sentence and was living with a woman named Alice Fry. After his exploits as a robber, Sam Byard had acquired notoriety in the county. His release from prison had fuelled local gossip.

"Who is this woman?" asked Grosvenor.

"She's an old friend of his," said the duty sergeant.

"Is she a prostitute?"

"No, she runs a stall in the market."

"Have you any idea where she lives?"

"She and her husband used to have a smallholding just outside the town. When he died, Alice started to run it on her own."

"How can we get there?"

"You need a cab, Superintendent."

It took them a matter of minutes to find one. They passed on the instructions they'd been given and the vehicle set off. Like the two other places they had been in that evening, Faversham was a pretty, medieval community with narrow, twisting streets, quaint cottages and impressive public buildings, all of which were now shrouded in darkness. Hinton raised a possibility.

"Byard may be armed, sir."

"His gun was confiscated at the time of arrest."

"He couldn't have abducted the superintendent on his own. He must have had a confederate."

"Then there'll be three of us against two of them," said Grosvenor. "Just follow my example and all will be well."

When the cab left the cobblestones of Faversham, it followed a road to the east then branched off on a dirt track. Already uncomfortable, the three passengers were jiggled up and down and side to side. They were relieved when the cab came to a halt. Obeying orders, the driver had stopped fifty yards or so from the smallholding. It comprised a straggle of old buildings.

The three men approached cautiously. When they got close to the house, the superintendent signalled that Hinton should go around the back of the property to prevent an escape that way. He and Legge gave him time to take up his position before they moved in. The first knock on the door was ignored. When Grosvenor knocked harder, a window opened above them and a woman's head poked out.

"We're trying to sleep," she said, peevishly.

"Mrs Fry?"

"Who's asking?"

"Superintendent Grosvenor. We believe that Sam Byard is living here."

"No, he isn't," she replied, withdrawing her head to speak to someone in the room. When she reappeared, her manner was more respectful. "I'm sorry, sir. Sam left here days ago, sir."

"We'd like to come into the house to verify that fact, Mrs Fry."

"Don't you believe me?"

"Frankly, we don't. We've come all the way from London to find him and we're not going until we do."

"He's not here, I tell you."

"If you can prove that, Mrs Fry, we'll be on our way."

She went back into the bedroom and closed the window behind her. A couple of minutes later, they looked through the downstairs window and saw her carrying a lantern. When she opened the door, she was revealed as a woman of middle years with an old dressing gown wrapped around her body and a nightcap on her head. Moth-eaten slippers were on her feet. She stood back to let them enter the house.

"Can you confirm that Byard has been here?" asked Grosvenor.

"Yes, sir. He didn't stay long."

"Why was that?"

"Sam was going off to stay with friends somewhere. He didn't say who they were or where they lived. He's always been peculiar like that."

"You do realise that sheltering a criminal is an indictable offence."

"He's not a criminal now. He served his sentence."

"Could you put your hand on your heart and say he's not here?"

"Yes," she asserted.

The next moment there was a loud yell from the rear of the house and they heard sounds of a scuffle. Legge immediately ran to see what was happening. In due course, he and Hinton dragged in a skinny, pale-faced man in his thirties with gaunt cheeks and close-cropped hair.

"This is Byard, sir," said Hinton. "He was trying to escape."

"Done nothin'!" howled Byard.

"Then why didn't you stay to speak to us?" asked Grosvenor.

"Don't trust the p'lice."

"We can see that."

"What's he supposed to have done?" asked Alice.

"He knows only too well. At his arrest," said Grosvenor, "he issued threats against my predecessor, Superintendent Tallis of Scotland Yard. On a visit to Canterbury, he was kidnapped. We've come to arrest Byard for orchestrating that kidnap."

Byard was bewildered. "Did nothin' of the kind."

"What have you done with him?"

"Who?"

"Superintendent Tallis."

"Know that name from somewhere," said Byard, frowning. "Can't remember where." He tapped his head. "Bein' locked away does terrible things to your mind."

His confusion was genuine. Hinton was the first to realise it.

"It's not him, sir," he said, letting go of the man.

"It must be," insisted Grosvenor.

"Sam hasn't got the strength to kidnap nobody," argued Alice, going to put an arm around him. "He's as weak as a kitten. It's why I took him in."

"But he swore to get even with the superintendent."

"That was years ago."

"Done nothin' wrong," bleated Byard.

"I believe him, sir," said Hinton. "He tried to escape because he's afraid of the police. When I grabbed him, he didn't put up a real fight. I'm sorry, sir, but you picked the wrong man."

"Can't you see?" asked Alice, holding the lantern up to her friend's face. "He's a sick man. All he wants is for the police to leave him alone."

"That's all," said Byard.

There was an awkward pause as the truth slowly began to sink in.

Somewhere in the gloom, Grosvenor was grinding his teeth in frustration.

# CHAPTER
# TWENTY-THREE

When the detectives turned up to question him, they noticed Cudlip's lack of surprise. He seemed rather pleased to see them as if anticipating with relish another war of words with the pair. Offering them seats, he took care to stay on his feet so that they were not talking down at him. Since the man was Leeming's choice as the killer, Colbeck let the sergeant begin the interview.

"What were you doing at the concert tonight?" asked Leeming.

"Unlike you, I went there to enjoy it."

"That's why *we* went."

"No," said Cudlip, "you spent more time looking around the room than watching what was happening onstage. You believed that Rodman's killer would be in the audience and might somehow give himself away."

"We also wanted to see what sort of musical entertainment people get here in the New Town. It helped us to understand what kind of community this is."

"We get by."

"Everyone else does but you're an outsider, aren't you?"

"That's my choice."

"Why do you look down on these people?"

"Is that what you think I do?"

"Yes, sir, it is. Everybody in that audience tonight looked as if they were at home there. You didn't. You stuck out, as if you were only enduring the concert and couldn't wait to get out. Apart from anything else, you hardly spoke to the people beside you."

"How can you claim to enjoy the entertainment if you were watching me all the time?" asked Cudlip with a knowing smile.

"Let me ask the questions, sir."

"It's a fair point, Sergeant."

"It is," conceded Colbeck, stepping in, "and it's typical of you to raise it. The answer is that it's perfectly possible to enjoy a Mozart overture without gazing at the band. To be honest, the music was just as enjoyable when I *wasn't* looking at them, leaving me free to keep one eye on the audience. Listening to music and watching people like you are not mutually exclusive activities. We did both simultaneously."

"And we saw that you didn't fit in," added Leeming.

"I don't make friends easily," said Cudlip.

"Doesn't that worry you, sir?"

"It's a source of great pleasure. Why should I let people with whom I have nothing in common come into my life?"

"That takes us back to where we started," said Colbeck. "Your principal reason for attending the concert was to sneer at what you perceive as the vulgar tastes of the inhabitants of this village."

"You're probably right," said the other, airily. "It's a trait in me that I share with you."

"Really?"

"Let's be candid, Inspector. You're far more educated than the average policeman. That must be an embarrassment to you at times. You must look with horror at some of the untutored oafs you have to acknowledge as colleagues."

Leeming was indignant. "Are you talking about *me*?"

"If the cap fits . . ."

"I had to work hard to achieve the rank of sergeant."

"Don't let him rile you," advised Colbeck. "It's one of the conversational tricks that Mr Cudlip uses to put people on the defensive. Also, importantly, it deflects attention from him and we're not going to allow that."

"You see?" asked Cudlip, waspishly. "That's a perfect example of your superior intelligence. While the sergeant took my bait, you saw it for what it was and refused to touch it."

"Let's concentrate on the matter in hand, sir. You are a suspect in a murder enquiry. The next time you try to play games with us by demonstrating the misplaced arrogance of a railway clerk, we'll arrange for you to spend the night in a police cell so that you can meditate on your stupidity."

"There was no need for you to bother me again."

"Yes, there was."

"I did not kill Rodman, Inspector. How many times must I say it?"

"You must carry on until you make us believe it."

"The burden of proof is with you, surely?"

"Be warned," said Leeming. "The inspector used to be a barrister. If you want a legal argument, he'll tie you in knots."

Cudlip tried to sound reasonable. "I don't see why you keep harassing me," he said. "It's not as if you have a scintilla of evidence to arrest me."

"There's your behaviour on the night of the murder."

"That was unforgivable," confessed Cudlip.

"You assaulted a prostitute that night. If she wished to press charges against you, it could lead to a conviction."

"Women like that don't get involved with the police because they're breaking the law themselves."

"Is that why you felt free to ravish her?"

"I've told you before. It was a rare lapse."

"You claimed that you were drunk at the time."

"To my shame, I admit it freely."

"Then why didn't Mrs Knight mention it? In her profession, she's used to seeing drunken men turn up on her doorstep. It's often because they'd never have the gall to go there sober."

"Alcohol loosens their inhibitions," added Colbeck. "I don't think it would be needed in your case, sir. You like to be in control at all times and that means keeping a clear head. So, if it wasn't drink that made you behave so badly, what was it?"

"That's my business."

"Can you see how it looks from our point of view?"

"Yes, I can," said Cudlip, "but I'm asking you to see it from mine. I've been working hard for the GWR and leading a life that appeals to me. All of a sudden, I'm a suspect in a murder case on the basis of an anonymous smear and an ill-timed visit to a brothel." He looked from one to the other. "Men are men. Have neither of you ever sought the comfort of a woman like that?"

Leeming was aghast. "I'm a happily married man," he said, "and so is the inspector. We'd never dream of —"

"Don't dignify his question with an answer, Sergeant," said Colbeck, cutting him off. "He's trying to talk his way out of it again."

"There's nothing for me to answer to," said Cudlip with exasperation. "There must surely be more likely suspects than me."

"You're the one who interests us at the moment."

"Why?"

"Because there are religious aspects to the murder," said Colbeck, watching him carefully, "and they suggest the work of an atheist. The killer decapitated his victim and the head turned up in St Mark's Church in grotesque circumstances. It's the work of a diseased mind, sir, and that's why you've come under suspicion."

Cudlip sounded appalled. "I'd never do a thing like that."

"You've poured scorn on organised religion."

"Yes, but only because it's a confidence trick played on the ignorant masses."

"Did you have to kill someone to make that point?"

"I hardly knew Rodman."

"You knew his wife," said Leeming.

"That's all in the past."

"I don't think you'd ever forget a woman like that. For her part, however, I fancy that she was rather glad to forget about you."

Cudlip was vehement. "That's not true."

"Whatever you offered had no appeal for her."

"You've no idea what happened."

"I believe that it soured you for life," said Colbeck.

"You know nothing whatsoever about me."

"We know that Frank Rodman got between you and the woman you doted on."

"Yes, he did," said Cudlip, losing his temper. "She preferred that lumbering ape to someone like me with an appreciation of the finer things in life. Betty was mine by rights. Why couldn't she see that? When I went to that brothel the other night," he continued, eyes glistening, "I didn't go to make love to Euphemia or to that mother of hers. I went there to take possession of a woman I once loved. Betty had to be punished, you see. When she married that dreadful husband of hers, she cast me aside as if I had no claim at all on her affections. It was cruel of her. She'd allowed me to get close to her then rejected me. That rejection has haunted me for years. My love for her has turned to hatred. I had this urge to punish her for condemning me to live the miserable life that I have. On the day before the murder, I'd seen her in the street and she'd looked straight through me as if I meant nothing at all to her. It was humiliating. When I went to that house at night, I pretended that Euphemia was Betty Rodman and she was at my mercy at last. I could make her suffer for all those long years of loneliness I've had because of her cold-heartedness. That's why I deliberately hurt her. I called Betty to account. I didn't need to get drunk to do that. It was *owed* to me."

Madeleine Colbeck had tried to keep herself awake by reading a book but her eyelids were beginning to droop. She fretted at being unaware of what was happening in the two separate investigations. Since her husband was leading the murder inquiry, she should have been thinking about that but it was the other crime that was uppermost in her mind. The disappearance of Edward Tallis had become general knowledge now. There was a report in the day's edition of *The Times*, praising him for his record at Scotland Yard but fearing for his safety. That worried Madeleine. While she knew that Tallis was strong, experienced and resourceful, she also remembered that he was close to her father's age. He was therefore an old man with many of the defects that the passage of time inevitably brought. She pictured her father in the same situation, held prisoner and able to do virtually nothing against younger and more powerful enemies. Having once been held as a hostage herself, she recalled the sense of hopelessness that had threatened to overwhelm her.

She had survived. There was no certainty that Tallis would do the same. The article in the newspaper had made no reference to a ransom note. Nobody was trying to trade the superintendent for money. That was the most frightening aspect of all. The whole event was shrouded in mystery. When, where and how had he been abducted? Why was he the chosen target in the first place? Where was he being held and how was he being treated? How successful was the search and was it bringing any credit to Alan Hinton? If he hadn't been found yet, could anyone realistically believe that Tallis was still alive?

Madeleine wished that Colbeck was in charge of the manhunt, using his experience, marshalling his men and taking decisions based on his instinct for the way that criminals behaved. He'd never forgive himself if he were still fettered to the case in Swindon while Edward Tallis, his old sparring partner, was being killed. It would haunt him beyond measure. Madeleine prayed once again that the superintendent was still alive and that he was not being tortured in any way.

Tallis was in a quandary. Too exhausted to stay awake, he was also in too much pain to fall asleep. It was not for want of trying but, the moment he drifted off, the handcuffs seemed to bite his wrists and the rope around his ankles intensified his cramp. He'd long ago given up any hope of release in return for a ransom. It was clearly not in the minds of the people who'd snatched him in Canterbury and spirited him away. In making him suffer, they'd achieved their objective. In all probability, they were now starving him to death and leaving him to rot in a foul-smelling stable. He could hardly move, let alone consider a means of escape. All he could do was to show some spirit by fighting off the fatigue and maintaining his self-control. Whatever they did to him, he promised himself, he'd face it with courage and defiance. Essentially, he was still a soldier, refusing to plead for mercy with an enemy. They'd never make him submit.

On the way back to Canterbury, the two constables retreated into silence, not wishing to provoke Grosvenor. He, meanwhile, was trying to find an excuse for what had turned out to be a minor disaster. Having sworn to capture the kidnappers, he was returning empty-handed to face Captain Wardlow. By the time they arrived at the police station, he'd been through every possible defence of his actions and found none that was remotely convincing. At the same time, however, there was something in his character that prevented him from admitting failure. Having explained that Sam Byard was not, after all, the man behind the kidnap, he did his best to sound an optimistic note.

"What it proves is that I'm on the right track," he claimed. "Though it may not have been Byard, it was certainly someone like him, a disgruntled prisoner who has nursed a grudge against the superintendent throughout his long incarceration. Byard was the obvious choice. When I do more research at Scotland Yard, I'll have other names."

"And while you're doing that," said Wardlow, sceptically, "my dear friend is in mortal danger with no hope of rescue."

"There *is* hope, Captain. That's what I'm telling you."

"You assured me that you'd unmasked the kidnapper."

"That was an informed guess."

"So what will you give us next — more informed guesses? We don't have time for guesses, Superintendent. Your two constables were struggling but at least they didn't raise my hopes by claiming instant success as you did. I know what Edward Tallis would want at this moment," said Wardlow, "and it is not your blundering. He'd want Inspector Colbeck."

"That's exactly who he'd want," ventured Hinton.

"We need the very best man for the task in hand."

"You *have* him," said Grosvenor, smouldering.

"What I have are three detectives who haven't made an inch of progress between them. I'll be reporting your failure to the commissioner and asking for Colbeck instead."

"He's not available," Hinton reminded him. "Inspector Colbeck is committed to a murder investigation in Wiltshire."

"Yes," said Grosvenor, venting his spleen, "and, because he refused to take my advice, he'll be there for very much longer. When I've solved this crime, as I most certainly will do, I'll go straight to Swindon to bail out the great Inspector Colbeck."

Leeming had been profoundly shocked by Cudlip's confession. Innocent of murder, he had, in the sergeant's opinion, nevertheless committed a revolting crime. He had wanted to arrest the man on the spot but Colbeck told him that they had something more pressing to do. Leaving the house, he led the way down the street.

"We can't let him get away with it, sir," said Leeming.

"We won't."

"What he did was verging on rape."

"Inspector Piercey can deal with that," said Colbeck. "This village is under his aegis. We'll pass on all the details to him but the arrest of a killer is paramount. That's why we came here in the first place."

"Are you convinced that it's Alford?"

"Not entirely, Victor, but he's the last man standing."

"I was so certain that Cudlip was the killer. When we both had a go at him, he was almost demented. Did you see the way his eyes blazed?"

"Yes, I did."

They walked on until they came to Alford's house. In response to their knock, Liza Alford came to the door. They were surprised to see her.

"We thought you'd be looking after Mrs Rodman," said Colbeck.

"She's not there any more. They've moved her to the parsonage."

"That was very kind of the vicar and his wife."

"We could have managed," she said, "but they didn't give us the chance."

"We need to speak to your husband, Mrs Alford."

"Fred's not come back from the concert yet."

"It was over some time ago," said Leeming. "We were there."

"Fred will have gone to the Glue Pot for a drink, I expect. He was very upset when he heard that Betty and the children had been taken away from us by the

**336**

vicar. I told him that we couldn't offer what she'll be given at the parsonage but it was no use. Fred is in one of his moods."

"Does that often happen?"

"My husband is a good, decent man," she said, loyally. "I couldn't ask for a better one."

"But he can be unpredictable," said Colbeck. "Is that what you mean?"

She bit her lip. "Yes, Inspector, it is."

"We're sorry to have disturbed you. Goodnight."

As they walked away, neither of them realised that she stayed on the doorstep, looking after them with an amalgam of concern and foreboding. The detectives went back in the direction of the Glue Pot, the pub to which Alford had obviously returned.

"He doesn't need to drink at the Queen's Tap any more," said Colbeck.

"No, sir," said Leeming. "Alford only went there when Rodman was barred from the Glue Pot. He's gone back to where the beer is supposed to be better."

"Who told you that?"

"Edgar Fellowes, the railway policeman."

"It's a matter of individual taste, Victor."

"I know, sir. At this moment, *my* individual taste is for a pint of beer in either the Glue Pot *or* the Queen's Tap. I don't care which. I'm parched."

"Let's save the drink until we have something to celebrate."

"It's going to come as a fearful blow to Mrs Alford."

"I doubt that somehow," said Colbeck, pensively. "She knows her husband better than anybody."

When they got within reach of the Glue Pot, they heard the unmistakable sound of Welsh voices raised in song. Llewellyn and his friends were celebrating his success at the concert. The detectives entered the pub to the strains of "Clychau Aberdyfi". Seeing no sign of Alford, they asked the landlord if he'd been there that evening and were told that he'd stepped in to have a pint of beer then gone straight out again.

"Fred Alford didn't seem himself tonight," said the landlord.

"What was wrong with him?" asked Colbeck.

"I don't know, sir. He was odd, that's all."

After thanking him, they went back out into the street so that they didn't have to compete with the choir inside the building. Leeming was curious.

"Do you think he's at the Queen's Tap instead?"

"No, Victor."

"Then where on earth, is he?"

Colbeck fell silent for a few moments then a slow smile began to surface.

"I think I know where we'll find him," he said.

Fred Alford was standing outside the parsonage, gazing upwards as he tried to guess in which room Betty Rodman was sleeping. It was colder than ever now but he was impervious to the low temperature and the swirling wind. He felt that he'd been robbed. The death of Frank Rodman had put Betty within reach of him at last but the vicar had intervened to whisk her away to the comfort of the parsonage. There'd be no more opportunities to be alone with her and to enfold her in his arms. With their immediate needs being taken care of, Betty and her children wouldn't need him and his wife to the same degree. The most he could hope for was a glimpse of her in church on Sunday. It was not enough.

Staring obsessively at the upper windows, he didn't hear the footsteps approaching him. All of a sudden, Colbeck and Leeming were standing either side of him. The inspector was excessively polite.

"Good evening, sir. I had a feeling you might be here."

"There's no law against it, is there?" said Alford, bristling.

"None at all — but there is a law against murder."

"Then why don't you find the killer and arrest him?"

"That's what we came to do, sir," said Leeming, a hand on his arm.

Alford was roused. "I didn't murder Frank. He was my friend."

"But he stood between you and Mrs Rodman. You were always more interested in her than in him. Why else are you keeping vigil out here in the cold while she and the children are inside the parsonage?"

"You wouldn't understand."

"In the course of our work," said Colbeck, "we've come to understand a great deal about human nature and we've been intrigued to see the way that people in this village behave. There was no better example of it than at the concert this evening. All five of the suspects we've identified were there — you, included. Each of you behaved in a way that told us a lot about your respective characters."

"Are you telling me that I've been a *suspect* all this time?"

"Your name was put forward by Mr Cudlip."

"Don't listen to that turd!"

"Four of the men on our list have now been removed from it."

"That leaves you," said Leeming, tightening his grip.

"Let go of me," cried Alford, trying to push him away.

"Don't struggle, sir, or I'll have to use handcuffs."

"But you've no reason to arrest me. I love Betty Rodman. I'd do anything for her. Why on earth would I kill her husband and cause her such unbearable pain? The poor woman's life has been ruined. You took me to identify the body, Sergeant. I *saw* what happened to Frank. His head had been sliced clean off. Only a maniac would do something like that. Is that what you think I am?" he asked in disbelief. "Do you honestly think I'm capable of doing that to another human being?"

"We believe that Mrs Rodman was treated badly by her husband," said Colbeck. "Is that true?"

Alford grimaced. "Well, yes, it is."

"Did you ever tackle him about it?"

"Of course I did."

"And did he change as a result?"

"No, Inspector, he didn't. Frank would agree to do something but, the moment he had a drink inside him, he'd forget all about it. In that sense, he could be a bit of a monster. I hated him for it," admitted Alford, "but I didn't want to kill him or leave his corpse in that state. It made me sick just to look at what someone had done to him. All I could think about was how to keep the truth from Betty."

Alford spoke with such passion and sincerity that he jolted them. Colbeck gave a nod and Leeming released his grip on the man. Alford had worshipped Betty Rodman from afar, knowing that she could never be wholly his. The murder had brought the two of them closer for a time but that's all it could achieve. Each of the detectives was forced to accept the same conclusion. Fred Alford was innocent of the crime. Leeming felt acutely embarrassed at their mistake but Colbeck took it in his stride.

"I believe that we owe you an apology, sir," he said, briskly.

Grosvenor was in a panic. After his failure in Canterbury, he'd taken the train back to London and gone straight to Scotland Yard, prepared to work all night in the interests of finding Edward Tallis. If he was to retain his reputation, he had to show his mettle. Otherwise, his hopes of a promotion would wither on the vine. Ensconced in Tallis's chair, he went through the ledger once more, searching for the man most likely to have fulfilled the threats made against the superintendent. There were suspects in abundance. Sam Byard had stood out from the crowd but was clearly in no position to kidnap anyone. In settling too soon on him, Grosvenor had dispensed with his usual caution. He was being much more circumspect this time, determined to find the right name so that he could pursue the individual in the certain knowledge that he'd now identified the kidnapper.

To aid his frenetic search, he opened the box of cigars that he'd bought and took one out. When he'd lit it, he puffed hard and felt his lungs warm and his sagging body revive. He was occupying a seat from which an untold number of crimes had been solved and he was holding a rank that he longed to secure permanently. As he leafed his way through the ledger, his sense of panic began to ebb away and a new vigour coursed through him. However many cigars it took, Grosvenor believed that he would retrieve the situation and gain well-deserved kudos. It would be the ideal way to prove his superiority over Robert Colbeck.

The Queen's Tap had closed for the night but, since they were residents, Colbeck and Leeming were allowed to stay up to finish their drinks. A pint of beer had made the sergeant feel gloomy and he began to wonder if they'd ever solve the murder.

"I said that we had too many suspects," he recalled. "Now we have none at all."

"That's not quite true, Victor."

"One by one, all five of them turned out to be innocent."

"You're forgetting something that *I* said a while ago," remarked Colbeck. "I warned you that the killer might be somebody else altogether. Evidently, he is."

"But we've no clues as to who he might be, sir."

"Oh, I think we do. I've been sitting here and piecing together little bits of information about him. We made the wrong assumption at the very start."

"What do you mean?"

"We didn't look beyond a uniform. Who first identified the body?"

"Edgar Fellowes."

"How did he happen to be on-site at that time of the day?"

"He must have been on the night shift."

"Quite so," said Colbeck. "How was he able to identify a man whose head had been cut off? According to Inspector Piercey, Fellowes told them that he'd recognised the tattoos on Rodman's arms. How could he be so certain? Hundreds and hundreds of men are employed in the Works. The chances are that a number of them will have tattoos of one kind or another. Is it at all likely that Fellowes could pick Rodman out so easily from the others?"

"Well, no, I suppose not."

"There are lots of other indications that point to Fellowes."

"Yet he was so helpful to us, sir."

"That's one of them, Victor. By keeping a close eye on the investigation, he could make sure that he was never in danger. Had he felt that he was, my guess is that he'd have disappeared from Swindon at once."

"But he's a married man with a family."

"That didn't stop him visiting Mrs Knight's house. That gave us an insight into his character. You saw the way he fawned over the vicar at the concert. Few men in his position would be hypocritical enough to do that. They'd be too conscious of their secret vices. Fellowes is not," decided Colbeck. "The most telling point of all is that he has access to the Works twenty-four hours a day. The sight of his uniform keeps suspicion at bay so he can come and go to suit himself. I believe that he used that freedom of movement to inveigle Rodman into going with him to the Erecting Shop."

"How could he possibly do that, sir?"

"We'll have to ask him, won't we?"

"But we don't know where he lives," complained the other.

"We don't need to know. If he's been on the night shift all week, then we know exactly where to find him. For the sake of appearances, he came to the concert with his wife but she'll be back at home now. Fellowes will have changed into his uniform and is patrolling the site somewhere."

Leeming needed time to absorb what he'd just been told.

"I think you're right, sir," he acknowledged. "Fellowes kept pointing us in the wrong direction. At the very start, he was the one who told me that Llewellyn was the most likely killer."

"He diverted your gaze," said Colbeck.

"Nothing is more despicable than a crooked policeman."

"He betrayed his uniform, Victor."

"And he certainly fooled me in the process," said Leeming. "I was taken in by that helpful manner of his when, all the time, the only person he was really helping was himself." Doubts lingered. Are you certain it was him, sir? "We don't want to arrest the wrong man again, sir."

"We're not going to, Victor."

"I felt dreadful when we pounced on Alford."

"You won't have that feeling this time. You'll have the deep satisfaction of knowing that you're making a vile criminal pay for what he did. Think of Rodman's mutilated body. That was the work of Edgar Fellowes," warned Colbeck. "We're dealing with a very twisted and violent man."

Edgar Fellowes had come to like the night shift. He was paid extra money and had nobody to monitor what he was doing. During the day, he was always visible to someone or other. In the darkness of night, he was invisible. Though it was freezing outside, the site was a more tempting place to be than in the arctic coldness of his wife's bed. To his mind, her indifference towards him had justified his decision to look for pleasure elsewhere, given freely in return for his promise not to report the location of the brothel. Fellowes was enjoying a deeper pleasure now. As he walked into the Erecting Shop, lantern in hand, he was celebrating the fact that he'd got the better of the famous Railway Detective. Having tricked both Colbeck and Leeming, he felt that he was completely safe. The murder would remain unsolved.

Reaching the spot where he'd killed Frank Rodman, he spat on the floor then grinned in triumph. He had no remorse whatsoever. His victim deserved everything that had happened to him. Fellowes spent minutes reliving the moments when he'd ended the life of his enemy. The sound of footsteps brought him out of his reverie and he turned round to see the fuzzy outline of a tall figure striding towards him. Only when the man got close did he realise that it was Colbeck. It made him step back in alarm.

"I'm glad to have found you at last," said the inspector, calmly. "I've been searching everywhere for you. You're very elusive." He was close enough to see the dismay on the other man's face.

"What are you doing here?" asked Fellowes, anxiously.

"Do I really need to answer that question?"

"You shouldn't even be on-site, Inspector. You're trespassing."

Colbeck smiled. "Then perhaps you should try to arrest me."

But Fellowes was not really listening. Mind aflame, he was looking for a means of escape. He hadn't managed to deceive Colbeck, after all. The inspector had finally seen through the battery of defences behind which Fellowes had been hiding.

"It's all over," said Colbeck, quietly. "You'll have to come with me."

"Stand back," ordered Fellowes, raising his lantern to use as a weapon, "or I'll dash your brains out."

"At least explain why you killed Rodman. I'm interested to hear that."

"Frank Rodman was loathsome. I had to get rid of him once and for all."

"Did he have some kind of a hold over you?"

"Yes, he did and he made me suffer a great deal as a result. Rodman knew how to torment a man. He . . . found out something about me."

"I think I can guess what it is."

"The sergeant no doubt told you."

"Yes, he did."

"Rodman happened to see me coming out of that house one night and he made it tell. That bastard was blackmailing me, Inspector. He was extorting money from me week by week. It's the reason I volunteered for the night shift. I needed the extra money to pay that bloodsucker."

"How did you get him to come in here with you?"

"That was easy," said Fellowes, contemptuously. "I dangled even more money in front of him. I told him how we could steal various items from the Works then sell them at a profit. He couldn't resist the temptation."

"And I daresay he was fairly drunk when you actually came in here."

"He was drunk, deranged and completely off guard. I'd concealed a cleaver in here on the previous night. All I had to do was to knock him out then hack off his head."

"Did you have to strip him naked?"

"It was his turn to be humiliated," said Fellowes. "I'd been the butt of his sneers for weeks on end. He taunted me about my wife and boasted that he was married to the prettiest woman in the village. He was cruel, Inspector."

"In terms of cruelty, I don't think he'd hold a candle to you," said Colbeck, moving closer. He held out his hand. "Give me that lantern, please."

"Keep away!" shouted Fellowes.

"The game is up."

"You're not even armed."

"I don't need to be. I can overpower you with ease. Unlike your victim, I'm neither drunk nor deranged, you see. I've come here to place you under arrest and that's what I intend to do."

Backing away, Fellowes hurled the lantern at him then ran off. Because he ducked quickly, all that Colbeck lost was his top hat. He retrieved it at once then picked up the lantern. Fellowes, meanwhile, was sprinting towards the main exit, confident that he'd got away. He knew every inch of the Works whereas Colbeck would have to grope his way around. There was no danger of his being overtaken. Then someone came out of the darkness to dive straight at him and knock him to the ground, jarring his whole body and taking all the breath out of him. Leeming turned him over in a flash and handcuffed him expertly. When he got up, the sergeant grabbed him by the collar and hauled him to his feet. Illuminating the scene with the lantern, Colbeck strolled up to them.

"My apologies," he said, breezily. "When I said that I was unarmed, I forgot to tell you that I'd brought Sergeant Leeming with me. He's a weapon in himself."

"How could you do it?" asked the sergeant, shaking his prisoner. "How could you put a severed head on the altar in St Mark's Church then chat to the vicar at the concert as if you were a true Christian?"

"I detest the man and all he stands for," snarled Fellowes.

"And what do *you* stand for?"

"I stand for freedom. I wanted to shock this place into life for once. Shifts, rotas, duties — every day is the same if you work for the GWR. We live in the same houses, work in the same places and all move at the same slow, boring, uneventful pace. We're like so many rabbits, retiring obediently to our hutches every night before getting up to do exactly the same thing the next day. And that's how it goes on without the slightest change. Frank Rodman gave me the chance to shake this village to its foundations," said Fellowes, unrepentant, "and so I did. Killing him made me feel very, very good."

"Then you have a distorted view of your fellow human beings," said Colbeck. "If the only way for you to feel very, very good is to make everyone else feel very, very bad then you've no place in society."

"Being in this particular society is like wearing a straitjacket."

"You'll be able to take it off now."

"I did pull the wool over your eyes, though, didn't I?" said Fellowes, laughing wildly. "You have to admit that."

"All you did was to delay the inevitable," said Colbeck. "Fortunately, the public hangman is a patient man. He was quite content to wait for you until you were ready to come." He pointed a finger. "Let's go,

Sergeant. We can't bring Mr Rodman back to life again but his wife will be pleased to know that we've arrested his killer. It will bring her a small measure of relief."

# CHAPTER
# TWENTY-FOUR

No matter how many times he tried, Alan Hinton was unable to persuade Captain Wardlow to go home to a warm house and a soft bed. The older man insisted on staying at the police station in Canterbury even though it meant sitting on an upright chair in a draughty room.

"Go back home," pleaded Hinton. "There's nothing you can do here."

"I'm staying until Major Tallis is found."

"That might be days away."

"I'll wait here as long as it takes."

Wardlow brought up a palm to conceal a yawn. He was plainly fatigued and had come close to dozing off a number of times, but his friendship with Tallis somehow made him find extra reserves of stamina. Hinton couldn't bear to see the pain etched into his features.

"The inspector said that we could use that empty cell," he said.

Wardlow was insulted. "I'm not going to be locked up like a prisoner," he declared. "I mean to remain here, fully awake. Any discomfort I suffer pales beside what the major is probably going through."

"But there's a bed and blankets in there, sir. You could lie down."

"That's not a bed, Constable. It's a bare, wooden board and it's usually occupied, I daresay, by some drunkard they've hauled in from the streets. If you're getting tired, you try sleeping in there."

"Mr Grosvenor told me to stay up until he returned."

"*If* he returns," muttered Wardlow.

"I'm sure that he will, sir."

"Well, I pray he doesn't start us off on another wild goose chase. It was unkind of him to raise our hopes like that."

"He hasn't been in charge of anything like this before," said Hinton, tactfully, "but he's a very experienced detective. In looking at cases in which Superintendent Tallis was once involved, I believe he was doing the right thing. He just happened to settle on the wrong name."

"What guarantee do we have that he'll ever stumble on to the right one?"

"I have faith in him, sir."

"Mine is rapidly disappearing."

His eyelids fluttered and he nodded off. Hinton was afraid that he'd fall off the chair altogether. Wardlow's head dropped on to his chest. His body sagged and he began to wheeze. Without any warning, he then started to keel over. Hinton was just in time to catch him before he hit the floor.

"Let go of me!" cried the older man, testily.

"You fell asleep, sir."

"I did nothing of the kind. I was merely resting my eyes."

"Then I apologise."

Easing him back up into a sitting position, Hinton retired to the other chair. The pair of them retreated into a cold silence. Wardlow was willing himself to stay awake while Hinton was going over the details of the case once again.

"There is an alternative explanation," he said, eventually.

Wardlow blinked his eyes. "What do you say?"

"Perhaps we are looking in the wrong place."

"That's self-evident."

"Superintendent Grosvenor is convinced that we're after a criminal with a vengeful nature and there's sound reasoning for that. Couldn't he also be from Superintendent Tallis's more distant past?"

"What do you mean?"

"The kidnapper could have once been in the army."

"That's arrant nonsense!" snapped Wardlow.

"How do you know?"

"It's because Major Tallis had an impeccable military record. The men held him in the highest esteem because they knew he never made mistakes. He'd never lead them into an ambush or take them unprepared into a skirmish. Our old colonel, Aubrey Tarleton, used to say that the major cared too much for his men. I consider that to be an admirable trait in his character."

Hinton was amazed. He'd had little direct contact with Tallis but, on the occasions when they had met, he'd always found the man abrasive. He made a mental note to tell his colleagues that, during his years in the army, Tallis was known for consideration towards the lower ranks. There'd be howls of incredulity.

"Did you serve in India with him?" asked Hinton.

"We served *everywhere* together. Our careers ran in parallel."

"I see."

"That's why I know that it's futile to look through his army career. The person — or persons — we're after belongs to the major's life as a detective. Damnation!" he exclaimed, using his stick to hit the floor several times. "Where *is* Grosvenor? He's been gone for hours."

"He's tied to the railway timetable, sir. What is certain is that he'll never give up. He'll find the name we need if it takes him all night."

Going through the records by the light of the oil lamp, Grosvenor was enveloped by the fug created by the cigars he'd been smoking. He had found two more former prisoners who'd vowed to punish Tallis when they were released. The problem was that neither of them had any connection with Canterbury. It had to be someone who came from, or near, the city. He was certain of that because he'd found a cutting from the local newspaper in the desk drawer. It contained a long article about Tallis's military career and explained why he would be given a special award at the forthcoming reunion. It was impossible not to be impressed by his achievements. His work at Scotland Yard was also praised. The most significant piece of information was in the concluding sentence.

*Our thanks are due to Captain R. D. H. Wardlow from Lower Hardres, who provided us with the foregoing detail and who is looking forward to meeting his old friend once more.*

Grosvenor felt the thrill of discovery. That was it. He now knew how the kidnapper had found out about Tallis's visit to the reunion and guessed that he was likely to stay beforehand with Wardlow. The pair of them had probably been kept under surveillance. If it was not by Sam Byard, by whom had it been?

He stared down at the two names and noticed a telling detail. Though he hailed from Derby, one of them, Nathan Ringer, had recently been released from Maidstone Prison. If he'd stayed in the area, he'd most certainly have been able to read the local press. Having spent his sentence plotting his revenge against Tallis, he might suddenly have found that the man was coming within reach at long last and seized the chance to strike.

Closing the ledger, Grosvenor got to his feet with the conviction that he'd discovered the right culprit this time. Nathan Ringer had been released after a long sentence. He'd had years of toil, misery and isolation to keep his anger bubbling away under the surface. Evidently, it had now been given full vent.

Having arrested, charged and taken Edgar Fellowes to the police station in the Old Town, the detectives waited until he'd been safely locked away then went straight to Inspector Piercey's house. Annoyed at first to be roused from his bed, Piercey was delighted to hear that the case had been solved and to receive the evidence on which he could arrest Simeon Cudlip. In order to do that, he'd have to close down Claire Knight's brothel yet again but, having done it before, he knew that it would soon reappear elsewhere. Like Colbeck, he believed that even prostitutes deserved the protection of the law and should not have to submit to sexual violence from crazed clients. Since the detectives were anxious to leave the town, it meant that the inspector was back in charge once more and that pleased him more than anything.

On the train back to London, Colbeck and Leeming were able to put one case aside for the time being and concentrate on the disappearance of Edward Tallis.

"Where is he?" asked the sergeant.

"I don't know where he is, Victor, but I know where he *should* be and that's among his army friends, receiving their congratulations and reminiscing about old times. From what I hear," said Colbeck, "reunions of this kind are virtual feasts. Wine and spirits flow very freely."

"I'd settle for a pint of beer and a meat pie, sir."

"You'll have to wait."

"What if Mouldy Grosvenor has already found him?"

"Then I'll be the first to shake his hand. Yet somehow I fancy that he's had no success so far," said Colbeck. "Had he rescued the superintendent, he'd have sent me a telegraph instantly to boast about his achievement."

"Are we going to Scotland Yard first?"

"There's no point. The search is being controlled from Canterbury."

"Mouldy may not be very pleased to see us."

"We're not going directly to him."

"Then where *are* we heading?"

"We'll take a train to Ashford," said Colbeck, "then take the branch line to Hastings. That will enable us to get off at Hythe."

"Why are we going there?" asked Leeming.

"It's where the barracks are situated. Members of his old regiment have been helping in the search so they'll know if there's been any development."

"But it will probably be midnight by the time we get there, sir."

Colbeck laughed. "This is a reunion dinner, Victor," he said. "They'll be drinking until dawn."

In the event, it was impossible for Captain Wardlow to stay awake. With his walking stick still in his hand, he faded off into a light sleep and, miraculously, stayed upright in the chair this time. All that Hinton had to do was to fight off fatigue so that he could keep a close eye on him. Darkness had brought the hunt to a stop but neither man dared to leave what had become the temporary headquarters of the search. The only refreshments on offer were cups of tea and slices of rock-hard cheese. As he looked at his sleeping companion, Hinton was glad that he'd defied his childhood ambition of becoming a soldier and joined the police instead. In spite of what the captain had said about Tallis's exemplary record in the army, Hinton would have hated serving under him. Whenever he'd aroused his wrath, he could always retire to the pub at the end of his shift and moan to the other constables. In the army, he'd never have been off duty and would certainly not have the relative freedom he currently enjoyed.

Though he knew that his mind should be focussed entirely on the search, his thoughts kept drifting to Lydia Quayle. Since she'd come into his life, she'd brought a pleasure he'd never enjoyed before. There was an unspoken affection between them that made even the briefest of meetings with her occasions of joy. Hinton wished that he could engineer such encounters without appearing to be too forward but he lacked the skill to do so. There was also the barrier of social inequality. Lydia inhabited a wholly different world and he could never hope to enter it. At the same time, she'd given him what he felt were clear indications that she wanted their friendship to develop. Exactly how that would happen, however, he was at a loss to understand.

Warm thoughts of Lydia made him feel pleasantly drowsy and he longed to fall asleep and meet her once again in his dreams. But the sound of raised voices jerked him fully awake. He stood up as Grosvenor came into the room but Captain Wardlow remained asleep. Grosvenor wanted a full audience for his announcement so he shook the old man unceremoniously by the shoulder.

358

"What's up?" said Wardlow, eyes struggling to open. "Is there news? Have we found him yet? What's happened?"

"I know who the villain is," asserted Grosvenor.

"You said that once before," Hinton reminded him.

"This time, there's no mistake. The man was recently let out of Maidstone Prison so we can be certain he's in the county. He knew that the superintendent would be coming here because I found a cutting from the local newspaper with details about the reunion."

"*I* sent that cutting to the major," said Wardlow, guiltily. "To some extent, I'm responsible for what happened. My name was mentioned, you see. Anyone reading the article would assume that Major Tallis would stay with me beforehand."

"That's exactly what Nathan Ringer did," said Grosvenor.

"How do you know?" asked Hinton.

"It's blindingly obvious, man."

"Not necessarily, sir. Many prisoners are illiterate. They certainly don't read newspapers. What sort of a person was Ringer?"

"He was an expert forger so he was clearly educated. As well as counterfeit, he was convicted of obtaining money by false pretences from wealthy widows, and there were other crimes that could be laid at his door — hence the long sentence."

"Why didn't you pick this individual out earlier?" said Wardlow.

"It was because he came originally from Derby and had no apparent connection with Kent. Sam Byard, by contrast, was a Kentish man."

"That depends on which side of the Medway he was born. If he hails from north of the river, like me, he'd be a Man of Kent. To be a Kentish man, he'd have to come from the south side."

"Let's not be pedantic, Captain."

"I'm still not convinced about this new name you've plucked out of the air,"

"That's because you haven't studied Ringer's case in the way that I did."

"Prison can have a profound effect on someone, sir." Hinton said to him. "It can either break a man's spirit, as it seems to have done in the case of Sam Byard, or it can send a prisoner out into the world, seething with resentment."

"Ringer belongs to the latter category."

"Did his sentence involve hard labour, sir?"

"Yes, it did."

"That can sour a man for life."

"Well," said Wardlow, grudgingly, "you seem to have found the right man at last — and not before time. I suppose I should commend you for that."

"Byard was a man of limited intelligence and low cunning, the kind of criminal that exists in large numbers in the slums of London. Ringer is from a different class of offender. He'll want to get even with the people who caught him in the first place."

"That will be Inspector Colbeck and the superintendent," said Hinton. "Does he have designs on the inspector as well?"

"That's irrelevant, Constable."

"How do we track this man down?" asked Wardlow.

"The first move is to visit Maidstone Prison itself. I'll take on that task," said Grosvenor. "They'll know the details of his discharge and may be able to provide an address for him. Having looked after the man for so long, they can also tell me about his behaviour while he was locked away there."

"Did you learn anything about this fellow's character during your researches?"

"I learnt one thing, Captain. Nathan Ringer has a mean streak. He'll want to make the superintendent suffer."

Tallis had no concept of time. Was it day or night? How long had he been there? Had Christmas come and gone? There was a more immediate question. How much longer could he survive? His limbs seemed to take it in turns to go into spasm or to lose all feeling. The only relief he could get was by shifting his position and rubbing the dead arm or the twitching leg against the stall. For the rest, it was a case of progressive agony. Just when he thought the pain was at its worst, the intensity would increase even more. He was being stretched on the rack of someone's malevolence until his joints were pulled irresistibly apart.

As predicted by Leeming, it was midnight before they finally reached the barracks in Hythe. Because they'd turned up at such an hour, it took them some time to persuade the sentries that they were there on legitimate police business. They were conducted to a room near the officers' mess where the reunion was taking place.

Sounds of jollity and drunken laughter percolated through to them. Celebrations were clearly still in full swing. They had a long wait before Captain Ardingley agreed to see them. Irritated at being dragged away from the reunion dinner, he was curt during the introductions.

"What, in God's name, do you mean by coming here at this ungodly hour to ask the same question that that young constable put to me?"

"Who was that?" asked Colbeck. "Constable Hinton or Constable Legge?"

"Hinton, I think. I sent him packing."

"Why was that, Captain?"

"He dared to suggest that private correspondence I'd received had somehow been read by people plotting to kidnap Major Tallis."

"That was enterprising of him in my view. But we come with a very different question. Before I put it to you, can you please confirm that Superintendent Tallis, as we know him, is still missing?"

"Unhappily, he is, Inspector."

"Then let me tell you what's brought us here."

"It's uncanny," said Leeming, staring at the captain. "Did you realise how much you resemble him? When you first walked in, I thought for a moment you were Edward Tallis."

"The resemblance is very faint," said Ardingley, dismissively.

"Did you serve with him?"

"Yes, I did and I was proud to do so. The major was an inspiring soldier."

362

"We, too, have profited from his inspiration," said Colbeck. "I'm glad to find something at last on which we can agree. The army moulded him and this regiment has remained an important part of his life."

Ardingley slowly mellowed. Looking resplendent in his dress uniform, he listened intently as Colbeck explained his reasoning. Because Tallis would only have been in Kent in order to attend the reunion, he believed that the kidnap might have some link with the regiment.

"That's a foul calumny!" said Ardingley, roused once more.

"I'm not saying for a moment that anyone here is in any way involved," said Colbeck, "merely that the roots of this crime may lie in the major's military past."

"I don't follow, Inspector."

"If you served with him for many years, you'll have known Major Tallis well."

"I revered the man."

Leeming was about to say that the captain even made an effort to look like Tallis but he thought better of it and held his peace. Colbeck developed his theory at length and gradually won Ardingley over.

"It's fortunate that you were brought to my office," said the captain, smiling.

"Why is that, sir?" asked Leeming.

"I know where the drink is hidden."

Ardingley unlocked the bottom drawer of his desk and took out three glasses and a bottle of brandy. Having poured a generous measure into every glass, he passed one each to his visitors then raised his in a toast.

"Let's drink to the safe return of Major Tallis!"

Colbeck and Leeming echoed the toast then took a grateful sip of their drinks.

"I owe you an apology, Inspector," said Ardingley, waving them to chairs and sitting down himself. "It was only when you were talking just now that I remembered where I'd heard your name before. You led the investigation into that tragic business of Aubrey Tarleton's suicide. He'd been the colonel of this regiment when I joined the army and we were sad to see him retire to Yorkshire. Then came the news of his death," he added, shaking his head. "Major Tallis wrote to me at the time to heap praise on the way that a certain Inspector Colbeck had handled the investigation."

"He didn't heap praise on us," grumbled Leeming.

"Solving the mystery behind the suicide was a reward in itself," said Colbeck. "It was a case that was very dear to the superintendent's heart."

"It was dear to all our hearts," said Ardingley.

Tarleton's suicide had come as a great shock to those who knew him. He'd walked along a railway track in the path of an oncoming train and was killed instantly, Tallis's emotional reaction had been a hindrance to the inquiry and it was only when Colbeck and Leeming were left alone that they were able to take the investigation to its conclusion.

"To return to the present situation," said Colbeck, "it was tempting to believe that Superintendent Tallis was abducted by a criminal he was instrumental in catching and convicting."

"That's the theory on which the search has been operating," said Ardingley. "His replacement, a fellow named Grosvenor, claimed to have discovered the culprit and went off to arrest him."

"Can you recall who it was, sir?"

"Byard — that was it. Sam Byard."

"I remember the case well. He robbed people on trains. The superintendent and I arrested him and his accomplice."

"Well, I heard from one of the soldiers deputed to help in the manhunt that Byard was not the man behind the major's kidnap. It was another failure for Scotland Yard. I have to say that I've not been impressed by the men sent to take charge of this case — though I excuse Constable Hinton. You were right about him, Inspector. At least he sought a connection between the army and the crime."

"What we need from you, Captain, is the name of a military Sam Byard."

"Soldiers don't rob people on trains."

"Perhaps not," said Colbeck, "but they do get into trouble and take umbrage at the way they've been treated by their superior officers. Can you think of any person who might have been severely disciplined by Major Tallis, as he was at the time, and who nursed a grievance thereafter?"

"I'm not sure that I can," admitted Ardingley. "The major was known as a fair-minded man. It explained his popularity with the lower ranks. Let me think for a few moments." He put his glass aside. "As you'll appreciate, my brain is rather clouded . . ."

When he'd been promoted, Grosvenor didn't expect that he'd be called upon to travel through the night to Maidstone Prison and have to pound on the door for minutes before it was finally opened. The governor's house was inside the precincts and he was tucked up snugly in his bed but, fortunately, his deputy was on duty and he saw at once the need for urgency. He took the newcomer to the office where the prison records were kept.

"What was the name?" he asked.

"Nathan Ringer."

"I don't remember him offhand. That means he behaved himself while he was with us. The ones who stay in the mind are the rebels or those who try to escape."

"Ringer was released only weeks ago."

"Then we'll soon find him."

The deputy governor was a tall, straight-backed man with a manner that suggested a military background. Opening a ledger, he used a finger to work his way down a list of names.

"Here he is," he said. "Nathan Isaac Ringer. It's strange how many deep-dyed villains have biblical names."

"What do your records say about him?"

"He seems to have caused us no trouble while he was here."

"Do you have any idea where he went when he left?"

"Oh yes, we always ask for an address before they depart."

"And what address did Ringer give?"

"He went from here to Stelling Minnis. He was going to stay at a pub there."

"Where is this place?"

"It's not far from Canterbury."

Leeming could not believe the captain's powers of recall. Ardingley was a human history of the regiment. While the sergeant was feeling dizzy after a glass of brandy, a man who'd been drinking all evening was thinking and talking with exceptional clarity. The captain couldn't remember anyone who'd shown outright hatred of Tallis but he was reminded of an incident that he thought might be relevant.

"It was during our time in India," he said. "The intense heat and the ever-present danger took its toll on all of us. Drunkenness was a constant problem and not just in our regiment. It was endemic in the British army and always has been. The case I'm thinking of concerns a man called Joseph Stagg."

"Who was he?"

"He'd joined the army young and seemed to take to the life at first. Then we were moved to India and he became something of a troublemaker. The major always said that he was more sinned against than sinning. Some of us disagreed with that assessment of Stagg. I thought that there was always a whiff of insubordination about him."

"What happened to Stagg?" asked Colbeck.

"He went too far one day," said Ardingley. "He broke into the stores and got uncontrollably drunk. When a lieutenant tried to arrest him, Stagg fought back and got the upper hand. If he hadn't been overpowered by two guards, there might have been a terrible outcome."

"Was he charged with attempted murder?"

"Yes, Inspector, and he was sentenced to three hundred lashes."

"That would have killed him!" exclaimed Leeming.

"Luckily for him," said Ardingley, "the major interceded on his behalf. He went to the colonel and pointed out instances where Stagg's behaviour reflected well on him. The man had shown heroism in the field and made light of the injuries he'd received there."

"How did Colonel Tarleton respond to that?"

"He heeded the plea because the major was very persuasive. As a result, the sentence was reduced from three to two hundred lashes. Stagg was quite unaware of what had happened. Because he'd been hauled up initially in front of Major Tallis, he actually blamed him for the punishment he received."

"Two hundred lashes," said Leeming, ruefully. "That's cruel."

"Flogging is essential in the army, Sergeant. It's quick, effective and, because it's in front of the whole regiment, it sends a signal to everyone else that discipline must be maintained. Importantly, it means that we retain an able soldier who will recover to take his place alongside the others. As for the number of lashes," said Ardingley, "Stagg would probably have passed out halfway through the flogging. The provost marshal had a very strong arm. When he wielded the cat-o'-nine-tails, every stroke told."

"Why did nobody tell Stagg that Major Tallis had actually helped him?"

"That was a private matter between the major and the colonel."

Colbeck saw the paradox at once. The person who'd intervened to reduce the man's sentence had, unjustly, been identified as being responsible for it. Because he was unaware of it, Tallis's act of kindness counted for nothing in Joseph Stagg's mind. Two hundred lashes would leave injuries that would take a very long time to heal and the mental wounds would never entirely disappear. Whenever he thought about the major, Colbeck decided, Stagg would feel something cutting into his naked back with vicious force.

"What happened to the man?" he asked. "Did he stay in the army?"

"Yes, he did. Stagg was discharged earlier this year."

"Have you any idea what happened to him?"

"I should imagine that he went back to the family farm."

"And where might that be?"

"It's down here in Kent. When he joined the army, Stagg chose the regiment whose barracks were closest to his home. He's a local lad."

Maidstone Prison was an unlikely place in which to have an early breakfast but that was what Grosvenor did. Anxious to confirm that he had the right man this time, he asked to speak to someone who knew Nathan Ringer better than the deputy governor. One of the older warders, a man with a face of granite and a gravelly voice, was called in to talk about the former prisoner. It transpired that Ringer had been surly at first but had quickly adapted to the demands of prison life and caused no serious problems. Thanks to the interest the prison chaplain had taken in him, he'd appeared to have some sort of religious conversion. The warder was cynical.

"The chaplain was taken in by him," said the warder, "but I've seen people like Ringer before. They'll do and say anything to get some small advantage. I never trusted him. Just because he had his head in a Bible, it didn't mean that he was reading it."

"What sort of mood would he have been in when he left here?"

"Every prisoner is glad to walk free at last, Superintendent."

"Had incarceration changed him in any way?"

"I don't think so. Deep down, he probably hated the lot of us."

"Would he feel embittered at the people who actually put him in prison?"

"Oh, yes, he'd never forgive them."

Grosvenor gave his sly smile. He'd been told exactly what he'd hoped to hear.

While he was tempted to return to Canterbury to collect Hinton and Legge, he saw an opportunity to keep all the glory to himself. If he arrested Ringer on his own, he'd get unstinting praise from the commissioner and, in the event of Tallis's death, he would almost certainly take his place. In effect, the decision was made for him. He had no qualms about

370

meeting resistance even if he had to take on two men. As a precaution, he'd brought a loaded weapon with him as well as two sets of handcuffs. Hinton and Legge wouldn't even know about the arrest until the superintendent delivered Ringer, with or without his accomplice, to the police station.

Having taken advice on how best to reach Stelling Minnis, he left the prison and made his way to the railway station. Since there was no direct line to Canterbury, he had to change trains on the way to get there, thereby creating a delay and making him irritable. As soon as he reached his destination, he hired a cab to take him to a village which was only six or seven miles away. After the speed of the railway, he was forced into a slower mode of travel. It gave him time to review his decision that Nathan Ringer simply had to be the culprit. At first glance, Sam Byard had seemed the more likely kidnapper but that had been an illusion. Ringer had the intelligence to set up an ambush for Edward Tallis when he read in the local newspaper about the superintendent's arrival in the area. Circumstantial evidence was strong. There was an added incentive for Grosvenor. In arresting Nathan Ringer, he would be obliterating the embarrassment of his earlier mistake in going after Byard.

To get to Stelling Minnis, the cab driver took the more direct route along Stone Street, a Roman road which, for the most part, was ramrod straight. It involved a long climb up a steep hill but it saved Grosvenor from a serpentine route through Lower Hardres, home of Captain Wardlow, Upper Hardres and Bossingham. When they reached Stelling Minnis, he had a stroke of good fortune. Though it was only a little after six o'clock, a delivery of beer was being unloaded from a wagon outside the Rose and Crown. There was enough light from the lanterns on the wagon and on the pub itself for him to see the two people heaving the crates into the building. One of them looked very much like the man described to him as Nathan Ringer. Unlike Byard, enfeebled by his time in prison, Ringer appeared to be fit and active. He'd certainly have had the strength to take part in a kidnap.

Grosvenor got out of the cab and watched from the shadows with rising excitement. This was his moment.

Having watched Captain Wardlow until he'd fallen asleep again, Hinton had himself dozed off and was snoring gently. Both men were rudely awakened when the door opened and Colbeck entered with a bleary-eyed Leeming at his heels.

"What are *you* doing here, sir?" asked Hinton in amazement. "I thought you were in Swindon."

"That assignment is happily at an end," said Colbeck, "so we can lend our assistance here. We were hoping to report to Superintendent Grosvenor."

"He's gone to Maidstone Prison."

"That's the best place for him," murmured Leeming, mutinously. His voice rose. "How long is his sentence?"

Hinton explained why the superintendent had gone there and Wardlow, still half-asleep, confirmed that the man behind the kidnap had finally been identified. It only remained to find his whereabouts. Colbeck was unconvinced. Having been there at the time of Nathan Ringer's arrest and trial, he felt he knew the man far better than Grosvenor.

"I can't believe that Ringer was implicated," he said.

"But the superintendent is certain that it's him," said Hinton.

"What do *you* think, Constable?"

"I'm not . . . quite so sure, sir."

"I was dubious at first," admitted Wardlow, "but he persuaded me in the end. Please don't tell me that it's another hideous mistake."

"We think we've found the real villain," said Leeming, "and we did it by visiting the barracks in Hythe."

"Yes," added Colbeck. "We spoke to Captain Ardingley." He turned to Wardlow. "He sent his warmest regards, sir."

The captain's head drooped. "Major Tallis and I should have spent last evening in Ardingley's company," he said, dejectedly, "drinking our fill and toasting the regiment. Such an opportunity may never arise again."

"We went to Hythe because I felt that the solution to this puzzle lay in the superintendent's military past rather than among criminals he might have arrested."

"I thought that as well, sir," Hinton interjected.

"And I dismissed the idea as nonsense," said Wardlow, huffily.

"Then you were wrong," Colbeck told him. "With the invaluable help of Captain Ardingley, we settled on a former soldier named Joseph Stagg."

"That name sounds vaguely familiar."

"He was flogged for attempted murder, sir. Apparently, Major Tallis got his sentence reduced by a hundred lashes but he never even thanked him because he didn't know there'd been a plea for mercy on his behalf. Mistakenly, he believed that the major was the man who'd imposed the sentence in the first place."

"I remember the incident now," said Wardlow. "It occurred in India."

"That's right." Colbeck glanced down at the map of Kent still open on the table. "We'll borrow this, if we may. It will help us to find Stagg."

"Where is he?"

"Hopefully, he'll be on the family farm. It's somewhere off the Dover Road."

Wardlow struggled to get up. "I'll go with you."

"No, sir," said Leeming, easing him gently back down on to his chair. "There could be violence. You stay here and leave it to us."

"Am I to come with you?" asked Hinton, hopefully.

"Yes," said Colbeck. "An extra pair of hands is always useful." He opened the door then turned back. "Goodbye, Captain. Please give the superintendent our regards."

"What do I tell him?" asked Wardlow.

"Advise him to work on his excuse for a second wrongful arrest."

Grosvenor waited until they'd finished unloading the wagon before he moved in. He confronted Ringer in the bar, where he was transferring bottles from the

374

crates to the shelves. While the man was pale, thin and hollow-eyed, he'd somehow kept many of the handsome features that had allowed him to prey on vulnerable women. Ringer was surprised to see him walk in unexpectedly.

"We're not open for hours yet, sir."

"I'm not here for a drink," said Grosvenor.

"If you want to speak to the landlord, you'll have to wait. He's still in bed."

"I came to see *you*, Ringer."

The other man blinked. "How do you know my name?"

"I'm Superintendent Grosvenor from Scotland Yard and I'm here to arrest you." Ringer was astounded. "Is your accomplice here as well?"

"What accomplice?"

"Don't lie to me, man. You were party to the kidnap of Superintendent Tallis and will be held to account for the crime along with whoever assisted you."

Ringer gaped. "I honestly don't know what you're talking about."

"If you resist arrest, your sentence will be lengthened accordingly."

"But I've just served my sentence, sir."

"I know. I was in Maidstone Prison earlier this morning. That was how I knew where to find you. The deputy governor told me you'd be in Stelling Minnis."

"You should have spoken to the chaplain instead."

"Why?"

"It was his brother who agreed to help me. He's the vicar here and as kind and understanding as the chaplain himself. When you've been to prison, it's difficult to find a job of any kind, let alone somewhere to live. Mr Hollings, the vicar, arranged for me to live and work here at the Rose and Crown. If you care to meet him," he went on, "I'm sure that he'll vouch for me."

Doubts began to form but Grosvenor pressed on regardless.

"I'll need to rouse the landlord to tell him I'm taking you to Canterbury."

"Please don't do that, sir. I've done nothing wrong."

"You were involved in the abduction of Edward Tallis. We know that you've harboured a grudge against him all these years."

"I did at first," confessed the other, "and I thought of nothing else. But the chaplain taught me there was such a thing as forgiveness. What the superintendent and Inspector Colbeck did was no more than what was expected of them. They arrested a man who was doing wicked things and causing a lot of grief. Well, I'm not that man any more and I bear no malice against either of them." He extended both hands. "Arrest me, if you must and handcuff me. All that you'll be doing is to ruin my one chance of a better life." Grosvenor hesitated. "I like it here, Superintendent. It's a lovely village. Apart from the vicar and the landlord, nobody knows about my past. People around here are starting to accept me. I might have been used to a more comfortable way of life at one time, but it was based entirely on deception. Those days are over. I've learnt my lesson the hard way."

Grosvenor gulped.

It was just after dawn when Edward Tallis heard the sound of a horse and cart outside. He was shivering in the cold and aching with hunger. Even the slightest movement was accompanied by a shooting pain. When the cart came to a halt outside, he knew that the two men were back again and that there wasn't even the faintest chance of release. Having put him through torment, they'd come to kill him off. They'd brought something to lever away the planks they'd nailed across the door. It was suddenly flung open and the two of them entered with lanterns. Sweeping off his hat, one of them stood close to Tallis and held the light near his face so that it could be seen clearly.

"Do you remember me now, Major?" he growled.

"It's Stagg," said Tallis in surprise. "Private Stagg."

"Yes, it's the man you had flogged half to death in India."

"But it wasn't my decision, man —"

"Shut up!" yelled Stagg, silencing him with a blow to the face. "Before my sentence was carried out, I spent two days locked up in a stinking hole with no light and in baking heat. In your case, it's been icy cold but at least you've found out what it's like to be treated like a wild animal."

"Now for the best part," said the other man.

"This is my brother, Leo."

"I'm good with my hands, you see, so I made this cat-o'-nine-tails for Joe." He thrust the whip in front of Tallis's face then handed it to his brother. "He told me exactly what it looked like."

"And exactly what it *felt* like," said Stagg. "String him up, Leo."

Realising what they intended to do, Tallis quivered inwardly but he showed no fear and he was certainly not going to beg. It was pointless trying to tell Stagg that he'd actually spoken up on his behalf. The man was so committed to his perverted idea of vengeance that he wouldn't listen to a word Tallis said. Leo had brought a rope with him and he stood on a rickety old wooden box so that he could loop it through the iron hook in the ceiling. The two brothers then lifted their victim to his feet, causing him tremors of agony. While Leo held him tight, his brother unlocked the handcuffs, brought Tallis's hands around to the front of his body and locked his wrists together again. Then they tied one end of the rope around the handcuffs and pulled on the other, hoisting him up until his feet were barely touching the floor. The pain was now indescribable and Tallis came close to passing out. When one end of the rope was tied off against a post, he hung suspended and defenceless.

"I'll show you what two hundred lashes feels like," said Stagg, gleefully. "Get the prisoner ready, Leo."

Taking out a sharp knife, his brother sliced through Tallis's waistcoat and shirt until they were no more than rags. He then grabbed hold of the strips of material one by one and tore them completely away, exposing the naked torso. When Tallis twitched involuntarily in the cold, the brothers laughed. Stagg held the cat-o'-nine-tails in front of his eyes then lashed the side of the stall with it by way of demonstration.

378

"I'm going to flay you alive, Major Tallis," he warned.

But the words died in his throat when he heard the sound of an approaching vehicle. Running to the door, Leo saw a cab haring towards them through the gloom. When it skidded to a halt, three men jumped out and ran towards the stable.

"Run for it, Joe!" he shouted. "It could be the police."

"It can't be," said Stagg, crossing to the door to look out. "How on earth did they know where we were?"

His brother didn't bother to reply. He simply charged off to the cart, leapt up into the seat and snapped the reins. As it began to move away, Hinton flung himself on to the back of the cart. Joseph Stagg didn't even reach it because Leeming moved quickly to intercept him, tripping him up then jumping on him to pummel him hard with both fists. Colbeck ran to the stable, lantern in hand. When he saw the way that Tallis had been strung up, he was appalled.

"Don't worry, sir. I'll get you down."

"Colbeck?" whispered the other. "Is that you?"

"I'll be as gentle as I can, sir."

Untying one end of the rope, he let it fall slowly through the hook so that Tallis's arms were no longer stretched upwards. Colbeck then helped him to sit down before taking off his own coat and putting it around his shoulders. When he untied the rope around Tallis's ankles, he brought a little more relief to the prisoner. It was clear that the man was too dazed and exhausted to explain what had happened to him but he rallied when Leeming dragged in Joseph Stagg, whose face was streaming with blood.

"I got him just in time," he said.

"Well done, Sergeant," said Tallis, teeth chattering. "He'll have the key to these handcuffs somewhere about him."

Leeming goggled. "Look at the state of you, sir!" he gasped.

"Don't just stand there," said Colbeck.

"What have they done to him?"

"He's still alive — that's the main thing."

"Just about," said Tallis, gamely.

Leeming shook Stagg hard. "You'll pay dearly for this."

"Find that key at once," said Colbeck.

After searching Stagg's pockets, Leeming located the key and handed it over. Colbeck immediately freed Tallis and helped him to his feet. After flexing his muscles and rubbing his sore wrists, the superintendent walked unsteadily but purposefully across to Stagg and grabbed him.

"Where are my cufflinks?" he demanded.

Alan Hinton, meanwhile, was clinging on to the side of the cart as it careered madly across the grass. Leo Stagg used his whip to get extra speed from the horse then he swung round and flailed away at Hinton, trying to dislodge him from the cart altogether. Taking care not to be hit in the face, the constable took most of the stinging blows on his arm. His top hat had blown off and, because of the grime, his clothing was filthy but he didn't stop to worry about that. Staying on the cart was all that he could think about at that moment. The driver tried a different way to shake him off, making the horse zigzag his way across the field so that there were sudden changes of direction. When the cart dipped into a hollow at full speed, Hinton was thrown inches into the air.

If he was going to be thrown off, he decided, he intended to take the driver with him. The next time that Leo swung round and lashed out at him, therefore, Hinton grabbed hold of the whip and tugged with all his might. Leo was pulled off balance, allowing the constable to scramble to his feet and dive at the man. There was a violent struggle with the cart bouncing its way over the ground. When one of the wheels hit a boulder, the whole cart lurched sideways and threw both men out on to the grass. Hinton was on his feet in a flash but Leo, who'd fallen awkwardly on one arm, took a little more time. He was a hulking figure with muscles hardened by farm work. Hinton, however, had fire inside him. Enraged that the man had dared to kidnap Tallis, he jumped at him courageously and landed some heavy punches to the face.

The fight was soon over. Though Leo fought back, he could only use one arm, the other one having been badly damaged in the fall. In spite of his smaller physique, Hinton fought like a man possessed, punching and grappling until he wrestled his adversary to the ground. Dazed and handicapped, Leo Stagg was gradually beaten into submission. Hinton was bruised and dripping with blood but he still had enough strength to handcuff the other man then yank him roughly to his feet.

On Christmas Eve, a few guests had been invited to the Colbeck residence for a drink. Victor and Estelle Leeming were there and so was Lydia Quayle. Being a member of the family, Caleb Andrews felt that he had to be the first to arrive and he was due to spend the night there as well. As they sipped their glasses of mulled wine in the drawing room, Andrews was still keen to talk about the two recent cases in which his son-in-law had been involved.

"So the killer was a villainous railway policeman," he said, pointedly. "Trust the GWR to employ such a man."

"It was Madeleine who made me look at the case from another angle," recalled Colbeck, "When I showed her the plan of the Railway Village, she was struck by its relentless uniformity. That made me think that someone might find living there quite oppressive. I was right. Fellowes, the man in question, hated the repetitive lives they were all forced to live in Swindon. Murder was a blow against what he claimed was the depressing sameness of the Railway Village where his whole life was timetabled to the last second. He did have a stronger reason to kill his victim, of course, but I was nevertheless grateful for Madeleine's initial comment."

"You solved the crime, Robert," she said. "I deserve no credit."

"It's very strange," said Leeming. "We spent all that time on a case in Wiltshire yet it's the night in Kent that really stays in my mind. We actually prevented a murder there. Stagg and his brother really meant to kill the superintendent."

Colbeck nodded. "They intended to flog him to death."

"How terrible!" exclaimed Lydia.

"It's a tribute to the superintendent's constitution that he stood up to being bound hand and foot and left for days in a freezing stable. The doctor has advised him to take time off to rest but I can guarantee that he's probably still at his desk."

"Victor told me what happened to Inspector Grosvenor," said Estelle.

"He's been reduced to the rank of sergeant."

"That's far too good for him," said Leeming. "When he was given power he didn't deserve, he made such a mess that he should now be pounding the streets in uniform."

"Let's forget about him and his woes," suggested Colbeck, "and dwell on the happier aspects of the events in Kent. Edward Tallis was rescued in the nick of time, Victor and I received fulsome praise and Constable Hinton was thanked personally by the commissioner. As a result, we're all safely back home in the bosoms of our respective families in time to celebrate Christmas." He looked down at the crib in which his daughter was sleeping. "Helen — God bless her — will have her father beside her tomorrow."

"I'm longing to see her face when she's given her presents," said Lydia. "I was with Madeleine when she bought some of them."

"Did she buy anything for *me*?" asked Andrews.

"No," said his daughter, "I bought nothing at all."

"Don't tease me, Maddy."

"Then don't ask a silly question. You know that I'd never dare to forget you." She indicated the parcels around the tree. "There's a gift for everyone." The doorbell rang and they all looked towards the hall. Madeleine smiled. "This is a present that we thought you might appreciate, Lydia."

She was surprised. "Why *me*?"

"You'll soon see," explained Colbeck. "Since he played an important part in foiling the kidnappers, I felt that Alan Hinton ought to join in the toast to our success. Why don't you go and greet him, Lydia?"

Torn between embarrassment and delight, Lydia looked self-consciously around the other faces then ran on tiptoe to the door and out into the hall. The others exchanged a knowing smile. It was a few minutes before Hinton and Lydia came into the room together. They were beaming happily. There was a flurry of welcomes then Hinton indicated the window.

"Have you looked outside?" he asked. "It's snowing hard."

"That's wonderful news!" said Colbeck.

Leeming laughed. "Our boys will be thrilled."

"Do you hear that?" said Madeleine, leaning over the crib to place a kiss on her daughter's head. "Daddy is back home and we're going to have a white Christmas."

384

# UNDER ATTACK

## Edward Marston

1916: While German Gotha bombers raid London from above, a man's body is fished from the Thames below. The man had been garrotted and his tongue cut out before he was left to his watery grave, and as the killer had taken care to remove identifying items and even labels, Inspector Marmion and Sergeant Keedy struggle to name the victim before they can begin properly with their investigation. As family and business associates are found, the list of suspects grows ever longer; and as Marmion wrangles with the case, he and his family must also contend with their anxieties for his now-missing son, Paul. With great care, Marmion must pick his way along a twisting path that will lead him towards the killer.

# THE CIRCUS TRAIN CONSPIRACY

## Edward Marston

1860: Following a string of successful performances, the Moscardi Circus is travelling by train to Newcastle for their next show. Amongst the usual railway hubbub, the animals have been loaded, the clowns — now incognito — are aboard, and Mauro Moscardi himself is comfortable in a first-class compartment with a cigar. Yet a collision on the track with a couple of sleepers causes pandemonium: passengers are thrown about, animals escape into the night, and the future of the circus looks uncertain. When the body of a woman is discovered in woodland next to the derailment, Inspector Colbeck is despatched to lend assistance, believing the two incidents might be connected. It is up to Colbeck to put the pieces together to discover the identity of the nameless woman and unmask who is targeting Moscardi's Magnificent Circus.